D0364485

WITHDRAWN

WITHDRAWN

993479048 3

RED LIGHT

GRAHAM MASTERTON was a bestselling horror writer for many years before he turned his talent to crime. He lived in Cork for five years, an experience that inspired the Katie Maguire series.

GRAHAM MASTERTON

RED LIGHT

HEAD of ZEUS

First published in the UK in 2014 by Head of Zeus Ltd.

Copyright © Graham Masterton, 2014

The moral right of Graham Masterton to be identified as the author of this work has been asserted in accordance with the Copyright, Designs and Patents Act of 1988.

All rights reserved. No part of this publication may be reproduced, stored in a retrieval system, or transmitted in any form or by any means, electronic, mechanical, photocopying, recording, or otherwise, without the prior permission of both the copyright owner and the above publisher of this book.

This is a work of fiction. All characters, organizations, and events portrayed in this novel are either products of the author's imagination or are used fictitiously.

9 7 5 3 1 2 4 6 8

A CIP catalogue record for this book is available from the British Library.

Hardback ISBN: 9781781856765
Trade paperback ISBN: 9781781856772
eBook ISBN: 9781781856758s

Typeset by Palimpsest Book Production Ltd, Falkirk, Stirlingshire

Printed and bound in Germany by GGP Media GmbH, Pössneck

Head of Zeus Ltd
Clerkenwell House
45-47 Clerkenwell Green
London EC1R 0HT

WWW.HEADOFZEUS.COM

For Dawn Harris,
with love and optimism

GLOUCESTERSHIRE COUNTY COUNCIL	
9934790483	
Bertrams	18/02/2015
AF	£18.99
GH0	

Coiméad fearg ar bhean a bhfuil foighne
Irish saying: 'Beware the anger of a patient woman'

One

The smell hit them as soon as Ciaran opened the front door. A ripe, sweet stench so strong that they both took a step back on to the pavement. Ciaran's prospective client dragged a crumpled handkerchief out of his raincoat pocket and held it over his nose and mouth.

'Holy Mary, Mother of God, that's some fecking benjy coming out of there,' he said, in a muffled voice, jabbing his finger towards the darkened hallway.

Ciaran said, 'That's fierce, isn't it? Jesus, I'll give you that.'

'Well, I'm not renting a place that stinks like that, I can tell you that for nothing. I'll be giving my customers the gawks before they've even eaten anything.'

Ciaran looked up at the faded red and green lettering over the front of the shop. 'I'll tell you what it is, most likely,' he said, clearing his throat and trying to sound authoritative. 'The last tenants we had here, they ran a Hungarian deli. Well, you can see by the sign. Hungarian Deli. I'd say that they probably left some of their stock in the freezer, like, when they moved out, but Bord Gáis would have shut off the electric and that was over a month ago. That's rotten sausage, or something like that, I'll bet you money.'

'I don't care *what* it is, boy,' said his client. 'I'm not even

1

going in there to have a sconce at it until you get rid of that smell.'

Ciaran said, 'Okay, Mr Rooney, grand. I totally understand. I'll get it sorted, no problem. But what do you think of the location?'

His client looked around. He was a short, broad-chested man of about fifty-five, with thick curly grey hair and deeply buried little eyes and silver prickles on his chin. He was wearing a belted grey raincoat that gave him the appearance of a human beer keg.

'Oh, the location's what I was looking for, near enough. I'll be doing kebabs and curry as well as fish and chips, like.' He paused for a moment, looking down the steeply sloping street towards the city centre. Then he turned and said, 'Jesus, will you ever close that fecking door?'

'Okay,' said Ciaran, but as he went to reach for the door handle he dropped his bunch of keys on to the mat. He was only twenty-two, skinny and awkward, with short ginger hair and a beaky nose and a raging red spot on his chin. He had always been clumsy, and since this was only his second week at Lisney's estate agent's, and only the third client he'd taken out on his own, he was still very nervous. It didn't help that the hallway next to this shop-front property smelled so foul. His stomach tightened up and he could taste bile at the back of his throat.

'Listen, Mr Rooney, I swear I'll have the place cleaned up by tomorrow for you. It's a great offer, you have the shop and the kitchen and the basement storeroom and there's WC facilities at the back, only twelve thousand euros the year. I know there's a rake of commercial rentals available in the city centre right now, but not many at this price.'

Ciaran's boss, Blathnaid, had told him that since the

recession the owners of this building had already dropped the rent by two thousand euros and unless they found a tenant soon they would probably have to reduce it even further. Lower Shandon Street still had its fair share of small businesses. There was Denis Nolan's butcher's to the left of the property with drisheen and pigs' bodices in the window, and Hennessy's newsagent to the right, and the Orosin African Restaurant directly opposite, but there were plenty of boarded-up shop-fronts further up the street and even the ones that were still open were struggling.

'What about that premises on the Ballyhooly Road?' asked Mr Rooney, with a sniff. 'Is that still available?'

'I'll be honest with you, Mr Rooney, you wouldn't get anything like the same footfall as you would here on Shandon Street. And if it's kebabs and curry you're talking about, you wouldn't get the same ethnic clientele.'

'Yeah, well, that's what they say about Shandon Street, isn't it? Just like a pint of Guinness – black at the bottom and black in the middle and white at the top.'

Ciaran didn't answer that. Lisney's had given him strict training in political correctness, and in any case the Chubb security lock in the door was stiff and he was having difficulty turning the key. He was still struggling with it when he heard a weird howling sound. It was quite high-pitched, like a woman or a child. Or maybe it was only a cat. But whatever it was, it was coming from *inside* the building.

'Right, let's get on with it, then,' said Mr Rooney, checking his wristwatch. 'I don't have any more time to waste. I'm supposed to be in Ballincollig by twelve.'

But Ciaran had his ear to the front door, and he was listening hard. 'Would you shush for a moment?' he said, lifting one hand.

'C'mere to me?' asked Mr Rooney, crossly.

'I'm sorry. Would you shush for a moment, *please*? I think I can hear somebody.'

'Come on, boy. I'm a very busy man and I'm running late already.'

'No, no, listen! There it is again! It sounds like crying!'

Mr Rooney tutted and rolled his eyes up into his head and walked back over to the front door. At the same time a Traveller's filthy old pick-up truck piled with lengths of timber and old washing machines came grinding up the street, with exhaust smoke billowing out of the tailpipe and cigarette smoke out of the windows.

'I can't hear nothing at all,' said Mr Rooney. 'It's your imagination playing tricks on you, boy.'

As the pick-up laboured its way up to Church Street, however, and the racket from its perforated silencer began to subside, another cry of pain or despair came from somewhere inside the building. The cry was so drawn out that it was almost operatic, and this time they both heard it.

'I thought you said the place was unoccupied,' said Mr Rooney, almost as if he were accusing Ciaran of a breach of contract.

'It's supposed to be, like. The two top floors are rented out separate, but there's nobody in them at the moment, so far as I know.'

'You don't know very much then, do you? I suppose we'll have to go in and see what's amiss.'

'I'd better ring the office first,' said Ciaran.

'Oh yeah, and what can they do? You'd be better off ringing the guards.'

Ciaran hesitated for a few seconds, and then he turned the key in the lock again, and opened the front door. The

4

smell seemed even worse this time. It was so strong that at first Ciaran thought that he could actually *see* it, like an orange fog, but that was only the light that was filtering down into the hallway from a stained-glass window at the top of the first flight of stairs.

It was so thick, the smell, that it made him choke. It filled up his nostrils and his throat and his lungs. It reminded him of the time a rat had died underneath the floorboards of his Auntie Kathleen's cottage in Clash, only a hundred times stronger.

The hallway was narrow, with embossed wallpaper which had been painted over in mustard-yellow gloss, and a floor covered in worn green lino. A doorway on the left led into the shop. It resisted at first, but Ciaran pushed it hard with his shoulder and it shuddered open. Inside, the shop was dark because of the slatted steel security shutters that covered its windows. Two glass-fronted food cabinets stood at right angles to each other, but their glass was dusty and they were both empty. In the middle of the floor there was a tipped-over wooden chair, and on the opposite wall a torn poster of a castle in Budapest was still pinned up, but apart from that there was no other reminder that this had once been a Hungarian delicatessen. Ciaran realized he must have been wrong about the sausage. The smell wasn't nearly as strong in here as it was in the hallway.

'This would make a grand chipper if you could just get rid of the stink, like,' said Mr Rooney, looking around. He was about to say something else when he was interrupted by yet another thin, high howl, almost a scream. It sounded as if it was coming from the room right above their heads, and Ciaran thought he could hear movement as well, somebody's heels bumping on the floor.

Neither of them said anything, but Mr Rooney went back out into the hallway and started to stump up the stairs, gripping the shaky banister-rail to heave himself up. Ciaran followed, feeling very immature. He was the agent's representative after all, and he was supposed to be in charge.

They reached the landing. The light from the stained-glass window mottled their faces as if they were both suffering from some kind of incurable skin disease. There was a door to their left with flaking brown paint on it, and in front of them another door, which was half open. Ciaran could see a washbasin, stained with rust, and an old-fashioned iron bathtub with a large dripping tap.

'Is anybody there?' Mr Rooney shouted out. 'I said, is anybody there?' He took a deep wheezing breath, but before he could shout out a third time he broke into a fit of coughing and had to punch himself on the chest before he managed to stop. 'Jesus. You wouldn't have thought I'd given up the fags.'

'I'd have said that it was coming from in here, that crying,' said Ciaran, nodding towards the door on the left.

'Well, go on, boy,' said Mr Rooney, suppressing another cough. 'We haven't got all fecking day.'

Ciaran took hold of the Bakelite door handle and eased the door open. The curtains were drawn, so it was hard for him to see if there was anybody in there, but even if the howling wasn't coming from this room, the smell certainly was. Ciaran actually retched, and he had to hesitate a moment before he pushed the door open any wider because he was afraid he was going to have to rush into that bathroom and be explosively sick.

'Hallo?' he said, cautiously. 'Is there anybody in there?'

He could hear bluebottles buzzing. Then he heard a

whimper, and another moan, on a low descending note this time, as if the moaner was terrified. Ciaran took a breath to steady himself, and immediately wished that he hadn't, because the stench was so bad. He reached across to the light-switch and clicked it, but nothing happened. As he had said himself, the power company must have turned off the electric.

'Oh, for feck's sake,' said Mr Rooney. He pushed past Ciaran and crossed over to the window, dragging back the thick green curtains so that the room was filled with bright grey morning light. At least a dozen bluebottles were flying around or crawling up the windows.

What they saw made both of them stand stock still with shock. Ciaran felt as if all the blood in his body had dropped to his feet. The room was a bedsit, with a purple sofa-bed along the wall behind the door. Apart from that, the only other furniture was a grubby, oatmeal-coloured armchair, a teak coffee table in the shape of an artist's palette, and a cheap veneered wardrobe. In the corner of the room next to the window there was a small triangular washbasin, and a shelf with a microwave oven and an olive-green plastic kettle.

On the wall above the sofa-bed hung a faded picture of Saint Patrick, white-bearded and smiling benevolently, with a mass of snakes around his feet, all slithering into the sea. On the sofa-bed itself lay the body of a naked black man, and kneeling beside the bed was a young black woman, wide-eyed, wearing only a purple satin bra. She was so emaciated that her arms and legs looked like black fire-pokers, and her stomach was creased with wrinkles.

She wailed again and raised one arm, shielding her face, '*Ba a cutar da ni!*' she said, in a voice so thin that it was more like a whistle. '*Ba a cutar da ni!*'

The sight and the smell of the man's body had shaken Ciaran and Mr Rooney so much that for almost a quarter of a minute neither of them could speak. When he did say something, all that Mr Rooney could manage was, 'Holy Mary, Mother of God. Fecking state of him, la.'

Both of the man's hands were missing and the blanket beneath his wrists was black with dried blood. The stumps were alive with maggots, wriggling and twitching as they struggled with each other to feed off his festering flesh. Worse, though, was his face – or what was left of his face. His lower jaw was intact, with a neat black goatee beard, but above that there was nothing more than a huge crimson flower with petals made of meat. Maggots were tumbling all over this blossom and bluebottle flies were clustered around it, busily laying more eggs.

Even more maggots and flies were crawling between the man's legs, scores of them, giving him the appearance of wearing a huge rippling nappy.

'Ring the guards, boy,' said Mr Rooney, in a husky voice, but Ciaran had already taken out his mobile phone and was prodding out 112.

Mr Rooney held out both hands to the girl and said, 'C'mere, girl, we're not going to hurt you. What in the name of Jesus are you doing in here with this dead feller?'

'You no kill,' said the girl. 'Please you no kill.'

'Hey, we're not going to *kill* you. Why would we want to do that?'

'Please, you no kill.'

'Of course we won't kill you. Come on, you need to get yourself out of here.'

'Lower Shandon Street,' Ciaran was saying on his mobile. 'The sign over the shop says Hungarian Deli. Well, there's a body here, a black feller with no head. And there's a girl, too, she's still alive but I'd say she needs a bit of help. She's black too. That's right. No, I don't think she's injured at all. Yes. Ciaran O'Malley. Yes.'

He turned to Mr Rooney and said, 'The cops are on their way. They said not to touch nothing and not to move the body.'

'Oh, I will, yeah,' said Mr Rooney. 'I'm going to pick him up and dance around the fecking room with him.'

'I think I'm going to have to get out of here,' said Ciaran. He raised his hand in front of his face to block the view of the body lying on the sofa-bed. 'I just can't take this smell any more. And them maggots.' Just saying the word 'maggots' made him bring up another mouthful of bile and his eyes watered.

Mr Rooney unbuckled his raincoat and wrestled himself out of it. He held it out to the girl and said, 'Here, love. Put this on. At least you'll be decent so.'

Weakly, the girl reached out for the arm of the chair and managed to lever herself up on to her feet. She was so thin that her pelvis looked like a plough blade. Mr Rooney draped his raincoat over her bony shoulders, but before he did so Ciaran could see that her back was patterned with lumpy diagonal scars, as if she had been beaten, or burned, or both.

They left the room and awkwardly made their way downstairs. As they reached the hallway, the girl stopped and said, '*Ba za ta komo, yana ta? Yarinyar?*'

'Don't know what the feck you're talking about, love,' said Mr Rooney. Despite her being bare-footed, he ushered her out of the front door and into the street. He looked over her shoulder at Ciaran and said, 'Shut that door, would you, boy, before my breakfast comes back for an action replay.'

It had started to rain, not heavily, but enough to make the road surface glisten and the shores start gurgling. The girl kept glancing around her, very agitated, as if she expected somebody to appear at any moment and attack her. A black man in a dirty red hoodie was sheltering in the doorway of the betting shop opposite, smoking, and Ciaran could see that his presence disturbed her, because she turned her back to him and pulled up the collar of Mr Rooney's raincoat to hide her face.

'The cops will be here before you know it,' he told her. He laid his hand on her shoulder, trying to be reassuring, but she flinched away.

'What's your name, girl?' he asked her. 'What do they call you? You understand some English, don't you?'

The girl nodded. 'Yes. Understand. That woman not come back?'

'What woman?'

The girl pointed upwards, towards the room where the body was lying. 'That woman kill Mawakiya.'

Ciaran looked at Mr Rooney and Mr Rooney's thick grey eyebrows went up.

'Your man was topped by a *woman*?' he asked her.

'With *bindiga*. Gun. Yes. Two times in head.'

'Well, that doesn't surprise me, the state of him. Face like a couple of meat cakes.'

'He was shot?' said Ciaran. 'It's pure amazing that nobody heard it.'

'Oh, that doesn't surprise me one little bit,' said Mr Rooney. 'Nobody never hears nothing in this city these days, not if they know what's good for them, any road.'

'Do you *know* the woman?' asked Ciaran.

The girl shook her head. 'I don't know her. But she say

to me, not move. Not move! If you come out of room, I will be waiting for you. I will do same to you like Mawakiya.'

'So that's why you stayed there?'

The girl nodded again, and then suddenly her lower lip curled down and she started sobbing. 'I so afraid. I so afraid. She say to me, if you come out of room, I kill you like Mawakiya. This is promise.'

'Jesus,' said Mr Rooney. 'So that's why you stayed in there. When did this happen? Like, how long have you been in there?'

The girl held up three long fingers with silver rings on them. Her nails were painted metallic-purple, though they were all badly chipped.

'Three days? Jesus. And all that time your man was getting stinkier and stinkier and you didn't have nothing to eat or drink?'

'I have water. I have biscuit.'

'Ah well, I don't suppose a feller with his face blown off could have done much to sharpen your appetite. I was going to have the bacon and cabbage at the White Horse Inn today in Ballincollig but I don't think I'll be eating anything at all anywhere for a while.'

'So what's your name?' Ciaran persisted. 'Where do you come from? How long have you been here in Cork?'

The girl stared at him over the top of Mr Rooney's raincoat collar. Her eyelashes were crusted with yellow and her left eye was bloodshot. She didn't answer, but just continued to stare at him as if she didn't trust him, or any man, or anyone – and never would again.

'You're not even going to tell me your name?' said Ciaran. 'Well, how old are you? You can tell me that, can't you? Or don't you know?'

The girl held up both hands, with all of her fingers spread. Then she held up only her right hand, with two of her fingers folded back.

When Ciaran frowned in bewilderment, she did it again. Two hands, ten fingers, then one hand, three fingers.

'Mother of God,' said Mr Rooney. 'She's only thirteen.'

At that moment, lightning flickered over the hills towards the south-west and the girl clamped her hand over her mouth as if she had just told the most dreadful lie.

TWO

Katie entered the interview room. It was gloomy but not dark enough for the light to be switched on. A middle-aged woman in a red tweed suit was sitting in one of the Parker Knoll armchairs that were crowded together at the right-hand side of the room. She had dyed ginger hair and fiery crimson cheeks, and the drawn lines around her mouth of a woman whose teeth had all been taken out as a wedding present.

She half stood up as Katie came in, but Katie made a patting gesture in the air to indicate that she should stay seated.

'Mary ó Floinn, superintendent,' she said, in a stage whisper. 'It was me that you talked to on the phone.'

Katie nodded. She was more interested in the young girl standing by the tall window, looking out. The window was speckled with raindrops and outside the dark slate rooftops were shiny and wet. Down in the area below, a man with a khaki windcheater covering his head was stacking bricks and smoking. Katie couldn't be sure if the girl was watching him or if she was staring at nothing at all.

She knew from the records that Nasc had given her that she was eight years old, but she looked no more than five. Her brown hair was unkempt and straggly, and Katie could see crusty brown scabs among the curls. She was very thin, and her emaciated state was exaggerated by the long grey cotton dress she was wearing, which was clean and well pressed, with pink smocking on the front, but two sizes too big for her.

Katie went over to the window and stood beside her. The girl didn't look up, but continued to stare outside. She had a high forehead and sharp angular cheekbones, and huge brown eyes. She reminded Katie of one of the fairies in the storybooks that her mother used to read to her, except that she had fading yellow bruises on her left cheek and around her mouth, and purple bruises around her neck, too, like finger marks.

'Corina?' said Katie, very gently.

The girl looked up at her, and then immediately looked away.

'Corina, I'm Katie. Have they given you anything to eat?'

'She had fish fingers for her lunch,' put in Mary ó Floinn. 'Mind you, she ate only the one. I had the feeling she'd never been given more than one before and she was afraid what might happen if she ate any more.'

Katie stood looking at Corina for a long time. She couldn't think of the last time she had felt pain like this. She had to turn away from the window because she had a *tocht*, a lump in her throat, and tears in her eyes.

After a while, though, she swallowed and smiled and said, 'Corina, why don't you and me sit together over here and we can talk?'

She went over to the sagging maroon couch on the opposite side of the room and sat down. Corina hesitated for a moment, and then obediently came over and sat next to her, with her head lowered, staring at the carpet.

'Would you like some chocolate?' Katie asked her.

Corina shook her head.

'Are you sure? You've had your lunch, haven't you, so you're allowed.'

Mary ó Floinn, in the same stage whisper, said, 'There's a bit of an issue with chocolate, superintendent.'

'What do you mean "a bit of an issue"?'

'She took a square of chocolate out of the fridge, only a dooshie piece, but Mânios smacked her so hard she hit her head on the concrete step, and then he half choked her. So ... as you can probably understand, she's a little wary when it comes to chocolate.'

'I see,' said Katie. She smiled at Corina, but behind her smile her pain had turned to anger, an anger that was stronger than almost any anger she had felt before, and in her mind she could see herself stalking out of the room and finding Mânios Dumitrescu at whatever bar in Cork he was drinking in this afternoon, The Idle Hour probably, taking out her .38 revolver and without hesitation shooting him between the eyes.

She unfastened the flap on her bag and took out the Milkybar she had bought at the newsagent's on her way here. 'Let's share this, shall we? Half for you and half for me.'

Corina stared at her with those soulful brown eyes. Then, at last, she nodded.

While they sat side by side, eating chocolate, Katie said, 'Do you know where you were born?'

Corina shook her head again.

'Do you know where you are now?'

Corina nodded.

'And where is that, Corina?'

Corina closed her eyes and recited, in a soft, hoarse voice, 'Number thirty-seven St Martha's Avenue, Gurranabraher, Cork. Telephone number 021 4979951.'

'Well, at least the Dumitrescus made sure they weren't going to lose her,' said Katie. She waited for a moment while Corina finished her chocolate and lifted up the hem of her dress so that she could wipe her mouth. Then she said, 'What's your mother's name, sweetheart?'

'Marcela.'

'Marcela is the woman you've been living with. I mean your real mother.'

Corina frowned as if she didn't understand. Katie looked across at Mary ó Floinn, who shrugged and said, very quietly, 'She believes that Marcela *is* her real mother, superintendent. Remember that she was only three when the Dumitrescus adopted her. We've contacted the social services in Bucharest but we were hoping that you could get in touch with the Romanian police to see if they can trace her real family.'

'Oh, we'll do that, for sure,' said Katie. 'They have a special directorate to combat human-trafficking, just like we do. Meanwhile I'd like to set up some interviews with Corina, when you think she's ready. We can't delay it for too long, though. As you say in your report here, the Dumitrescus have adoption papers and they've already lodged a complaint to get her back.'

'The courts won't make us hand her over, though, will they? Look at her.'

Katie shrugged. 'I don't know, Mary. Unless we can find some really sound evidence against them there's not a lot we can do. Well ... you're the legal experts when it comes to immigrants. If they can get their hands on her again, the Dumitrescus could up sticks and head off to England or back to Romania or wherever in the world they wanted and then we'd never see her again.'

'God forbid,' said Mary ó Floinn. 'The ISPCC have lodged

her for the moment with some really grand foster parents in Douglas, Mr and Mrs Brennan. I'll be taking her there after this. She should be able to talk to you in two or three days, maybe sooner. She just needs to get over the fear that she's going to get a beating if she tells you what the Dumitrescus have been doing to her. Meanwhile I've given you the name of the neighbour who first called us. I don't know whether she'd be prepared to give evidence in open court, but maybe she could give you some leads to other witnesses.'

Katie took hold of Corina's hand and squeezed it, and smiled. 'I'll see you again, Corina, yes? Some nice people are going to take care of you. You'll have your own bed to sleep in and you won't have to do any more cooking or cleaning or changing babies' nappies, and we're not going to let Marcela or Mânios hit you any more. You're safe now.'

She didn't know if Corina understood everything that she was saying, but the little girl looked up at her and gave her a wide grin. It broke Katie's heart to see that all her teeth were rotten right down into her gums.

While she was putting on her dark red waterproof jacket, Katie had a few quiet words with Mary ó Floinn in the corridor.

'Fair play to you, Mary, you've shown some real neck, doing this,' she told her. 'Most people don't dare cross the Dumitrescus. We've had Mânios Dumitrescu up in front of the court three times in the past four years on charges of assault and extortion and every time our witnesses have been threatened with being cut or beaten up and they've all conveniently decided to lose their memories.'

Mary ó Floinn said, 'You don't think we're scared at Nasc? We've already had some very nasty phone calls from the Dumitrescus. Not openly threatening, as such. They're vicious, but they're not stupid. And of course this isn't the usual kind of case for us. Mostly we're trying to keep Roma families together, not split them apart. In the end, though, yes – I suppose it's all going to depend on what you can coax little Corina to say to you and what witness statements you can get.'

She paused, and then she said, 'By the way, superintendent, I wasn't expecting you to come here in person. I very much appreciate it.'

Katie gave her a quick, tight smile. 'I was going to send Detective Sergeant ó Nuallán – you've met her, haven't you? But I wanted to come and see Corina for myself. I'm allergic to those Dumitrescus but I wanted to remind myself exactly why, and just how much. Mânios, he's the devil incarnate, that fellow, that's the only word for him, and that mother of his, what a witch!'

She looked back towards the interview room and saw Corina sitting alone on the couch, her head down, playing some game by wiggling her fingers. Detective O'Donovan had reported to her that when Corina was taken from the Dumitrescu house in Gurranabraher last Friday, the officers had found that she had no spare clothes, only the filthy T-shirt and shorts she was wearing at the time, no shoes apart from a pair of worn-out rubber dollies that were two sizes too small for her, and no toys. She wouldn't have needed books, because she had never been sent to school and couldn't read or write. She couldn't even count up to ten in Romanian.

Katie made her way down the steep concrete steps of Ferry Lane to Pope's Quay, overlooking the River Lee, where she had parked her metallic-blue Fiesta. The sun was shining, so that the pavements and the road surface were almost blinding. After she had climbed into the driver's seat she pulled down the sun visor and looked at herself in the mirror. The weather had been unseasonably cold in the past few weeks and her lips were chapped. She thought she looked tired, and her short copper-coloured hair was a mess. Sometimes she wondered what John had ever seen in her, though he had always told her that she looked as if she were related to the elves, petite and green-eyed and 'impossibly pretty'. 'Don't you mean "pretty impossible"?' she had always retorted.

She applied some Lypsyl to her lips and tugged at her hair. She made up her mind not to go to Advantage again to have it cut, although it probably wasn't her stylist's fault that she had chopped it about so much. While the poor girl was trying to layer it and trim it straight Katie had been constantly talking on the phone, and when she talked on the phone she always got agitated or angry, and she never sat still.

No wonder her late mother had always called her 'Fairy Fidget'.

Three

Her phone rang now, playing the chorus of 'The Wild Rover' by The Dubliners. *And it's no, nay, never – no, nay never no more—*

She lifted it out of her jacket pocket and said, 'Yes, Liam? What's the story? Did you get to talk to Gerrety?'

It was Inspector Liam Fennessy. He was supposed to have been meeting Michael Gerrety and his lawyer this morning to discuss the thirty-nine charges that were being brought against Gerrety for operating the city's most profitable online sex service, Cork Fantasy Girls. It was a convoluted case that had been dragging on for months.

'Gerrety didn't show,' said Inspector Fennessy. 'No big surprise, I'd say. His lawyer made some lame excuse about his mother being poorly. But that's not the reason I'm ringing you. A feller's been found dead in a flat over a shop in Lower Shandon Street. Horgan's there already and ó Nuallán's on her way. Horgan said your man's been lying there for at least three days, but it could be anything up to a week. Both of his hands have been amputated and it looks like he's been shot point-blank in the face with a twelve-bore.'

'Jesus.'

'That's exactly what I said. He was a black feller, apparently. We have a name for him because there was a young

20

girl in there with him, although it's not a name I'd recognize. The girl claims she was an eye-witness to him being shot but she was too scared to come out of the room. Apparently the perp threatened her that if she did, she would blow *her* head off, too.'

'Come here to me? 'Did you say *she*?'

'That's right. The girl told the two fellers who found her that it was a woman who did it, for definite.'

'Did she *know* the woman?'

'They didn't think so. They weren't sure.'

'Did she give them any idea what she looked like? Would she recognize her if she saw her again?'

'No. They said she clammed up after telling them that. Didn't say another word.'

'What number Lower Shandon Street?'

'I don't think you'll have any trouble in finding it, ma'am. We have three cars and a white van there and more on the way. The technical team should be there, too, at any minute. Horgan says that there's a fierce crowd already.'

'Okay, Liam. I'll go there directly. How about you?'

'I still have all of the statements on that Ringaskiddy drugs case to go through. It's up in court in the morning. Michael Gerrety's lawyer said that he might be available tomorrow afternoon, but I doubt I'll be able to meet him then. I'll have to make it Friday, if I can.'

'In that case, don't worry. I'll go. It's high time I had a less than friendly chat with Mr Gerrety.'

'Cancery bastard. I know exactly why he vexes Dermot so much.'

'Watch your temper, Liam. Just leave the file on my desk, and I'll have Shelagh fix the appointment for me.'

'Yes, ma'am. I'll catch you later so.'

Katie started up her car, backed out of her parking space in front of the old Cork Button Co., and drove along the quay to Lower Shandon Street. Earlier this morning she had been wishing she had eaten something before she had left home. She usually found that if she missed breakfast she was beginning to flag by eleven o'clock and become irritable, particularly in the week before her period. After what Inspector Fennessy had told her, though, she was relieved that she hadn't. There were few things she found more unpleasant than lukewarm coffee and half-digested Alpen spurting out of her nose.

Fennessy had been right – Lower Shandon Street was already crowded with three patrol cars, a yellow ambulance, a white Mercedes Vario van from the Technical Bureau, an outside broadcast van from RTÉ, two Garda motorcycles and at least seventy or eighty bystanders, many of them black and Asian, all standing on the pavement opposite the Hungarian Deli as if they were expecting a minor celebrity to show up.

A motorcycle garda waved Katie through and pointed to a space where she could park outside O'Donnelly's Turf Accountancy, with two wheels tilted on to the kerb. Detective Horgan was standing outside the Hungarian Deli, talking to Dan Keane from the *Examiner* and a woman reporter in a silvery fur-collared anorak whom Katie didn't recognize. He immediately came up and opened her door for her. Katie saw that he had a blue surgical mask tied around his neck.

'Well, wow, you really hurled it here, ma'am. Didn't break the speed limit, I hope?'

Katie ignored that remark. She was used to Detective Horgan's terrible sense of humour. He was blue-eyed and fresh-faced, and his high quiff of wiry blond hair made him look like a member of a second-rate boy band. In spite of his puerile quips, though, he was developing into a very acute and persistent young detective, who was almost impossible to fob off with blustering excuses or hastily cobbled alibis.

'So what's the story?' asked Katie, as they walked towards the shop.

Detective Horgan pointed to Ciaran O'Malley and his client, Mr Rooney, who were standing under the awning of the next-door premises looking fed-up and anxious to go. 'The young feller works for Lisney's and he was showing the old feller the shop to rent it out as a chipper. The way they tell it, they opened up the front door and the stink almost knocked their socks off.'

'The body's where?'

'Upstairs, first floor.' Horgan pointed to the window over the Hungarian Deli sign. When she looked up, Katie could see blue laser lights criss-crossing the ceiling, and then, momentarily, the back of one of the Garda technicians in his white Tyvek suit.

'I'll tell you for nothing, ma'am, it hums in there like St Mary's church choir. You'd be advised to put a dab of the old Mentholatum under your nose.'

'Inspector Fennessy mentioned a girl,' said Katie.

'Yeah, that's right, they found her sitting on the floor next to the body, practically naked. She's in the back of the ambulance now. I talked to one of the paramedics and she doesn't appear to be suffering from any injuries, like, but she's badly undernourished. She's been living off tap water and Bolands Raspberry Creams for the past three days. They'll be taking her off to the Wilton Hilton in a minute for a check-up.'

Katie said, 'Okay, I'll see her first. Have you interviewed those two fellers?'

'I have, yeah, both of them. Not that they could tell me much. When they first found the body the girl said a couple of things in some language they didn't understand. The old fellow said it sounded like African.'

'African? What kind of African?'

'Well, he wasn't too sure about that. But the kind that black people speak.'

'Off the top of my head, detective, I don't know how many languages they speak in Africa, but it must be more than one. We speak about twenty different languages in Cork, for God's sake. You'd think so, anyway, by the sound of it.'

Detective Horgan said, 'He did catch the victim's name, though, or what he thought was the victim's name, because the girl repeated it two or three times. Mah-wah-*kee*-yah.'

'Mah-wah-*kee*-yah? He was sure of that?'

Detective Horgan nodded and held up his iPhone. 'I made him say it over, and I recorded it, and the young fellow agreed that was what it sounded like.'

'All right,' said Katie. 'I think you can tell them they can go for now. They both look like they've had enough for one day. Have you tried to talk to the girl yourself?'

'I did, but she wouldn't say a word to me. Those two fellers said that the last thing they got out of her was her age. They asked her how old she was and she stuck up thirteen fingers. Well – I mean she stuck up her fingers thirteen times. Ten, and then three.'

This was one of those moments when Katie couldn't be sure if Detective Horgan was joking or not, but she let it pass. She walked around to the back of the ambulance and knocked. After a moment the doors were opened and a young woman paramedic appeared, in her bright yellow and green uniform, with a pale angular face and dark hair shaved so short that she almost looked as if she were undergoing chemotherapy.

'Detective Superintendent Maguire,' said Katie, holding up her ID. 'I'd like to have a few words with your patient, if I may, before you take her off to CUH. I presume that's where she'll be going?'

'That's right, yes,' said the paramedic.

'What condition is she in? I mean, generally speaking?'

'We've checked her for heart rate and blood pressure and any obvious physical trauma. She's dehydrated and she's at least twenty-five pounds underweight for a girl of her height. Apart from that, she appears to have two fractured ribs, as well as multiple bruises and dozens of historic scars.'

Katie climbed up into the ambulance and sat down next to the girl lying on the trolley. The girl stared up at her, clutching the light blue cotton blanket that covered her, as if she were terrified to let go. Her hair was filthy and tangled and she had weeping red cold sores around her lips. She obviously hadn't washed in a long time, because she smelled of stale body odour and urine.

'Hallo, sweetheart,' said Katie, giving her a smile. 'How are you feeling?'

The girl said nothing, but pulled the blanket up further under her chin.

'This fine lady is going to take you to the hospital,' said Katie. 'The nurses will give you a shower there, and wash your hair for you, and then they'll give you something to eat and drink. Believe me, you'll feel a hundred times better.'

'She hasn't spoken at all,' said the paramedic. 'She won't even tell me her name.'

'Well, that's not unusual,' said Katie. 'Ever since she was taken away from wherever she's come from, I doubt if a single person has done anything but lie to her and threaten her and thrash the daylights out of her if she wouldn't do what she was told. Why should she think that you and me are going to treat her any different?'

She was tempted for a moment to ask the girl about 'Mah-wah-*kee*-yah', but she decided against it. Even if she could persuade her to say anything at all, it was obvious that she was deeply traumatized and in Katie's experience witnesses in that state were almost always unreliable. She didn't want to devote hours of valuable police time trying to distinguish between what had really happened and what might have been nothing more than a young girl's nightmare.

'I'll come and see you later, when you're settled in the hospital' she said, and gave the girl a smile. The girl only stared back and dragged the blanket up so far that only her eyes were showing.

As Katie stepped down from the back of the ambulance, however, the girl did say something, though her voice was so muffled that Katie could hardly hear her. There was noise from outside, too, a police siren suddenly yipping and dozens of people talking.

'Say that again, sweetheart, would you?' Katie asked her.

The girl lowered the blanket a little, took two or three breaths, then whispered, '*Rama Mala'ika!*'

'I'm sorry, girl, I don't understand you. What does that mean? That's not your name, is it? *Rama Mal-ah-eeka?*'

She waited, but the girl didn't repeat it. Katie looked at the paramedic and shrugged.

'Okay if we take her off now?' said the paramedic.

'Of course, yes. Thanks a million.'

It was starting to rain again, so Katie hurried across to the deli and went inside. Detective Horgan was waiting for her and Detective Sergeant ó Nuallán had arrived. They were both standing inside the shop, talking to the technician whose back Katie had seen in the upstairs window.

Kyna ó Nuallán had joined Katie's team only a month ago, from Dublin, to replace Detective Sergeant Jimmy O'Rourke who had been shot and killed while on duty. She was a thin, tall, sharp-faced young woman with a prominent chin, a geometric blonde bob and almost colourless eyes. Detective O'Donovan had said he would have quite fancied her if she didn't always make him feel that he had said something gauche, even before he'd said it.

That was one of the reasons that Katie had selected her, though, apart from the fact that she was a woman. She had a way of listening to witnesses – nodding, not interrupting, but with one finely plucked eyebrow constantly raised as if she didn't believe a single word they were saying. She made them work harder and harder to convince her that they were telling her the truth, and that was a very rare talent. Horgan had already dubbed her Sergeant O'Polygraph.

'I got here as fast as I could, ma'am,' she told Katie. 'I'm almost done with Councillor Parry. You should have my full report on that by Friday, once I've talked to the Cremin brothers. I'm still trying to trace where the payment for that Donnybrook development went to, but I'll find it.'

Katie turned to the technician. He was fortyish, grey-haired, and she had never seen him look anything but weary – as if he went home every night and tried to watch television with his spaghetti supper on his lap but couldn't see anything in his mind's eye but glistening intestines, and couldn't taste anything but Vicks VapoRub.

'Well then,' she said, 'we'd better take a look at this unfortunate feller. How long do you think he's been dead?'

The technician handed her a surgical mask and passed another to Detective Sergeant ó Nuallán. He raised a jar of Vicks, but Katie shook her head and took an aerosol of Lancôme Miracle out of her bag. She sprayed the inside of the mask and then knotted it around her neck. Although most technicians and coroners used Vicks, it opened the nasal passages as well as masking the smell of putrefaction, and she found it made it linger in her lungs for longer. She didn't want to be lying on her pillow tonight still breathing in the stench of death.

'Judging by your *Calliphora vomitoria*, I'd say that three and a half days was about right,' said the technician. 'The weather hasn't been too warm but it's been long enough for them to lay their eggs and for their larvae to hatch out and the first batch to grow to maturity. They've plenty to feed on, after all. Flesh and faeces, their favourites.'

They climbed the stairs, the technician leading the way and Katie following close behind him.

'I've been in touch with Lisney's,' said Detective Horgan, as they reached the first-floor landing. 'This whole property's been empty for about a month. The downstairs was rented by the Hungarian Deli people and Clancy's after tracing them now to see if they went back to Hungary or not. The two upstairs flats were both rented by some company called Merrow Holdings, based in Limerick.'

'Any idea who's behind them?' asked Katie. The perfume inside her surgical mask was so strong she had to sneeze, twice. It made her nose run but she knew better than to take it off, so she sniffed.

'Merrow Holdings? Not yet. But Lisney's said they'd get back to me before the close of business.'

The technician led them into the bedsit. It was lit so

brightly with tungsten lamps that it looked like the set for a morning television show. The technician's young assistant was down on his hands and knees with a Labino Nova torch light with a blue filter on it, searching for bloodstains or any stray fibres that might have been caught under the skirting board. He sat up on his haunches as they came into the room. He had such raging red acne on his forehead that Katie had always thought he looked as if he had been shot in the face with a pellet gun, but compared to the body on the sofa-bed his face was simply speckled.

Katie stood beside the sofa-bed and stared at the body for a long time. He was very dark, with a slightly dusty look about his skin, so she guessed he was probably Somali or Nigerian, since they made up most of Cork's African immigrant population. She could see that he had been shot twice in the face at point-blank range with a shotgun – possibly a double-barrelled shotgun – once in the right cheek and the second time in the left eye. Above his chin, with its precisely trimmed goatee beard, there was nothing but the concave red labyrinth of his sinuses. The technicians had cleared the mature bluebottles from the room, but there were still a few random maggots crawling around inside the victim's face, like cave explorers.

The man was very thin, though his stomach was hugely swollen with gas from his decomposing bowels. His bony right shoulder was covered by a tattoo of a black widow spider in its web, and his long flaccid penis was tattooed to resemble the head of rattlesnake, with scales and eyes, and even a forked tongue licking out of the side of it. The snake continued up through his woolly black pubic hair until it wound itself around his waist and its rattle finished up on his breastbone.

A single brown star was tattooed on each of his knees.

Katie leaned forward and stared at his face more closely. 'His lip's very *pink*,' she commented. The technician came up behind her to take a closer look at it.

'It is, yeah, I'd say it's been tattooed that colour. It's a bit of fashion, apparently, among the young Nigerians. They think it makes them more attractive to girls.'

'What, bright pink lips?'

'Oh yeah. A friend of mine works for Tattoo Zoo on South Main Street. He was telling me about them the other day, those Nigerians. They have a fad for having their mickeys decorated, too, like this feller.'

'What about his hands?' asked Katie, looking at the stumps at the ends of his arms. The bones that protruded from his left hand had been roughly and erratically sawn through at a right angle, while the bones of the right hand had been cut very cleanly, at a slant.

'His hands? Well, they've both gone missing,' said the technician. 'A couple of the guards went searching through the whole house top to bottom but they couldn't find a trace of them. It looks like your man must have taken them away with him for a keepsake.'

'It was a woman, according to the witness.'

The technician looked back down at the grisly hollow of the dead man's face. 'A *woman*? Jesus. She must have taken some rabbie, and no mistake. I'll tell you what's interesting, though. Whoever did it, they shot this feller while he was lying down, right here. *In situ.*'

'Both shots?'

The technician nodded. 'The both of them. Straight through his head and into the sofa cushions.'

'But she used a shotgun ... and even if it was a sawn-off shotgun ...'

'That's right, ma'am. She would have had to be standing on the bed with her feet either side of him, pointing the gun down at his face. Especially since she was a woman, and probably not so tall as a man.'

'So, any sign of footprints?'

'That's what's interesting – no. No indentations in the cushions, no dirt smudges on the sheets from somebody's shoes, nothing.'

Katie slowly raised both hands as if she were holding up a crucifix beside the altar in church. 'Maybe she simply stood where I'm standing now and held up the shotgun vertical with the muzzle downwards and the stock up in the air. Then she could have pushed the trigger up with her thumb.'

'It's possible. They have a fair recoil in them, though, those shotguns. Your average twelve-bore can kick back at you with anything up to twenty foot-pounds – even more, depending on your load. That's like being punched by a middleweight boxer.'

Katie looked around the bedsit. 'I see,' she said. 'Any other forensics you want to show me?'

'There's over a thousand blood spatters, ma'am, as well as flesh fragments and bone fragments and brain tissue. There's also urine and excrement and stray hairs that probably came off the young girl who was hiding in here. Until we move the body off the bed we won't know the full extent of it for sure, but all of the exposed areas of the sheet and the blanket that we've been able to examine so far have numerous semen samples on them.'

'Numerous? How numerous?'

'Too many to give you even a guesstimated figure yet, but I'd say they run into hundreds.'

'It doesn't take a genius to work out what's been

happening in here, then,' said Katie. She went across to the window and looked down into the street, where even more crowds had gathered. 'God, don't these people have anything better to do? Don't they know that *Elev8* starts in a minute?' She was talking about the children's programme on RTÉ2.

She turned around. 'How about the door?' she asked the technician.

'Well, look at it, the lock's not up to much, Hickey's cheapest, but it wasn't forced and the key's still in it.'

'Okay, that might help,' said Katie. 'But it's no good trying to recreate a scenario simply from what we have here. We have no way of telling if the perpetrator came into the room and surprised the victim and the girl together, or if the perpetrator brought them both here from some other location, or if the girl and the perpetrator were here first and the victim burst in on them.

'According to those two fellers who found her, the girl knew the victim, or at least she knew what his name was, but we don't know if she knew who the perpetrator was. That's our number one priority. The sooner we can find out the victim's identity, the sooner we'll have some idea of why he was killed and who might have killed him.'

Sergeant ó Nuallán was jotting in her notebook. 'I'll go to the Tattoo Zoo and ask them for a list of African clients who might have had their lips tattooed lately, and if any of those had their genitals tattooed, too. That'll be a start.'

'There's a few more tattoo places you can try if you don't have any luck there,' said Detective Horgan. 'Body and Soul on Rahilly Street and Magic's on Robert Street. Oh, and there's Dark Arts on Maylor Street ... I know *they* do a lot of Nigerians.'

'"Nigerians" may be *spelled* with a "g", Horgan,' Katie retorted, 'but you *pronounce* it soft, like a "j".'

'Oh, sorry, ma'am,' said Detective Horgan, feigning surprise. 'Don't want to be accused of inadvertent racism. Or even advertent racism, whatever that is.'

'Shut up, Horgan. And start knocking on doors, both sides of the street. We want to know if anybody was seen coming in or out of this building, and when – and if anybody heard anything unusual, whether it sounded like two gunshots or not. Also, if they heard any arguments or shouting or screaming.'

'Yes, ma'am.'

The technician sucked in his breath behind his surgical mask and said, 'We'll be here for three more hours, at least, probably more. I'll let you know as soon as we've had the victim wheeled off to the path lab.'

'Thanks,' said Katie. 'I'd better get on to the state pathologist. Oh God, if it's Reidy, he's really going to hate this one. If there's one thing that gets up his nose, it's a blindingly obvious cause of death.'

When she came back out on to the street, Dan Keane from the *Examiner* was waiting for her, as well as the woman reporter in the silvery anorak with the furry collar. Dan had his usual cigarette hanging out of the side of his mouth, which waggled when he talked, and his face looked even more prune-coloured than ever.

'What's the form, Dan?' she asked him. 'Didn't I hear you were retiring?'

'Can't afford to, superintendent. Not with the price of Powers these days.'

'You could always give it up.'

'Oh yeah, and I could give up breathing, too.'

'Aren't you going to introduce me?'

'Sure, yes, sorry. This is the lovely Branna, superintendent. She's just joined the *Echo*, although I can't imagine she has half an idea what she's let herself in for. Detective Superintendent Maguire, meet Branna MacSuibhne. Branna, girl – meet the highly respected and extremely scary Detective Superintendent Maguire.'

Branna held out her hand but Katie was busy untangling her surgical mask and didn't take it. 'Whatever you do,' she said, nodding at Dan, 'take everything this man tells you with a bucket-load of salt.'

Branna MacSuibhne was much younger than she had seemed at first sight. Perhaps it was the bouffant ash-blonde hair which had been sprayed rigidly into place on either side of her face like two water-buffalo horns, or the thick black mascara on her eyelashes. She had a plump, heart-shaped face and was actually quite pretty, though her chin was a little weak, and Katie would have guessed she wasn't much older than nineteen.

'Do we know who's gone to higher service yet?' asked Dan, nodding towards the upstairs room. Branna tugged a new notebook out of her anorak pocket and stood close beside him with her freshly sharpened pencil poised.

Fionnuala Sweeney came over to join them, with her gingery curls and her trademark green windcheater. Her unshaven cameraman hovered behind her shoulder, repeatedly coughing. Fionnuala held out her RTÉ microphone and smiled sweetly.

Katie was suddenly conscious of how messy her hair was and she gave it two or three tugs to try and tidy it. Fionnuala widened her eyes and kept on smiling, as if to reassure her that she looked grand and not to worry about it.

Katie cleared her throat and said, 'The victim – the victim is an African male of indeterminate age who appears to have been fatally injured by gunshot wounds, although we'll have to wait for the coroner to establish the precise cause of death.'

'His fecking head was blown off,' said Dan, blowing smoke out of the corner of his mouth. 'That would be a precise cause of death for most people, wouldn't you say?'

'For all we know, he may have already been dead before he was shot,' said Katie. 'So, like I say, we're waiting for the coroner.'

35

'There was a girl locked in with the body,' said Fionnuala. 'Do you know who she was? Is she a suspect?'

'An African female was discovered in the flat along with the victim. She wasn't locked in, but it appears that she had been there ever since he was killed.'

'How long was that?'

'We don't know for certain, but seventy-two hours at least, possibly longer.'

'If she wasn't locked in, why didn't she try to get out of there? The body must have been bealing by then!'

'Again, we don't know for sure.'

'When you say "African", what was she?' asked Dan. 'Nigerian? Senegalese? Somali?'

'We haven't established that, either. She's deeply traumatized, as you can imagine, and we haven't had the opportunity to interview her yet. We will, though, when she's up to it.'

'Did she actually witness the victim being shot?' asked Branna.

Katie thought: *Good question, girl.* But in reply she said, 'We don't have any way of knowing at the moment, not until she talks to us.'

She paused, and made a point of looking straight at Fionnuala's cameraman. 'If you saw or heard anything unusual around Lower Shandon Street in the past three or four days, please don't hesitate to get in touch with us. Just dial 021 452 2000. Your identity will be kept secret and it doesn't matter if you think it was important or not, it's surprising what small bits and pieces of information can help us to make an arrest.'

'This African girl,' Branna persisted. 'Was she a prostitute?'

Jesus, aren't you the blunt one, thought Katie. She turned back to Branna and said, 'We don't yet know who she is or where she came from, and so we have no idea if she was a sex worker or not.'

'She was almost naked when she was found.'

'Branna, in this job we come across plenty of people with their pants down. That doesn't necessarily mean they're sex workers.'

'But that will be one of your lines of inquiry?'

Katie gave her a brief, uncommunicative smile. 'As soon as we have any firm information, we'll be sure to pass it on to you.'

'But it is a major problem in Cork, isn't it? Vice, and prostitution? I mean, some people are calling Cork the sex-trade centre of Ireland.'

'That's all for now, Branna,' said Katie. 'We'll be holding a full media conference at Anglesea Street when we have something concrete to tell you.'

'There's at least ten brothels operating in the city centre alone, though, right this minute while we're talking, and more than a hundred prostitutes, easy. I mean, what are you doing about them?'

Katie went over to Branna, took her arm, and drew her aside.

'Branna, if you want to talk to me about vice, then you're welcome to make an appointment and come to Anglesea Street and we'll talk about vice. Right now, I'm dealing with a violent homicide and I'm not going to stand here in the street speculating who might have done it or whether it's connected with the sex trade.'

'But –' Branna began, but Katie lifted a finger to shush her.

'How long have you been with the *Echo*?'

'A week. Well, last week and yesterday, and this morning.'

'I wish you the best of luck, but just remember that this is Cork, not Limerick, or Dublin, and you're not Donal Macintyre. Get to know your contacts first, build up some trust. Then you can start crusading.'

Branna's cheeks flushed pink. 'I'm sorry, superintendent. I didn't mean to overstep the mark, like.'

'That's all right. And don't worry. I'm as much concerned about the vice in this city as you are. But it isn't easy to put a stop to it, for a whole lot of different reasons, and if you come and talk to me about it I'll tell you why.'

Fionnuala Sweeney came up to Katie and said, 'Sorry, superintendent. Can we just do a couple of quick reaction shots?'

'How do you want me?' asked Katie. 'Grinning or grim?'

'Oh, just your normal expression, please.'

For a brief moment, Katie closed her eyes and thought: *My normal expression, what in the name of all that's holy is that? Martyred? Disillusioned? Exhausted?*

She returned to her desk at Anglesea Street, carrying a skinny latte and an iced doughnut, as well as a green manila folder of case notes tucked under her arm. She hadn't even sat down when her mobile rang. *And it's no, nay, never – no, nay never no more—*

'John?' she said, clearing a space on her desk. 'Hold on a moment, John.' Then, 'How did it go with ErinChem?'

Detective O'Donovan appeared in her open doorway but she lifted her hand to indicate that she needed a few minutes before she could talk to him.

John sounded depressed. 'How do you think it went?'

'I don't know. Didn't they want you? I thought you would have been perfect.'

'Well, that was the word they used.'

'What? *Perfect*?'

'Come on, Katie, you know I'm a genius! They did a whole lot more than give me the job. They want me to set up and run a whole new internet marketing division.'

'You're *kidding* me.'

'No, you heard it here first! They're giving me a free hand to hire my own team of web designers, data analysts, product managers, you name it. My official title will be International Online Sales Director.'

'John, I'm so, so pleased for you. Well, I'm pleased for *me*, too. I can't pretend that I'm not.'

'Come on, sweetheart, if it hadn't been for you –'

'What *I* did is totally beside the point. They wouldn't have hired you if they hadn't thought you were exactly the kind of person they were looking for. You have it all, John, you know that. You have the experience. You have the talent. You have those chocolate-brown eyes.'

'Careful, I won't be able to get my head out of the door.'

'We'll have to celebrate,' said Katie. 'But not tonight, I'm afraid. I don't know if you've heard, but there's been a homicide on Lower Shandon Street, so I'll probably be working very late tonight. Well, no, the victim's body was discovered this morning, but it's probably been there for three or four days. Yes. Don't ask. No. *Faugh*. I can still smell it now.'

'So what time can I expect you home?' John asked her.

'I don't know for sure. But don't wait up. I love you, and congratulations. Oh – and by the way – how much are they paying you?'

'Eighty k basic, but with excellent bonuses, and if the online sales do really well, the sky's the limit.'

'I love you, John. You've made my day.'

'I love you, too, detective superintendent.'

Katie put her phone down. She was so pleased that she couldn't stop herself from smiling, even when Detective O'Donovan came back in. He looked at her quizzically, but said nothing. She had always made it clear that her personal life was private. Everybody at Anglesea Street knew about John Meagher, of course, and Katie's relationship with him was the subject of daily gossip in the canteen, but nobody would have dared ask her to her face how she and John were getting along together.

John Meagher had been born and brought up in Cork, but he had emigrated to America and up until three years ago had been running a successful dot.com pharmaceutical business in San Francisco. Then his father had suddenly passed away, and he had been called back to Knocknadeenly, north of Cork, to take care of his elderly mother and to run the family farm. Because he was the oldest, the rest of the Meaghers had expected it of him, and he hadn't felt able to refuse.

A series of murders had brought Katie to Knocknadeenly, and that was when she had met John for the first time. In the rain, and the mud, under the most stressful of circumstances. But after Katie's first husband, Paul, had died, she and John had started an affair, and their affair had gradually grown fiercer, and stronger, and more passionate.

'You're my Greek god,' she had written to him in a note – because that was what he reminded her of, with his curly black hair and his straight nose and his muscles that had been sculpted by months of ploughing and raking and toting bales of hay.

But no matter how hard John worked, eking a living out of the farm had been a losing battle, even before the recession. When the Irish economy collapsed, John had been forced to sell the farm for a loss. He had planned to go back to the United States and join some of his friends in a new online pharmacy business, and he had asked Katie to resign from An Garda Síochána and come with him. He had even arranged a job for her with Pinkerton's detective agency.

Katie's father had advised her to go. You have only the one life, girl. Don't end up a miserable old spinster with nobody but cats for company. But she had found it impossible to think about quitting the senior position that she had struggled so hard to achieve. More than that, she felt that she had sworn to give her life to protecting the people of Cork, and what was she going to do, turn her back on them, just because she had fallen in love?

She had called Aidan Tierney, the chief executive officer of ErinChem, the pharmaceutical company out at Ringaskiddy, and they had met for lunch at Isaac's. Only a few months before, Katie had helped to keep Aidan's daughter Sinéad out of the courts when she was arrested along with several other teenagers for organized shoplifting in Penneys, of all places. The clothes in Penneys were so cheap they were practically giving them away anyhow. Aidan had been toying with the idea of setting up an online sales division at ErinChem, and Katie had suggested that John might be just the man to do it for them.

Now John could stay in Ireland, with a job that he was really good at, and a respectable income, and Katie could stay at Anglesea Street. She felt so happy she could have gone for a drink, instead of a lukewarm latte from Costa Coffee.

'Ma'am?' said Detective O'Donovan, at last.

'Sorry, Patrick, yes, what is it?'

'You're smiling, ma'am.'

'Yes, detective, I'm smiling. Is that a crime?'

'No, ma'am. Just to let you know that we interviewed the staff in Nolan's the butcher's and the African restaurant opposite. One of the lads who works in the butcher's says he was laying out sausages in the window on Friday morning when this black feller comes past in this bright purple suit. The lad looks up at him and the black feller looks back, and he's wearing a beard. The black feller, not the lad.'

'Well, our victim had a beard, but he didn't have a purple suit. In fact he didn't have any clothes at all. Did the boy remember what time this was?'

'About midday, he said. But a few minutes later, just before they opened, he sees a black woman walk past, too.'

'That's not unusual for Lower Shandon Street. If you stand there long enough, half of Africa's going to walk past you.'

'He only noticed her because of what she was wearing,' said Detective O'Donovan. 'Like, the African women, they're usually wearing some kind of wrapping, what do they call them, *abayas*, and a headscarf. And I'm not being racist or nothing but most of them seem to have arses the size of Cork and they walk very slow and deliberate like they own the place. I was trying to get past one of them in Penneys the other day and it was like trying to push my way in through a fecking turnstile at Páirc Uí Chaoimh.'

'*Patrick*,' Katie admonished him.

'Well, yes, no, I know I shouldn't say that, but you know. It's like it's a national characteristic, like.' He held out both hands as if he were measuring something about four feet wide.

'But this girl—?'

'This girl was skinny, and all dressed in black. Black jeans and a black jacket, with a black scarf tied around her head. He said she was very black herself, like, but very pretty. That

42

Rihanna, that's who he said she reminded him of.'

'Okay, I see. Did he see where either of them went?'

'After the girl had gone by, he stepped out into the street to take another look at her, but she was gone. So either she was a real quick walker, because it's all uphill there, or else she disappeared into one of the shops.'

'How about the man in the purple suit?'

'No sign of him, neither.'

Katie sat down. The pale sun that had come out briefly had been swallowed up behind the clouds again and her office became so gloomy that she was tempted to tell O'Donovan to switch on the overheard light. A few drops of rain sprinkled against the window.

'Did the butcher boy see if the girl was carrying anything? Like a bag, or a sack? Maybe a golf bag, something like that?'

'If he did, he didn't say so. You're thinking how she got the shotgun into the premises, if it was her who did it?'

'Well, of course. And you should have thought of that.'

'I'll go back and ask him. I have to go back anyway because one of the fellers who works in the African restaurant saw the feller in the purple suit and he thinks the cook there knows who he is, but the cook hadn't come on for his shift yet and the feller didn't know where he lives.'

'Okay, Patrick, if you can do that, please. Anybody else see them? The girl, or the purple suit man?'

'If they did, they're not saying. But Horgan's asking around the various African communities to see if anybody knows who they are. There can't be too many black fellers strutting around in purple suits now, can there? And if we don't have any luck there, we'll canvas the menswear shops and the tailors'.'

Katie said, 'I'll have a word with Maeve Twomey.' Maeve Twomey was her ethnic liaison officer and closely in touch with the various immigrant groups who had settled in Cork, especially the Poles and the Lithuanians and the Africans. 'She can talk to Emeka Ikebuasi, he's the big cheese in the Nigerian community. And that Somali, whatever his name is. Geedi something. The one who keeps jiggling up and down while he's talking to you like he's doing a rain dance.'

'A rain dance, that's rich. In Cork, how would you ever know if it had worked or not?'

As if to emphasize his point, rain lashed against the window, hard and brittle, and the hooded crows on the car parked opposite took to the air, as if at last they had lost their patience with being rained on.

Once O'Donovan had gone, Katie eased the lid off her coffee and opened the manila folder in front of her. This contained a list of all the charges they had brought against Michael Gerrety relating to his sex website, Cork Fantasy Girls, as well as his financial connections to at least seven brothels and three so-called massage parlours and fitness clubs, including the notorious Nightingale Club on Grafton Street.

Gerrety had contended that he had done nothing legally or morally wrong. By allowing girls to advertise on his website, he said, he was making sure that their business was all out in the open and they were much safer than if they had been obliged to rely on cards in newsagents' windows or small ads in the local papers, or walking the streets.

Women's and immigrants' support groups in Cork had combined together to start a campaign called Turn Off The Red Light, the aim of which was to eradicate local prostitution and the trafficking of women for sex. In retaliation,

Gerrety had launched Give It The Green Light, to fight for the decriminalization of sex work.

Give It The Green Light had produced posters of pretty, smiling women saying 'I'm Happy In My Job – And I'm a Sex Worker'. If Gerrety hadn't been making so much money out of prostitution, Katie could almost have believed that he was sincere.

She finished reading through the file and sat back. She knew that advertising brothels and prostitution was prohibited by the Criminal Justice (Public Order) Act of 1994. But if a girl didn't specifically offer sex on Gerrety's website, was her advertisement in breach of the law?

And what if a man answered the girl's advertisement and had sex with her, could Gerrety be said to be living off immoral earnings, since he charged her 200 euros a month to post it? Or could he protest that what two people decided to do together once they had met on a social website had nothing to do with him whatsoever? You might just as well prosecute an online dating agency for living off immoral earnings. Or the *Examiner* even, for running a lonely hearts column.

It was Chief Superintendent O'Driscoll who had insisted on charges being brought against Michael Gerrety. He was a deeply religious man and he despised Gerrety with a passion – he almost considered his disdain for the laws of brothel-keeping to be a personal insult. In Katie's opinion, though, they had charged Gerrety prematurely, before they had gathered enough evidence that would stand up in court, and on reflection Chief Superintendent O'Driscoll had been inclined to agree with her. With his approval, Katie had set up Operation Rocker to dig out even more substantial proof that Gerrety was breaking the law.

She took her cup of coffee to the window and stared out of it for a long time. Only one street away she could see the tall greenish tower of The Elysian. It was seventeen storeys high and the tallest building in the whole of Ireland. It had been built in the boom days of the Celtic Tiger, before the financial crash of 2008, and even now almost half of its apartments and offices were still empty. The people of Cork had been quick to nickname it 'The Idle Tower', after The Idle Hour pub nearby. But there was one apartment that she knew was occupied, right at the very top, with a commanding view of the whole of the city, and that was where Michael Gerrety lived.

She couldn't stop herself from thinking about little Corina, too frightened of punishment even to take a single square of chocolate – or of the girl who had been found with the headless, handless body in the bedsit in Lower Shandon Street, too terrified to leave the room.

It was raining almost insanely hard now, as if God were trying to wash all of the city's sins away. Katie's jubilation at John's finding a job at ErinChem had subsided, and she felt flat. She almost wished she had given up on Cork and gone to San Francisco with him.

At least in San Francisco it wouldn't be raining as if it were never going to stop.

Five

Zakiyyah was woken up by the sound of somebody whistling and drumming a complicated rhythm on a tabletop.

She lifted her head from the bed and looked around. Her eyes were unfocused and her ears were ringing, as if she had fallen over and hit the back of her head. She was lying in a large gloomy room with sloping dormer ceilings that were blotched with damp. The carpet was a dirty bright green and fraying at the edges. Through the grimy windows at either end of the room she could see wet slate rooftops, so she guessed they must be three or four storeys up.

In the street below she could hear traffic and people's feet pattering and clicking along the pavement, and somebody shouting '*Echo*! *Echo*!' The man who was whistling and drumming was sitting at a table beside the door, bent over a newspaper, which he was reading with all the intensity of somebody studying an instruction manual. Every now and then he stopped whistling and drumming, sniffed, and turned a page. He was bald and bulky, a light-skinned African, wearing a yellow flowery shirt that was straining across his shoulders.

Zakiyyah said nothing, but sat watching him. She had no idea where she was or how she had got here, but she felt completely detached, as if she wasn't really there at all, but was just dreaming about it. The smell of damp carpet wasn't a dream, though, and neither was her headache, nor the stiffness in her shoulders and elbows, as if she had been sleeping in the same position for a very long time.

She thought she recognized the tune the man was whistling and drumming – 'Sex Tape' by Tamaya. They had been playing it in the Z-Club where she had been working on Victoria Island in Lagos. That all seemed so far away and long ago, and her home village near Shaki seemed to have shrunk even further into the distance. Her father had grinned at her with his three front teeth missing, but her mother had been weeping and she had repeatedly reached out to touch Zakiyyah's face with her fingertips, as if she would never see her again as long as she lived. Her younger sister, Assibi, had been standing a little way away, staring at her in bewilderment. Why is Zakiyyah leaving us and going with those men? It had been a grey, humid day and she remembered the acrid smell of diesel fumes from the men's Land Rover.

Zakiyyah's left arm felt sore and she slowly rubbed it. She was wearing nothing but a knee-length sleeveless slip of pale turquoise satin, spattered with a few dark stains. She reached up and felt her hair, which was braided in its usual cornrows, with coloured glass beads. She was still wearing the pink glass bracelet around her wrist that her mother had given her on the day she had left the village. She had said that it contained the spirit of her *Orisha*, her guardian spirit Ochumare.

The man at the table turned to the last page of his newspaper, read it intently, then folded it neatly in half and looked across at her. 'So! You are awake at last?' he said.

He had almost no neck, and his face appeared to be squashed so that his eyes had almost disappeared and his nostrils had spread wide and his lips bulged out. He reminded Zakiyyah of the wooden gods that her uncle used to carve.

He stood up and waddled over to her. 'Do you know how *long* you been *sleeping*?' He had the strangest sing-song accent, like nothing that Zakiyyah had ever heard before. It was half Cork, half Nigerian.

Zakiyyah shook her head.

'Twenty-seven hours, near enough. Still, not really surprising considering the dose that Mister Dessie give you. You hungry? You thirsty? Bet you busting for a piss, right?'

Zakiyyah looked up at him but didn't answer him. She didn't know what to say. She had no idea who he was or what she was doing here or why she should have slept for so long.

The man lifted an iPhone out of his shirt pocket and tapped out a number, breathing heavily as he did so. As he waited for an answer, he gave Zakiyyah a wink and a thumbs-up sign and said, 'You going to do good, girl. You *real* pretty, let me tell you that. And wow, them little diddies! You going to have them queuing round the corner.'

Zakiyyah touched her lips and said, 'Drink? I can have drink?'

'Sure, sure you can, what would you like? I got Coke. Or water. Or there's Murphy's if you feel like something stronger.'

'Water,' said Zakiyyah. She didn't understand what he meant by the other drinks.

'Just a second,' the man told her. 'Mister Dessie? Yeah. Bula here. Yeah. How's it hanging? Well, the girl's woke up now. Grand, from what I can tell. No, fine. No, absolutely fine. Yeah. Okay. I'll see you in five, then.'

He switched off his phone and crossed over to the other side of the room, where he opened a door that led to a small kitchenette. Zakiyyah could see a sink with a Baby Belling oven on the draining board, and a window covered with a broken Venetian blind.

The man filled a red china mug with water and brought it back to her. He stood over her while she gulped it down, and then said, 'More?'

She shook her head. She didn't know what she wanted. She just wished that she didn't feel so dizzy and unreal.

'Look,' said the man. 'Mister Dessie's going to be here in a minute. He's a good man, Mister Dessie, so long as you do what he tells you. You understand me? He will always treat you right and give you all the stuff you want, so long as you work hard and don't give him no trouble.'

'I always work hard,' said Zakiyyah. 'I never give my boss no trouble.'

'In that case, you and Mister Dessie will rub along fine.'

Zakiyyah looked around the room. 'Where is this place?' she asked him. 'They tell me I am coming to work in a club, dancing, like Z-Club.'

'Well, that's right. Kind of. I think you have one or two financial things to sort out first. Mister Dessie will tell you all about it.'

'But this is Ireland?'

'Yes, girl. This *is* Ireland.'

Zakiyyah shook her head again, but it still wouldn't clear. 'I don't remember coming here. I came on a plane?'

'No, you came on a ship. But don't you worry about it. You're here now, girl. Your new life starts here'

'I still can't think.'

'Like I said, don't worry about it. Mister Dessie won't be paying you to think.'

'What about my clothes? Where is my suitcase?'

'Mister Dessie will sort out something for you to wear.'

'But in my suitcase was not only clothes. I have pictures of my family. I have other things. My make-up. Things that my friends in Lagos gave me.'

The man went back to the table, picked up a red and white carton of Carrolls cigarettes and lit one. Smoke blew out of his wide-apart nostrils as if one of her uncle's carved wooden gods had come to life.

'All that kind of thing, you'll have to ask Mister Dessie about all that. Me, I'm just here to keep an eye on you.'

'But I want to get dressed.'

The man looked amused. 'I don't think you'll be worrying too much about that, darling. Not in your line of work.'

Zakiyyah stood up. Her head was gradually beginning to feel clearer. She had been promised a nightclub job in Ireland, as a hostess and dancer, just like her job at the Z-Club. Her manager, Benjamin Bankole, had been talking to an Irishman who had visited the club. He had called her into his office and asked her if she wanted to make ten times as much money as she was making in Lagos.

The Irishman had been standing next to her manager's desk. He had been fat and balding and wearing a sweat-stained shirt with palm trees and monkeys on it. He had grinned at her and said, 'Who knows, girl? You wait till my friend Michael Gerrety claps his eyes on you. You could even be famous.'

She still wasn't clear what had happened after that. She could remember packing her suitcase. But then the Irishman had come round to the house where was staying on Oluwole Street to pick her up and told her that she needed a rabies inoculation before the immigration authorities would allow her into Ireland. Luckily enough, he had some vaccine with him.

She remembered sitting on the side of her creaky bed and baring her arm for him, but that was all.

'I need toilet,' she told the bald African man.

'There – through there,' he said, pointing to a door opposite the kitchenette.

Zakiyyah went into the cramped windowless lavatory and closed the door, although there was no lock on it. The wooden seat was loose and the cistern was gurgling. This wasn't how she had imagined Ireland at all. She had imagined a dark, plush club with twinkling lights and smartly dressed customers. She had imagined dancing between the tables and beaming men tucking banknotes into her garters, just like they had at the Z-Club.

At first she could urinate only in fits and starts, but then it seemed as if she were never going to stop. She still hadn't finished before the man opened the toilet door without knocking and said, 'How long are you going to be, girl? Mister Dessie's here!'

There was toilet paper, but nowhere for Zakiyyah to wash her hands. She came out of the toilet and started to cross the room towards the kitchenette. She was only halfway there, though, when a loud, twangy voice said, 'And where the feck d'you think *you're* going? Come here, girl!'

She stopped and turned. A podgy man in a grey double-breasted suit was standing in the middle of the room, with his hands deep in his jacket pockets and his legs spread apart. He had black wavy hair which was short on top but curled over his collar at the back in a mullet. His eyes were bulbous and his nose was an odd bifurcated blob and his lips were red and rubbery. He wore a wide red zigzag necktie but it did nothing to hide his belly, which hung pendulously over his belt.

Zakiyyah hesitated, but the man in the grey suit flapped his hand to beckon her over, once, twice, and then again, much more irritably, so she slowly approached him. She was very conscious that she was wearing nothing but this thin turquoise slip and she crossed her arms protectively over her breasts so that he wouldn't see her nipples.

'This is Mister Dessie,' said the bald African man, as if that weren't obvious. 'Say hallo to Mister Dessie, Zakiyyah.'

'That's your name, Zakiyyah?' asked Mister Dessie. He stuck his thumb up his right nostril and tugged at it, as if he had some dried mucus up there that he was trying to dislodge. 'What does that mean? Anything? I know what *this* meb's name means, Bula-Bulan Yaro. Fat Boy.'

'Zakiyyah means pure,' said the bald man, blowing out smoke. 'Like, never touched by nobody, never.'

'Ha!' said Mister Dessie. 'I like that! Usually we change the girls' names, but I really like that! That's what-do-you-call-it? Ironic.'

The bald man smiled and nodded, though it was obvious he didn't have the faintest idea what 'ironic' meant.

Mister Dessie went over to the bed and sat down and patted the blanket beside him to indicate that Zakiyyah should sit down, too. She did so, very cautiously, although she kept as far away from him as she could.

'You have my suitcase?' she asked him.

He blinked at her with those bulbous eyes, like a toad. 'Your suitcase? Why would I have your suitcase?'

'It has all my clothes in it, and my shoes, and pictures of my family.'

Mister Dessie slowly shook his head. 'Don't know what would have happened to that, girl. Not my department. But don't you worry, I can fix you up with something to wear.'

'But in my suitcase is everything.'

'No, no, no, that's where you have it wrong. Whatever you had in your suitcase, that *used* to be everything, but that was before you agreed to come here. The thing is, like, you're in considerable debt to us, financially, and you're going to have to find a way to pay us back.'

Zakiyyah frowned at him, and crossed her arms even more tightly across her breasts. 'I do not understand you,' she said. 'How am I in debt?'

Mister Dessie slapped his sausage-tight trouser leg and turned to Bula-Bulan Yaro. 'Did you hear that, Bula? "How am I in debt?" Would you credit the naivety?'

'Pure amazing,' said Bula, in his strange Nigerian-Irish accent, although it was obvious that he didn't know what 'naivety' meant, either.

Mister Dessie turned back to Zakiyyah and said, 'How much do you think it cost us to get you here? Your boat ticket? All of our other expenses? And just remember that you agreed to come here voluntary, like. My friends assured me that nobody forced you. But you could hardly expect us to bring you here for free.'

Zakiyyah was beginning to feel anxious now. 'I do not know how much it cost,' she said. 'Those men told me that I would make a lot of money in Ireland, much more than in Lagos.'

'Well, you will, darling, I can assure you of that,' said Mister Dessie, patting her thigh. 'For starters, though, you have to reimburse us. As much as we'd like to think of ourselves as a charitable institution, we're a business, and we can't afford to be shelling out boat tickets left, right and centre.'

Bula grunted in amusement. He must have heard all of this so many times before.

Zakiyyah was beginning to feel shivery, even though the room was so warm and stuffy. She touched her forehead and she was perspiring. She felt as if she could hardly breathe, especially since the air was so thick with Bula's stale cigarette smoke.

'How much do I owe you for the ticket?' she asked Mister Dessie. 'If I owe you, yes, I will pay you back.'

'Two thousand seven hundred and fifty euros, all told,' said Mister Dessie, without even blinking. 'But for you, we'll say two thousand five.'

'How much is that in dollars?' Zakiyyah asked him.

Bula had been prodding at his iPhone. 'Three thousand three hundred and sixty-four dollars, give or take,' he called out.

'I can pay you back every week, when the club pays me,' said Zakiyyah.

'What club?' asked Mister Dessie.

Zakiyyah felt even chillier now, and she was beginning to tremble. 'The club I came to dance at.'

'You won't be dancing at any clubs, darling, not until you pay us back what you owe us.'

'What do you mean? How can I pay you back if I cannot dance?'

'Simple. You can work for us, that's how. We have a club where men come along to be entertained by pretty young women like you. If you do that for two or three months, you should have cleared your debt, and then you can take yourself away and dance your rear end off wherever the fancy takes you. But not until then.'

Zakiyyah was shaking. 'I do not understand you. I do not know what you mean. Please. I need my suitcase. I need my clothes. I do not feel very good. I feel sick.'

'It's not difficult to understand, darling,' said Mister Dessie. 'A man feels the itch for some female company, like, so he comes along to our club and chooses a female to give him some company. That's all there is to it. Depending on how much your man's prepared to pay, she'll give him a hand-job, or a blow-job, or intercourse, front or back or both, and everybody's happy.'

Zakiyyah couldn't believe what he had just said to her. 'You want me to be a *bagar*? A hooker?'

'A *hooker*? We don't call them that in Ireland. We call them *hostesses*, or sex workers. It's a very respectable way of life altogether in Ireland, believe you me. It's not quite like being a nun, I'll grant you that, but it's not so much sluttier than serving behind the cosmetics counter at Brown Thomas. And, like I say, you won't have to do it for more than two or three months.'

'I think I need doctor,' said Zakiyyah. Her stomach knotted up and she unexpectedly retched, although nothing came up except a mouthful of sour-tasting saliva.

'Oh, you need something to eat, that's all,' said Mister Dessie. 'Bula can send out for a pizza for you. We'll have to add it on to your bill, mind. But that's business. You'll never get rich if you don't watch the pennies.'

'I am sick,' said Zakiyyah. 'I cannot work for you. I cannot be *bagar*. Please, I feel very sick.'

'You don't have a choice, I'm sorry to tell you,' Mister Dessie replied. 'If you don't work for me, I'll report you to the immigration authorities and you'll be arrested as an illegal immigrant and locked up in the Dóchas Centre. That's the prison for women who don't behave themselves, and believe me, you won't like it in there.'

'I can go back to Lagos. Please.'

'Go back to Lagos? How? How are you going to pay for it? And just for the moment I have your passport for safe keeping, in case you think of skipping the country without settling up what you owe us.'

Zakiyyah retched again. She felt as if her whole stomach lining was being turned inside out, like the sleeve of a jacket.

Mister Dessie stood up. 'I know what you need, girl,' he told her. 'You've caught the rabies, that why you're feeling so sick. It was Charlie's fault. He didn't give you enough of the vaccine. Here.'

He reached into his inside pocket and took out a flat black leather case. He laid it on the table, unzipped it, and slid out a hypodermic syringe and a small glass bottle. Zakiyyah glanced over at him once or twice, but now she was shaking too much to care what he was doing. Bula stood by, with his arms folded, smiling placidly.

Mister Dessie sat down beside her again and lifted up her left arm. She felt a sharp prick, like a mosquito sting, and then Mister Dessie said, 'There. You're grand. You'll be feeling much better before you know it.'

He turned to Bula and said, 'You can take this one over to Washington Street. I think Mairead's ready for her now. Any road, Michael will be wanting to take a sconce at her later.'

Zakiyyah's shakes were gradually subsiding, though her thigh muscles continued to twitch now and again. She felt a warmth rising up inside her, and a calmness. In fact she felt almost light-headed.

'I must have my suitcase,' she said.

Mister Dessie ignored her. He stood up and zipped the hypodermic syringe back in its case and returned it to his inside pocket. Then he said to Bula, 'As soon as you've

57

dropped this one at Mairead's, I want you to go over to Carroll's Quay and see what the feck that Lindsey has been up to.'

'What's the story there, like?'

'I don't know for sure, but there was some kind of a shimozzle with one of her customers last night and he called for the guards. That's the last thing we need, being haunted by the shades. As if we don't pay the bastards too much as it is. They'll all be taking themselves off on holliers in the Canaries before we know it, at our expense, with their blue lights flashing!'

'I must have my suitcase,' Zakiyyah repeated. 'It has all my clothes – everything!'

Mister Dessie turned to her and said, 'Will you ever shut the feck up? I know you come from Africa, like, but you don't have to pester me like a fecking parrot.'

'But I need my clothes! And I am not going to work for you as *bagar*!'

Mister Dessie paused for a moment, looking at Bula as if to say what am I going to do with this girl she's giving me a pain where I didn't even know I had a window.

Then he walked across to the bed and clamped his hand around the back of Zakiyyah's neck, hauling her on to her feet. She yelped out in pain but he gripped her even tighter and shook her head until the beads in her cornrows rattled. Without saying a word, he pulled up her turquoise satin slip and forced his right hand between her legs. She tried to clench her thighs together and bend herself forward, but he wrenched her neck up even further so that she actually felt her tendons crackle.

Breathing furious onion fumes into her face, he hooked two fingers up inside her, and then pressed his thumb against her clitoris, as hard as he could. He kept up the pressure relentlessly for nearly ten seconds, all the time staring at her with those bulging eyes and breathing noisily through his nostrils.

Zakiyyah could do nothing but stare back at him, her mouth wide open in pain. Bula meanwhile wasn't even taking any notice of her, but prodding on his mobile phone again, as if he was used to seeing Mister Dessie treat girls like this and thought nothing of it.

After a while, Mister Dessie abruptly released her neck and took his fingers out of her. Still without saying anything, he went over to the kitchenette and washed his hands with Fairy Liquid. He came out again, shaking droplets of water all across the room. Zakiyyah could only stand where she was, her head bowed, one hand slowly massaging the back of her neck. He had hurt her between her legs, too, but she didn't want to touch herself there, not in front of him.

Mister Dessie went to the door. As he opened it, though, he stopped and said, 'Hey!'

Zakiyyah didn't respond. She hadn't wanted to cry, but now she couldn't help herself. The tears slid down her cheeks and dripped off her chin.

'Hey, are you hearing me, girl?' Mister Dessie demanded. 'Because let that be a fecking lesson to you! Don't you ever try to take the piss out of me, girl, because that's what you'll get, or worse.'

Still Zakiyyah didn't answer. Instead, she turned away and shuffled over to the bed. She eased herself painfully down on to its worn-out springs and curled herself up like a child.

Six

It was nearly 10.30 p.m. when Detective O'Donovan knocked at Katie's office door again. He looked scruffy and tired. The shoulders of his khaki trench coat were still sparkling with raindrops and his tie was crooked. Katie was in the middle of shuffling all of her papers straight, in preparation for going home.

'What's the story?' she asked him. 'You look all flah'd out.'

He sat down heavily in the armchair on the other side of Katie's desk, took out a crumpled Kleenex and loudly blew his nose. 'I hope I'm not getting one of them summer colds, that's all. I was interviewing that feller who'd been cutting and shutting them motors down at Victoria Cross yesterday and he was sneezing all over me like he was trying to blow me out of the door.'

'So, any luck with Maka-wiya?'

'Mawa-*kiy*-a, ma'am, and it's the feller's nickname, not his actual real name. The cook in the African restaurant knows him – well, at least by sight. He goes in there at least once a week to eat, on account of they cook this special Nigerian dish he likes, pepper soup with hot chilli and fatty lamb and big slices of tripe.'

'Please, Patrick! My stomach hasn't recovered from

smelling your man's decomposing body today, let alone finding out what disgusting food he used to eat.'

'Oh, sorry, ma'am,' said Detective O' Donovan. He tugged his notebook out of his coat pocket, licked his thumb, and flipped it open. 'From what the cook was telling me, like, he's a real cute hoor, this Mawakiya. He's got his sticky black fingers into almost everything you can think of. Drugs – especially the party stuff like Es and ket and miaow-miaow and GHB. Stolen copper wiring. Stolen mobile phones. But his main line of business is pimping. He has contacts in Sierra Leone and Benin and Nigeria and he brings a steady stream of girls over. The cook said he always has two or three sexy young girls with him whenever he comes in to eat, and it's never the same girls twice. And *very* young. He reckoned that some of them couldn't have been older than fourteen or fifteen.'

'But we only know his nickname?'

'Mawakiya, that's right. It means the Singer, according to the cook, on account of the feller never stops singing. Well, he's stopped singing now, of course, for permanent.'

'What language are we talking about? And don't just say "African".'

'Hausa, that's what the cook told me. He speaks it himself. But they speak Hausa all over the shop in West Africa, not just one particular country.'

Katie tapped her pencil against her teeth and frowned. 'I don't understand how he's never shown up on our radar before. A black feller in a purple suit pushing drugs and getting himself involved in low-level larceny and pimping underage girls from Africa. You'd think our alarm bells would have rung the moment he first stepped out on the street.'

'Maybe they did,' said Detective O'Donovan.' There's at

least three black pimps that we know of, aren't there? With his head missing, he could be easily be one of them and how would we know? Maybe he didn't wear a purple suit *all* the time. I've got a yellow leather jacket myself, like, and I hardly ever wear it.'

'Thank God for small mercies.'

'Well, yeah, the missus is not too keen on it, either. Every time I put it on she calls me Hell's Canary.'

Katie said, 'At least we're sure of a name now, even if it is only a nickname. That means I can put out an appeal through the media tomorrow morning, asking for anybody to come forward if "Mawakiya" rings a bell, or if they ever saw a black feller walking around the city in a purple suit, or if they remember seeing anybody answering that description at the restaurant or anywhere else around Lower Shandon Street.

'We can also ask if anybody noticed that black girl in black – the one the butcher boy saw. The one who looked like Rihanna. If she really *does* look like that, somebody must reck her.'

She scribbled a note to herself and then said, 'I'll go to the hospital first thing and try talking to the girl again. You and Horgan and Dooley see if you can find those three black pimps, if only to eliminate them. There's that Johnny-G, isn't there? And the one who calls himself The Spider. Terence Somebody.'

'Terence Chokwu. The other one is Ambibola Okonkwo, although don't ask me how in the name of Jesus I can ever remember that.'

'If you can't find them, or you can't find all of them, you can start asking around the brothels and massage parlours. In fact, you can do that anyway.'

'Do you know how many brassers we've got on our books as of yesterday?' said Detective O'Donovan.' Seventy-six in the city centre alone. That's going to take us forever. Besides,' he said, taking out his tissue again and wiping his nose, 'I can't see any of them telling us much. There's usually only one reason they open their mouths and it's not to grass on anybody.'

'Oh, come on, Patrick,' Katie cajoled him. 'I know how persuasive you can be, especially with the ladies.'

'What about the autopsy?' O'Donovan asked.

'A pathologist is coming down tomorrow afternoon. Not Dr Reidy, I'm sorry to say – or on the other hand, perhaps I'm not.' She peered at the notepad on her desk and said, 'Dr O'Brien. Never met him before. He doesn't like to fly, so they told me, so he's coming on the train. He can start by doing some DNA tests. Since our victim has no hands he has no fingers, and since he has no fingers we have no fingerprints. The technical boys didn't find any at the scene, did they? Only the girl's.

'Meanwhile, I'll have Kyna talk to INIS and the UK Immigration Service, too. And the Nigerian embassy of course.'

Detective O'Donovan dry-washed his face with his hands. 'Okay then, unless there's anything else you want me to do I'm going to shave a bullock.'

'No, you go. I'll see you in the morning.'

Before he went, though, O'Donovan stopped and said, 'You do realize something about this woman who allegedly blew this feller's head off?'

'What?' said Katie. She was already skimming through a report about farm machinery that had been stolen from Coolyduff and Templehill. O'Donovan didn't answer immediately, and so after a while she looked up.

'What?' she repeated.

'Well, I'd say that she's done us a considerable favour, ridding the city of a scumbag like that. Wouldn't you?'

By the time she turned into the driveway in front of her single-storey house in Cobh it had stopped raining. The clouds had cleared away and the moon was reflected like a broken plate in the half-mile stretch of water that separated Cobh from Monkstown on the opposite shore. A soft breeze was blowing and it was unusually warm, almost as if somebody were breathing on her face.

She paused in the porch for a moment with her front-door key held up to the lock. The breeze had made her think of little Seamus breathing against her face, and it had given her one of those terrible and unexpected pangs of grief. She knew there was no point in grieving. She could cry for the rest of her life and it would never bring him back again. She just hoped that he could see her now, wherever he was, in some baby's heaven, and that he knew how desperately she missed him.

She was still standing there when the door opened and John appeared, accompanied by a billow of acrid smoke, as if he were a demon making an entrance in a pantomime.

'Ah, Katie! I thought I heard your car.'

'Holy Mary, Mother of God, what's going on?' said Katie, flapping her hand at the smoke. 'You haven't set fire to the place, have you?'

'Oh, that, no, everything's fine. I just let the potatoes boil dry, that's all. I've opened all the windows in the kitchen. Come on in.'

Barney, her Irish red setter, came trotting out of the living room to greet her. 'Don't jump up, Barney,' she told him. 'I'm a little too tired for jumping up.'

'Hard day, huh?' John asked her. He kissed her and then helped her out of her red waterproof jacket.

'Yes, well, I'd rather talk about your day than mine.'

'Hey, come take a load off, and I'll pour you a drink. I bought champagne, to celebrate.'

'I'll just have a vodka to start with, if that's okay. Jesus, how many potatoes did you burn?'

'Oh, I think I managed to rescue most of them. I forgot all about them, that was the trouble. You know me, I can only think about one thing at a time and most of the time that's you.'

'Get away out of here, you spoofer,' she smiled, but she put her arms around his waist and lifted up her face for them to kiss. She had grown to love him so much. He was tall, with dark curly hair, though he had been to the barber's to have it cut shorter and neater for his interview with ErinChem. His eyes were brown but in some lights they could look agate or even garnet-coloured. Although she thought he was Greek-god handsome, Katie was always taken by the way he never seemed to take himself too seriously, and was never arrogant. At the same time, she had seen for herself how determined he was. He had come within an inch of persuading her to resign from An Garda Síochána and accompany him to San Francisco.

She kissed him again and again. He looked so attractive in his crisp white shirt and he still smelled of the 1881 aftershave he had worn for his interview, although he smelled of burned potatoes, too.

'Hey, are you *hungry*?' he asked her, as she kept on kissing him.

'I'm in love. And I'm so happy you've got that job.'

'Well, me too. If it all works out well, there's no reason

why I shouldn't do fifty times better than I would have done in the States. That CEO thinks a whole lot of you, doesn't he, that Aidan Tierney? He was praising you up to the sky.'

'I did him a favour once,' said Katie, and then immediately wished that she hadn't. She gave John one more kiss and went over to the drinks table and poured herself a double measure of Smirnoff Black Label. She took a large swallow, and coughed, and for a moment she couldn't breathe.

John stopped in the doorway. 'Hey, are you okay? Not going to choke to death on me, are you, before I can serve you my celebratory supper?'

Katie shook her head, lifting her glass to show him that she was all right, just trying to get her breath back.

Then – 'What favour?' he asked her.

'Oh, it was nothing much. His daughter got into some trouble and I had a word in the right ear, that's all.'

'What kind of trouble?'

'She was caught shoplifting, that's all. Nothing too serious. I think her boyfriend egged her on. A right piece of work he was.'

'So Aidan Tierney owed you?'

'You could say that. Stop looking so grim!'

'I'm not looking grim. I just wanted to get this straight. Aidan Tierney agreed to interview me because he owed you a favour. It wasn't just because you happened to know each other socially and you suggested that I might be the best person for the job?'

'But you *are* the best person for the job – you know that. Whatever favour Aidan might owe me, he wouldn't have taken you on if he hadn't thought you were going to be brilliant at it!'

John said, 'I'd better go see how my pie's doing. I don't want to cremate that, too.'

He went into the kitchen, but Katie followed him. The windows were all wide open and most of the acrid smell had eddied away now. She could see that one of her best stainless-steel saucepans was perched on the window sill, filled with cold water, its interior stained with dark brown circles.

'John,' she said, 'hundreds of people in this city owe me favours of one sort or another, from councillors down to shoplifters. Part of being a good detective is knowing when to turn a blind eye, and when it's more important to keep somebody obligated to you than it is to bang them up for some minor misdemeanour.'

'Okay, I get it,' said John. He opened the oven door and peered in at the lumpy-looking pie that was sitting on the middle shelf, dripping some of its filling on to the baking sheet beneath it. He checked his watch and said, 'Ninety minutes ... I guess it's ready now. How about we sit down and eat?'

'You made that yourself?'

'Don't sound so amazed. I have been known to cook more than baked beans on toast. You're always saying how much you miss the ham and leek pie they used to serve in Henchy's, so I made you one.'

'I don't know what to say.'

She saw now that John had laid the kitchen table with knives and forks and napkins, and two champagne glasses, as well as a new red candle in a floral holder.

'You didn't have to do all of this,' she said. 'I'm happy that you're staying, that's all.'

He put on a pair of gingham oven gloves and lifted his

pie out of the oven. 'There, look at that, a culinary work of art! I'll just put the cabbage on to boil. Where do you keep your matches?'

Katie went to the living room and took the cigarette lighter out of her bag. As she lit the candle, John said, 'For the sake of argument, supposing you *hadn't* been able to fix me up with a job. Would you have come with me to San Francisco?'

She shook her head. 'John darling, I *have* fixed you up with a job. Or rather, you've fixed yourself up with a job. If ErinChem hadn't wanted you, they wouldn't have hired you. And it's not some potty little pretend job, either.'

'Yeah, you're right. I should stop sounding as if I'm not grateful. I *am* grateful. I love you, Katie, you know that, and that's the beginning and the end of it.'

He lifted out the two dinner plates that had been warming in the oven and cut them each a large slice of pie. Then he strained the cabbage and the potatoes that he had managed to salvage and carefully arranged them next to each slice. Katie sat down while he went to the fridge and took out a bottle of Lanson champagne. Once he had eased out the cork, he filled their glasses and raised his own in a toast.

'Here's to us, Katie. I love you. And thank you for making it possible for us to stay together. I mean it.'

Katie clinked glasses with him and took a sip.

'Tuck in, now, sweetheart,' John told her. 'Believe me, once you've tasted this, you will never hanker for one of Henchy's pies ever again.'

Katie picked up her fork. The pie smelled strongly of ham and leeks and celery, but somehow its pungency brought back the overwhelming smell of that rotting headless body in Lower Shandon Street, and the smell of the girl who had stayed with it all that time. When Katie put a little of the pie in her mouth and started to chew it, it was sweet and lumpy, and she began to think of maggots.

She tried to swallow, but she couldn't. She picked up her pink paper napkin and quietly spat her mouthful into it, and folded it up. John hadn't realized what she had done, and he smiled at her and said, 'Okay? You enjoying it? Sorry if the potatoes taste a little burned.'

He dug up another large forkful and put it in his mouth, but Katie laid her fork down at the side of her plate.

'I'm sorry, John. I can't eat this.'

'What? You don't like it? Really? I didn't think I was *that* bad a cook.'

'I'm sorry,' she repeated, and then she pushed back her chair and hurried out of the kitchen to the toilet. She only just managed to lift the seat before she brought up the only things she had eaten and drunk all day – the iced doughnut and the skinny latte. After that she sank to her knees and stayed there, her head bowed, retching, and then retching again, until her ribs ached.

After a while there was a gentle knock at the toilet door.

'Katie? Are you okay, sweetheart?'

She tore off some toilet paper and wiped her mouth. 'I'm grand, John. It wasn't your pie, I swear to God. I've had a stressful day, that's all.'

'I've thrown it away now, anyway.'

'What?'

'The pie.'

'Oh, John,' said Katie. She took hold of the edge of the washbasin and pulled herself up on to her feet. She was surprised to see in the mirror that her cheeks were only slightly flushed, though her eyelashes were stuck together with tears, which gave her the appearance of a pretty but surprised-looking doll.

She opened the toilet door. 'You didn't really throw it away, did you?'

He nodded. 'Yeah. I guess I could have given it to Barney, but I didn't want to make him sick, too.'

Katie wrapped her arms around him and held him tight and wondered if she would ever manage to do right for doing wrong.

They didn't make love that night, although they lay very close together before they went to sleep, and John repeatedly stroked her shoulder and her hair. Katie was too tired and too disturbed by what she had seen, and she wondered yet again if she had done the right thing by staying in An Garda Síochána, or whether her stomach was telling her something that her mind still refused to acknowledge – that she had seen enough cruelty and unhappiness, and enough human beings shredded to a pulp, or burned to ashes, or floating bloated in the River Lee.

When she eventually fell asleep, she dreamed that she was standing on the platform at Cork Kent railway station, waiting for Dr O'Brien, the pathologist, to arrive from Dublin. The morning was grey and colourless, although it wasn't cold. A train pulled into the station in utter silence. It stayed there with all of its doors shut, but the platform was suddenly jostling with hundreds of people, mostly men in raincoats, and anxious-looking women wearing headscarves.

One of the men lifted a furled umbrella and called out, 'Katie! Katie Maguire!' – but as he did so Katie saw little Corina being dragged away through the throng by Mânios Dumitrescu. Corina kept turning around and staring at Katie, wide-eyed in desperation, but when Katie tried to elbow through the crowd after her, Dr O'Brien stepped into her way and dodged from one foot to the other so that she couldn't get past him.

'Now then, Katie!' he admonished her. 'One thing at a time!' She knew he was grinning but she couldn't clearly see his face.

She tried to force him aside, but then she found she was pushing against John's shoulder and that she wasn't at the railway station at all. She thought, though, that she could hear a baby crying, and that was what must have woken her up.

'Seamus?' she said, and sat upright, listening intently for another cry.

She waited and waited, but of course she heard nothing but the sound of an occasional car passing outside and the doleful hoot of a ship leaving the harbour.

John sat up, too. 'What is it?' he asked her.

'Nothing,' she said, lying back on her pillow. The moon was watching her, cold and cynical, through the curtains. 'Nothing at all.'

Seven

The dirty grey Range Rover drew up right outside Niamh Dailey's house while she was cutting back her privet hedge with a pair of kitchen scissors.

She stood up straight and shaded her eyes with her hand. She had seen the Range Rover several times a week since those Romanians had moved in next door at number thirty-seven, seven months ago, but it had never parked directly across her own front gate before.

Niamh waited for the driver to get out, so that she could ask him to budge up a few yards in front of his own house. Her son, Brendan, would be home for his lunch in half an hour and where was he going to park, what with the Shaughnessys at number thirty-three taking up half the street with that second-hand ambulance they used as a grocery van and that old Toyota that was always up on bricks? But almost half a minute went by before she heard the driver's door open and that skinny Romanian appeared.

Ever since she had first seen him, Niamh had thought that if a rat could grow to human size and walk around on its hind legs, that's exactly what Mânios Dumitrescu would look like. He had black, slicked-back hair with grey stripes in it, and glittery little eyes, and a long pointed nose. Underneath his lopsidedly trimmed moustache his two front teeth stuck out at opposing angles, but his chin was so weak that it seemed to have collapsed into his neck before it had been given enough time to set.

He was wearing a shiny brown nylon shirt and skinny black jeans, with brand-new Nike buffers, so that he seemed to bounce as he walked up to Niamh's front gate. Without being invited, he opened the latch and stepped into her front yard. He came right up to her, staring at her all the time, and then he prodded her in the chest with his finger – once, twice, three times. He wasn't tall, only five foot six inches or so, but Niamh was only a small woman herself, and he was twitching and jerking his head and sniffing with pent-up aggression.

'What do you think you're doing, like?' she said, tightly clasping her kitchen scissors in both hands. 'Get away out of here before I call Dermot from next door!'

'You can call anybody you like, you nosey witch,' Mânios Dumitrescu hissed at her. 'You tell the police about my mother? It was you? I know it was you. Who else?'

'Your mother was treating that little girl something shocking,' Niamh retorted, even though she was finding it hard to keep her voice steady. 'She was beating her, and making her do all the housework, and keeping her up past midnight because she didn't have a bed of her own. And I've heard *you* shouting at her, too, the poor little creature!'

'Is not your business!' said Mânios Dumitrescu. 'What happen in your house is your business! What happen in my mother's house is my mother's business! Not yours, you nosey witch!'

'Just get away out of here,' said Niamh. 'I'll have you for trespass, and for jabbing me, too.'

'Oh, you don't like jab!' said Mânios Dumitrescu, prodding

her again. She backed away from him, but her yard was so small and steeply inclined that she could only press herself into her hedge. 'This is nothing, let me tell you! You say bad words about my mother, I will make sure you never say no bad words about nobody never again! *Nu înțelegi?* Understand? *Am tăiat limba și să-l mănânci la micul dejun!* I cut out your tongue and make you eat it yourself for your breakfast!'

Niamh said nothing, but simply stared back at him. She was trying to look defiant, but she was terrified and she had wet herself a little bit.

Mânios Dumitrescu stayed in her front yard for a few moments longer, with that glittery look in his eyes. Then he spat on the ground and walked off, leaving the gate open. He went into number thirty-seven next door, leaving his Range Rover parked where it was.

Niamh went into her own house and stood in the kitchen, trembling as if she were cold. She used to be frightened when her husband, Frank, came home from The Flying Bottle on a Friday evening, but that had been nothing but shouting and punching and slapping her and pulling her hair. She really believed, though, that Mânios Dumitrescu would seriously maim her, or even murder her. If the Dumitrescu family had been able to abuse a defenceless little girl the way that they had abused Corina, then they obviously had no human feelings whatsoever.

She went over to the dresser and picked up the phone. She found the number she wanted in her dog-eared little notebook and carefully dialled it. It rang for a long time before it was answered, but she waited patiently. At last a woman's voice said, 'Yes?'

'Is that Detective Sergeant ó Nuallán?'

'It is, yes. Who's calling?'

'It's Niamh Dailey, from number thirty-five St Martha's Avenue in Grawn. I was the one who rang you about the little Romanian girl next door.'

'Oh yes, sure, of course. How are you, Niamh? We're expecting a hearing up in front of the court either tomorrow or Friday, depending on their calendar. I'll give you plenty of notice when we need you to give evidence, and I'll send a car round for you.'

'The thing of it is, though, to be honest with you, I think that I made a mistake.'

In her mind's eye, Niamh could visualize Detective Sergeant ó Nuallán on the other end of the phone, frowning.

'Mistake? What kind of mistake?'

'All those things that I said that I saw, I'm not at all sure now that I saw them at all, like. And all those things that I said that I *heard* – I'm not at all sure that I heard those, neither.'

'What are you telling me, Niamh?'

'I can't give evidence, that's what I'm telling you. How can I swear on the Holy Bible to things that I'm not at all sure of?'

'Which particular parts aren't you sure about? We can still build a strong case even if you only *heard* Corina being abused, or even if you only saw her doing housework and changing the babies' nappies when she should have been at school. Her physical and psychological conditions speak for themselves.'

'I'm not sure about any of it,' said Niamh. 'I'm sorry.' She felt like putting the phone down because she knew how disappointed and frustrated Detective Sergeant ó Nuallán must be feeling, but at the same time she knew that nothing was going to make her change her mind and give evidence against the Dumitrescus.

'They've got to you, haven't they?' said Detective Sergeant ó Nuallán. 'Which one of them is it? The mother? Or is it that Mânios? Or one of his brothers? Niamh – you know that threatening a witness is a criminal offence in itself?'

'I'm not saying they've threatened me. I just can't remember clearly anything that happened next door, and that's an end to it.'

'I'll come round to see you. We can talk this over. Are you at home now?'

'No, no, I'll be going out for the messages in a minute,' Niamh lied. She couldn't begin to imagine what Mânios Dumitrescu would do if a detective turned up on her doorstep only twenty minutes after he had threatened to cut out her tongue. He might be arrested, but it would only be her word against his, and he would probably be let out on bail. Even if he were held in custody, there would still be his mother and his two brothers to be afraid of, as well as an assortment of other unshaven Romanians who came in and out of number thirty-seven at all hours.

'I'll meet you in the cafe at Dunne's, if you like, at three o'clock,' she told Detective Sergeant ó Nuallán. 'But you won't be changing my mind, I swear to God.'

Eight

John came blinking into the living room in his blue towelling bathrobe, his hair sticking up at the back like a cockatoo. Katie was already dressed in her sandy-coloured linen suit and a coppery blouse to match her hair. She was checking the Iarnród Éireann timetables on her mobile phone to see what time Dr O'Brien was expected to arrive, and eating a shortbread biscuit.

'Is that all the breakfast you're having?' he asked her.

'I'll have something decent when I get to work. I'm late enough as it is.'

'You didn't eat anything last night.'

She put down her phone and gave him a smile. 'Yes, I know, and I'm so sorry about that. I'll bet that pie was probably ten times tastier than anything I ever ate in Henchy's. It's the job, I'm afraid. Sometimes I can see something during the day that turns my stomach and I can't get it out of my mind.'

John held her close and kissed her and ran his fingers into the back of her hair.

'Hey, don't mess up the coiffure!' she protested, although she was kissing him back just as enthusiastically as he was kissing her. 'That took nearly half a can of hairspray to get it to stay like that!'

'Are you going to be late again tonight?' he asked her.

'I wish I knew,' she said, picking up her bag. Barney kept circling around and around her, thumping her legs with his tail and almost tripping her up. 'It depends if we make any headway with this headless feller, if you know what I mean.'

'You're a comedienne and you don't know it,' said John. 'I love you, Katie Maguire.'

'So what will you be doing? You don't start at ErinChem until Monday, do you?'

'Working out my business strategy. And getting in touch with my friend Buzz Perelman in Oakland. What Buzz doesn't know about online marketing hasn't been invented yet. Then I'll probably go see my mother. Well, I *might* go see my mother.'

Katie held on to both of his hands and didn't want to let him go and didn't want to take her eyes off him – but then she turned and looked around the living room. It was still decorated in the same ornate 1990s style that Paul had considered to be classy, with Regency-striped wallpaper and gilded Regency furniture from Casey's in Oliver Plunkett Street, and reproduction seascapes on the walls.

'There's something else you could do,' she said. 'This is *your* home now, as well as mine. Why don't you choose a new colour scheme for us? And some new carpets and curtains and furniture? It's long overdue for a change, and it reminds me of things I don't want to be reminded of, not any more.'

'Are you serious?' John asked her. 'I'm not so sure you'd like my taste.'

'Oh, I like your taste, John Meagher,' she told him, and gave him another kiss.

* * *

The train from Dublin was ten minutes late and Katie was beginning to grow impatient. Since Dr O'Brien was only a junior pathologist she normally wouldn't have met him in person, but she was going to the hospital in any event so that she could talk to the girl who had been found with Mawakiya's body. Apart from that, she preferred to keep every available member of her team on the job today, trawling through the bars and the brothels and the massage parlours and trying to find out who Mawakiya actually was.

Shortly after ten-thirty that morning she had sent out an appeal on RTÉ and Cork 96FM radio, as well as the *Examiner* and the *Echo*, asking for anyone who had known or seen Mawakiya to contact the Gardaí as a matter of urgency. However, although HEADLESS, HANDLESS HOMICIDE had been headline news, only three people had called in so far and none of them had been able to offer anything helpful. 'I think I might of seen your man in Waxy's about a week ago.' 'It wasn't The Spider because I saw him yesterday afternoon on Pana and in any case he wasn't wearing purple.' 'I'm a hundred per cent sure that I distinctly heard a couple of loud bangs on Lower Shandon Street when I was coming out of O'Donovan's but I can't remember exactly when.'

Katie knew from her own experience how hard it was for the Gardaí to persuade any of the prostitutes who worked in the city's brothels to talk to them, because they were so afraid of what would happen to them if they spoke out. Either that, or they were so drugged up and exhausted that they scarcely knew what day of the week it was. It was almost as difficult to persuade freelance sex workers to come forward, the single mothers who did a bit of oral sex on the side to help pay the bills, because they were reluctant to admit what they did for a living in case their neighbours found out. All the same, a man had been murdered and it was more than likely that he was the kind of man who had his fair share of enemies. When somebody like that was killed, Katie could usually expect a tip-off from some grass or some barman who kept his eyes and ears open in exchange for a few hundred euros.

At last the yellow-fronted train pulled into the platform. Unlike her dream, the doors opened, but very few people disembarked. There was a bunch of lads who kept pushing and pulling each other, and two nuns, but the only passenger who looked remotely like a pathologist was a short, rotund young man with heavy-rimmed glasses and a comb-over, wearing a creased green jacket and wheeling an overnight case behind him in fits and jerks, as if it were a disobedient dog.

'You must be Dr O'Brien,' said Katie, walking up to him, with her hand out.

'Oh!' he exclaimed. He changed hands with his overnight case so he could shake hands with her, and promptly dropped the magazine he had been carrying under his arm. As he bent down to pick it up, his mobile phone fell out of the breast pocket of his jacket and clattered on to the platform.

'Detective Superintendent Maguire,' said Katie. 'Thank you for coming down so promptly.'

'Oh! Detective superintendent, eh? Well!' He picked up his phone and pressed the on button to make sure that it was still working, and then he shook her hand. His handshake was surprisingly firm and direct. 'This is an honour! Usually I'm lucky if they send a taxi for me!'

'I was on my way to the hospital anyway. And I wanted to talk to you before you started your examination, too.'

They walked across the car park to Katie's Fiesta. Dr

O'Brien clumsily heaved his case into the back and they climbed in.

'Did you know Dr Collins?' Katie asked him, as he struggled to fasten his seat belt.

'No, no, I didn't. I was appointed to replace her. But I know the circumstances. You were there, weren't you, when she was shot? She was very highly thought of. Very sad.'

Katie started the engine and backed out of the car park. 'This victim that you're going to be examining, he's African, but we don't have any clues yet as to his identity. It doesn't help that most of his head has been blown away with a shotgun blast and both of his hands have been severed.'

Dr O'Brien was rummaging inside his jacket pocket. 'Sorry – I could have sworn I put my train ticket in my wallet. I hope I haven't lost it.'

Katie said, 'We have one witness who says that she actually saw the victim being shot. She's a young African girl, only about thirteen years old. She spoke to the two people who first found the victim, and she told them that he was shot by a woman, but she hasn't said anything else. So far, nobody else has come forward to give us even a clue to his identity.'

'I read a bit about it in the paper,' said Dr O'Brien. 'Obviously, I can take samples of the victim's DNA, but even DNA won't help us if there's nothing to match it with. And if we don't have any fingerprints, well—'

'It's early days yet,' said Katie. 'It's just that I'm always uncomfortable until I know who murdered somebody, and why. But I'm even more uncomfortable if I don't even know who it is who's been murdered.'

Dr O'Brien was still hunting for his ticket. 'It would seem that your murderer has gone to some considerable lengths to stop you from finding out. I'd say that she's a highly controlling personality. You *may* discover who your victim is, but only when she decides to tell you, not before.'

Katie glanced at him as she drove along Penrose Quay and then turned left to cross the river on Brian Boru Street. The surface of the river was a faultless mirror, with upside-down red-brick buildings in it, and an empty sky.

Dr O'Brien caught the way she had looked at him and said, 'Oh … I studied psychiatry at Trinity College as well as histopathology at St Patrick Dun.'

'Oh yes? So why didn't you become a psychiatrist? It's not nearly so gruesome.'

'I could have been. In the end, though, I decided I preferred the certainties of death to the vagaries of life.'

'All right, then,' said Katie. 'So why do you think our murderer doesn't want us to know who our victim is?'

'Why do *you* think?' asked Dr O'Brien. 'You're the expert, after all. I bow to your greater practical experience.'

She turned left down St Patrick's Street, the main shopping street, past Marks & Spencer's and Brown Thomas. Unexpectedly, she was beginning to warm to Dr O'Brien. He may have been chubby and clumsy, but he was making her think clearly. She had so many cases to deal with simultaneously that she sometimes became mentally entangled, but he was insisting that she considered this murder very analytically and in isolation. Stop worrying about Michael Gerrety's legal shenanigans and Mânios Dumitrescu and his child abduction and pimping, not to mention all those thousands of euros' worth of stolen farm machinery and that home invasion in Ballyvolane and those two rape cases in Ballintemple. Stop worrying about John, too, and your guilt at not eating his pie.

'All right,' she said, 'she doesn't want us to know who the victim is because that would enable us to work out what her motive was for murdering him, and if we knew why she murdered him it would probably be easy to work out who she is, too.'

'So what do you think her possible motives might be?' asked Dr O'Brien.

'Revenge, more than likely. I doubt if you would blow anybody's head off simply for the pleasure of it, even if you're a sadist. It could have been to punish him for stealing something. That's what they do in sharia law, isn't cut, cut a thief's hands off?'

'Yes, that's called *hudud*,' said Dr O'Brien. 'But even your hard-line Islamists usually amputate only one hand, for the first offence anyway. And it's unlikely that a woman would carry out a sharia punishment. In some Islamic courts, women aren't even allowed to give evidence in cases of theft, let alone carry out the sentence.'

'Perhaps he was muscling in on somebody else's territory,' Katie suggested. 'We had some of that last year when some crack pushers from Limerick tried to undercut one of our local dealers. Three of them were found in the river with their noses cut off – the implication being, don't come sniffing around in places where you're not welcome. We're pretty certain who did it, but we could never prove it for sure.'

Dr O'Brien nodded vigorously. 'I don't think there's any question that the victim's hands being amputated is symbolic. Exactly what it's symbolic of, I couldn't tell you for certain, though I expect I'll be able to tell you more when I've had a chance to examine him. For instance, *how* the hands were amputated could be important. But if we can find out what the amputation meant, I think we'll be very close to finding our killer.'

'Perhaps you should have been a detective, instead of a pathologist,' said Katie.

'Oh, no,' said Dr O'Brien. 'As I told you, I much prefer certainties, and there's nothing as certain as somebody who's dead. The dead don't argue. They don't tell lies. They're never unfaithful.'

Katie was turning into the car park of Cork University Hospital. She didn't ask him why he had made that last remark, but she could guess.

'I'll see you later so,' she said. 'You have a room booked at Jury's on Western Road – just give them your name at the desk. Give me a call when you've finished your autopsy. I'm very impatient to know what you come up with.'

Katie found the African girl in a private room on the third floor of the hospital, with an armed garda sitting outside reading the racing pages in the *Irish Sun*. The officer stood up when he saw her approaching, but she said, 'You're grand,' and he sat down again.

The girl already looked much better. She was sitting up in bed in a fresh pink nightdress watching television. The cornrows had been taken out of her hair and it had been washed and brushed into a black fluffy bush. She looked even prettier than she had when Katie had first seen her in the ambulance, but also much younger. She was really no more than a child.

Katie lifted a chair over and sat beside her bed. 'Well then,' she said, 'how are you feeling today?'

The girl said nothing, but simply stared at her, twisting the sleeve of her nightdress.

'Do you remember me from yesterday? I spoke to you in

84

the ambulance. My name's Katie. Look, I brought you some sweeties.'

She held out the bag of Haribo jellies that she had bought at the hospital shop downstairs. The girl made no attempt to take them and so she laid them down on top of the blanket, on her lap.

'Can you tell me your name?' Katie asked her.

The girl remained silent, but continued to stare.

'I've come here to help you get better, and to find your family, if I can. Your mother and your father. Do you know where they are?'

Still no response.

'Do you know which country you came from? Was it somewhere in Africa? Somalia? Sierra Leone? Nigeria? The Congo?'

The girl opened her mouth as if she were about to say something, but then she closed it again.

Katie took hold of her hand and squeezed it and smiled at her. 'Fair play to you, sweetheart, if you're not ready to talk to me yet then that's up to you. But it would be nice to know your name, so I know what to call you. Maybe I should give you a name for now. Maybe I should call you Isabelle. Do you like the name Isabelle? I first met you under the bells of Shandon, after all.'

As Katie sat there, holding the girl's hand, two large tears welled up in the girl's eyes and slid down her cheeks. Katie reached over to the bedside table and tugged out a tissue for her and gently dabbed them away.

'You're going to be all right now, Isabelle. Nothing bad is going to happen to you ever again. You're going to be taken care if. If we can't find your parents, then we'll find somebody kind to look after you, I promise.'

At that moment a doctor came in through the door, holding a clipboard under his arm. He was small and neat and Indian, with a shiny bald head and a trim black beard.

'Ah, detective superintendent! I'm sorry I'm a few minutes late! Anaphylactic shocks wait for no man, I'm afraid!'

He held out his hand and said, 'Dr Surupa. How are you? I believe we have met before. People are always being brought to me in a terrible condition, and you are always having to find out who did it to them.'

He gave Isabelle a brief smile and then said to Katie, 'Perhaps it is better if I speak to you outside.'

They left the room and walked together along the corridor until they reached the window at the end, overlooking the car park.

'She is under the supervision of Dr Corcoran, who is one of our six psychiatric consultants, and also a key nurse for her physical welfare. Dr Corcoran is a specialist in treating the trauma associated with cases of human-trafficking or sexual slavery. Unfortunately, in recent years these cases have become increasingly common. I suppose this is the price we pay for opening borders and giving people more freedom to move between one country and another.'

'So how is she?' asked Katie. 'Has she spoken to anybody? She won't say anything to me. She won't even tell me her name, or where she came from.'

Dr Surupa shook his head. 'She is very deeply disturbed, and in Dr Corcoran's opinion it may take weeks or even months for her to recover.'

'According to the two men who found her, she said she was only thirteen years old.'

'Well, having examined her, that seems likely, although we have no way of telling exactly because girls vary in the age of their sexual maturity. Her breasts have started to develop, but typically African girls show signs of breast development a year earlier than Caucasian girls, although nobody knows why. However, she has been desperately under-nourished and because of that her menarche has not yet started.'

'How about her general physical condition?'

'She has some patterned scarring on her back and arms, which looks like lizards or scorpions and appears to be tribal decoration of some kind. If you can find somebody who is an expert on such scarring you might be able to identify where she has come from. But she also has severe diagonal scarring, which is almost certainly the result of having been whipped or beaten with a stick.'

'I see. Any genital mutilation?'

Dr Surupa turned over the page of his clipboard. 'No, no FGM, although that surprises me a little in the light of all the rest of the tribal scarring. However, she *has* been sexually abused, and very violently. She has both vaginal tears and anal fissures, both comparatively recent. I don't like to imagine what objects must have been forced up inside her.'

Katie stood looking out of the window at two young nurses running and laughing across the car park. Then she said, 'Thank you, doctor. I'd appreciate it if you'd keep me up to date with any changes in her condition – especially if she starts to talk. I'll come back to see her as often as I can.'

She walked back to Isabelle's room. To her surprise, Branna MacSuibhne, the new young reporter from the *Echo*, was standing next to Isabelle's bed, taking pictures with her iPhone.

'What in the *name* of Jesus are you doing in here?' she demanded. Then she turned around to the armed garda and said, 'Why did you let *her* in? She's a reporter, for God's sake! I thought you were supposed to be taking care of this young woman's security?'

The garda stood up, dropping his newspaper on the floor. 'I'm sorry, ma'am!' he protested. 'She told me she was one of the medical team.'

'I did not so!' said Branna.

'Well, she didn't tell me she wasn't.'

'Oh, I see,' said Katie. 'So long as somebody doesn't actually introduce themselves as a reporter, or a criminal, or a homicidal maniac, they're all right to come waltzing in, are they? Does she *look* like one of the medical team, with her handbag and all?'

'I only wanted to get the human side of this story,' said Branna.

'You'll get the human side of my hand if you don't get away out of here. And give me that phone.'

Branna reluctantly handed over her iPhone and Katie ushered her out of the room, looking back at Isabelle as she did so. Isabelle was staring at the television, seemingly oblivious to all this disturbance.

Out in the corridor, Katie methodically deleted all Branna's pictures of Isabelle from her camera. Before she handed her iPhone back, though, she said, 'What about recording?'

Branna's cheeks were flushed with frustration. 'There was nothing to record.'

'She didn't say anything to you?'

'Not a word.'

'Then push on, girl, and don't think of coming back uninvited.'

'You can't stop me getting my story,' Branna challenged her.

'I'm not going to try to, Branna. But I *can* stop you from making a holy show of this young girl. In the whole of your lifetime, you will never have to suffer what she's already been through, so don't you forget it!'

'We'll have to see about that, won't we?' said Branna, and stalked off along the corridor with her water-buffalo hairstyle bouncing.

Nine

As soon as he saw Mânios Dumitrescu appear out of number thirty-seven, lighting a cigarette as he came, Niamh's son, Brendan, said, 'Right, that's it!' and went for the front door. Niamh, however, caught hold of his sleeve to hold him back.

'Don't, Brendan! They're not worth it, those people! They'll bring you nothing but grief!'

'Name of Jesus, mam, you've torn me shirt!'

He struggled to free himself, but she pushed past him and stood in front of the door so that he couldn't get out unless he lifted her bodily out of the way.

'I said *no*, Brendan! I'm not having you hurt for the likes of them!'

'Oh, I see! So your man thinks he can threaten me mam and then leave his scabby Range Rover blocking up our front gate so that I can hardly get in for me dinner and that's all right, like?'

Niamh said nothing but stayed where she was with her arms pressed against the side of the door frame, breathing deeply and staring steadily at Brendan as if she were challenging him to risk everything she had ever put into his upbringing – every cup of milk, every kiss, every song, every day by the sea.

They heard Mânios Dumitrescu's Range Rover start up

with a roar and a rattle of a loose exhaust, and then he was gone.

Brendan went back into the living room, shaking his head. Niamh lifted up his torn shirtsleeve and said, 'If you take that off, I'll sew it for you now. It's a small price to pay, you know that. Those people will cut the tripe out of you as soon as wink at you. I'd sooner be sewing the shirt of a boy who swallowed his pride than standing over the grave of a boy who wouldn't.'

'Mam, you can't let these people treat you this way. I don't care what fecking country they come from, they're tinkers, and I'll not be having no fecking tinkers putting my own mother in fear of her life.'

'Wash your mouth out and give me your shirt.'

Mânios Dumitrescu drove down to Pope's Quay and then along by the river. He was slapping his fingers so that his heavy silver rings clattered on the steering wheel and singing 'Dragostea din tei', which had done so well for Romania all those years ago in the Eurovision Song Contest, although he interrupted himself now and again to cough and sniff noisily up his left nostril.

He was feeling much more pleased with himself now. He had just received a phone call from his solicitor's telling him that the circuit court hearing about his custodianship of little Corina had been brought forward until next Tuesday afternoon, and that one of the key witnesses to her alleged mistreatment had unreservedly withdrawn her evidence. Unless there were any dramatic developments, Corina should be back at home at number thirty-seven with him and his mother by Wednesday.

He sucked at the last of his cigarette and threw the stub

out of the Range Rover's window. He knew that he had only two or three left in the packet, so he stopped outside the Spar grocery halfway along McCurtain Street to buy himself some more, and some chocolate, too. For some reason, he had a craving for chocolate.

He was no longer than three or four minutes in the shop, but when he came out a garda was carefully tucking a ticket under his windscreen wiper.

'Hey! *Hey*! What are you doing?' he demanded. 'Anybody can park anywhere in this street!'

The garda was large and placid, with blond eyelashes and a face like a pink boiled ham. He pointed to the Range Rover's windscreen with his pen and said, 'Nothing to do with parking, sir, although this street is a clearway between 4 and 6 p.m. Your insurance is three months out of date and you don't have your NCT certificate on display.'

'What? NCT? What is that? I am foreign visitor, I don't need such a thing!'

'You need to have valid insurance, sir, wherever you come from, and since this vehicle is over four years old and registered in Ireland, it needs to be tested. On this occasion, sir, I'm going to allow you to drive it away, mostly because it would be a fecking nuisance to have to call for a truck to tow it. But you must immediately insure it and test it as soon as possible and produce evidence of both at your nearest Garda station.'

Mânios Dumitrescu was so angry that his narrow nostrils flared and he squeezed the Kit Kat he was holding in his hand so hard that he crushed it. He had enough self-control, though, not to argue with a garda. He had done it before, once, in The Idle Hour, when he was very drunk. He had agreed then to pay an on-the-spot fine of 140 euros, so he hadn't been given a criminal record – but after two gardaí had explained his legal rights to him behind one of the dockside cranes across the road, he had also come away with two black eyes, a perforated eardrum and a fractured thumb.

He said nothing more but snatched the ticket from under his windscreen wiper, climbed back into the driver's seat, and headed along McCurtain Street to the traffic lights at the junction with Summerhill. When he got there, he tore open the Kit Kat wrapper with his teeth and a shower of chocolaty crumbs dropped into his lap.

'*Pula mea*!' he snapped, brushing them off his trousers.

Unnervingly close to his left ear, a strongly accented female voice said, 'I would laugh, Mânios, if anything that you ever did could be funny.'

Startled, Mânios Dumitrescu twisted himself around, but whoever it was ducked down behind his seat so that her face was hidden. All he could see was the sleeve of a black leather jacket and the leg of a pair of black denim jeans.

'Who the *fuck* are you and what you do in my car!' he shouted. He started to unbuckle his seat belt, but at that moment the lights changed to green and a truck blew its two-tone horn right behind him.

'Okay! Okay!' he screamed, but the truck blew its horn again, and now the cars behind joined in, too.

He drove slowly up Summerhill, trying desperately to find a space to pull into the kerb, but it was a narrow road with a narrow pavement and the first hundred yards were bordered by the stony perimeter wall of Trinity Presbyterian Church. There was a bus stop fifty yards further up, but a 207 bus had just pulled into it, and the lay-by immediately beyond it, which served O'Donovan's off-licence, was blocked by a council refuse truck.

Meanwhile, the truck that had blown its horn at him stayed only about two feet behind the spare wheel of his Range Rover, aggressively revving its engine.

Mânios Dumitrescu slowed down even more as he approached St Luke's Cross, thinking he would turn left into Wellington Road and park outside the bookmaker's. As they neared the junction, however, the woman behind him said, 'Don't even think about stopping, Mânios. Keep going. Go to the house where you were meaning to go anyway.'

'Listen – who the fuck *are* you?' Mânios Dumitrescu demanded, twisting around in his seat again. He slowed down almost to a standstill and this time he was treated to a deafening five-second blast from the truck. He turned back immediately and angrily stamped his foot down on the accelerator, so that he surged past St Luke's Cross and kept on climbing up the Ballyhooly Road, his exhaust-pipe rattling like maracas.

'Mânios – it does not matter to you who I am,' said the woman after a while. In spite of her strong accent, she sounded quite cultured. She also sounded distracted, as if she were thinking about something else altogether, something much more important – or maybe somewhere else altogether, somewhere very far away, where everybody spoke like her.

'So how do you know my name, hey?' said Mânios Dumitrescu. 'How do you know where I am supposed to be going?'

'The Avenging Angel knows everything.'

'And who the fucking *fuck* is the *what*? The Avenging Angel?'

'Be patient, Mânios. Ssh! Don't be in such a hurry to get to hell.'

'What crap do you think you talk about, *scorpie*? What

is to stop me from pulling over right up ahead here, then to drag you out of my car and throw you into road in front of bus?'

It was a long, steep ascent up the Ballyhooly Road and the green hills of the surrounding countryside were beginning to rise into view all around them above the grey city rooftops. Because of that, Mânios Dumitrescu had gained at least two hundred yards on the truck and it was no longer tailgating close behind him. Dillon's Cross was coming up, where there would be space for him to park outside the pharmacy and heave this unwelcome intruder out of the back of the Range Rover. He was so angry he was doing that sniffing, head-jerking thing again, and that made him even angrier. When he was younger, his school friends had teased him by calling him *marionetă*, or 'puppet', whenever he grew angry.

'I told you,' said the woman. 'Keep going until you reach the house where you wanted to go. Do not stop. Do not turn around again to look at me. I am here. You will be able to see me soon enough, and then you will wish that you had not.'

'Well, all I say to you is fuck you,' said Mânios Dumitrescu. '*Pizda mă-tii!*'

They had reached Dillon's Cross now and he could see a space on the opposite side of the junction where he could pull in, but the traffic lights had just turned to red and he had to wait.

As calmly as before, with no sense of urgency at all, the woman said, 'All I say to *you*, Mânios, is that you can curse me as much as you like. But curses I can brush away like flies. What *you* cannot brush away is the gun that I am aiming at the back of your seat.'

She paused for a moment, to allow this to sink in. Then

she said, 'I promise you that I do not lie to you, Mânios. If you try to stop before you reach 14 Glendale View, or if you turn around to look at me again, you will have more to clean out of your lap than chocolate biscuit crumbs.'

Mânios Dumitrescu adjusted his rear-view mirror, trying to see her face, but the sun was shining in at a sharp angle through the rear window of the Range Rover and he was dazzled. At the same time, the traffic lights had changed to green. The truck had caught up with him now and blasted its horn again to get him moving.

It took no more than three or four minutes for them to reach Glendale View, a terrace of eleven small houses, each of which stood at the top of a steeply sloping front garden. All the houses were painted different colours – pink, raspberry, green and grey, although two or three of them still displayed their original sandy-coloured pebbledash. Most of the gardens were crowded with green recycling bins and discarded building materials, but there were one or two small rockeries, and fibreglass plant pots, and even a concrete fountain like a cherub, although it dripped rather than splashed and its head was covered with a sinister blindfold of green slime.

'You know where to park,' said the woman.

When they reached the end of the terrace, Mânios Dumitrescu turned into a narrow alleyway and drove up to a small courtyard of dilapidated lock-up garages.

'So what do you want me to do now?' he asked. He switched off the Range Rover's engine and sat in the driver's seat without moving. 'I only believe that you have a gun because you tell me you have a gun, and I am always cautious when it comes to taking risk with my life. But maybe you *don't* have a gun.'

'You want to try to run away, and find out if I am lying to you or not?'

'I would prefer to beat the *cacat* out of you.'

'Try whichever one you like.'

Mânios Dumitrescu didn't have an answer for that. He sniffed, and then he gave an unexpectedly girlish sneeze.

'Right,' said the woman, 'I am going to get out of the car now. I will stand back a little distance. Then – when I make the signal to you, *you* will get out of the car. Once you have shut the door you will drop your keys on to the ground. Then you will start to walk down the path and around the corner to number fourteen.'

Mânios Dumitrescu started to say something, but then he must have realized the futility of saying anything, whether the woman had a gun or not, because all he managed to come out with was, 'How do I—?'

'You will let yourself into number fourteen. The door is on the latch, not locked, if that is what you were going to ask me. You will go straight up to the big bedroom which is on the left at the top of the stairs. I will be very close behind you. You will go into that bedroom and stand by the window. Then I will tell you what I want you to do next.'

The woman opened her door and was about to step down from the Range Rover when Mânios Dumitrescu said, 'So – are you going to tell me what you want me from me? I don't even know who the fuck you are. Is this kidnap? You want money from my family? We are not rich people. You waste your time.'

'It is not money I am looking for,' said the woman. 'You will find out.'

'Is it drugs? If it is drugs, then what is all this circus for?

97

I can get you all of the drugs you ever heard of, and I can get you some you *never* heard of.'

'I am not interested in your drugs.'

'Did you ever take LucY? I will bet money you never took LucY. Once LucY hit your brain, your whole life is change forever. You will fuck *anybody*, and it does not matter if they are pretty or ugly or thin or fat or nine years old or ninety, you will fuck them *all* and every fuck will feel like heaven.'

'Mânios—'

'Hey, why do you think all of the prostitutes take it? From February it was illegal in Ireland but I can get you all the LucY you want.'

'I told you, I am not interested in your drugs.'

'Then *what*?' he raged, punching his thighs so that the biscuit crumbs jumped up. 'I do not understand! You want a piece of my business? *That* is it, isn't it? You want a piece of my business! I should of know! It is always the same with you *negris*! You are too lazy to start a business of your own, so you steal the business of honest people who work fingers down to their bones!'

'Honest people?' said the woman. 'Where? I do not see any honest people. I see only you.'

With that, she climbed down from the Range Rover and walked away from it, at least twenty-five yards, before she eventually turned around and beckoned to him.

Mânios Dumitrescu hesitated before he opened his door. He didn't look at her, almost as if he didn't want to acknowledge that she existed. For her part, she waited patiently, while the large white cumulus clouds slowly rolled overhead and the hooded crows soared around and around in leisurely circles, as unflustered as she was.

His door clicked open and he stepped down from the driver's seat.

'*Keys,*' she called out.

It was only then that he raised his eyes and looked at her. She was an ebony-skinned young black woman, no more than twenty-three or twenty-four years old, with her hair shaved up on either side of her head and a tangled topknot of corkscrew curls. She wasn't tall, no more than five foot six inches, but she was broad-shouldered, with large breasts and narrow hips and proportionately long legs.

She was wearing black drainpipe jeans and black boots and a black T-shirt, with a sleeveless black leather waistcoat slung over it. Around her neck she was wearing a necklace made of beads and shells and claws, and both of her wrists were decorated with silver bracelets.

'So – who are you?' demanded Mânios Dumitrescu. He narrowed his eyes, but she was wearing huge wraparound sunglasses that hid most of her face and reflected the sunlight in two dazzling stars.

'Keys,' she repeated.

'I don't see no gun,' Mânios Dumitrescu challenged her. 'Where is this famous gun you say you got?'

'You really don't believe me?'

'Ha! I believe my eyes, that is all. If my own mother said that she was the one who gave birth to me, I would not believe her, either.'

The young woman reached into the right-hand pocket of her waistcoat and tugged out a flat grey pistol, not much larger than an iPhone 5.

Mânios Dumitrescu lifted up both hands and said, 'You joke me. That is toy.'

'Try me,' said the young woman.

Mânios Dumitrescu took two or three moonwalking steps back, jingling his keys as if he were taunting the young woman to shoot him – that's if she really *could* shoot him with a gun so small.

She held the pistol up in both hands and pointed it at his midriff.

'Keys,' she said. 'I am not the best of shots but I will try to blow off your dick.'

There was a long moment of high tension. Mânios Dumitrescu stopped jingling his keys and stood absolutely still. He could have been one of the human statues who pose outside Brown Thomas in Patrick Street while passers-by pull faces at them, trying to break their concentration.

The young woman remained motionless, too, keeping her pistol aimed between his legs.

After almost a quarter of a minute, Mânios Dumitrescu dropped his heavy bunch of keys on to the concrete.

'Okay,' he said. 'I play your game. What do you want me to do now?'

'I told you. Walk slowly to number fourteen. Go inside. The door is not locked. Go upstairs to the main bedroom.'

Mânios Dumitrescu reluctantly did as he was told, walking in a jerky, stumbling marionette way that betrayed how angry and frustrated he really felt, even though he was trying to give the young woman the impression that she didn't bother him at all.

Years ago, the front garden of number fourteen must have been the homeowner's pride and joy. There were two flower-beds, with borders made of terracotta rope-top tiles, and a large concrete gnome in each of them. Now, however, the garden was overgrown with bindweed and all the red and blue paint had been weathered from the gnomes, so that they looked like two lepers.

The front door had originally been painted lime-green, but all that paint was blistering and peeling. It juddered on its hinges when Mânios Dumitrescu pushed it open and stepped inside.

Once he was standing in the hallway, he called out, 'Bridget! Rodika! Miski!'

'You are wasting your breath, Mânios,' the young woman told him. 'Your girls have all gone out for the day.'

Mânios Dumitrescu stared at her, and now he was really astounded. 'They have gone *out*? Where? Who the fuck said that they could go out? They are not allowed to go out! They are supposed to be working! What has happened to their clients? Those girls can't go *out*!'

'They can and they have and all their appointments for today have been cancelled.'

'What! You can't fucking do this to me. This is my business, *scorpie*! This is my bread and butter!'

'I know,' said the young woman. 'Why do you think I am here? Now, get upstairs.'

There was another moment of tension. Mânios Dumitrescu stood with his hand on the banister, breathing deeply and evenly to control himself. The tense feeling was accentuated by the narrow, claustrophobic hallway, with its faded floral wallpaper and the bead curtain hanging over the kitchen doorway to try and give it the atmosphere of a brothel. A dried-up yucca plant crouched in a planter at the foot of the stairs, as if a huge dead crab had suddenly dropped down from the landing above.

The whole house smelled of damp and musky perfume and stale sweat and bleach. Through the wall, they could hear the muffled sound of a television comedy from next door, with occasional waves of canned laughter.

Eventually, Mânios Dumitrescu began to climb slowly up the stairs, with the young woman only three or four steps behind him. When he reached the landing he hesitated again, but then he turned into the main bedroom on the left-hand side and she followed him.

'Now what?' he said.

Although the curtains were drawn, they were of cream-coloured loose weave and so the sunlight filtered in. Most of the bedroom was taken up by a king-sized bed, covered with a shiny pink satin quilt which had innumerable stains on it. On the ceiling above the bed was a mirror with smudges and fingerprints on it, and on the bedside table stood three dildoes of different sizes – one maroon one, which was gigantic, almost the size of a man's forearm with its fist clenched, and two thinner ones, with a fourth dildo curled around them, which was long and snake-like and double-ended. There were also several bottles of Durex Play lubricant and a pack of baby-wipes, a lamp with a pink frilly shade, and a clock.

On the wall facing the bed hung a framed Jack Vettriano poster of a nude woman. Something was smeared across her face, which could have been chocolate.

Mânios Dumitrescu looked around. 'So what happen now?' he demanded. 'Why did you want to come with me here? I come here anyway. But my girls, I have to get them back. Every hour they don't work, it cost me money. It cost *them* money, too. Ten appointments a day, at least, that is the rule.'

'How old is Miski?' asked the young woman.

'What? Young, of course. Who is going to want to fuck some old granny? But how should I know?'

'Miski is fifteen years old.'

'And? So? She likes what she does. She is good at it! Best gobble-job in Cork, that is what they say! And what else could she do? She cannot read. She cannot write. She cannot add up number! So what are you? Some friend of Miski?'

'Take off your clothes,' said the young woman.

'What? Are you crazy?'

She pointed that small grey gun at him again, directly at his face this time.

'Take off your clothes, Mânios. All of them.'

Ten

Mânios Dumitrescu turned away, one hand lifted, shaking his head.

'You think I would take off my clothes just because you ask me? Like I say, you're crazy.'

'No, Mânios, I am not *asking* you. I am *telling* you.'

'Oh, you with your toy gun? Well, the answer is of course no. You can go and fuck yourself. I have enough of this game now. I want to know where my girls are and I want you to go. Enough of this *cacat*. Look—'

He reached into his pocket, took out a flick-knife and sprung it open. 'What is it to be? Huh?' he said, circling it around and around, loose-wristed, like somebody used to fighting with knives. 'I think real knife beat toy gun, how about you?'

The young woman lifted up her sunglasses and tucked them into her corkscrew curls. She had strikingly unusual looks, with high cheekbones and wide-apart brown eyes. Her nose was short and straight and she had a strong, prominent chin, as if she had a very slight underbite. Even though he was so angry and so irritated, Mânios Dumitrescu could recognize an exceptionally attractive woman when he saw one.

'Hey ...' he said, suddenly grinning his rat-like grin. 'Why don't we just say quits, yes? You go, you get out of here, and we will leave it like that. No hard feeling either side. How about that?'

'Don't come any closer,' she warned him.

'Oh yes? And you are *really* going to stop me, are you, with that pea-shooter?'

The young woman reached into the left-hand pocket of her waistcoat and produced a slim black shotgun shell. She held it up and said, 'You must know what this is.'

Mânios Dumitrescu stared at it without saying anything.

'Maybe you have not heard of these guns,' the young woman told him. 'They are called personal protection pistols and they take just one of these shotgun shells. But one is enough if you are standing in the way when one of them is fired, which *you* will be.'

Mânios Dumitrescu thought about that, with his eyes narrowed. Then he slowly folded up his flick-knife and held it tight in the palm of his hand.

'Throw it on the bed,' said the young woman. '*Now*, take off your clothes. All of them.'

He tossed the flick-knife on to the quilt and she immediately picked it up and tucked it into the back pocket of her jeans. Then she stood back and watched him as he unbuttoned his shirt, baring his white concave ribcage and the long grey hairs that grew out of his nipples. He prised off his beige leather loafers and then dropped his crumpled grey trousers and stepped out of them. He was left in nothing but a pair of yellow-stained boxer shorts with black and white pictures of Felix the Cat all over them, and a pair of white calf-length socks.

'Come on,' said the young woman. 'Everything.'

Mânios Dumitrescu let his boxer shorts drop to his ankles

and trod his way out of them. Then he balanced on one leg after the other to roll down his socks.

He stood in front of the young woman completely naked, his pubic hair wild, his penis dark and diminutive, but he kept his arms folded defiantly across his chest and made no attempt to cover himself.

'Go and sit on the bed,' the young woman told him. 'No, not here – over there.'

He went around to the opposite side of the bed and sat down, round-shouldered. The young woman picked up all of his discarded clothes between finger and thumb and tossed them out of the door on to the landing.

'I curse you to death for this,' Mânios Dumitrescu told her. '*Trăsni-te-ar moartea, săte te trăsnească!*'

The young woman took no notice. She went over to the dressing table by the window, opened the left-hand drawer, and took out a pair of steel handcuffs.

'Put your feet up on the bed,' she told him.

'So – I know what you plan to do,' said Mânios Dumitrescu. 'You plan to call back my girls, and then to shame me, in front of them! Look, here is your boss, no clothes, tied up like chicken!'

'Put your feet up on the bed,' she repeated.

'Okay, whatever you like. But I tell you, this will make no difference! Those girls, they respect me! No matter what you do to me, they will still respect me!'

'I know,' said the young woman. She took hold of his hairy left ankle and clicked one of the handcuffs around it. 'That is because you will beat them until they bleed if they don't.'

She fastened his ankles together, and then she stood back

for a moment. 'Look at you now,' she said, shaking her head. 'Just look at you.'

'All right, I look like fool!' snapped Mânios Dumitrescu. 'Well done! You make big boss look like *tâmpit*!'

'But you are not looking!' insisted the young woman.

'I do not have to look! I do not *want* to look!'

'*You are not looking!*'

With that, she pushed him hard in the middle of his bony chest with the heel of her hand. He fell back on to the quilt and found himself staring up at his reflection in the mirror on the ceiling. For nearly five seconds he remained transfixed, as if he couldn't believe what he was seeing.

'That is *you*, up there!' said the young woman. 'That is Mânios the big boss man. Mânios who likes to hit women and cut people's throats if they make him angry and treat little children like slaves. Look at you! You said you looked like a chicken! No, you do not look like a chicken! You look like a *spider*!'

Mânios Dumitrescu closed his eyes tight. After a while, through gritted teeth, he said, 'Is that it? Are you finish with me now? What are you going to do now? Take photograph, yes, so that you can show them to all of my girls? Well, do it. I don't care. I don't give a shit for you and I don't give a shit for anybody.'

The young woman sat down on the bed beside him. 'That is exactly why I am here, Mânios. When somebody has no feeling for anybody else except themselves, they are a danger to the world. That is when the Avenging Angel has to visit them.'

'Oh, and *you* are the Avenging Angel, are you? Ha! First *negri* angel I ever saw!'

'Think whatever you like. But the Avenging Angel has to visit people like you to punish them for their evil. And more than that, the Avenging Angel has to *prove* that she has punished you.'

'*Eşti nebun! Eşti complet nebun!* You are totally mad!'

'No, not at all. In most countries in Africa, if somebody has been caught for doing wrong, and punished, it is always necessary to produce evidence to the authorities that the punishment has been carried out.'

'What punishment?'

'Of course, it depends on what they have done. Maybe they didn't manage to tap enough raw rubber, in the rubber plantation, according to their quota. Then again, it could have been something worse, like stealing somebody's goat, or having sex with their own daughter. Or maybe something even worse than that, like you have done. You have murdered a few men in your time, haven't you, Mânios?'

'What are you talking about? I don't have to listen to this mumbo-jumbo!'

The young woman reached inside her waistcoat and drew out a junior hacksaw, with a tubular metal frame and a finely serrated blade about six inches long.

'My evidence that *you* have been punished will be your hand.'

Mânios Dumitrescu looked at the hacksaw, and then he let out a sharp barking sound, as if he had been trying to laugh to show his contempt but his throat had tightened with panic before he could let it out.

'You are *serious*? You are going to cut off my hand?'

'No, Mânios. You are.'

'I told you. You are *crazy*! Why do you think I would cut off my own hand?'

The young woman gave the faintest of shrugs. 'It is your choice.'

She lifted up the small grey pistol and pointed it at his groin. 'If you don't cut off your hand, I will shoot you between your legs and turn you into a woman.'

'You joke. This is bad joke, yes?'

'I think it is a very *good* joke, after the way you have treated women all your life. Now you can find out for yourself what it is like.'

'You could *kill* me, shooting me there.'

'Yes. But that would be a pity. What is the Romanian word for "eunuch"?'

Mânios Dumitrescu tried to sit up, but the young woman pushed him down again.

'If you let me go now,' he said, 'I will make sure you have one hundred thousand euros in cash by the end of today. I mean it.'

'I thought you said you were not rich.'

'I am not, but I can lay my hand on money when I need to. I have friends.'

'I told you. I am not interested in your money.'

'A hundred fifty thousand euros. *Two* hundred thousand!'

The young woman stood up and carefully laid the hacksaw on the quilt next to his right hand. 'You *are* right-handed?' she asked him.

'Two hundred fifty thousand! I swear it! I will get it for you by midnight tonight, in cash! Quarter of million! And afterwards no more questions!'

The young woman nodded towards the cheap, silver-plated carriage clock next to the dildoes on the bedside table. 'Look, it is two minutes to three o'clock. When it comes to three o'clock, I will shoot you.'

Mânios Dumitrescu was breathing deeply now. He tilted himself towards her, hesitated for a moment, and then threw himself sideways off the opposite side of the bed. He dropped heavily on to the bedside rug, but snatched at the quilt and made a grab for the bedside table to pull himself upright. The clock and the lamp and the dildoes tumbled and clattered on to the floor.

He managed to stand up, but all he could do with his ankles fastened together was to try and hop towards the door, and after two awkward hops he realized that trying to get away was both futile and ludicrous, as well as being painful. The handcuffs had scraped the skin from both his ankles and they were bleeding.

He shuffled awkwardly back to the bed and sat down. During his escape attempt the young woman had remained where she was, unruffled, watching him with a remote expression in her eyes. As she had said at the bottom of Summerhill, if it had been anybody else but him, it would have been funny.

'I think you have had your two minutes' grace,' she said. She came around the end of the bed and pushed him back down again, heaving his legs up on to the quilt. Then she stood back and aimed the small grey pistol directly at his scrotum.

'You want to say one last word as a man?' she asked him.

He closed his eyes and then his penis swelled up a little and a small fountain of urine rose out of it. It went on and on, drenching the pink satin quilt and trickling down his thighs. The young woman waited until he had finished, and then she said, 'I wish your girls and your children could have seen that. You are disgusting. You hurt *them* all the time and think they deserve it, but when somebody threatens to hurt you, all you can do is piss yourself.'

She levelled the gun again, but he lifted both hands and said, 'No. *În numele lui Isus.* Please.'

'Too late, Mânios. Time is up!'

'No!' he screamed. 'No!'

He jerked his knees up into the foetal position. At the same time he groped frantically across the bed and picked up the hacksaw. He raised his left arm stiffly in front of his face, as if he were telling the time, and then he dragged the hacksaw blade across the back of his wrist, just above the stainless-steel bracelet of his Rolex. The tiny teeth ripped through his skin and into his flesh with a sound like somebody tearing a cotton handkerchief in half, and his face was instantly spattered all over with blood.

'*Ah-ah-ah-ah-ah-ah-ah*,' he stuttered.

'Go on,' the young woman encouraged him. 'Now you have started, you might as well finish. Maybe you will find it easier if you sit up, and take off your watch.'

Mânios Dumitrescu stared at her with bulging eyes, but he didn't say anything, and when she helped him to swing his legs off the bed and sit up straight he didn't struggle or try to lash out at her. He was trembling with shock and he didn't even protest when she slid his watch off his blood-smeared wrist.

'Go on,' she coaxed him. 'So far – look – you have hardly scratched yourself.'

Outside, the clouds must have been drifting over the sun, because the bedroom gradually became gloomier. Mânios Dumitrescu lined up the hacksaw blade with the cut that he had already sawn across his wrist, closed his eyes for a split second, and then dragged it again across the same line.

As he started sawing, he began to utter an extraordinary high-pitched howling sound, like a mongrel being run over.

Even so, he soon seemed to realize that he was failing to cut hard enough or deep enough. After five backward and forward strokes he had sawn no deeper through the skin than the cartilage that connected the two bones in his forearm to the bones in his hand. He stopped, panting, as if he were trying to summon up more resolve.

'Go on,' the young woman told him. 'If you don't finish doing this, I will still shoot you, and that is my promise.'

Mânios Dumitrescu didn't say anything. Still panting, he dragged the bedside table close up beside him, so that he could lay his left forearm on top of it. Blood was welling out of the groove that he had cut so far, but he managed to insert the hacksaw blade into it. He gripped the tip of his tongue between his teeth and started sawing again. This time, he sawed relentlessly, with harsh, quick strokes that tore right through the flesh and the tendons and the cartilage, and which forced the bones to separate.

Like a large red flower blossoming, runnels of blood slid in all directions across the top of the bedside table and then ran down its legs. Blood was dripping off Mânios Dumitrescu's chin, too, because his crooked front teeth had almost severed the tip of his tongue. The pain he was feeling was nearly enough to make him black out, but he had suffered pain many times before in his life. During his early years in the Ferentari district of Bucharest, when he was selling drugs, he had been beaten with baseball bats and stabbed and once he had been whipped with barbed wire. No matter what they did to you, though, you never let your enemies realize how much they were hurting you, because if they did the bastards would have won, they would have humiliated you. What kept you focused through your pain was the thought that as soon as you had the chance you would do the same to them, only worse. That is what he thought now. *I will get my revenge on this black woman, and the things I will do to her will make Satan go pale.*

Mânios Dumitrescu kept on sawing until he had cut right through to the last shred of skin, and with each of the last few strokes his bloody hand flopped from side to side. Then, quite suddenly, it dropped off the table on to the rug.

His face was ashy-grey, all except for a crimson beard of blood, because now he had bitten off the tip off his tongue. He was shaking even more violently with shock – in fact, his skin seemed almost to ripple. In spite of this, he managed to lift up his left arm and brandish his stump in front of the young woman's face. He had severed both of the arteries in his wrist, but because of the self-protective constriction of the blood vessels it was only dribbling blood at the moment, like a garden hose with a leaky washer.

'*There!*' he croaked, although he had to stop and cough up blood before he could say any more. 'And you thought I do not have balls to do it! *Futu-ti crucea matii!*'

'I will have to tie your arm up for you,' said the young woman, quietly. A gold Japanese-style bathrobe was hanging on the back of the bedroom door and she went over and pulled out the sash from around its waist. 'Otherwise you will bleed to death.'

'What do you care?' He nodded down towards his detached hand, lying on the rug. 'There! There is your proof that you punish me! That is what you wanted! Now you go! Get out of my life!'

'Lie down,' said the young woman.

Mânios Dumitrescu tried to resist her at first, but he was in too much of a state of shock and much too weak. He let her push him back flat on the quilt and then use the gold sash to tie a half-knot around his wrist, tighter and tighter, until the blood stopped flowing altogether.

'Press your thumb on there and keep it there,' she told him. She went into the small en-suite toilet and came back with a toothbrush, which she twisted into the sash and wound around like a clock key to make a tourniquet.

Mânios Dumitrescu lifted it up to look at it, and said, 'You want me to thank you for this?'

'Wait until I have finished with you, Mânios, before you think of thanking me.'

'*Finished* with me?' he said, and for the first time that afternoon there was genuine dread in his voice.

The young woman walked around the bed and used a folded copy of yesterday's *Echo* to pick up his severed hand. 'Yes, good,' she said. 'This hand is proof that you have been punished. But ... we have to provide *two* proofs. One for God, and one for the police.'

'What?' he said, blurrily. For a few seconds his eyes rolled up into his head and he was unconscious. The young woman laid his severed hand down on the dressing table and waited patiently for him to come round. When at last he did, about three or four minutes later, he stared at her as if he couldn't think who she was. Then he held up his bloodied stump, with its toothbrush tourniquet, and stared at her in horror.

At first he did nothing but pant, but she could see from his face what he was thinking. *Oh God, don't let this be real. Oh God, please don't let this be happening to me.* With his right hand he even managed to make the sign of the cross, and after a while she heard him whisper. '*Oh, Isus va rog sa ma salveze.*'

She went up to the side of the bed and looked down at him. 'I need one more proof of your punishment. But you cannot give me that proof yourself. I shall have to take it for you.'

He let his head drop back on the quilt and looked up at her dully.

'When I have done this,' she said, 'I promise that I will give you peace.'

He still said nothing. She wasn't even sure that he could hear her.

'I am going to cut off your other hand now. Do you understand me? They always say that the devil finds work for idle hands. But if you *have* no hands, Mânios, you cannot get up to any more mischief, can you?'

The bedroom suddenly filled up with sunlight again. Mânios Dumitrescu half closed his eyes and tried to persuade himself that he had died, and gone to heaven. The trouble was, he couldn't imagine that heaven smelled like this, of blood and urine and Estée Lauder perfume, or that heaven could be such agony.

'*Alo, salut, sunt eu, un haiduc* ...' he whispered, from the song '*Dragostea din tei*'. *Hello, it's me, an outlaw* ...

Eleven

Katie parked her Fiesta on Anglesea Street right outside the front entrance of Garda headquarters, instead of in the main car park. A warm breeze was gusting as she got out of the car and almost blew away the folder of evidence she was carrying.

She had parked here because she would have to go straight back out again as soon as she had dealt with any outstanding messages and eaten the cheese salad sandwich she had bought in Marks & Spencer's. She had made an appointment that afternoon with Cois Tine, a charity that supported immigrant African women. She was hoping to find somebody there who could help her to get through to Isabelle. Cois Tine in Irish meant 'by the fireside' and the charity's whole purpose was to make African women feel that they had a place of warmth and safety to go to, where they could tell their story and make friends.

As she crossed the pavement, her attention was caught by a man standing on the corner of Copley Street, no more than thirty feet away. Although it was so warm and windy, he was wearing a long black raincoat with a pointed hood, and goggles like an old-fashioned motorcyclist. A tatty grey mongrel was sitting beside him, its fringe intermittently blowing into its eyes.

Katie stopped for a second and narrowed her eyes and stared at him, but because of his goggles she couldn't be sure if he was looking back at her. He made no move to walk towards her or to cross the street. He just stood there with his raincoat flapping in the breeze.

Oh well, she thought, it takes all sorts. She wasn't particularly superstitious, though she did see hooded crows as an omen of ill luck, and if she spilled any salt she always threw two pinches over her left shoulder in case the devil was standing close behind her. Her father had been a Garda inspector, though, and he had always told her that if anything looked unlucky, no matter what it was, then it probably was unlucky, so she should tread carefully. She had once seen a broken window in Togher that looked like a witch, and when she had entered the house to investigate she had been attacked by a crack-crazed burglar who had almost taken her eye out with a chair leg with a nail sticking out of it. She still had a small triangular scar next to her right eye, even today.

As she climbed the red-tiled steps in front of the Garda headquarters, a hoarse voice called out, 'Katie! Wait up there a moment, would you?'

It was Chief Superintendent Dermot O'Driscoll, puffing towards her like a red-faced steam engine, his white hair flapping like the smoke from its funnel. His tie was askew and he was carrying his linen jacket over his shoulder, with his shirt sleeves rolled up and his belly hanging over his belt.

'Thought you were having the day off, sir,' said Katie, as he caught up with her.

He dragged a green spotted handkerchief out of his trouser pocket and mopped at his forehead and the back of his neck. 'I was. I am. I haven't come in to do any work. I needed to come in and have a word with you and some of the others.'

He opened the door for Katie to enter the building and then they went up in the lift together to his office. On the way up he smiled at her once or twice but said nothing, which was unusual for him. Usually he couldn't stop talking about last Saturday's disastrous hurling match against Clare, or what a mountain of pasta he had eaten the previous evening at Kethner's, or how his wife's sister had visited again and never stopped talking and in the name of Jesus that woman would break your melt.

'Have a seat,' he told her, when they entered his office. He dropped his jacket over the back of his chair and then quickly shuffled through the messages that had been left on his desk, sniffing as he did so. He picked up one message and read it and grunted in amusement, but he didn't make any attempt to read the rest.

'I've, ah …' he began. Then he stopped and said, 'You and me, Katie, we've worked together for quite a good many years, haven't we, considering that you're so young and I'm so old?' He stopped again and then he said, 'There used to be a song about that, didn't there, I seem to remember?'

Katie smiled, but she didn't answer. She could tell that there was something badly wrong. Chief Superintendent O'Driscoll was never hesitant and he was never evasive. He always came out and spoke his mind directly, no matter how unpopular his opinion might be. That was what he had always admired about Katie, and why he had so vigorously backed her promotion to detective superintendent, against determined opposition from other senior Garda officers in Cork, and even from Dublin Castle.

Assistant Commissioner Pádraig Feeney had publicly commented in the *Examiner* about Katie's appointment: 'Women should be at home, hoovering and baking barm brack and wiping the children's snotty noses, not detective superintending.'

Chief Superintendent O'Driscoll drew out his chair but he didn't sit down. 'The reason I took the day off today was to go to my doctor to get my results,' he said. 'The thing is, like, I've been having symptoms for some time, but, you know ... I assumed they were the natural consequence of growing older and putting on a bit of weight.' He slapped his stomach as if to emphasize the point, and then he said, 'The thing of it is, I've been having a bit of difficulty with the waterworks.'

Oh God. The waterworks. Of course, Katie knew what was coming next, but she could only wait with her cheese salad sandwich in her hand while Chief Superintendent O'Driscoll found the words and the courage to tell her what his doctor had told him. She knew with a terrible inevitability that this was one sandwich that she was never going to eat.

'It's prostate cancer,' he said. 'Quite advanced, so far as they can tell, but I'll have to be given some more scans before they can know for sure how far it's spread.'

'Oh, Dermot,' said Katie.

Chief Superintendent O'Driscoll shrugged and smiled as if to say, 'Oh well, that's life for you,' but Katie could see that he was gripping the jacket on the back of his chair so tightly that it was crumpled and his knuckles were spotted with white, and from the way he kept blinking and sniffing she could tell that he was very close to tears.

'I'll be going off on indefinite sick leave from tomorrow onwards,' he said. 'They're taking me into the Bon Secours on Monday morning first thing, and then we'll just have to see where it goes from there.'

Had he been anybody else that Katie knew, she would

have stood up immediately and put her arms around him and hugged him to comfort him. She stayed where she was, though, because she knew that hugging him would only make him feel uncomfortable. He was her superior officer, after all, and for all that he had fought so ferociously for her appointment, she still respected his rank. She knew, too, that he was far from being a feminist. He simply believed that women had far keener noses for sniffing out cheats and liars than men.

'Tadgh McFarrell is still on his holliers until the end of next week,' said Chief Superintendent O'Driscoll. 'I thought he might take over, but they've already told me that they'll be bringing in somebody from outside to run things, at least until I'm fit enough to come back.'

There was a long silence between them. Katie couldn't think what else to say, except that she was sorry. She couldn't really ask him how long he had been suffering from painful or difficult urination, or how long it had been since he had experienced an erection.

She couldn't even ask him how long he expected it to be before he came back, because she knew that he had no way of telling and that the likelihood was that he would never come back at all, even if he survived.

But Chief Superintendent O'Driscoll smacked his hands together as if to say, 'That's enough of that maudlin nonsense. Let's get on.'

'How's it going with that black feller?' he asked. 'The one who had his napper shot off?'

'Oh – well, yes, him,' said Katie. 'The pathologist hasn't sent through the results of his autopsy yet, but I should get them later today. As far as identifying your man is concerned, a few witnesses have told us that they've seen him around the city from time to time, and judging by the company he was seen in, which was mostly young brassers, it seems highly likely that he was a pimp. But nobody's come up with a name, except for Mawakiya, the Singer.'

'That doesn't tell us anything, does it? He could have been handy with a sewing machine for all we know. How about the girl?'

'The one who was found with him? Isabelle? Well, that's what I've called her for now. Not a squeak out of her so far. But the therapists are working on her, and I'm going to see Father Dominic at Cois Tine at three o'clock. I'm hoping he can find us one of his warm motherly African women – somebody who speaks her language and who can coax her into talking to us.'

'Okay, then, grand. And what about Michael Gerrety? I'd give anything to see that skanger sent down.'

'We're supposed to be meeting with him and his lawyers at 1 p.m. tomorrow. But to be honest with you, sir, I don't think we're going to get very far with that.'

'Well, no, we didn't think we would, did we? All this Green Light shite. The trouble is, Gerrety has half of the city council in his pocket. If he's not paying them off, they're round at one of his massage parlours having their knobs gobbled, excuse my language. Even some of the social workers speak up for him, "Oh, at least he's keeping the poor girls safe off the streets." And none of his girls are going to say a word against him, are they? Not unless they want three shades of shite beaten out of them – or worse.'

Katie said, 'We'll still be going ahead with Operation Rocker? I mean, even after you've gone off on sick leave?'

'Operation Rocker! Of course. Why not? What's to stop it? It's the only way we're going to be sure of shutting Michael

Gerrety down, after all. He can hardly deny living off immoral earnings if we bust into his premises and catch his prozzies and his punters in mid-fornication, can he?'

'It's his laptops I want to get my sticky fingers on,' said Katie. 'His laptops, and his iPhones, and the contents of his safe. We'll never nail him under the Sexual Offences Act, not in the present climate. It's public order we need to go for – that, and trafficking. We've got some pretty solid evidence of that, so long as the witnesses hold up in court. No – it's his accounts I'm after. That's how we put Terry Buckley out of business, after all. Four million euros to the Criminal Assets Bureau, that's what Buckley had to pay. I'll bet you Michael Gerrety will have to cough up at least twice that.'

'Don't you worry, Katie,' said Chief Superintendent O'Driscoll, shaking his head so that his jowls wobbled. 'There's nothing going to stop Operation Rocker. I'm not tolerating Cork being known as the vice capital of Ireland, not while I'm still in charge.'

For nearly six months now, Katie had kept three of her detectives assigned almost full-time to Operation Rocker, as well as two part-time. It was a smaller but more intelligence-led follow-up to Operation Boulder which had raided fourteen brothels in Cork last year. Detective Horgan had chosen the name: a 'rocker' was what children called a very heavy stone, but one that they could just about manage to pick up and throw.

The team working on Operation Rocker had been gathering incriminating evidence from every possible source. They had kept watch on every suspected brothel and every individual hooker. They had interviewed prostitutes in the women's wing of Limerick Prison, and in the Dóchas Centre in Mountjoy Prison in Dublin. With legal authority, they had hacked into mobile phones and internet connections. Not least, they had kept their ears open to casual conversations in pubs and clubs, and between lawyers in the district court.

In three weeks' time all of this work would culminate in simultaneous raids on seven premises in the city centre – not just sex shops and massage parlours, but accountants' and solicitors' offices.

Chief Inspector O'Driscoll sat down at last, wincing, and looked thoughtful.

'That informant of yours,' he said. 'You know. The one with the eyes like a goat.'

'Denis Costigan, is that the one you mean?'

'That's your man. Is he still sure he knows where Gerrety keeps his records?'

Katie nodded, and couldn't help smiling, Denis Costigan did have eyes like a goat. Not only that, his jaw moved rhythmically from side to side when he chewed, just like a goat chewing grass. But he knew everybody and everything that was going on in Cork. His goat's eyes were always open when money or drugs or stolen property was changing hands.

'He called me yesterday,' said Katie. 'He's ninety-nine per cent sure that Gerrety is still using the basement of that sex shop on Oliver Plunkett Street, Amber's. We've been keeping it under observation, but only very discreetly, because we haven't wanted to spook him. He was there on Friday afternoon, with that wife of his, Carole. His girls are still bringing their earnings there, too, according to Denis. Half for Michael Gerrety and half for the girls, minus the two hundred euros he charges them to advertise on his website, or the five hundred euros he charges for the rent of one of his scruffy rooms.'

'Good,' said Chief Superintendent O'Driscoll. 'I know I

can rely on you to see this through. You and Tadgh McFarrell or whoever else it is they put in charge. I just wish I could be here to supervise it.'

'Don't worry,' said Katie. It was nearly ten to three now and time for her to go. 'It's too close to my own heart to let it go wrong.'

She stood up, with her cheese salad sandwich in her hand.

'You're not going to have time to eat that, are you?' he asked her.

'No, I don't think I am. Besides, I'm not very hungry. Do you want it?'

'What is it?'

'Cheese salad.'

He suddenly looked old and tired and sad. 'No, Katie, I don't think so. My salad days are over.'

Twelve

It was 9.30 p.m. before she arrived home that evening, and she hoped that John had remembered to take Barney for his walk. She would have done it herself if she had still been living her own, but her mind was being jostled by the day's events and all she wanted was a drink and something to eat and bed.

John must have seen her headlights through the curtains in the living room because he opened the front door as she climbed out of her car. Barney came tumbling out from between his legs and barked, and jumped up at her. She tugged at his ears and said, 'Whisht! Whisht! Calm down! You'd think I hadn't been home in a week!'

John smiled and kissed her and said, 'Good evening, pig-in-chief. How are things at the pigsty?'

'Stressful as usual,' she said, as she came into the hallway and took off her jacket. 'What's that smell?'

'Supper. I hope you'll be able to eat it.'

'Well, to be truthful, it smells really, really good, and I'm hungry. Not only that, I haven't had to look at any decomposing bodies today.'

She went through to the spare bedroom, which she still called the nursery, unfastened her holster and laid her Smith & Wesson revolver in the top drawer of the linen chest.

When she came back into the living room John was already standing by the drinks table, holding up a cut-crystal tumbler of vodka, tinkling with ice. 'There, I poured you one already.' He handed it to her and kissed her again. '*Slainte*. May bad luck follow you all of your life, but never catch up.'

'Where's your drink?' she asked him.

'In the kitchen. I've nearly finished cooking. Do you want to come join me? My God, I'm getting so domesticated, it's unbelievable. Do you know what I did today? I dusted the window sills. I have a PhD in computer science and I dusted the window sills.'

She followed him into the kitchen, laying her hand on the back of his white cotton shirt as she did so. He was so tall and slim and godlike and she loved his curly black hair, even when it was cut short like this. What she loved about him so much was that he was physically strong but emotionally sensitive, and that he always seemed to be able to sense when something was worrying her.

He went over to the stove, lifted the lid of an orange casserole and peered inside. 'Doing great,' he said. 'Give it twenty minutes and it'll be ready.'

'What is it? Spaghetti bolognese?'

'Meatballs Mexican-style, the way my cleaner, Nina, taught me to cook them in San Francisco, in chipotle-tomato sauce. Believe me, when you cook these, you never get any leftovers.'

'That sounds wonderful. I haven't had anything all day. I could eat the back door buttered.'

'So what's the story?' said John, giving his sauce a stir and then replacing the lid on the casserole.

'Nothing special. Why?'

He came up to her and laid his hands on her shoulders.

She loved that dark brown liquidity of his eyes and the coal-dust darkness of his six-o'clock shadow. A real dark Irishman, from romantic days, when there were fairies and kings.

'I think I know you well enough by now,' he smiled.

'You know what my life's like,' she told him. 'Somebody's always doing something they shouldn't, and I have to find out who they are and catch them. Day in, day out. There's never a day when everybody in Cork decides just for twenty-four hours to stop drinking and robbing and fighting and vandalizing and selling drugs and prostituting themselves. Not one day, never! But that's what I signed up for.'

'Okay,' said John, kissing her hairline, and then her fore-head, and then the tip of her uptilted nose. 'So do you know what I did today? Well, apart from housework.'

She put down her glass on the kitchen counter and then twisted open the top button of his white shirt. 'Go on. What did you do today? If it was anything to do with the internet, I probably won't understand a word of it.'

'In simple terms, I've been designing a website that will enable doctors and pharmacists to see the test results of ErinChem's newest products not just as charts and statistics, but visually. For instance, a speeded-up video of somebody's skin rash clearing up.'

Katie undid his second button, and then his third, and slid her hand inside his shirt. 'Yuck! I hope you're not going to put me off my supper again.'

He kissed her long and deep, his tongue exploring her teeth and then tussling with hers. Then he kissed her again. When he stood back from her, his chest was rising and falling as if he had been running to meet her along the seashore. 'I think I might turn off my meatballs for a while,' he said.

'This wasn't part of the method that Nina the cleaner showed me.'

He went over to the hob and switched off the gas. When he came back to her, Katie was already unbuttoning her own blouse. She caught hold of him fiercely and kissed him again and again, pulling open his shirt and wrenching it off his shoulders. Although it had been months now since he had last worked on his late father's farm, and he had put on at least ten pounds in weight, his chest was still muscular and his stomach was still taut. She grasped his penis through his trousers and she could feel that it was growing already. She squeezed it even harder and he said, 'Ow!' and flinched, but both of them laughed in mid-kiss.

John lifted off Katie's blouse and then unfastened her bra. Her late husband Paul had always struggled with bras, for all that he was a womanizer, and had usually ended up blaspheming at whichever fecking eejit had invented them. But John put his left hand smoothly behind Katie's back and her bra opened as if by magic, and her large rounded breasts fell free, with the subtlest of double bounces, and her rose-pink nipples already starting to crinkle.

They kissed again for a long time, until Katie could hardly breathe. What a way to die, she thought, with her eyes closed, and her mind completely in darkness, kissed to death. At last, gasping, she pulled away from him and said, 'Barney.'

'Barney?'

She went over to the kitchen door and closed it. 'I don't want him spying on us.'

'He's a dog.'

'Exactly. Didn't you ever hear of dogging?'

She unbuckled John's tan leather belt and tugged down his zip. He was wearing grey David Beckham briefs which

Katie had bought for him in Gentleman's Quarters, and they clung closely to his erection. She went down on one knee to help him pull off his trousers, and then she rolled his briefs down, too, so that his penis rose up in front of her, so hard that it pulsed slightly with every beat of his heart. She took it into her mouth and sucked it, and rolled her tongue around it, and poked her tongue tip into it.

John stood upright, rigid, both hands covering his face, and when she cupped his testicles in her hand and gently prickled them with her fingernails, and then sucked his penis harder and deeper, he groaned like a man who has realized for the first time the dreadful truth – that happiness never lasts forever.

Katie stood up, her lips glistening. 'Sit,' she said.

'Sit? You make me sound like Barney.'

She grinned and said, 'Sit down, you gom. There – on that chair.'

Naked now, John did as he was told, and sat down on the plain wheelback kitchen chair, holding his erection in his hand like a newly crowned king with a purple sceptre. Katie unzipped her skirt, peeled off her tights and stepped out of her panties. Usually, she never wore panties when she wore tights, but it was close to the twenty-seventh of the month.

'You know what you are, Katie Maguire?' said John, as she came up to him and stood in front of him, with her hand resting on his right shoulder.

'Pig-in-chief, that's what you called me before.'

He smiled and gave the slightest shake of his head. The expression on his face was almost beatific. 'You're a dream, that's what you are. You're some incredible dream that I shouldn't even be dreaming. Look at you.'

Katie kissed him, and then very carefully she climbed

aboard him, opening her legs wide so that he could position his glans between the lips of her hairless vulva. When she was sure that he was positioned comfortably, she gradually lowered herself down, so that his penis slid deeper and deeper inside her. At last he was so deep that it looked as if she had black pubic curls, too.

She put her arms around him and rested her head against his shoulder and they stayed like that for over a minute, just feeling each other and smelling each other.

'I don't want this to end,' John whispered, his breath hot and thunderous in her ear.

'All things must end, my darling,' she murmured.

'Please God, not this.'

Katie didn't say anything to that. Her life was all endings rather than beginnings, and here they were sitting on a kitchen chair while they were whirling around the Sun at 67,000 miles an hour, and it seemed so ridiculous and passionate and tragic all at the same time that she could have cried.

Slowly, she raised herself up, until John was right on the brink of slipping out of her. But then, very slowly, she sat down again, until she felt his hair between her thighs again. This time he slid so deeply inside her that his penis touched the neck of her womb, and she gave a snuffle and a nervous little jump. She continued to ride him up and down, up and down, keeping the same even rhythm, even though John was thrusting himself upwards now, his legs out straight, his thighs rigid and his buttocks clenched hard.

Katie could feel a climax gradually rising between her legs. The wooden chair seat was cutting into the sides of her knees, but she could hardly feel it. All she could feel was John inside her, and the pressure building inside her, building and building, as if her whole existence was about to implode.

John gasped, 'Oh my God, Katie! Oh my dear God!'

She felt him shake, and then he jerked violently up and down as if he were having a seizure. She could feel his warmth and his wetness flooding inside her. She clung to his shoulders, her whole body locked with tension, her face contorted, her teeth gritted, her climax so close that she could have screamed.

Then her mobile phone buzzed on the tabletop. *And it's no, nay, never – no, nay never no more—*

It was Inspector Liam Fennessy. He sounded very calm, but then he always sounded very calm. He had a coldness and a detachment about him that she had admired at first, almost envied, until she had discovered that he was coping with the stresses of his job by bullying his wife, Caitlin.

'Sorry to disturb you, ma'am. We have another feller with his hands cut off and his face gone missing.'

'Oh, God in heaven,' said Katie. She was still breathless and she picked up a tea towel to pat the perspiration from her face and neck. John got up, went through to the bedroom and came back with her dark green dressing gown, which he wrapped around her shoulders, and then kissed her on the forehead.

Inspector Fennessy said, 'A woman phoned Mayfield Garda station just before it closed and said that there was a body in a house on Ballyhooly Road, somewhere between Glen Avenue and Sunview Park East. Then she hung up.'

'She didn't give her name?'

'No. But it didn't take the lads long to find the right house. It was the only one where nobody was watching the telly. The door wasn't locked, though, so they were able to go straight in. Sergeant ó Nuallán and Detectives O'Donovan and Horgan are on their way up there now, as well as the technical team.'

'Do we have any idea who the victim is?'

'Not so far. He's a white male, early to mid-forties. He hasn't yet been moved, of course, but he has two distinctive tattoos visible on his upper arms, and a fair few scars, but that's all. He was naked, like the black feller, with both hands severed and missing, and what would appear to be a point-blank shotgun blast to the face. Or possibly *blasts*, plural. According to the lads who found him, there wasn't too much left of his head, like.'

'Give me the address and I'll go up and take a look for myself.'

'There's no need to, ma'am. I'll make sure you get a comprehensive report in the morning, videos and all. I can fend off the media, too, if they get any wind of it.'

'Thanks, Liam, but I want to see this first-hand. I'm beginning to get the feeling that this might not be the last of these, if we don't find our perpetrator pretty quickly.'

'Okay, then. I'll tell Sergeant ó Nuallán to be expecting you.'

She put down her mobile phone. John was buckling up his trousers with a rueful expression on his face. 'You're going out again? Another great supper down the toilet.'

'You dare. I want to eat that when I come home.'

'Katie, if that call was about what I guessed it was about, then you're going out to take a look at another dead body, am I right?'

Katie fastened her bra at the front and twisted it around to the back. 'Yes, you are. Liam says that his hands were cut off and then he was blasted in the face with a shotgun, just like that black feller in Lower Shandon Street – only *this* victim's white. That tells us it probably wasn't racist. So either it's a copycat killer, or somebody carrying out a vendetta, or just some gas woman who gets her kicks out of chopping men's hands off and then blowing their heads off.'

'Whatever the motive, Katie, don't tell me that you'll come back here later tonight with an appetite for meatballs?'

She went up to him and fastened the last two buttons of his shirt. 'No,' she said, 'I suppose you're right. But don't throw them away, whatever you do. They'll probably taste even better tomorrow, when they've had a chance to mulch for a while.'

John kissed her. 'Story of my life, isn't it? You can't have it today, John, but never mind. It's going to be ten times better tomorrow. And the word is "marinade", not "mulch". Mulching is what you do with compost.'

'I know.' said Katie. 'It was supposed to be a joke, you being a farmer and all. Well, a former farmer. I'm sorry.' She pressed her forehead against his chest and said it again. 'I'm sorry.'

She wondered, if they stayed together, how many times she would have to say that. Perhaps she ought to have it tattooed on the palm of her hand.

Thirteen

Detective Sergeant ó Nuallán met her outside the house, wearing a faded denim jacket and jeans, and a rainbow-coloured silk scarf tied around her head.

'Like the scarf,' said Katie. 'Very hippie.'

'I need to wash my hair, that's all.' She was wearing no make-up and the purple circles under her eyes made her look as tired as Katie felt.

Between Glen Avenue and Sunview Park East, the 200-yard pavement was cluttered with patrol cars and vans and an ambulance, and so many blue and red and white lights were flashing that it looked like a fairground. Almost every front door along the road was open and the residents were standing on their steps in the warm evening air watching the gardaí and the technicians coming and going. Even small children were standing out in their pyjamas.

Katie could see Detective O'Donovan talking to people in the small crowd that was gathered behind the blue and white *Garda: No Entry* tape. She also recognized Dan Keane from the *Examiner*, wearing the saggy grey linen jacket he always wore in summer. Dan raised his cigarette to her in salute, but she only gave him the briefest of nods in return.

'Who tipped off the media?' she asked Detective Sergeant ó Nuallán. 'Jesus, look, there's Fionnuala Sweeney, from RTÉ.

Tell your friends to watch out for you on the Morning Edition.'

'It wouldn't surprise me one bit if it was our perpetrator herself who tipped them off,' said Detective Sergeant ó Nuallán. 'If you ask me, she's trying to make a point.'

'Oh yes? And what point is that?' asked Katie, as she stepped into the hallway and looked around.

Upstairs, on the landing, so many halogen lights were flashing that it looked as if they were holding an exorcism up there. A technician called down to them, 'Could you wait there just a moment, please, ladies! I'm just untangling me cables.'

'It's the hands,' said Detective Sergeant ó Nuallán, 'Not only is she cutting them off, she's taking them away with her, so that we don't have any fingerprints. And because she's shot the victims point-blank in the face it's almost impossible to identify them from photofit pictures. You wait till you see your man upstairs. Apart from that, she's made it a nightmare checking their dental records – that's if they have any dental records in this country. Going by the state of that African man's teeth, I'd say that he'd never been to a dentist in his life, in any country.'

'So what's the point she's making? Always assuming that she *is* a she.'

'I think it's all about us. I think she's making a show of us for not doing our job. Maybe she's trying to tell us that we should have known a long time ago who these men were and what they were up to. So now she's a kind of vigilante, trying to make us look as if we couldn't beat nails into a bog with a saucepan. Since we can't punish them, then she's going to, and we *still* won't know who they are.'

'We don't have any substantive proof yet that either of

the two men were criminals,' Katie reminded her. 'We don't know *what* they were.'

'Oh, I'm fully aware of that, ma'am. I'm only theorizing. Our perpetrator probably killed them out of plain old revenge, more like. Maybe they conned her elderly mother out of her manage money, or maybe one of them made her pregnant and left her without any child support but she didn't know which one. But who knows? I'd lay odds on both of them being bent. There aren't too many respectable men who go around with boa constrictors tattooed on their mickeys – or if there are, I've never met them.'

Katie smiled tiredly and nodded. Detective Sergeant ó Nuallán was beginning to grow on her. More than anything else, she liked any detective who had the imagination to come up with a high-flown theory but the pragmatism to know that most criminals were too stupid to commit offences out of anything but greed or plain viciousness. Perhaps the cleverest thing that this perpetrator had done was to leave them so little forensic evidence that they had to theorize.

The technician beckoned that they could come up, and they climbed the stairs and entered the bedroom.

Because he was so recently dead, the man's body had only just started to decompose, although his skin already looked mottled. All the same, the room reeked so strongly of stale urine and faeces that it was suffocating. It was that smell that Detective Horgan called Essence of Old Folks' Home. Katie covered her nose and mouth with her hand. She had remembered her latex gloves, but she wished she had brought her Miracle perfume spray with her. The two technicians were wearing surgical masks and Detective Sergeant ó Nuallán took off her scarf and tied it around her face like a bandit.

The body was lying on the bed with his arms straight down, so that if his hands had still been there they would have been discreetly covering his genitals. A tourniquet had been fastened around his left wrist, with a pink toothbrush to tighten it, but his right wrist had bled out all over the quilt, and the bleeding had been so copious that the quilt was still shiny and wet. Although both stumps were clotted with dried blood, Katie noticed that the left wrist had been cut quite raggedly, with stray shreds of skin, while the right wrist had been cut as sharply and neatly as a log for the fire.

The man was white-skinned, with hairy arms and legs and a wild hairy tangle on his chest. From the way that his body hair was beginning to show signs of grey, Katie guessed his age at mid- to late forties. He had six or seven diagonal weals across his ribcage, like dried brown caterpillars, which indicated that he had been severely beaten at some time in his life, probably with a cane or a metal rod. He also had several silvery scars, some with suture marks, which indicated that he might have been stabbed.

On each of his bony shoulders was tattooed a triumphantly grinning blue skull, surrounded by a star.

His head had been even more spectacularly blown apart than that of the black man on Lower Shandon Street. There was no face, only a crimson cavern with two ears either side of it, at least twenty-five centimetres apart. A triangular flap of skull was still sticking up from the top of his head, but his brains had been sprayed across the quilt and pinkish lumps were still creeping slowly down the white wooden bedhead.

The senior technician leaned close to Katie and peered down into the remains of the man's head. 'Good evening to you, ma'am. This unfortunate individual was shot at least three times, I'd say, whereas we now know that the black feller was shot only twice.'

Katie raised an eyebrow but didn't ask him how he was sure about that, because she knew that he was going to tell her.

'This afternoon Dr O'Brien sent us over all the ammunition that he had recovered from his remains, so that we could count it and weigh it in conjunction with the ammunition that we dug out of the mattress. In total, six defence discs and twenty-one copper-plated BB pellets, which means we missed three, because there should have been twenty-four.'

'Defence discs?' said Katie. 'That means those new Winchester shotgun shells.'

'That's right. The PDX1. And the beauty of the PDX1 is that you can use them in handguns like the Taurus Judge which can take .410 shotgun shells as well as ordinary .45 cartridges. They're specifically intended for self-defence at very close range. The sort of gun that neurotic Americans like to keep in their bedside tables in case an intruder breaks in.'

'So ... if you can fire these shotgun shells from a handgun—' said Katie.

'You've got it, ma'am. It's in my report already ... the one I'll be sending you by lunchtime tomorrow if I ever get finished here. It solves the question of how a woman could have shot your man in the face at point-blank range without standing on the bed to do it. It also solves the question of how your perpetrator could have entered the premises on Lower Shandon Street without being seen to carry a full-length or even a sawn-off shotgun.'

Katie turned to Detective Sergeant ó Nuallán and said, 'Right. We need to check every firearms dealer in the country to see if they've sold any of these particular shotgun shells.' She turned back to the senior technician and said, 'They're made by Winchester, aren't they, but what did you say they were called?'

'PDX1 Defender,' the technician told her, poking around inside the victim's face with a shiny pair of tweezers. 'They're very distinctive because they have a black hull, unlike most shotgun shells. And you see here, inside the victim's sinus cavities? This grey plastic powder. It's called Grex. They pack it into the shotgun shell to keep the blast pattern tighter.'

'Okay, thanks,' said Katie. 'We also need to know if any of the dealers have sold a handgun that might be capable of firing these shells, although I'd be surprised if it was acquired legally. Oh – and get in touch with the shooting clubs, too, Lough Bo and Fermoy. You never know, their members are all mad about guns so one of them might have heard something. I'll have a word myself with Eugene Ó Béara. If anybody knows which guns in Cork happen to be where, he does. Either that, or he knows somebody who knows somebody who does.'

Detective Sergeant ó Nuallán had made a note of all this on her iPhone. With her voice muffled behind her bandit mask, she said, 'Fine. I'll get on to it tomorrow as soon as they're open.'

Katie stood very still for a while, her hand still pressed over her nose and mouth, looking around the bedroom inch by inch. She had already seen the dildoes lying on the bedside rug, and the clock, and the broken lamp. After a while she went slowly over to the dressing table and opened the drawers one after the other. Eyeliner, nail scissors, glittery nail varnish, elastic bands, hairgrips, Nurofen tablets, Durex condoms.

Nothing to tell her who might have used this bedroom, even if they probably had used it for prostitution.

Detective O'Donovan came stumping up the stairs, out of breath.

'I've talked to all the neighbours along this row,' he said, flipping open his notebook. 'The house is rented, but none of them knows the name of the owner. They've suspected for about six months now that it was being used as a knocking shop because there were so many strange men coming and going at all hours of the day and night.

'The woman next door, Mrs Cooney, she complained one night because of all the screaming going on when her kids were trying to get to sleep. The next morning some feller came around and told her that if she ever complained again he'd pour petrol all over her and put a match to her.'

'Name of Jesus, why didn't she report him?'

'You want her exact words? "I believed that your man would actually burn me alive if he found out that I'd shopped him, while the guards wouldn't get off their arses until I was nothing but ashes."'

'There's public confidence for you. Could she describe him, this feller?'

'She thinks he was foreign, because he spoke funny.'

'Oh well, that's helpful. The people round here think you're foreign if you come from Midleton. What did he look like, did she say?'

'She said he was one skinny malink. In fact, she said he was so thin that the one eye would have done him. But he still made her afraid of her life.'

Katie nodded towards the body lying on the bed. 'He's skinny enough, wouldn't you say? It could have been him.'

'Well, yes. It could have been. But I don't think there's a lot of point in asking Mrs Cooney to take a look at him.'

'All right,' said Katie. 'I don't think there's much more I can do here tonight. I'll look forward to your report in the morning, Bill, and hopefully we'll have the coroner's report on our black friend, too.'

As she left the house, Dan Keane came up to her, closely followed by Fionnuala Sweeney and her cameraman.

'So, what's the form, detective superintendent?' asked Dan Keane. 'We hear another pimp has had his head blown off.'

'I don't know who told you that, Dan,' said Katie. 'An unidentified male has been found deceased at this address, but so far the cause of death has not been officially established. There is no evidence so far to connect this death with the suspected homicide earlier this week of an unidentified male at an address in Lower Shandon Street.'

'Oh, there's a pity,' said Dan Keane. 'I had my headline all ready for tomorrow's paper, "The Headless Whores' Man"!'

'So far we have no proof that either victim was connected in any way with prostitution or the sex trade. Sorry. But I'd like to know who gave you that idea.'

'I'm sure you would, detective superintendent. As usual, however, my sources must remain confidential.'

Fionnuala Sweeney held out her microphone and said, 'Is there any truth in the suggestion that both victims had their hands cut off, too?'

Katie gave her a tight smile and said, 'I can't say anything more at this stage. I'm still waiting for the coroner's report. Once we've fully established the cause of death and the extent of any injuries, we'll let you know of course. It's likely that

I'll be holding a media conference late tomorrow afternoon at Anglesea Street.'

Fionnuala Sweeney held up a small piece of notepaper and frowned at it. 'Do you happen to know what "*Rah-ma-malah-eekah*" means?' she asked.

'Where did you hear that?' said Katie, shielding her eyes from the cameraman's lights.

'I can't reveal my source, I'm afraid. That was told to me in confidence.'

'Well, that's helpful. Do *you* know what it means?'

'No. We tried it out on Google Translate, in every possible language they do, but we came up with nothing at all.'

'In that case, there's nothing more that I'm prepared to say to you at this stage,' Katie told her. 'The press office will get in touch with you tomorrow.'

'Are you *sure* you've never heard that before?' Fionnuala Sweeney persisted, but Dan Keane laid a hand on her shoulder and said, 'Don't waste your breath, girl. If Detective Superintendent Katie Maguire doesn't want to give you an answer, Saint Peter will be asking you what good you've ever done, before she'll give you one.'

Katie and Detective Sergeant ó Nuallán walked together to Katie's car.

'I think you're right, and it *was* the perpetrator who tipped off the press,' said Katie. 'That girl they found with the body on Lower Shandon Street, the one I call Isabelle, she said that exact same thing to me before they took her off to hospital.'

'She didn't give you any idea what it meant?'

'No, she didn't, and it was the last thing she said to me. But I met with Father Dominic at Cois Tine this afternoon and he's sending two African women to talk to her tomorrow, one Nigerian and one Somali. Most of the African immigrants in Cork come from one or other of those two countries, so there's a fair chance that at least one of them can persuade her to open up.'

Detective Sergeant ó Nuallán was tying her scarf around her head again. 'I don't know if you picked up my message yet, but Horgan got no joy from immigration. There's no trace at all of the girl entering the country, wherever she's originally from.'

'Why doesn't that surprise me one bit?' said Katie. 'Listen, I'll see you in the morning so. We have a meeting with Michael Gerrety and his lawyers in the afternoon. Perhaps *he* might tell us who she is.'

'Patrick O'Donovan was telling me all about Michael Gerrety,' said Detective Sergeant ó Nuallán. 'From what I gather, I'm sure he'll tell you, yeah.'

Fourteen

'So this is your little nest, girl,' said Mairead, opening the last door at the end of the corridor. Zakiyyah peered inside. The buildings on the opposite side of Washington Street faced almost due south, so the room was filled with reflected sunlight from their upstairs windows. It was so narrow, however, that the king-size bed was pushed up against the wall on one side and there was space for only one bedside table, with one pink-frilled table lamp, although there was a reading light clipped to the opposite side of the headboard.

The window was covered with a plastic venetian blind, with alternate lavender and white slats, and the bed was covered in creased purple velveteen, with heaps of cushions in various shades of purple and violet. The corner of the room behind the door was curtained off, presumably to give Zakiyyah somewhere to hang her clothes – not that she had any, now that her suitcase had been taken away from her.

On one wall hung a large poster of a salacious young witch, naked except for a pointed hat and a cloak, her eyes closed in ecstasy as she pushed the handle of her broomstick up inside her. Her black cat was watching her and licking its lips.

On the facing wall there was a framed photograph of

Blarney Castle, faded by years of sunlight until it was almost colourless.

'What do you think, then?' said Mairead. 'Home from home. Better than some mud hut in Africa, I'll bet.'

Mairead was a short, bosomy woman with long lank silver-blonde hair that draped over her shoulders. She had a heart-shaped face and a turned-up nose and she could have been pretty in a plump, waitressy way, except that her cheeks were blotched and puffy and underneath the thick pink gloss her lips were cracked. Her eyes were cornflower-blue, but Zakiyyah saw some indefinable lack of focus in them, as if she had long forgotten who she was and what she was doing here.

She was wrapped in a gold satin gown and was wearing high-heeled gold slippers, but underneath Zakiyyah could see that she was wearing only a black lacy corselet, with some of the lace ripped around the side of one cup.

Mister Dessie was standing in the corridor close behind them, smoking and talking to a girl in the room next door. 'I'll be off now, Mairead,' he said, after a while. 'Himself will be dropping by later, he said, after his round of golf. He said not to let anyone touch her until he's taken a sconce at her and the doctor's been.'

'Oh, I will, yeah,' said Mairead. 'Listen, would you nip across the road for me and get me a packet of Johnny Blue before you go? I've been gasping.'

'Go and get them yourself, you idle slag. What do you think I am?'

'You're all fecking heart, that's what you are, Dessie. That's the last time you get a gobble.'

'After the last time, I'd rather stick it down a mincer.'

Mister Dessie went off, and Mairead put her arm around

Zakiyyah's shoulders and said, 'Don't take any notice of that gobdaw. He's all mouth and no trousers.'

'He frightens me,' said Zakiyyah. 'He will not let me have my suitcase and he hurt me.'

'Don't you worry, girl. I won't let him hurt you again. Well, so long as you behave yourself, and do what you're told, like.'

'I was supposed to dance in a club. I do not understand any of this.'

Mairead looked towards the window, at the buildings opposite, and her eyes seemed even more unfocused, as if she had X-ray vision and could see right through them, to the hills beyond. 'No, love, I don't think any of us do. I keep asking myself how I got myself into this, and to be honest, I don't really remember. I know that I was stone-broke. Dessie lent me some money, and then he lent me some more money, and before I knew it I owed him seven hundred euros and I didn't have any way to pay him back except for this.'

'I share a bed only once with a man,' Zakiyyah told her. 'That was my boss in Lagos, and I did not want to do it, but he said that I would lose my job.'

'Oh, you'll get used to it. It's not half as bad as some of these Holy Joes try to paint it. Fair play, some of the punters we get are totally crustified, or else they're langered and they stink of the drink, but in that case they usually can't get it up any road. Either that or they'll ask you to do something pervy. But you don't have to do anything you really don't want to, especially if it's unhygienic. Mister Dessie will usually back you up if a punter's giving you grief. But if a punter asks *me* to do something that's pure disgusting, what I usually tell him is it'll cost him double.'

She laughed, although her laugh sounded completely flat,

like a broken bell, with no humour in it at all. 'Most of the time, though, they cough up, and then I wish I'd charged them three times as much.'

Zakiyyah said, 'What if I do not like the man at all?'

'Then you open your legs and close your eyes and think of what you feel like for your dinner tonight.'

'I cannot say no, I do not want you?'

'No, girl. You're here to pay back what you owe. If you turn down a punter, or upset him at all, then you're liable to get yourself a beating, believe me.'

'I am so frightened,' said Zakiyyah. She had to sit down on the bed because she was trembling so much and she felt as if she were going to be sick. She retched twice, while Mairead stood beside her, watching her patiently.

'Let me tell you how it works,' said Mairead. 'What happens is, the punter sees your picture on Michael's website. He phones up the number, like, and we send him to the courthouse there across the street. That's so that we can see him standing on the steps, just to check out that it isn't the shades or a fecking one-legged leper or something. If he looks okay we phone him back and we tell him how to get up here.'

'Then what?' asked Zakiyyah. She had never felt such dread in her life, and she found it even more terrifying because of the matter-of-fact way in which Mairead was describing what she was expected to do.

'There's four girls here most of the time. I'll introduce you to the others in a minute. If your punter hasn't already taken his pick from the pictures on the website, he'll make his choice after we let him in. He'll tell us what he wants, like, and we tell him how much it's going to cost him. It's a hundred euros for a hand-job, or a hundred and seventy for oral, or two hundred for full sex, with another fifty for anal. Then of course it's extra for anything like bondage or lesbian or special requirements.'

Zakiyyah closed her eyes. She wished that somehow she could be magically transported back to her home village – that when she opened them again she would see her mother stirring Akamu custard and her father raking the yard and her sister laughing in the sunshine. If that was impossible, she would rather not open her eyes, ever again, and never see that purple bedspread, or those cushions, or those orange brick buildings opposite with their dazzling windows. She would rather be dead.

But she opened them again, and she was still alive, and Mairead was still talking to her. 'Renting this room will cost you two hundred euros a week, and your advertisement on the interweb will cost two hundred and fifty. On top of that, Michael takes sixty per cent of everything you make, which goes towards paying him back. I'll help you to work that out.

'House rules: none, really, except that you must always use a condom. Michael's very particular about that, even for oral. It doesn't matter how much the punter offers you to do it without. It's all part of Michael's Green Light campaign, so that he can prove to the world that he keeps his girls healthy and safe, that's what he says. You have to buy your own condoms, though, and your own baby-wipes.

'You'll be starting in the morning as soon as the first punter rings, and finish whenever the last one wants his end away. That usually means you'll service ten or maybe twelve punters a day, sometimes more. You'll be extra busy when Cork's playing at home, I can tell you. Sometimes you won't even have time to wash your mouth out.'

Zakiyyah managed unsteadily to stand up. 'I would like a drink of water, please.'

'Oh, of course, girl! I'll bet you haven't had a drink all day, have you? And did that Bula give you anything to eat? I'll bet that he didn't, the gowl. Jesus, he's as thick as two short planks tied together. Come into the kitchen and I'll knock you up a hang sangwich.'

Zakiyyah followed Mairead into the tiny kitchenette, where a moulting green budgerigar was perched in a cage on the window sill. Mairead poured her a glass of red lemonade and made her a sandwich with white bread and Spam. As she sat at the glass-topped table, two other girls came in, a small flat-faced Thai girl with very long black hair who was wearing nothing but a thong and a quarter-cup bra, so that her prune-like nipples were exposed, and a tall, thin blonde in a stained pink dressing gown. The blonde's hair was braided in a tight coronet and she looked as if she might have been Czech or Ukrainian.

'This is Lotus Blossom and this is Elvira,' said Mairead. 'Girls, this is Zakky.'

Lotus Blossom came up and kissed Zakiyyah on both cheeks and said, 'Welcome. You call me Lawan, that is my real name, not work name.'

'Zakiyyah,' said Zakiyyah.

Elvira smiled and gave her a little finger-wave, but Lotus Blossom said, 'Elvira does not speak good English yet. She has been here only one month now. For me it was very hard to understand Irish people when I first come here, even though I speak good English already. Sometimes I still don't know what they say. Everything they say is "like" and good is "how bad" and even old man is "boy".'

She pressed her sparkly-polished fingertips to her lips and

tittered. Elvira smiled, too, in a dreamy, drugged-looking way, although it was obvious that she didn't know why.

Zakiyyah drank her red lemonade and tried to eat her sandwich, although she found it difficult to swallow. The phone rang and Mairead picked it up and said, 'Oh. Sure. You'll be there in five minutes, will you? Well, give us a ring when you get there, darling, and I'll tell you where to go next. That's all right.'

'Who was that?' asked Lotus Blossom.

'Not for you, girl. It's some culchie who's just come up on business from Kenmare and he fancies Elvira. Do you know what he said, the stupid cake? "I've only seen her picture online and I'm desperately in love with her already." Jesus.'

'So long as it's not that old man who sells fish in the English Market,' said Lotus Blossom. 'Every time he always wants *me*. "Oh, Lotus Blossom you're so sweet like your name!" But he stinks of kipper! He says he washes but he always stinks of kipper!'

She tittered again, although there was no real humour in her laugh at all, just like Mairead's. Zakiyyah felt that they were laughing only because crying wasn't going to change anything. She pushed her plate away and said, 'I am sorry. I cannot eat any more. My stomach is not good.'

'Oh, don't you worry about that, girl,' said Mairead. She picked up one of the sandwiches herself and took a bite. 'You'll soon get used to the delights of Irish cuisine. And most of the time we get takeouts from one of the local Chinkies.

'Here ...' she said, with her mouth full. 'I'll show you the rest of the place.'

Zakiyyah finished her drink and got up to follow her. As

she did so, Lotus Blossom laid her hand on her arm and said, 'Don't you worry, Zakky. It's not so bad. Better than working in a shop, or a restaurant. Most of the men are very nice to you. You only get a few bad ones, and that's because they're drunk.'

'How long have you been here?' asked Zakiyyah.

Lotus Blossom shook her head. 'I don't remember! Maybe two years. I will still be here when I am old and all of my teeth fall out! Men like that! Blow-job with no teeth! Not so worried you will bite it off!'

'You have not paid them back yet, in two years, the money you owe them?'

'I don't remember. They always say I still owe them more. Besides, what else am I going to do? They have my passport, all my papers.'

Mairead took Zakiyyah into the living room. The sunshine showed up the dust on the purple velvet curtains and the worn-out black carpet. Three black leather couches were arranged around the walls facing a 42-inch flat-screen TV, and in between the couches there stood a black-painted coffee table with dog-eared copies of pornographic magazines like *Private* and *Color Climax* arranged in a fan shape – like *Irish Country* and *Woman's Way* in a dentist's waiting room.

'This is where a punter can come in and have a drink and make his mind up which one of us he wants,' said Mairead. 'We charge twenty-five euros for a beer, thirty for a glass of wine, and fifty for spirits. Well, those are the basic prices. Usually, we charge as much as we can get away with.

Mairead's own bedroom was almost as large as the living room. It was furnished with a four-poster bed and a red plush chaise-longue and a white Regency-style dressing table with a marble-patterned top, although its edges were chipped.

There was a built-in wardrobe opposite the bed, with mirrored doors.

'That's so the punters can watch themselves getting their money's worth,' said Mairead. 'Mind you, they all want to take selfies these days, right in the middle of it, so they can show their mates afterwards. Michael's thinking of charging them extra for that.'

She showed Zakiyyah the bathroom on the opposite side of the corridor. This was gloomy and smelled of damp, and the grouting between the tiles had turned black. Underneath the frosted-glass window stood a narrow, old-fashioned bathtub with rust stains in it, and next to it a washbasin crowded with bottles of shampoo and conditioner. The ceiling was patchy with mould and looked as if it was about to collapse at any moment.

Mairead said, 'We'll go out shopping for you tomorrow and get you everything you need, like toiletries and make-up and that, and something for you to wear, like – although, believe me, you won't be wearing much for most of the time. Saves on the laundry, I can tell you!'

At that moment there was a chime from the doorbell downstairs. 'That'll be Elvira's punter. And I expect Michael will be here before we know it. Why don't you throw yourself down for a while, girl, and have a rest? You won't be getting much of that from now on, I can tell you!'

She lay on the purple bedcover, but she didn't close her eyes. The velveteen smelled sour and musty, as if it hadn't been cleaned in years, or ever, and from the angle at which she was lying she could see that there were shiny silvery splotches all over it. She heard the front door of the flat being opened, and a man's gruff voice, and then Mairead saying something, and laughing, although she could only make out the word 'darling'.

After that, she heard the door to Elvira's room close and the television in the living room being switched on. She couldn't hear that distinctly, either, only Irish women arguing with each other, and then music. Sad, lilting pipe music – the kind of music the Irish play to make themselves cry. It seemed to go on and on, until her eyes began to close.

She didn't want to fall asleep, but she did. She might have dreamed, but if she did, she didn't remember what her dreams were. All she knew was that she was abruptly woken up by a knock on her door, and a man saying, 'Well, well, what do we have here? The sleeping beauty! The sleeping *black* beauty!'

Immediately she opened her eyes and sat up, tugging down the hem of her slip to make sure that she was decent. She tried to primp up her hair as well, because she knew that all her glass beads had become tangled.

A tall, broad-shouldered man was standing in the doorway, wearing a camel-coloured summer jacket, with a green silk handkerchief in the breast pocket. He had thick chestnut hair, combed back in a wave, and he was suntanned in that freckly way that fair-skinned people tan. He was green-eyed, with a wide, generous face, and a deep Celtic cleft in his chin. He was smiling, although one of his front teeth had caught on his lip, so Zakiyyah couldn't be sure if he was smiling or snarling.

Mairead was standing very close behind him, and she said, 'Zakky, this is Mister Michael Gerrety. He's come to take a look at you.'

Michael Gerrety approached the side of the bed and stood between Zakiyyah and the window, so that she could see only his silhouette.

'Well, now, Mister Dessie said you were a cutie, and he wasn't wrong for once, was he, Mairead?'

'Oh, they'll be flocking in, Michael, once they see her on the interweb.'

Zakiyyah didn't know one Irish accent from another, but Michael Gerrety spoke very warmly and melodiously, and he sounded all the ends of his words with the tip of his tongue, like a trained actor.

'I can't say that I've ever been partial to black girls before now, but you are something very special, aren't you? What did you say her name was, Mair? Zakky?'

'Zakiyyah,' Zakiyyah corrected him. 'It means pure.'

'Oh yes! I think Dessie was blethering about that. Well, that's how we'll advertise you. Zakiyyah, the Pure Black Beauty. How old are you, Zakiyyah?'

'Seventeen. But I do not want to be hooker. I do not want to go with so many men.'

'When's your birthday, gorgeous?'

'August the fifteenth.'

'Then you're only days away from being legal, and that suits me down to the ground. I'm not a pimp, Zakiyyah. I'm not a criminal. I'm a respectable man who happens to believe that sex should be sold openly and cleanly, like anything else that people want to buy and sell. There should be adequate protection for the young women who want to sell themselves, and both sympathy and understanding for the men who feel the need to buy them. It's as straightforward as that.'

'But I do not want to sell myself,' said Zakiyyah. Her eyes filled with tears but she defiantly brushed them away with her fingertips. 'I thought I came here to dance.'

Michael Gerrety stepped back, away from the window, so that she could see him clearly again. 'But you *did* come here to dance, Zakiyyah! And you *will* dance! I have scores of contacts in nightclubs all across Ireland, and in the dance companies, too! Me and Michael Flatley, we go golfing together almost every weekend! But unlike him, I'm not a millionaire, sweetheart! You came here all the way from Lagos, and do you know how much that cost me?'

'Mister Dessie told me,' said Zakiyyah. 'But I will pay you back everything I owe you. I promise.'

Michael Gerrety was still smiling but he shook his head. 'What job? Stacking shelves at Dunne's Stores? Washing dishes at McDonald's? Changing beds at Jury's Hotel? Do you know how little money those jobs pay? Because you're not qualified to do any other kind of work, are you?'

'I promise I will pay you back!'

'I *believe* you, sweetheart, but the question is *when*? Jobs like that pay 8.65 euros an hour, while working here could earn you more than two thousand euros every single day. You would have to work more than eleven days at one of those minimum-wage jobs to make that sort of money. Not only that, where would you live? What would you eat? What clothes would you wear? You'd have to pay for those out of your wages, too, and that wouldn't leave very much for me, would it, if anything at all?'

'I would have clothes if you had not stolen my suitcase.'

'Nobody's stolen your suitcase, my darling. We have it in safe keeping as security, that's all. You can have it returned to you when you've paid off everything you owe me.'

'I do not believe you. I do not believe anything you say to me. I was supposed to come to Ireland to dance, not to be *bagar*.'

'You don't believe me?' said Michael Gerrety. 'Well, I thought you might say that, and I suppose I don't blame you. Mair – Mair! Fetch me my briefcase, will you? It's in the kitchen, on the chair.'

Mairead appeared with a chequered Louis Vuitton brief-case and handed it to him. Michael Gerrety took out a brown manila folder and opened it up. Inside were six or seven photographs of varying sizes, some coloured and some black and white.

'Those are my pictures!' said Zakiyyah, sitting up straighter. 'That is my family!'

Michael Gerrety held up a photograph of a smiling woman wearing a huge green and yellow Nigerian gele, or head-tie.

'That is my mother!' Zakiyyah protested. 'That is the only picture I have of her! Give it to me!'

She jumped up from the bed and tried to snatch it, but Michael Gerrety held it up high, out of her reach, and passed the manila folder back to Mairead.

'Give it to me! Give it to me! It is mine! Please, give it to me!'

With his left hand, Michael Gerrety pushed Zakiyyah back on to the bed. She tried to scramble up again, but he pushed her again, harder this time.

'I'm telling you, sweetheart, you're a very beautiful girl, and you and me are going to get along together like a dream – but only so long as you do what I ask you to do and behave yourself. You have no money, you have nowhere to stay, you have no friends at all. There's something else you're going to start feeling soon, and that's the itch to have more of that vaccine we gave you to protect you against the rabies. If you don't get that vaccine soon, you're going to start getting sick, I tell you. Then you'll be *begging* me to be a brasser. Begging on your black hands and knees.'

'Please – that is my mother,' said Zakiyyah. 'Please give me her picture.'

Michael Gerrety held up the photograph in front of her and then tore it in half. He tore it in half again, and then again, and then again, and tossed the pieces around the room.

'Every time you give me trouble, I'm going to come in here and I'm going to do the same to another one of your family pictures. Do you understand what I'm saying to you? And when I've run out of pictures, I'll have to think of something else to make you behave yourself ... like tear up your passport, for starters, and report you to immigration. You know what they do to illegal woman immigrants in Cork? They lock them up in Limerick Prison, and compared to the women's wing of Limerick Prison this place here is heaven on earth.'

Zakiyyah miserably picked up two torn fragments of her mother's photograph and tried to match them together, but Michael Gerrety had ripped them up too small and scattered them all around the room. All this time, Mairead was standing in the doorway, with her arms folded over her bosom, but the look in her eyes was just as far away as it had been before.

'You're clean, are you?' asked Michael Gerrety.

'I have not washed yet,' said Zakiyyah. 'Now I am here, I will wash.'

'I didn't mean that kind of clean. I mean you don't have any STDs?'

'Diseases,' Mairead explained. She pointed to her crotch and said, 'Diseases down below. Like the clap, like.'

Zakiyyah said, 'I only go with one man. My boss, Mister Bankole. Nobody else. Mister Bankole was very clean man.'

'Well, that's no guarantee at all,' said Michael Gerrety.

'But the doctor will be calling by later to have a look at you and take a blood sample, just to make sure you don't have the HIV. We don't want anybody accusing the Green Light of spreading STDs.'

Zakiyyah didn't know what to say to that. She felt angry at Michael Gerrety, and intimidated by him, but in a strange way she found him reassuring. Whatever he expected of her, he was going to make sure that she had somewhere to sleep, and that she was going to be fed, and that she wouldn't be locked up in prison. She had disliked what Mr Bankole had done to her, his sweating and his panting and the harsh dry feeling of his skin, but it had all been over in minutes, and he had thanked her, after all, and given her a thousand naira in cash. By the time she had taken a long hot shower she had felt physically as if nothing had happened to her, although she was sure that her friends could read in her eyes that she was no longer a virgin.

Maybe Lotus Blossom was right. Maybe it wasn't so bad, being a hooker. Maybe you could simply wash it off, at the end of every day, as if it had never happened.

Michael Gerrety checked his heavy gold Rolex. 'Right, then, I have to go now. Let's take a look at you.'

Zakiyyah frowned at Mairead. What did he mean by that? He *was* looking at her.

Muichael Gerrety caught the frown and said, 'The slip,' making a lifting-off gesture with his arms. 'I need to see you in the nip.'

Zakiyyah hesitated, but Mairead said, 'Go on, girl, he only wants to see what your figure's like, for your advertisement.'

Very hesitantly, Zakiyyah climbed off the bed and stood in front of Michael Gerrety, looking directly into those sea-green eyes. '*Ya zama jarumi*,' her mother had always told her. 'You must always be brave.'

She lifted off her slip and stood naked in front of him. Her skin was very dark and the sunlight gave a slight sheen to it. Her breasts were small but very firm and her waist was slim, although her hips flared out and she had a high, rounded bottom. Michael Gerrety didn't touch her. He looked her up and down and the only clue to what he was thinking was the way he pursed his lips, more like an accountant looking through a set of figures than a pimp. After a while he twirled his finger to indicate that he wanted her to turn around, which she did.

'Plenty to grab hold of there,' said Mairead, from the doorway, lighting a cigarette and blowing two tusks of smoke out of her nostrils.

'All right,' said Michael Gerrety, 'I'll have Dessie take a few pictures tomorrow and then I think we're in business. You can get dressed again now, young lady. You're a beautiful girl and I believe you're going to do us proud.'

How can he say that to me? thought Zakiyyah. *How can he tear up my only picture of my mother right in front of my face, and then tell me that I'm beautiful?* No man had ever confused her so much in her life.

'Just one more thing,' said Michael Gerrety, as he turned to leave the room. 'Ask Mairead here to lend you her razor, until you get one of your own. Don't want to be advertising a safari in the African bush, do we?'

Mairead laughed her cracked-bell laugh. Michael Gerrety looked back at Zakiyyah over his shoulder and gave her a mocking smile that made her shudder. She sat down on the bed with her slip in her lap and felt as empty as if she had just sold her soul to the devil.

Fifteen

Bula-Bulan Yaro shouldered his way out of Burger King on Patrick Street and immediately took the Whopper he had bought out of its box and started to eat it as he walked along, sniffing and wiping his nose with the back of his hand in between bites.

Mister Dessie had given him the afternoon off and he intended to spend it playing snooker at the Quay Side Club, but he had been moving beds all morning from one of Michael Gerrety's houses to another and he was so hungry he could have eaten a horse between two bread vans.

An elderly nun in rimless spectacles came hurrying after him and tapped him on the back.

'You forgot your box, young man,' she said, pointing to the cardboard takeout carton that he had tossed on to the pavement.

Bula turned around and stared at it as if he had never seen it before. 'I didn't forget it, sister. I didn't want it, that's all. See? I'm eating this burger. There's no way I'm going to be eating the box that it came in.'

'You could have dropped the box into a bin.'

'I could of, yeah. But I didn't. And if you're so worried about it, why don't *you* drop it into a bin? Then we'll both be happy.'

'I'll pray for you tonight,' said the nun. 'I'll pray that God shows you how sinful it is, to drop your rubbish in a beautiful city like this.'

Bula looked around. 'Sister,' he said. 'If you think this city is beautiful, you need new glasses, urgent-like. There, see – it probably looks a little fuzzy to you, but there's a Boots Opticians right across the street.'

With that, he carried on walking, taking another huge bite from his Whopper.

He hadn't even reached the end of the block, though, before a woman's voice alarmingly close behind him said, '*Bula*! Take the next right, Bula! Can you hear me, Bula? Take the next right down the lane there!'

Bula spun around, hopping on one foot, so that he nearly lost his balance. A young black woman was standing less than three feet away from him. She was dressed all in black, except for a necklace that looked as if it was made of triangular pieces of ivory, and she had a topknot of black snake-like curls. She was staring at him with such wide-eyed ferocity that he thought somebody must be setting him up for a practical joke. He looked all around him, still chewing, but he couldn't see any of his drinking acquaintances anywhere and none of the passing shoppers were taking any notice of him at all.

His mouth was so full that he could only mumble in protest and shrug his shoulders. But the black woman stepped towards him and prodded him in the chest. 'You heard me, Fat Man! Down the lane there, now! And keep going until I tell you!'

Bula swallowed, and coughed, but before he could manage to cough out any words the woman leaned closer to him and said, quietly but clearly, in a strong Nigerian accent, 'I know who you are, Bula, and I know who you work for, and I have a gun in my pocket, and I will not for one second hesitate to shoot you, even out here, in the middle of the street.'

Bula took two or three defensive steps back, his tongue chasing half-chewed burger around his mouth, and then swallowing, and swallowing, and swallowing yet again. He was trying to work out how this skinny young woman in nothing but jeans and a T-shirt and a sleeveless waistcoat could be carrying a gun, even though her right hand was pushed deeply into her waistcoat pocket.

'Hey,' he said, warily. 'Suppose I tell you to go and take a running jump.'

By now they were standing right in the middle of the narrow entrance to Mutton Lane, which runs from Patrick Street into the covered English Market, so that other people had to push past them. Bula wasn't at all sure if he ought to take this woman seriously or not. This must be a joke. But if it was a joke, what was funny about it, from anybody's point of view?

The woman said, 'I want to talk to you, Bula, that's all.'

'So how do you know my name? Who the feck are you? What do you want to talk about, anyway?'

'You'll never find out if you make me shoot you.'

'Oh, get away out of here. You don't have a gun.'

'That's what Mânios Dumitrescu said to me. Almost those exact same words.'

'Mânios? You mean *Manny*? Manny Dumb-arse? That septic little Romanian shite?'

'He's dead, Bula. Didn't you see it on the news this morning? Mystery man found with both his hands missing and his head shot off, up at Ballyvolane?'

Bula looked around again, still half suspecting that this
was a set-up. Then he turned back to the woman and said,
'That was *Manny*? Serious? How do you know? Any road,
what does it have to do with me?'

'Block the whole passage, why don't you?' said a beery-
breathed drinker who had just lurched out of the Mutton
Lane Inn.

'Oh, go and screw yourself,' said Bula.

'Hey, watch who you're talking to, you fat bastard,' the
drinker retorted.

'I said go and screw yourself. Are you deaf or something?'

The drinker pointed at Bula and took an unsteady step
forward, but the black woman raised her left hand in front
of him and gave him a look that meant, *Don't cause trouble,
can't you see that there's enough trouble going on here
already?* The drinker opened his mouth, but then he got the
hint and closed it again, and weaved away down Patrick
Street as if he were walking across the deck of the Cross
River ferry.

'Go on, Bula,' said the young woman, nodding her head
down Mutton Lane. As she did so, two gardaí came strolling
past them, a man and a woman, so close that Bula could have
reached out and tugged at the woman garda's shirtsleeve, but
he watched them go by without saying a word. He was here
in Ireland illegally, and if the Garda Immigration Bureau found
out that he was working for Michael Gerrety, without papers
or tax being paid, he would be lucky if Mister Dessie only
beat the dust off him. He had witnessed Mister Dessie
punishing a cute young entrepreneur from Dublin who had
tried to cheat Michael Gerrety on a property deal in
Rochestown. Both his legs had been broken and he had
suffered irreparable brain damage.

'All right,' he told the young woman. 'I'll give you five minutes, but that's your limit, whatever it is you want to say to me. You've already spoiled my dinner for me.'

He made his way down Mutton Lane, his cargo shorts flapping and sandals shuffling on the grey brick pavement, and the woman followed close behind him. He passed the doorway of the Mutton Lane Inn, which was so gloomy inside that it was lit by candles even in daytime, and he could hear a woman laughing so hysterically that she was almost screaming. Because the lane led directly into the English Market, he could already smell fresh pork and cheese in the air. Before they reached the market entrance, however, the young woman said, 'Here, Bula! Stop! This doorway here.'

Set in the right-hand wall was a flaking, maroon-painted door, with a tarnished brass plaque beside it: O'Farrell Furnishings.

The woman took two long keys out of her waistcoat pocket and used one of them to unlock the door. Then she stepped back and said, 'Go on, open it, and go inside.'

Bula looked at his half-eaten Whopper. 'And what do you suggest I do with this?'

'Eat it. Or don't eat it. It's entirely up to you.'

Bula hesitated, and then he dropped the burger on to the ground. 'Whatever you want to talk about, it had better be fecking worth it.'

'Well, I'll let you be the judge of that, Bula.'

Bula opened the door and stepped over the threshold, and the woman immediately followed him. She switched on the lights and then she closed the door behind her. As the fluorescent tubes blinked into life, Bula could see that they were in a narrow workshop, crowded with chairs and sofas, most of which were still only half upholstered, with white kapok stuffing bulging out of their criss-cross canvas webbing.

The workshop had been built up against the Mutton Lane Inn, so twenty feet above their heads it had a high, lean-to ceiling with long spiderwebs trailing from the rafters. Along the left-hand side ran a long, cluttered workbench, and the wall behind it was hung with saws and chisels and pliers and mallets. In the corner stood a blue metal table saw. The air was pungent with the smell of varnish and glue, and Bula felt that every breath he took was thick with sawdust.

'Right then, what's this all about?' he demanded. He checked his watch and said, 'You have four minutes and not so many seconds left, although to be straight with you, I don't know why I'm giving you any time at all.'

'You are giving me time for two good reasons,' said the woman, very calmly. 'One, because you are burning to know why I want to talk to you. Two, you think it just possible that I really *do* have a gun, and you are not the kind of man who likes to take unnecessary risks.'

Bula nodded and sniffed and wiped his nose again. 'You're right there. About the gun, any road. Why don't you show me? Then I might really be scared.'

The woman took her right hand out of her waistcoat pocket and held up the small stainless-steel pistol that she had used to threaten Mânios Dumitrescu. Bula stared at it, and then laughed.

'What the feck is *that*? A scuttering-gun? So long as you haven't filled it with piss, that doesn't scare me at all! I'm out of here! I don't give a toss what you want to talk to me about!'

The woman broke open the pistol and took out a black shotgun shell. 'Look! It is a pocket shotgun. It is loaded with only one round, Bula, as you can see. But one round is enough to kill you, or to hurt you very bad.'

She pushed the shell back into the chamber and clicked the gun shut. Bula said, defiantly, 'You're having a laugh, aren't you? That's the most ridiculous gun I ever saw. Not that I ever saw one like that before.'

'Well, I am not surprised by that. It is very new. It is called a Heizer. It is made so that you can carry it in your pocket and nobody knows you have it, unless they try to rob you or give you trouble.'

'And that's what you use to shoot Manny Dumb-arse?'

The woman didn't answer that, but continued to stare at Bula so intensely that he had to look away. Bula wasn't easily scared. He had been brought up in the waterfront slums of Port Harcourt in Nigeria and he had always been bulky and loud and ready to punch the first person to upset him. It wasn't the woman's little pistol that disturbed him so much as the way she seemed to be looking straight into his soul. His grandmother had practised juju and he had seen how she could steal people's spirits and make their lives unbearable, all without touching them, just by staring, the same way that this woman was staring at him.

'You know a girl called Nwaha?' the woman asked him.

'What if I do?'

'In February, Nwaha was found drowned in the river.'

'So what? They fish more people out of the river here in Cork than fish.'

'You knew Nwaha?'

'When was this? February? Jesus. I see new girls almost every day. How do you expect me to remember that far back?'

'Nwaha was very beautiful. Nwaha had flowers tattooed

on her hands and her wrists. Blue and red flowers. You would remember Nwaha if you had seen her.'

Bula shrugged. 'I don't know. Maybe I remember her, maybe I don't.'

'If I say that I will shoot you between your legs if you try to pretend that you don't remember her, will you remember her then?'

'*What*?'

'I know that you remember her, Bula, but I want to hear you say it from your own lips. I want to hear you say, "Yes, I remember Nwaha, and yes, we made her become a prostitute, me and the man they call Mister Dessie, and Mister Dessie's boss, Michael Gerrety."'

'Oh, no! Feck that! You won't hear me saying that! Not in a lifetime! I might as well dig my own grave and lie down in it and bury myself!'

'So you choose that I shoot you between your legs? Maybe that will help you remember?'

She pointed the small grey pistol directly at the fly of Bula's baggy cargo shorts. Bula couldn't help letting out a short yelp of hysterical laughter, like a startled bull terrier, but then he lifted both hands in surrender.

'No, come on, serious. You wouldn't for real, would you?'

The woman raised one of her finely plucked eyebrows. 'Nobody can hear us in here. The furniture man, he is away on holiday for five more days. I could shoot you and then leave you locked up here and nobody would hear you. What a terrible way to die that would be.'

Bula said, 'Fair play. You win. I admit it. I *did* know a girl named Nwaha. I wish I fecking hadn't. We *all* wish we hadn't, she was so much trouble. Mister Dessie said that he had to give her so much smack to keep her quiet that she cost him more than she ever made.'

'She had the red and blue flowers tattooed on her hands and on her wrists?'

Bula nodded. 'That was the girl all right. The guards came around and showed us the photos from the mortuary and asked us if we knew who she was. Of course, we all swore blind that we'd never seen her before, and so they couldn't prove nothing. But they were sniffing around our premises for days after and Michael Gerrety was throwing a rabbie about it.'

He paused. He was becoming highly stressed, and it was very warm and stuffy in the workshop, so that his bald head was dripping with perspiration and he could hardly catch his breath.

'You're not *recording* this, are you?' he asked.

'I have no need to,' said the woman. 'I am not going to report this to the guards.'

'You're not? Well, that's one relief!'

'No, Bula. I have no need to report this to anyone. I am the judge and I am the jury, and I am the executioner, too.'

'Well, that's what *you* think. But what I think is, you've had your five minutes, and I've had enough of this shite.'

Bula leaned slightly to the left, and then feinted to the right, and then suddenly lurched forward and made a grab for the woman's right arm. As he did so, however, one of his sandal buckles snagged in a rucked-up length of upholstery fabric that was lying on the floor and he stumbled.

The woman fired and there was a deafening bang. The shotgun shell with its three defence discs and its twelve BB shots blasted into Bula's bare knee from less than six inches away. His kneecap exploded and the scarlet flesh was ripped away from the top of his tibia and his fibula. Blood sprayed all over the hessian covering of the couch right behind him, and Bula pitched back on to it, too shocked at first even to scream.

He seized the arm of the couch, trying to heave himself upright, and then he looked down and saw his knee and shouted, in a high, hysterical voice, 'Look what you've done to me! Look what you've fecking done to me, you witch! You've blown my fecking leg off!'

The woman opened up her pistol and pinched out the empty shotgun shell with her fingernails. She loaded it with another and snapped it shut. Only then did she look down at Bula's ruined knee. His lower right leg had been almost completely severed, so that his right foot was pointing inwards, as if he were knock-kneed. Bright red blood was rapidly soaking the couch and dripping on to the floor, and amongst the tatters of muscle and dangling tendons his bones were glistening white.

'You've blown my fecking leg off,' he repeated, but very much quieter this time, almost reflectively.

'I gave you enough warning,' the woman told him. 'And you did admit to killing Nwaha.'

'What? It wasn't *me* who pushed her into the fecking river! None of us did! She threw herself in! Now call me an ambulance before I bleed to death here!'

'I know she threw herself in. There were witnesses. But *why* did she throw herself in? Tell me that.'

Bula struggled to unbutton one of the pockets of his cargo shorts so that he could tug out his iPhone. As soon as he had done so, however, and punched his code into it, the woman stepped forward and snatched it out of his hand. She slung it across the workshop so that it clattered against the opposite wall and dropped out of sight behind the chairs.

'*I need an ambulance*!' Bula shouted at her. His face was already taking on the pallor of a death mask, modelled out of wax. 'Look at this blood, it's pouring out of me!'

'I warned you. You cannot say that I did not warn you. But you did not believe that I would really shoot you, did you? I am not a liar like you and Mister Dessie and everybody else who works for Michael Gerrety. I am not a liar like Michael Gerrety himself.'

'Please, look, I'm sorry! Whatever I'm supposed to have done, I'm sorry! Just call an ambulance for me. I can't stop this bleeding, and it *hurts*, for the love of God! It hurts like all fecking hell!'

'But you attacked me, Bula. I shot you only to defend myself. Nobody is going to blame me for shooting you.'

'Who cares? Call for an ambulance. Please, *please*, will you call for an ambulance!'

'What do you think Nwaha said when she was taken by three men at once? Do you think *she* said please? Three men, all at once! Did anybody take any notice of *her* saying please?'

Bula said nothing. He was gripping his bloodied thigh in his right hand, just above his shattered knee. With his left hand he was trying to pinch his severed artery between finger and thumb, but it was too slippery for him to be able to keep it squeezed together.

The woman watched him for a few seconds, and then she said, 'Very well. I will stop you from bleeding to death. But only so that you do not escape your punishment.'

'Oh Christ, do whatever,' said Bula. His eyelids were flickering and his chest was rising and falling as if he were breathing his last. If his knee hadn't been giving him such excruciating pain he might have lost consciousness. Dully he watched as the woman went over to the workbench and came back with a ball of fine sisal twine and scissors.

She tucked her gun deep into her waistcoat pocket and then she knelt down and tightly tied up Bula's artery. When she had finished her fingers were smothered bright red, but the blood had stopped squirting.

'If you think I'm going to thank you for doing that, you've got yourself another thing coming,' said Bula, as the woman went over to the sink and rinsed her hands.

'I do not want your thanks,' she said, using an offcut of raspberry-coloured velvet as a hand towel. 'Soon you will be cursing me for saving your life. Soon you will be praying for me to kill you and put you out of your misery. Soon you will be wishing that it was you who had drowned in the river.'

'I still need an ambulance. If a doctor doesn't stitch this leg up soon, I'm going to lose it.'

'First, you have to be punished for what you did to Nwaha, and all of the other girls you have hurt so much.'

'Oh yeah, and losing my fecking leg isn't punishment enough?'

The woman looked away for a moment, absent-mindedly fingering the bones and the shells and the claws that made up her necklace. Then she turned back to Bula and said, 'You talk about punishment? Nwaha died, and what had she done to deserve that? Not only that, she was not given the burial ceremony that she should have been, according to our beliefs. She was not dressed in cotton robes, and none of the traditional songs were sung. I do not know if she is lying with her head towards the west, as it should be for a woman. All I can say is that she was at least buried in black earth, and not red, and that is only because *all* of the earth in this country is black, like the hearts of the people who live here. She was not given a second burial, either, which means her spirit will come back to haunt us.'

'I told you before,' croaked Bula. '*I* didn't push her in the river. None of us did. She jumped in, of her own accord.' He took two or three more wheezing breaths and then he said, 'You don't have any fags on you, do you?'

'Fags? Oh, you mean cigarettes. No. Smoking is so bad for your health.'

'Would you believe it, I'm not particularly worried about dying of lung cancer right now. Come on, I'm gasping. I think there's a nobber in my pocket if you can get it out for me.'

The woman ignored him. 'Now is the time for you to choose your punishment. I am giving you that much, which is more than you ever gave to Nwaha.'

'Well, thanks for nothing.'

'I can shoot you between your legs, like I said I would do before.'

'Hey, *what*? You said that you wouldn't do that if I told you that I knew Nwaha.'

'No, I did not say that. I said that I *would*, if you did not admit to me that you knew her. I never said that I would *not*, even if you did admit it.'

Bula said, 'You can't do that to me. Look what you've done to my leg already. I'm going to be a cripple now, for the rest of my life. Now you're going to make me into a gelding, too. What kind of a fecking sadist are you?'

'I told you what I am. Judge, and jury, and executioner, too. Do you think I like doing this? I hate being in the same country as you, and those vermin you work for, let alone being close enough to smell you. But, like I said, you can pick your punishment.'

'Nobody would have their balls shot off for choicer, would they?' said Bula. 'So what else is there?' He winced, and squeezed his eyes tight shut for a moment, and then he said, 'God almighty, my leg hurts. Can't you just call me an ambulance? I'm dying of the pain here.'

'Are you right-handed or left-handed?'

'What difference does that make? Left-handed, if you must know.'

'Then instead of me shooting you between the legs, you can choose to cut off your right hand.'

'*What?*'

'It is your choice, Bula. Which would you rather lose, your manhood or your hand?'

Bula sat on the couch for a long time, breathing deeply and slowly in his effort to control the pain in his knee. The woman stood watching him, and he knew that she was serious and that she wasn't going to let him go until she had punished him, one way or another. He had seen too many gang members being punished in Port Harcourt to think that she wanted only to frighten him. He had seen ears cut off, noses cut off, even a woman's lips cut off, so that they had fallen into her lap like the red rubber ring from a pickle jar.

'So, what is it to be?' the woman asked him, at last. 'You are lucky that I brought you here. In fact, that is the whole reason I brought you here, so that your punishment could be quick and easy for you.'

'I don't understand what you're talking about,' said Bula.

The woman used her pistol to point towards the corner of the workshop, to the blue table saw. It had a circular steel blade, with fine alternating teeth for cutting oak and mahogany and other hardwoods.

'Mânios was not so lucky. Mânios had to cut off his hand with an ordinary hacksaw. He did not cry out too much, but I know that it was not easy for him. For *you*, though – all you have to do is lay your arm across the table, press the switch, and *zzzztttt*!'

Bula twisted his head around and stared at the table saw. Then he turned back to the woman and said, 'Is there anything in the world that I can do to show you that I'm sorry about Nwaha? That if I had my time back, I'd jump in the river after her, and save her?'

'No,' said the woman. 'Nwaha is gone, and "sorry" cannot bring her back. And if it had not been for you, she would not have thrown herself in the river in the first place.'

'I could pay you,' said Bula. 'I could manage at least two thousand euros. Maybe even two and a half, if I sold this bracelet.'

The woman smiled faintly and shook her head. 'You are paying me already, Bula. This is your payment. I do not want your money.'

'Then I hope you go to hell, you witch. I hope you go to hell and get screwed by three devils for ever and ever, amen.'

Sixteen

Katie was sorting through the papers she needed for the meeting with Michael Gerrety and his lawyers when Detective Sergeant ó Nuallán knocked at her door.

'Kyna, come in. I thought for a moment there I would have to go without you.'

Detective Sergeant ó Nuallán was wearing a loosely woven white cotton sweater and a short grey skirt. Katie thought she was dressed a little informally for a confrontation with one of Cork's leading solicitors. She herself was wearing a blue and white striped shirt and a navy-blue knee-length skirt. But then she thought, Kyna's smart enough, and she's young enough, and there's nothing like a short skirt to distract a lawyer's attention from the subject in hand.

'Sorry if I'm late, ma'am,' said Detective Sergeant ó Nuallán. 'Detective Ryan's just this minute come up with something.'

With the help of the Crime Prevention Unit, Detectives Ryan and Dooley had been sitting through hours of city-centre CCTV for the past two days, concentrating on the time frame in which the African man had probably been murdered on Lower Shandon Street.

'There's this African feller in a purple suit, crossing Oliver Plunkett Street. And can you guess where he's going into? Amber's ... Michael Gerrety's sex shop.'

Katie snapped her briefcase shut. 'Is it up on screen now?'

'Come and see for yourself. There's no guarantee that it's him because you can't see his face clearly, and even if you could we don't have much of a face to compare it with. But there can't be too many Africans in Cork with purple suits.'

'You didn't have any luck with the tattoo parlours?'

'Not so far, though there's one place on Cook Street I'm going to go back to. Their head tattoo artist wasn't there when I called, and his assistant was decidedly shifty, as if he knew something but wasn't prepared to tell me.'

Katie looked around her office to make sure that she had everything she needed for her meeting, then she followed Detective Sergeant ó Nuallán along the echoing corridor and down the stairs to the main CCTV control room. Detective Ryan and a young female garda were sitting in high-backed chairs in front of the bank of thirty-six screens that were fed from cameras located all over the city. Crime prevention officer Sergeant Tony Brennan was there, too, in his shirt-sleeves, noisily slurping milky coffee and frowning at what appeared to be the beginnings of a drunken brawl outside An Spailpín Fánach on South Main Street.

On every one of the smaller screens, traffic was silently crawling to and fro, and pedestrians were thronging the pavements. On one of the larger screens, however, the image was frozen.

'Here he is, ma'am,' said Detective Ryan, rising from his seat so that Katie could sit down and take a closer look.

Conor Ryan was one of the youngest detectives at Anglesea Street, but he had already made himself a reputation for doggedness. When older and more experienced detectives had abandoned a lead because it seemed to show no promise at all, he would go over it again and again until he had found the evidence he was looking for, or until he was convinced there really *was* no evidence. He was chubby, with short brown hair that stuck up at the back, and flaming red cheeks, and his jackets always looked too tight for him. He could easily have been mistaken for a trainee bank teller or the assistant manager of a stationery shop, but Katie preferred to have detectives on her team who didn't look like detectives.

'Full marks for persistence, Ryan,' she said, leaning forward and peering at the monitor. It showed an angled view of Oliver Plunkett Street looking westwards from the Post Office towards Robert Morgan Street. Amber's sex shop was on the corner, with an orange awning. An African man in a purple suit had stepped off the high raised kerb opposite and was waiting for a taxi to pass before he crossed. He was wearing a grey fedora hat which, from that angle, partially covered his face.

Katie looked at the time at the foot of the picture: 11.17.14 a.m.

She squinted at the screen even more closely. 'It could just be shadow, but I'd say that your man has a goatee beard, like Mawakiya. But that still isn't one hundred per cent proof that it's the same feller, purple suit or not.'

'Of course, we'll be blowing it up and enhancing it, like,' Detective Ryan told her. 'I just thought you'd want to see the whole sequence first.'

'Yes. Go on.'

He ran the recording in reverse until the African man had jumped backwards on to the kerb and then walked jerkily back as far as Cook Street, where he disappeared. Then he played it forwards, so that the African man reappeared, waited at the kerb again and then crossed Oliver Plunkett

177

Street. He didn't hesitate for a moment outside Amber's but walked straight in.

'I'd say that he knows Amber's more than reasonably well,' said Detective Sergeant ó Nuallán. 'If you watch them, almost all of Amber's customers hesitate outside the shop for a while before they pluck up the nerve to go in, and even then they look up and down the street to make sure they can't see anybody who knows them. But this feller – no, he walks right in with no hesitation at all.'

Katie said, 'Eleven seventeen. Our man on the street would have probably called it a day by then, wouldn't he?'

'That's right. Most of the girls bring their takings in early, around nine, and it's soon after that when Michael Gerrety shows up, if he shows up at all. Sometimes he sends that gowl Dessie O'Leary, and O'Leary stays longer as a rule, but even he's usually out of there by ten or ten-thirty.'

'I'm pretty certain that's when they tot up their ill-gotten gains,' said Katie. 'I'll bet they keep them in their safe on the premises, too. Don't tell me that Michael Gerrety would risk leaving the building unaccompanied with that amount of cash on him. I very much doubt that we're the only ones lamping him, and if one of his rival pimps robbed him, like Johnny-G or that Ambly-bambly one that only Patrick can pronounce – well, he could hardly come to *us* to report it, could he?'

'What time exactly did purple suit *leave* Amber's?' asked Detective Sergeant ó Nuallán.

Detective Ryan ran the recording forwards until the black man in the purple suit reappeared from under the awning. The time was 11.41.32 a.m. He turned right and crossed back over the street, heading east towards Winthrop Street, which was a pedestrian precinct leading through to Patrick Street.

'The butcher boy in Denis Nolan's said he saw the black man in the purple suit around midday, didn't he?' said Detective Sergeant ó Nuallán. 'So the timing would fit, wouldn't it? It shouldn't have taken him more than ten minutes to walk from Winthrop Street to Lower Shandon Street, would it, if he went there directly?'

'If that,' said Katie. 'But what about the black girl in the headscarf who looked like Rihanna? There's no sign that she was following him from here, is there?'

'I've seen no sign of her so far,' said Detective Ryan. 'But there's a camera on Mercer Street opposite the GPO and that feeds through to one of the monitors next door, so I haven't had time yet to look at the recordings from that. I'm hoping it'll show us which direction your man went in next – whether he turned up Winthrop Street or carried on straight along Oliver Plunkett Street. But you never know. They might show us more than that.'

Katie said, 'We're pushed for time right now. But I'd appreciate it if you can run through those Mercer Street recordings as soon as possible – even if they only tell us which way he went. It could make all the difference. Like, if he carried straight on, then where was he going? If he didn't have enough time to get to Lower Shandon Street by midday, then are we looking at a different man, though I can't think how we could be.'

Detective Ryan made the image of the black man in the purple suit run forwards, and then backwards, and then forwards again. 'Like you say, ma'am, it's highly unlikely, but if there *were* two different African men walking around the city on the same morning, both wearing purple suits, then I'll make sure that I find out who they were, if it kills me.'

*   *   *

They were ten minutes late for their appointment on South Mall at the offices of Moody & McCarthy Solicitors. A receptionist showed them through to the oak-panelled conference room, where Michael Gerrety was already sitting with his lawyer, James Moody, smoking a cigar so that their air was pungent and bluish-grey.

Michael Gerrety and James Moody both stood up when Katie and Detective Sergeant ó Nuallán were shown in. Michael Gerrety was wearing an immaculate cream suit with a white rosebud pinned to his lapel, and as usual he looked extremely pleased with himself. James Moody was a large man with a stoop and sloping shoulders. He had dyed black hair slicked back from his craggy forehead and eyes that looked like two malevolent trolls hiding in the caves under his eyebrows. His lips were crimson and blubbery and he had a tendency to spit when he talked, but Katie had encountered him many times before and she knew him for a very wily and uncompromising lawyer, apart from being one of the most expensive in Cork.

'What's happened to Inspector Fennessy?' asked Michael Gerrety. 'I was looking forward to crossing swords with him. Very sharp-witted, Inspector Fennessy. So what are the Garda trying to do now, *charm* me into submission?'

'At least we're not trying to *choke* you into submission,' said Katie, flapping her hand at his cigar smoke.

'Oh, my apologies, superintendent,' he said. He went across to the sash window and opened it, so that the smoke shuddered out and they could hear the traffic noises from the street below. 'Carole doesn't allow me to smoke my cigars indoors or in the car, so I don't have many opportunities to pollute the atmosphere.'

'I wouldn't say that, Mr Gerrety,' said Katie, sitting down

at the conference table and opening up her briefcase. 'I'd say that you pollute the atmosphere with every breath you take.'

'Now then, detective superintendent,' put in James Moody. 'Let's keep this amicable, shall we? I realize that we can't leave this table today as friends, but we can at least leave with all of our differences resolved.'

'There's only one way we can leave this table today with any of our differences resolved, and that's if Mr Gerrety agrees not to deny any of the charges that we've brought against him and to come to a negotiated settlement with the Criminal Assets Bureau for the surrender of the profits that he and his wife have made from prostitution.'

Michael Gerrety smiled broadly but said nothing. James Moody raised one of his eyebrows and said, 'Well, now, is *that* all?' although it was obvious that he was being sarcastic.

'As a matter of fact, no, it isn't all,' said Katie. 'He must immediately close down his website, Cork Fantasy Girls, and undertake never again to advertise the sexual services of either women or men. He must close all of his premises that are used for purposes of prostitution and cooperate with all the relevant agencies and charities for the rehabilitation of the women involved – or their repatriation to their native countries if they're here in Ireland illegally.'

'Have you had a response yet from the Director of Public Prosecutions?' asked James Moody, spitting a fleck of saliva on to the middle of the polished mahogany table. 'I mean, you have actually *filed* the charges with the DPP, haven't you, along with whatever evidence you claim to possess?'

'Of course, and Inspector Fennessy and I have been discussing them with her directly. I know it's unusual for us to meet like this, but the DPP is very sensitive to the political complications that will inevitably arise from this case – apart from the number of people whose reputations could be compromised.'

Michael Gerrety's sea-green eyes widened in amusement. 'You mean some of the eminent local councillors who might prefer not to be named in open court?'

'Fair play to you, there's that to it,' said Katie. 'I won't pretend that there isn't. But the DPP has two main concerns. One is to spare the girls the humiliation of having to admit publicly to what they do, because there's no question that it's going to make headlines for weeks all over the media. Two, she wants to spare the taxpayer the expense of what could be a very complex and high-profile trial, with scores of expert witnesses having to be called.'

'But that's *precisely* what's needed, a high-profile trial,' James Moody interrupted her, spitting out the word 'precisely'. 'My client is looking forward to it with relish. For the first time he will have the opportunity to air his views on the protection of sex workers and his campaign to turn on the Green Light. He considers that he has advanced the cause of feminism in Ireland by *decades*, single-handedly, and he has done this by giving sex workers over the age of consent the opportunity to sell their services safely, respectably and hygienically, in secure environments.'

'Do we really want to go back to the days of street-walking?' added Michael Gerrety, still with that self-satisfied smile. 'Do we really want to go back to women having it in alleyways and up against pissy-smelling bus shelters, with no condoms to prevent them from catching all sorts, and nobody to chaperone them if a client turns nasty?'

Katie opened her briefcase and took out a thick green document wallet. 'Don't try to pretend that you're some kind of a saint, Mr Gerrety. We have first-hand evidence that in return for your so-called protection you exploit women by drugging them, by blackmailing them, and by threatening them with physical punishment if they refuse to do what you tell them.'

Michael Gerrety turned to James Moody with his hands held out, as if he had never heard any suggestion like this before and was totally innocent, but Katie continued. 'Cork Fantasy Girls purports to be a dating and escort and massage website, but you would have to be upstairs in a bungalow not to know what's really on offer.

'We also have first-hand evidence that you traffic in girls illegally from Eastern Europe and West Africa and that you confiscate any identity documents that they might happen to have to prevent them from leaving. We have evidence that you farm girls out to other pimps, especially girls you think are less attractive, or older women who have lost their looks. You run a cattle market, Mr Gerrety, that's what you do. You and your Green Light! It's a cattle market and you're the auctioneer, and the only thing green about it is the money that's pouring into your pockets.'

'My client strongly objects to being bracketed with "other pimps",' put in James Moody.

'I apologize,' said Katie. 'The trouble is, I don't know of any other word that describes men who live off the profits of prostitution. Procurers, perhaps?'

James Moody ignored that. He dragged out a handkerchief and wiped his mouth, and then he said, 'Of course, we're aware of the majority of your so-called evidence against my client already, since it was itemized in the thirty-nine charges that for some reason the Garda saw fit to bring against him. But he believes very strongly that public and political opinion is in favour of his Green Light campaign and that it is time for Irish law to catch up with the times. Besides that, he doesn't see that by posting advertisements for these young women's companionship on his website that he is in any way contravening the Criminal Justice Act 1994. If their clients happen to have sexual relationships with them, it is hardly *his* responsibility, is it?

'You must be aware that Canada's supreme court has unanimously struck down the country's anti-prostitution laws in their entirety, including keeping a brothel, living off the avails of prostitution, and even street soliciting. They did it because sex workers were seeking safer conditions. A similar ruling is bound to happen here in the Republic, in the not too distant future. Perhaps this case will be the catalyst for such a ruling.'

Michael Gerrety stood up again and walked towards the window. As he looked down at the passers-by in the street below, he reminded Katie of Orson Welles in *The Third Man*, looking at the people down below him from the top of the Vienna Ferris wheel. '*Would you really feel any pity if one of those dots stopped moving forever?*'

'I fully understand that it's your duty to uphold the law, superintendent,' he said, without turning to look at her. 'But certain laws have been rendered obsolete by technological advances like the internet, and even more so by the rapid changes in our moral attitudes.

'We are *kinder* towards each other these days, more tolerant. We are much more understanding that we all have needs, both physical and psychological. It's over a decade now since gay sex was decriminalized in Ireland. Surely it's time that we accepted that everybody has God-given desires that need to be satisfied, but that some of us have no partner we can satisfy them with.

'If a man is prepared to pay for sex with a woman, and a woman is prepared to sell herself to him, where is the harm? The only harm comes when such a transaction is illegal and has to be carried out clandestinely, which leaves the woman unprotected against sexually transmitted diseases or unwanted pregnancy or random violence. Worse than that, it means that sex workers are ruthlessly exploited by the vilest kind of low life and become entangled with all kinds of sordid criminality, such as drug-running and slavery. Sex should be a natural and healthy form of commerce, no less natural and healthy than the restaurant business, for example. Restaurants satisfy a natural hunger in return for money. Is that immoral? What's the difference between serving up a pork chop and prostitution?'

'Very eloquent, Mr Gerrety,' said Katie. 'Is that the closing speech that you've prepared for your defence?'

'How many of the women on your website are addicted to hard drugs?' asked Detective Sergeant ó Nuallán, in that flat, toneless voice that had earned her the nickname of Sergeant O'Polygraph.

'Don't answer that, Michael,' said James Moody, immediately, without even looking up from his notes.

'How many of the women on your website are illegal immigrants?' Detective Sergeant ó Nuallán persisted.

James Moody shook his head at Michael Gerrety and Michael Gerrety said nothing, although he kept on smiling.

'Of those women who are illegal immigrants, how many of their passports or other identity papers are you holding?'

'My client declines to answer that,' said James Moody.

'How many of them owe you money or believe they owe you money?'

'My client declines to answer that, too, and I strongly

object to this line of questioning. These women are not my client's personal responsibility and you cannot hold him liable for any addictions they might have or for their status as foreign nationals. It was my understanding that we were meeting here today to come to some broad agreement about these thirty-nine extremely shaky charges of living off immoral earnings.'

Katie said, 'We are, yes. If your client agrees to all of the conditions that I listed at the beginning of our discussion, then I'm prepared to go back to the DPP and tell her that we're prepared to suspend all charges against him, provided he complies with them and undertakes that he will continue to comply with them in the future.'

'You're asking far too much, detective superintendent,' said James Moody. 'Essentially, you're expecting my client to admit without due process of trial that he has committed an offence and to accept punishment by surrendering a very substantial amount of his assets to the CAB. You're also asking him to abandon a campaign for human rights in which he fervently believes.'

Michael Gerrety sat down and folded his arms. 'I will fight you on this one, believe me. Not for myself, but for all of those women who rely on me for safer working conditions. I treat my sex workers like royalty. I will fight you, and you just watch me – I will win, because I *always* win.'

Katie stowed her document wallet back into her briefcase, clipped it shut, and stood up. 'In that case, gentlemen, I have nothing more to say to you. The DPP will be in touch with you in due course, I'm sure.'

As James Moody opened the door for her, however, she stopped and said, 'Mr Gerrety, there *is* one thing I was meaning to ask you.'

'Not for a date, I should imagine,' smiled Michael Gerrety.

'Oh, I would, yeah. Do you think I'm a masochist? It's that African friend of yours I wanted to ask you about – the one who wears the purple suit. When was the last time you saw him?'

Michael Gerrety kept on smiling, but Katie could see that all of the amusement had drained out of his expression. 'I have no idea at all who you're talking about.'

'Oh well, don't worry about it. They say that the camera never lies, don't they? But in this case perhaps the camera was a bit guzz-eyed. We'll see you in court.'

'What camera? *What* camera?' asked Michael Gerrety, but Katie walked off along the corridor without answering him, and without looking back.

They had been given a lift to James Moody's office by Detective O'Donovan, but Katie chose to walk back to Anglesea Street because the afternoon was so sunny and bright and she needed to calm down. Michael Gerrety always made her feel like grinding her teeth. She wanted to text John, too, to tell him that she shouldn't be late home tonight, and that she had bought a lamb stew dinner for two from Marks & Spencer's. He had frozen the Mexican-style meatballs.

As they walked back along South Mall, Detective Sergeant ó Nuallán said, 'I was reading through the files on Michael Gerrety this morning.'

'Oh yes?' said Katie, jabbing away at her iPhone.

'Almost all of the evidence against him comes from the women who work in his brothels or rely on his website. No wonder he's so cocksure.'

Katie finished her message to John with a row of XXXs

and dropped her iPhone back in her pocket. 'You're right, of course. That's exactly why we've been planning Operation Rocker. Gerrety is smooth enough to persuade a jury that he only has the women's best interests at heart. And like you say, we have plenty of witness statements, but most of them come from women who depend on him in one way or another.'

'Couldn't we have waited until we had more material evidence before we charged him?'

'Well, I wanted to. But Dermot O'Driscoll was dead set on charging him as soon as we had witness statements. He's been burning to nail Michael Gerrety for years, like it's almost been a holy crusade. Maybe he suspected that he wasn't well, and wanted to see Gerrety convicted before he had to quit.'

'I don't think it's going to be at all easy to get a conviction with what we have so far,' said Detective Sergeant ó Nuallán. 'Like, some of the statements of drug abuse and beatings are pretty damning, aren't they? But now I've met Gerrety ... Jesus. He's a cute hoor, isn't he?'

'And then some,' said Katie. 'He may come on all saintly, but he won't hesitate for a moment to send his scobes around to threaten any of those women who have spoken out against him. No – we need much more hard evidence, even Dermot recognizes that. We need medical reports on how many of the women who work for him are addicted to drugs, and how many of them rely on him for a regular fix. We also need independent witnesses to say how many of those women he's coercing in other ways to act as prostitutes. We need to be sure how many of them are illegal immigrants, who he should have reported to the Immigration Bureau. How many of them don't even speak English, for instance? How many of them have passports or ID papers, and how many of them have had their papers taken off them? I'll bet you money that Operation Rocker will find their papers in Gerrety's safe at Amber's – or maybe even James Moody's safe. Now, that really *would* make my day!'

They crossed the Parnell Bridge and a warm south-west wind made Katie's hair blow across her face. Twenty or thirty gulls were screeching and flapping over something tattered and brown that was floating slowly down the river. Detective Sergeant ó Nuallán paused for a moment and shaded her eyes so that she could see what it was.

'Don't worry,' she said, catching up with Katie. 'It's only a dead dog.'

Seventeen

Bula said, 'You can't make me do it. You don't have the neck.'

The woman shrugged, as if he could think whatever he liked and it would make no difference to her. 'That is what Mânios Dumitrescu said at first. But I changed his mind. Soon he was sawing at his wrist like it was the middle of winter and he was freezing and he had to have wood for the fire.'

'You won't change *my* mind, you witch.'

'You do not believe that I will really shoot you between your legs?'

Bula let out a dismissive *pfff!* and shook his head. He was slurring his words now and hiccupping, and every now and then he would jolt with pain, but his eyes kept darting towards the workshop door. He was working out a plan to knock this woman over, snatch her gun from her, and then hop over to the door on one leg, using the backs of dining chairs and sofas to support himself, like a series of crutches. A mahogany table leg was resting against the opposite end of the couch he was sitting on, and he reckoned that if he could lunge over and seize that and then swing it around and smack her hard enough on the side of the head, he might be able to concuss her. He might even be able to kill her. At school, he had once smashed a classmate on the head with half a brick and he had seen his brains squirt out. He even remembered the boy's name, Abayomi. The boy had survived, but he had never been the same again. He had never been able to stop dribbling.

'So ... are you going to do it?' asked the woman. 'You can stay where you are if your leg hurts too much. I can move the saw over to you, so that you can easily reach it.'

'You really think I'm that fecking stupid, to cut my own hand off?'

'As I said, Bula, the choice is yours. But you cannot escape your punishment.'

Bula thought: *I'll take five deep breaths, and then I'll go for the table leg. Grab the thin end of it and swing it around, so that I hit her with the thick end – whakkk! She's moved in much closer now, I should be able to catch her on the cheek, or the eyebrow. Maybe I can even knock her eye out.*

Three, four, hold it, then five.

Bula rolled himself sideways and snatched the table leg. He lifted it up, but as he did so the thicker end of it got caught under the arm of a nearby chair. He managed to jostle it free, but the woman had smartly stepped back and when he reared up from the couch and flailed at her, he missed. His damaged leg gave way and he dropped heavily on to the floor.

He lay on his side, breathing harshly, but still gripping the table leg. The woman stood over him and said, 'Let go of it.'

'I swear I'm going to kill you,' Bula panted, although he was staring at the floor. 'I swear to God I'm going to beat the fecking shite out of you.'

'I *said*, let go of it,' she repeated.

Grunting with pain from his mangled knee, Bula attempted to use the table leg to lever himself up. Without hesitation the woman lifted her high-heeled boot and stepped on his wrist. With an audible crunch of tendons his fingers opened up, so that she was able to kick the table leg across the floor with her other foot and out of his reach. He tried to seize her ankle with his free hand, and shook it, and then punched it, but he was too weakened with shock to force her foot off his wrist.

'You are a fool, Bula,' she said. 'You are cruel and you are stupid and you do not even know how to atone for what you have done. You thought you were such a big man when you abused Nwaha, and all those other girls you treated no better than animals. I know all about you. But look at you now. You are not even man enough to choose your punishment, even though you know you deserve it.'

'You are so dead,' murmured Bula, with saliva sliding out of the side of his mouth. 'I promise you. You are so fecking dead.'

The woman bent forward, and with her boot still firmly planted on his wrist she pressed the muzzle of her small grey gun against the palm of his hand and fired.

He screamed like a girl. The flesh was blasted from his hand in a fan-shaped spray of scarlet and the bones of his middle two fingers were shattered into sharp white splinters. The woman lifted her boot off his wrist and stepped away from him, and he lay there staring wildly at his devastated hand.

The woman thoughtfully licked her lips. Her eyes remained hooded and she showed no emotion at all. She glanced towards the workshop door as if she was reassuring herself that no passers-by in Mutton Lane had heard the shot. Then she reloaded her pistol and tucked it into her waistcoat pocket.

'It seems that you have made your choice,' she told Bula. 'That hand will have to come off. So, in a way, you are lucky. Better to lose your hand than your *azzakari*.'

She forced her hands under the hot, sweat-soaked armpits of his yellow Hawaiian shirt and pulled him up. Although he was so bulky, she was very strong, and he didn't try to resist her. Once she had managed to manoeuvre his left buttock back on to the bloodstained couch, he even straightened his right leg to make it easier for her to shift him into a sitting position.

Sitting there, he now looked more like a giant toad than a human being, in spite of his Hawaiian shirt and cargo shorts. His face was grey, but it was so shiny with perspiration that it was almost silver. His eyes were bulging and his mouth was dragged downwards, and he spoke in croaks that the woman could barely understand. His eyes kept rolling upwards, and his head dropped and then jerked back up again, but he didn't lose consciousness. The pain in his knee and his hand was too overwhelming.

The woman went over to the corner of the workshop and dragged over the table saw, positioning it right in front of Bula and flopping his arms up on to it. There was a long extension lead attached to it, which she plugged into the socket in the wall. She took off the plastic blade guard and then tested it with three quick bursts, so that the circular blade spun around with a soft, high-pitched screech. While she was doing this, Bula sat numbly on the couch, staring down at his smashed right hand and occasionally twitching.

'There, Bula!' said the woman. 'Can you hear me?'

Bula looked up at her and nodded.

'Do you understand what you are going to do now? You are going to cut off your hand.'

Bula nodded again.

'I will turn on the saw for you, and then all you have to do is hold your right arm good and tight with your left hand, and push your wrist forward into the blade. Do it slow or your bones may catch in the teeth of the saw, so that your arm jumps back at you and hits you in the face.'

'This hand's wrecked whatever happens, right?' said Bula, in a dull matter-of-fact voice.

'Yes,' said the woman. 'Even if you went to the hospital, no doctor could save it. Look at it. There is hardly anything left to save.'

'If I cut it off, will it stop hurting so much? It has to.'

'You will have to try it and see.'

'You're a fecking witch, do you know that? You're like something out of a fecking nightmare.'

'You can call me what you like.'

'But you're not going to shoot me in the mebs?'

'I promise.'

'You swear on the Bible?'

'I swear.'

'How did I get myself into this?' Bula asked her.

'You mistreated Nwaha. The gods could not forgive you for what you did to her. Neither could I. I am *Rama Mala'ika*.'

'You're an angel? The angel of what? You're no fecking angel. I told you. You're a *mayya*. You're a witch.'

'I have nothing more to say to you, Bula. It is time for your punishment.'

She reached down and switched on the table saw and the thin whine of its electric motor drowned out what Bula

said to her next. He may have been cursing her or he may
have been praying. When his lips had stopped moving he
sat there staring at the keenly shining blade for almost ten
seconds, his tongue going around and around inside his
toad-like mouth as if he were chasing the last fragments of
his burger.

Then, with great deliberation, he laid his right forearm
flat on the metal surface of the table, with his elbow pressed
against the side-fence to guide it. He gripped his forearm
with his left hand, as she had told him, and slowly edged it
towards the blade. His shattered hand hardly looked like a
hand at all, but like a pigeon that had been crushed by a
car.

The woman took three or four paces back, and for the
first time since she had captured Bula and brought him into
this workshop, her head tilted back a little and her eyes
widened and her lips parted. She was holding her breath,
but Bula didn't see that. He was concentrating on inching
his wrist towards the circular blade, which was singing a
high metallic song at more than 3,000 rpm.

There was a sound like lumpy vegetables being blitzed in
a food processor. Bula's hand flew off the table and bounced
on to the floor, while Bula himself tipped sideways on the
couch, waving the stump of his right hand into the air, with
blood spraying out of it.

The woman quickly went over to the table saw and
switched it off. All she could hear now was the shuffling of
pedestrians' feet along Mutton Lane, and the muted strains
of fiddle music from the Mutton Lane Inn, and Bula's self-
pitying keening.

'Look what you've done to me!' he whined. 'Just look
what you've fecking done to me!' He was covered in blood.

Even his face was speckled with blood. He was holding up his right arm and it looked like a blood fountain.

'No, Bula-Bulan Yaro,' she said, although her voice was tighter now, as if watching him cut off his hand had excited her. 'Look what you have done to yourself.'

Eighteen

Katie had only just returned to her office when both Detectives Horgan and Ryan came knocking at her door.

'Who's first?' she asked, dropping the Gerrety files on to her desk. 'Ryan, you couldn't fetch me a Diet Coke, could you? I'm parched. Get yourself a coffee while you're at it, or whatever you want.'

'No problem at all,' said Detective Ryan.

Detective Horgan said, 'That feller up on the Ballyhooly Road, we've narrowed his identity down to three possibles, and I reckon I know which one of them he is. Or *was*, before he had his face blown off.'

'Okay. Have you heard from Dr O'Brien yet?'

'He rang about twenty minutes ago and said he was dropping by to see you later, before five if he could make it. He's completed his autopsy on the black feller, apart from some DNA test results. They're going to take a few days longer. But he's made a start on the other white feller, too. He's confident that he can tell us *what* the two victims are – their nationality, like – even if he can't tell us *who* they are.'

'But the white one, you think *you* can?'

'I checked up on his tattoos. The skulls inside the stars, they're Romanian prison tattoos. They mean something like, "Mess with me, you gobshite, and the stars foretell your sudden extinction." At the moment there's only three Romanian pimps in Cork unaccounted for. I've heard that Cornel Petrescu is probably in Limerick, touting some of his girls around the clubs. That leaves only Radu Vasilescu and Mânios Dumitrescu. Unless there's some other Romanian pimp that we don't know about, which I think is unlikely.'

'You can't locate either Vasilescu or Dumitrescu?'

'Not in their usual haunts, no. Vasilescu's almost always in The Ovens and Dumitrescu spends most of his afternoons in The Idle Hour. The barman in The Ovens thinks that Vasilescu may have gone back to Romania, although he couldn't swear to it. I called around at Dumitrescu's house in Grawn, but there was nobody home. His neighbours said they hadn't seen any member of the family for at least twenty-four hours. And very thankful they were, I might add. The woman next door said she was allergic to the lot of them, especially Mânios.'

Katie very nearly said, '*Please, God, let it be Dumitrescu*,' but she held her tongue. If it was Dumitrescu, then little Corina would stand much more of a chance of staying with her new foster parents and Katie herself would be saved the trouble of arresting and charging one of the nastiest and most sadistic people-traffickers in Cork.

Detective Ryan came back with a bottle of Diet Coke and a can of Red Bull for himself. 'I need the caffeine,' he explained, popping the top. 'That's fourteen and three-quarter hours of CCTV footage I've sat through, and Jesus, that would be enough to send a tightrope-walker to sleep.'

'But you have a result, by the look of it?' Katie asked him, nodding at the plastic folder he had laid on her desk.

'Oh yes, absolutely. You wanted to see which way the purple suit feller went after he left Amber's, and if a black girl was following him.'

He opened his folder and took out more than a dozen large photographs, which he fanned out in front of her.

'These first five images, I printed them out from the camera on Mercer Street. See – there's the purple suit feller turning up Winthrop Street, which is the way he would have gone if he had been heading for Lower Shandon Street. And look, after he's passed the doorway of The Long Valley, this young black woman steps out and she starts to follow him, only about five metres behind. She's all dressed in black with a black scarf tied around her head, just like the butcher boy described her.

Katie picked up the printouts and examined them closely. The woman was wearing a black T-shirt, a black sleeveless waistcoat, black jeans and knee-high black leather boots. A few stray curls stuck out of the top of her scarf, like the tangled roots of some exotic plant. Katie would have guessed her height at five foot five inches. She was very slim, too, no more than 125 pounds.

Detective Ryan laid out the next seven pictures. 'These were taken from the camera on top of A-Wear on Patrick Street, opposite Debenham's. They're the clearest ones and they show the young woman's face. They also confirm that she *is* actually following the purple suit man, not just randomly walking behind him – see – because he crosses the road here and she crosses right behind him. When he reaches the opposite side he hesitates for a moment, searching in his pockets, like maybe he's making sure he hasn't forgotten his wallet, or his keys, or something like that. She stops a few metres away from him and waits for him to carry on.'

'She's very pretty,' said Katie.

'I think she's gorgeous,' said Detective Horgan, leaning

over Katie's desk. 'I'm just praying that she's not the perpetrator, that's all, because if she's not, I'm fixing up a jag with her, for definite.'

Katie couldn't help smiling. 'That's the trouble with this job. Some of the worst scumbags are really attractive. I have to admit that Michael Gerrety is a fine-looking man, and a right charmer, too. Butter wouldn't melt. But when I think what he gets up to, and how he treats women, he makes my skin creep.'

Detective Ryan held up two more photographs. 'Here's a couple more images taken from the AIB Bank on the north side of the river on the corner of Bridge Street. They're not very good quality because of the way the sun's shining into the camera, but you can see the purple suit feller crossing the bridge and turning left along Camden Place, and the young woman following not too far behind him.'

Katie opened her desk drawer and took out a large magnifying glass. She held it over one of the pictures of the young woman as she was walking past Debenham's storefront. She was wearing a very striking necklace of beads and triangular white shapes and what looked as if they might be animal claws.

'What do you make of that?' she asked, passing it across for Detectives Ryan and Horgan to take a look.

'Those are tropical seashells, those conical things,' said Detective Ryan. '*Conus berdulinus.*' He blushed even redder than usual, and added, 'I used to keep tropical fish. Well, until they all died from the fin rot.'

'At a guess, I'd say that necklace came from Africa,' said Detective Horgan. 'I mean, apart from the tropical seashells, you don't find a lot of animals with claws that size in Ireland.'

'Well, I agree with you,' said Katie. She could never quite

tell if he was serious or not. 'But Africa is quite a big place and I'd like to know what specific part of Africa it came from, and whether it has any special significance. You know, tribal or religious. There's something about these two killings that's quite ritualistic. The hands cut off, the faces obliterated. Dr O'Brien thinks that the perpetrator is not just punishing her victims but making some kind of a point.'

'Just because our suspect is black and she's wearing an African necklace, that doesn't necessarily mean that these homicides are in any way ethnic,' said Detective Ryan. 'Like, the first victim may have been African, but if Horgan's right, then the second was Romanian.'

'Of course,' said Katie. 'I'm not jumping to any conclusions. Until we have more evidence, I'm not even saying for certain that the perpetrator is African, or a woman. But I'm going to show these pictures to the two African women from Cois Tine that Father Dominic sent to talk to young Isabelle. One's Nigerian and the other one's Somali. Maybe one of them can tell me if this necklace has any special meaning. Who knows, one of them might even recognize her.

She sat back and sorted through the CCTV images again. 'Good work, Ryan. I'm really beginning to think we may be getting somewhere now.' She held up one of the pictures and said, 'This is the best full-face picture of her, wouldn't you say? If you can enhance it as much as possible, we'll send it out to all units tonight. What's the time? I'll talk to the press office. We should even be able to get it on the Six One news.'

She turned to Detective Horgan and said, 'Well done to you, too. If that does turn out to be Mânios Dumitrescu, I'll treat you to a glass of champagne at Suas to celebrate. In fact, I'll buy you a bottle.'

201

Nineteen

She rang Father Dominic at Cois Tine, but his secretary said he had left the office and wouldn't be back until later the next morning. Next, she tried ringing Dr O'Brien's mobile number to find out when he expected to arrive at Anglesea Street, but his phone was dead. She thought she might as well call it a day and go home. Before she did that, however, she went along the corridor to Inspector Fennessy's office to see what progress he was making with the Ringaskiddy drugs case.

Inspector Fennessy was sitting at his desk in his shirt-sleeves, surrounded by files and papers, his hair sticking up on end so that he looked like a harassed James Joyce after yet another scathing review of *Finnegans Wake*.

'What's the story, Liam?'

'Oh, I'm getting there, I reckon. Three out of the five of them have admitted involvement, but there's conflicting evidence between the customs officers and the drugs unit as to what the actual quantities were. At the moment I'm nearly a kilo adrift. It might be down to some gom who didn't know how to use a weighing scale, or some of the stuff might have accidentally gone "missing" in inverted commas.'

'Well, let me know if you can't reconcile the figures. I don't want us having to admit to the judge that we don't know where a hundred thousand euros' worth of heroin has mysteriously disappeared to.'

Inspector Fennessy took off his glasses and tiredly pinched the bridge of his nose. 'Don't worry ... I'll find it, wherever it's gone. I'm just hoping it's incompetence rather than corruption.'

'How's things with Caitlin?' Katie asked him.

He put his glasses back on but didn't look at her. 'We're having a bit of a break from each other, as a matter of fact.'

'Oh, I'm sorry. How long for?'

'I don't know yet. Until she decides that she can forgive me, I suppose, or until she decides that she can't stand the sight of me any longer.'

'You talked to the psychiatrist, didn't you? Did she help at all?'

'Yes and no. She told me that I definitely wasn't bipolar. I almost wish I was. You can take medication for that. No, she said I simply take all of my workaday stress out on Caitlin, even though I love her. Or maybe it's *because* I love her, and expect her to understand how I'm feeling, and get frustrated and angry when she doesn't. I don't know ...'

'Well ... good luck,' said Katie.

Fennessy tossed a file across his desk and opened up another one. 'Thanks,' he said. Katie stood and watched him for a while, wishing she could think of something to say that would console him, or at least make him feel that his life wasn't all pressure and disappointment, but for the most part her life was like that, too. Pressure and disappointment were part of the job description, along with boredom and fear and thanklessness.

* * *

She was crossing the reception area on her way to the car park when Dr O'Brien came bursting in through the front door, dishevelled and hot, with a large tan canvas bag slung around his shoulders.

'I'm so glad I caught you,' he said. 'I'm always forgetting to charge my phone. You couldn't possibly lend me twenty euros for the taxi, could you? I've been stuck in the hospital all day and I couldn't get out to the ATM.'

Katie opened her bag and gave him two ten euro notes. He pushed his way out of the door and then returned a few seconds later, looking even more flustered than before.

'Sorry about that. So sorry about that. Do you want the change?'

'Pay me back when you've been to the cash machine. What do you have there? Is it going to take long?' She checked her wristwatch. 'The thing is, I've pretty much finished for the day.'

'Oh yes, I'm sorry I'm a little late. I had to wait for the results of some blood tests. I'll try and keep it short and sweet. But I really think you'll be interested to know what I've found out so far.'

'All right. Let's go up to the canteen. You look as if you could do with something to cool you down a bit.'

They went up to the canteen and sat by the window. It was sunny outside and down below in the car park a young mechanic in a white T-shirt and jeans was washing a Toyota patrol car. Dr O'Brien wrestled himself free from his canvas shoulder-bag and ordered himself an iced tea.

'You're not having anything?' he asked Katie, but all Katie could think of was getting this over with and going home. She knew how critical these autopsies were. It could well give her all the answers she was looking for. In spite of that, she was feeling flushed and tired and tense. All she really wanted was to go home and change and take Barney for his evening walk, and then relax with John in front of the television. Sometimes she secretly agreed with all of those chauvinistic officers who had told her that women aren't cut out for police work.

Dr O'Brien opened his bag and took out photographs and X-rays and a sheaf of untidy notes.

The first pictures he slid across the table were close-ups of the severed left wrist of the African victim who had been found in Lower Shandon Street, the one named as Mawakiya, the Singer.

'You'll notice that this was a very crude amputation, with several ragged hesitation marks on the skin of the upper side of his wrist. It looks as if the person who did it was either inexperienced or reluctant, or perhaps both.'

'Can you tell what was used to do the cutting?' asked Katie.

'Oh yes. If you look at these very fine serrations on the protruding ends of the radius and the ulna, you can see that the cutting was almost certainly done with a small hand-held hacksaw. A junior hacksaw, they call it. The first few cuts were extremely hesitant, hardly ripping through the skin, and it would appear that the cutter didn't know exactly where the bones were. Once the ligaments had all been cut through, however, the last four or five strokes were very much vigorous, as if the cutter was gaining confidence – although it's equally possible that he simply wanted to finish the amputation as quickly as possible.'

'You say "*he*". You don't think that a woman did this?'

'No, I don't. This is by no means conclusive, but judging from the angle of the cut and the hesitation marks, I would say that the victim cut off his own hand.'

'Mother of God. Are you serious?'

'Look at the way it was severed. The cutting was done from right to left, at a sharp diagonal, almost forty-five degrees. I'm not ruling out the possibility that somebody else cut this hand off, but it would have been quite awkward for them to cut it at that angle. Another person would have been more likely to have cut straight across the wrist, at ninety degrees. You might also have expected some bruising on the forearm where they held it firm, or where the victim was secured with ropes or a belt to prevent him from struggling, but no – there was no bruising at all to speak of.'

Dr O'Brien sipped his iced tea and watched as Katie held up the photographs to examine them more closely. She laid one of them flat on the table and placed her own forearm on top of it, using the back of a dinner knife to simulate sawing her own hand off. She had to agree with him that the angle made it more than likely that Mawakiya had cut through his wrist himself.

'You could be right,' she told him. 'But why on earth would he have done it? And *both* of his hands were amputated. He couldn't have cut off the other one, too.'

Dr O'Brien rummaged in his canvas bag and produced more photographs, this time of Mawakiya's right forearm.

'Of course, yes. Once he had lost his left hand, whoever cut it off, it would have been impossible for him to amputate his right. He may not even have been conscious. But the amputation of his right hand further confirms my suspicion that he cut off his left hand himself. See here – the right wrist has been cut through at a right angle, directly across from right to left. Our victim couldn't have done this himself, even if he had amputated his right hand first, before his left. He would have had to stand next to himself to do it, if you understand what I mean. Also, there are no hesitation marks, and the cutter has gone clean through the ligaments with hardly any abrasions to the radius or ulna or the metatarsals. Whoever severed his right hand had a fair idea of what they were doing. Not a surgeon, I'd say, but somebody who had cut a hand off before, or at least seen it done by somebody else.'

'Any bruising on his right wrist?'

Dr O'Brien shook his head. 'Like I say, he could well have been unconscious after losing his left hand. Shock, loss of blood.'

'Maybe the perpetrator had already shot him in the face.'

'Your technicians' report doesn't bear that out. The left side of the mattress was soaked, which meant that there was considerable loss of blood *after* the amputation of his right hand. His heart was still pumping.'

Katie sat back. Down in the car park, the young mechanic washing the patrol car had finished now. Before he turned off the hosepipe, though, he turned it on himself, and splashed himself in the face, and soaked his white T-shirt. He looked up at her, and she immediately looked away.

'Detective Horgan told me that you had some idea of our victims' nationalities.'

'Yes,' said Dr O'Brien. 'They both have tattoos, of course. Our African friend carries this extensive tattoo on his body, all the way from his genitalia to his sternum, but because of the colours and the composition of the inks used I suspect that it was done in Europe rather than his native country. It may even have been done here in Ireland. Detective Horgan told me that he has already identified the shoulder tattoos on our other victim, but our African friend's may prove more problematical, since it looks like a one-off.'

'But you still think you have a good idea where he came from?'

'Oh yes. Among other things, he had a considerable quantity of partially digested food in his stomach. Cassava fufu.'

'I see. And what exactly is cassava fufu when it's at home?'

'It's mostly at home in Nigeria. Fufu is a very character-istic Nigerian dish. You mix cassava powder with warm water and roll it into into a small ball. Then you dip it into a soup or a sauce and swallow it whole. Chewing it is a no-no. It's also made out of yams and plantain and semolina. You could say that it's the African equivalent of mashed potato.'

'That doesn't conclusively prove that that our victim was Nigerian,' said Katie. 'Just before I died I might have had chow mein for lunch at the Golden Chopsticks, but that wouldn't be proof that I was Chinese.'

'True,' said Dr O'Brien, 'although you don't find too many Chinese with hair your colour, do you? Or eyes as green as yours. Or freckles.'

Katie was taken aback by that, but Dr O'Brien carried on talking before she could think what to say to him.

'As it is, the stomach contents are only part of the picture. It was the various blood analyses that were most revealing. Our victim was a heroin user, and there was evidence that he had been smoking cannabis before he died. More than that, though, I found unusually elevated traces in his blood of tannins, phlobatannins, saponins, alkaloids, flavonoids, cardiac glycosides and sterols.'

'That means about as much to me as cassava fufu.'

'It tells me that he was a regular user of Agbo jedi-jedi. It's a herbal remedy which is very popular in Lagos. It's very bitter. In fact, it tastes disgusting. But among other ailments, it's supposed to cure piles and give men a much-improved erection. In fact, it sometimes gives men such a lasting erection that they have to go the doctor and have blood drained out of their penises. It's like Nigerian Viagra.

He leafed through his papers until he found the scribbled report that he was looking for. 'Taken in quantity over a long period of time, Agbo jedi-jedi can cause kidney and liver damage, and there were signs of that, too.'

'All the same, this isn't one hundred per cent proof that he's Nigerian, is it?'

'No, it isn't. But I reconstructed as much of his face as I could. Do you want to see that?'

'Go on. I haven't eaten yet.'

Dr O'Brien passed Katie a photograph of the dead African's reassembled features. He had painstakingly tweezered together all of those fragments of skin that had been blasted apart by the two shotgun shells and arranged them over a clear plastic mask. The result was a lumpy jigsaw of the African man's face. He was eyeless, and his nostrils were flared grotesquely wide. Half of his upper lip was missing, so that he appeared to be sneering.

'Best I could do, I'm afraid,' said Dr O'Brien. 'His skull was so badly smashed that it was impossible to tell for sure what he really looked like.'

'Obviously there's no way that we can hand *this* picture out to the media,' said Katie. 'We don't want to be giving everybody nightmares. I'll send a copy to our sketch artist, though, Maureen Quinn, and see what she can make of it. She's brilliant when it comes to recreating faces from autopsy photographs. Some young woman may have been floating in the river for three days and blown up like a balloon, but

Maureen can make her look like somebody you'd whistle at in the street.'

'Ah! But look *here*, and *here*!' Dr O'Brien interrupted, triumphantly. 'The most important thing that this reconstruction shows us is the scarring on the victim's cheeks. See? Two teardrop scars, one on each cheek. Those are tribal marks, which would have been inflicted when our friend was a baby. Yoruba, most likely, from north-western Nigeria. They don't do it so much these days, except in rural areas, but it would have been the accepted custom when our friend was born. A priestess would make the cuts with a ritual knife and then rub snail secretion into the cuts to cool them, followed by charcoal to stem the bleeding. Nigerian, no question.'

'Fair play to you,' said Katie. 'Apart from having a Nigerian nickname, I think we can now say with certainty that Mawakiya *was* a Nigerian. That's really going to help us actually, because we can narrow our enquiries down to the Nigerian community and forget about the Somalis and the Ghanaians and all the rest of them. There's less than seven hundred Nigerians living in Cork – at least one of them must recognize him. Once we know who he is, it's going to be very much easier to find out who had enough of a grudge against him to make him cut off his own hand and blow his brains out.'

'I haven't yet completed all the blood tests on the Romanian,' said Dr O'Brien. 'Again, though, I'm almost totally sure that he *is* a Romanian – and not just because of his tattoos. His teeth are the obvious giveaway. His jaw was shattered, but I've begun to put his dental work back together again and he had six implants, all of them very high quality. Without any doubt they were done in Romania. The enamel is almost certainly Romanian and the dental practices around

Bucharest are some of the best in the world – easily as good as American dentists, and very much cheaper, too. Stomatologists, they call them. In the UK or America, six implants would have cost at least twenty thousand euros. In Romania, probably a third of that, so even an ex-con would have been able to afford them. Obviously I'm only theorizing at the moment, but I would be very surprised if he didn't turn out to be Romanian.'

'Right,' said Katie. 'It may be jumping the gun, but I'll have some questions asked among the Romanians, too. You've done some grand work here, Dr O'Brien. I'll get in touch with our sketch artist right now and see if she can't produce a likeness of Mawakiya by the morning. We think we've made some progress with the possible identity of our perpetrator, too. We have CCTV pictures of an African girl following an African man in a purple suit, recorded on the morning we believe he was murdered. They should be shown on the Six One news tonight, and in the papers tomorrow morning.'

'Well, that's encouraging,' said Dr O'Brien, as he stowed his photographs and papers back in his bag, Then, with unexpected shyness, 'You don't *have* to call me Dr O'Brien, you know. Nobody else does. Not even the dreaded Dr Reidy. The name's Ailbe.'

'Ailbe. The patron saint of fishermen.'

'That's right. My old feller named me that because he was always mad on fishing. Not me, though. I always found fishing too boring, and when I did catch a fish I always felt sorry for it. I mean, imagine what it would be like if you were walking around minding your own business and suddenly a great hook came down out of the sky and caught you in the mouth and hauled you up into the air?'

'I'm not so sure that I want to,' said Katie.

'Oh well, that's just me,' said Dr O'Brien. 'I suppose it's the job. I often look at the people lying on the autopsy table there in front of me and try to imagine what they must have gone through before they died. The pain, you know. The thought: *Why me?* I should be more detached, I suppose, but a human being is a human being after all.'

Katie picked up the photograph of Mawakiya's reconstructed face. 'I can keep this one? But send me a JPEG of it, too – and the pictures of his forearms.'

'Of course.'

'I expect I'll hear from you tomorrow, then. Right now, I have to see if I can contact Maureen Quinn and get the press office all geared up.' She paused and then she said, 'Thanks, Ailbe. Good man yourself.'

Twenty

It was past 9.30 p.m. when she eventually arrived home. It wasn't raining, but it was misty and there were luminous haloes around the street lights, like dandelion puffs.

Barney came to the front door to greet her when she let herself in, but John didn't. She found him in the living room in front of the television watching the evening news. Next to him on the coffee table was a thick maroon folder and a half-empty glass of whiskey.

'Well, you're back at last,' he said, without looking at her and without getting up from his chair.

She crossed the room and gave him a kiss on the forehead, but he didn't lift his face to kiss her back. 'I *did* text you,' she said. 'I was about to leave the station when Dr O'Brien came in with his autopsy reports on those two homicide victims.'

'Those guys are dead. Couldn't it have waited till tomorrow?'

'Look – I'm sorry I'm so late, but it couldn't wait, no. There's a young woman out there mutilating people and blowing their heads off and I have to find her before she does it to anybody else.'

'*If* she's planning on doing it to anybody else. You don't know that for sure.'

'I can't take the risk. It looks like she may have had a serious grudge against these two victims and it's quite possible that somebody else has upset her. It's not like these killings were family-related or even race-related. She has some other agenda.'

'I saw her picture on the news just now,' said John. 'She didn't look like the vengeful type to me. In fact, I hate to say it, but I thought she was quite a looker.'

He held his hand out to her. 'Listen, Katie, I don't mean to be grouchy, but I'm only thinking of you. You've been working so goddamned hard lately. I'm thinking of *us*, too. We hardly seem to see each other these days. You're up at six and not back until nine or ten. I've practically forgotten what you look like.'

'You'll be starting work yourself on Monday,' Katie reminded him.

'That's one of the reasons I was hoping you'd be home early. I've drawn up all my plans for online marketing for ErinChem and I'd like you to take a look at them and tell me what you think.'

'I will. I promise. Just let me change and get my head back together. Has Barney been for his walk yet?'

'I took him about an hour ago. And, yes, he did his business.'

'How about you? Are you hungry?'

'I was, but I'm not so much now.'

'I've got that lamb stew if you want me to heat it up.'

'No. I don't think so. I think I'm past lamb stew. Maybe we could just have a pizza or a sandwich or something.'

Katie went into the bedroom she still called the nursery, unfastened her holster and locked her revolver away in the top dresser drawer. Then she went into the main bedroom, undressed, and went into the bathroom. When she reappeared, wrapped in her pink towelling bathrobe, John was waiting for her, sitting on the side of the bed.

'Sorry. Forgot to tell you. Your sister Moirin called about an hour ago.'

'Moirin? What did she want?' Moirin was five years younger than Katie, the fifth of a family of seven, all daughters. She was small and pretty, in a sharp-faced way, but she was incorrigibly bossy. She lived in the seaside town of Youghal, fifty kilometres east of Cork city, with an estate agent called Kevin, who seemed permanently sad and was very bad at golf. Katie and Moirin had never got on well and Katie hadn't seen her since last Christmas.

'She's staying with your dad for a few days, with Siobhán. She wants to know if we can go over there for lunch on Sunday. She says your dad has something important he wants to tell us.'

'Oh Jesus, I hope she's not cooking. She's a terrible cook. Why didn't she call me at the station?'

'I suggested it, but she said she doesn't like to interrupt you at work because your work's so important.'

Katie shook her head. 'Never changes, Moirin. Always sarcastic.'

'We don't have to go. You could do with a quiet day off.'

'I should, though. What's this "something important" that Dad has to tell us? Did she give you any idea?'

'No.'

'You didn't ask her?'

'I'm not the detective. And it's your family, after all.'

'Jesus, you could have asked her.'

'Don't take it out on me. You don't want to go there any more than I do.'

'It's Moirin, that's all. I'm not in the mood for her.'

'Well, don't go, then.'

'I have to.'

John stood up. 'I would really like it, you know, if once in your life you stopped feeling that you're responsible for everybody.'

'You resent me getting you that job. That's what this is all about, isn't it?'

'I don't resent it. Of course I don't resent it. It's a great job and it means I can stay here with you. But I'm like any other man. I need to do things for myself. I don't like to feel that I'm being manipulated.'

'I got you that job because I love you, not because I wanted to manipulate you!'

'Then why do I feel like some kind of fucking puppet?'

Katie stood looking at him, tired and shocked. He raised both hands as if to say that he was sorry, that he hadn't meant to say that, that he didn't really feel like that, but with his hands lifted he actually looked as if he was impersonating a puppet.

'I think I need a drink,' said Katie.

'I'm sorry,' said John. 'No, I'm not. Why do I have to keep saying I'm sorry?'

Katie went through to the living room and poured herself a large glass of Smirnoff Black Label. She took a swallow and shivered. John came into the room and stood behind her. He laid his hand on her shoulder, but she turned away from him.

'It's all right,' she said. 'I'm just a little off, that's all. I'll read your plans later. I promise.'

She sat down. Barney came up to her and rested his head in her lap, and she tugged at his ears. John stayed where he was, biting his lip.

'Why don't you put the oven on,' said Katie, after a while. 'I don't think it would do either of us any harm to have something to eat.'

'Sure,' said John.

'That's not an order, though,' Katie told him. 'I don't want you to think that I'm pulling your strings.'

John took a breath as if he were about to come back at her, but he went into the kitchen without saying anything.

'Two hundred!' she called after him.

Later that evening, as Katie slept, John reached across the bed and eased his folder out from under her elbow. She had read as far as page three: *Attracting Professional Endorsements for Online Medication.*

Twenty-one

Before she left home the next morning, she called Father Dominic at Cois Tine. Outside, the sky was dark grey and it was raining hard. John was standing in the kitchen with a bowl of muesli, staring at the raindrops dribbling down the window.

'I'm very glad you called, Katie,' said Father Dominic. 'Faith Adeyemi and Amal Galaid visited the hospital yesterday. Faith is Nigerian and Amal is Somali. They were soon able to establish that your girl Isabelle is Nigerian.'

'Well, that's a start, anyway.'

'Faith will be calling in to see her again at about ten o'clock before she goes to work. You'll like Faith. She was a sex worker herself once, but she was saved by Ruhama, God bless them for the work they do, and she still helps them to rescue other women from prostitution. She told me that she didn't make an awful lot of progress with Isabelle yesterday, but she believes she's managed to win her trust. Your girl is very frightened, she said, and not only of physical retribution.'

'So what else is she frightened of?'

'She's very superstitious, apparently. Faith can tell you more about it. I can ask her to call into the Garda station later this afternoon, if you like, when she's finished at Dunne's Stores. She works in the cafe at lunchtimes.'

'No – what's the time now? I can meet her at the hospital if she's going to be there at ten. I'd like to see the girl again anyway. Does Faith have a mobile number?'

'I'll call her if you like, Katie, and tell her you're coming.'

John finished his muesli and put the bowl in the dishwasher. 'Any idea when you'll be home tonight? Or is that too speculative? I was hoping I might be able to take you out for dinner, even if we only go to Gilbert's.'

Katie went up to him and put her arms around his waist and looked up into his eyes. 'Don't be angry with me. I'll get home as soon as I can. I'll call you. And I swear on the Holy Bible I'll finish reading your plan tonight.'

John kissed her, and smoothed his hand over her coppery hair. 'I'm sorry about the puppet thing. We Meaghers have always been a prickly lot. Actually, I get it from my mam. She thought that everybody was out to take advantage of her – even God.'

By the time she reached the hospital the rain had begun to clear, and when she reached Isabelle's room a watery sun was shining through the window. Isabelle was sitting up in bed, while a large African woman in a jazzy red and orange dress was sitting close to her. The woman was wearing a red silk scarf which had been folded into a high, complicated headdress, and huge hoop earrings. She had a broad, pleasant face, with a wide gap between her front teeth.

She lifted herself out of her chair when Katie came in and held out her hand.

'Hallo, I'm Faith,' she said. 'And you must be Katie. Father Dominic rang me to say you were coming. I'm sorry. I know your title is chief detective something, but Father Dominic said you wouldn't mind me calling you by your first name.'

'Katie's grand, Faith. Don't worry about it. How are you this morning, Isabelle? You're looking much better.'

Isabelle smiled, and Faith said, 'She is *so* much better. She knows now that she is safe. You know that you are safe now, don't you, Lolade?'

'That's her name? Lolade?' asked Katie. 'I'd better stop calling her Isabelle.'

The girl smiled even more broadly and said, 'I tell Faith that you are a very kind person.'

Faith said, 'It took a little time, but Lolade is no longer afraid to say what happened to her, are you, Lolade? She has been telling me so much this morning.'

'Father Dominic said something about superstition,' said Katie.

'That's right. Lolade believed that she was cursed. She was trafficked from her home village near Ibadan, in south-west Nigeria. That was about eight months ago, as far as she can remember.'

'How was she taken?'

'Her aunt said that she was going to find her work as a cleaner for a wealthy family in Lagos and that she would be able to send her parents money every month. But her aunt was involved in trafficking and she was flown here. More than likely she was given false documents. There are plenty of officials in Nigeria who will give you travel documents in exchange for the right payment.'

'Mother of God. It's the same old story. It's enough to make you cry.'

'There is worse, though. Before she was sent here, her aunt took her to a juju priestess. The priestess held a special ceremony and then she took clippings of Lolade's nails and hair and wrapped them up in front of her. She warned Lolade that if she tried to run away or to tell anybody that she was being forced to be a prostitute, she would be struck dead by lightning and all of her family would fall sick.'

Katie nodded. 'Our immigration people were telling me all about that not too long ago. They say it's quite a common way that traffickers make sure that their girls all do what they're ordered to and don't try to run off. When you come to think about it, I suppose it's no more bizarre than us Catholics believing that our souls will die if we have sex with a goat, or cheat at poker, or commit some other mortal sin. So that's why the poor girl wouldn't talk to me.'

'That's right,' said Faith. She reached across the blanket and held Lolade's hand. 'I told her, though, that I too was threatened by a juju priest before I was sent here to Ireland. I was forced to work for two years in a brothel on Pope's Quay and I will tell you it was like a living death. I was a prisoner, no person to speak to. I became useless, meaningless, helpless and hopeless. I felt I had to do whatever my minders told me, because I was terrified, just as Lolade was. The juju priest had warned me that I would burst into flames and all my skin would shrivel up, and that back in Nigeria my father and mother and all of my brothers and sisters would choke to death.

'Ruhama saved me from the brothel, and it was a Nigerian sister from Cois Tine who finally convinced me that the juju curse could not harm me. In the end I told everything to the guards, *everything*. I didn't catch fire. Father Dominic managed to contact my family through the Roman Catholic diocese in Oyo and none of them had been harmed because I had spoken out.'

'What happened to your minders?'

'Some of them were arrested and I think that one was

ordered to be deported. Of course, they were not punished nearly enough for what they had done to me, but I try not think about that. The most important thing is that now I have my life and my freedom, and I believe in my true value as a person.'

Katie turned to Lolade and said, 'You hear that, sweetheart? You're going to have a very good life from now on. You have people around you who are going to help you now, and treat you with respect – not use you as if you're worth nothing at all.'

Lolade nodded. 'I feel happy now. I did not feel happy in a long time.'

'I wanted to ask you about something you said to me in the ambulance. It sounded like 'Rama Mal-ah-eeka', if I remember it correctly. I didn't know what it meant.'

Lolade glanced anxiously at Faith and gripped her hand tight. Whatever it meant, it obviously still disturbed her.

'It means Angel of Revenge,' said Faith. 'The woman who killed Mawakiya, that is what she called herself. Lolade was not only frightened because this woman said she would shoot her like Mawakiya if she left the room, but because she was sure that she was a juju witch.'

Lolade made a quick side-to-side gesture two or three times across her chest. 'She was wearing a juju necklace same like the witch who put the curse on me,' she said. 'I thought that even if she had gone away she could still kill me from a distance.'

Katie opened her briefcase and took out the CCTV blow-up that Detective Ryan had given her of the suspect following the purple-suited man along Patrick Street.

'*That* is the woman,' said Lolade, furiously nodding her head. '*That* is *Rama Mala'ika*.'

Katie showed her another picture, this time of both the suspect and the purple-suited man.

'The man there – that is Mawakiya. He was wearing those clothes when he came to my room. He was coming for my money. He comes every day for my money. He told me also that two men were going to come in the evening. They want to have me at the same time, front and back, and I should be nice to them because they are his special friends.'

'But then this woman appeared?'

'Yes! She came in through the door *bang*! like thunder. And she point a gun at Mawakiya. And Mawakiya is very, very frightened! He gets down on his knees and says, don't hurt me, don't hurt me! But she says I will kill you if you do not do as I say.'

Lolade was growing agitated now, and Faith stroked her hair and said, 'Ssh, ssh, it is all over now. Nobody can hurt you any more.'

'If it upsets you too much to talk about this now, Lolade, I can come back later,' Katie told her.

'I *want* to tell you,' Lolade insisted. 'I was very frightened of the woman, too, but she did not hurt me, and I hated Mawakiya. It was horrible, how she killed him, but I am happy that he is dead. I could sing a happy song that Mawakiya is dead.'

'Did you see her cut off his hands?'

Lolade shook her head. 'The woman said to me to sit down in the corner and to turn my back and to cover myself with my blanket. I did not see. I only hear. I hear the woman tell Mawakiya to take off all of his clothes. Then I hear her say that she would shoot him between his legs and turn him into a woman so that he would know what it was like to be treated like a slave.

'I heard Mawakiya weep. I never hear a man weep like that before, only my grandfather when my grandmother died. I could not hear everything that the woman say to him next, but a long time pass, and then I hear him weep again, but this time it was different, and he say again and again "*ah*!-*ah*!-*ah*!", like something hurt him very bad.

'Next, another long time pass. I hear noises like "*sheee-sheee-sheee*", but I do not know what is happening. I pull away my blanket and I turn around to see if the woman is still there. Mawakiya is lying on the bed and there is so much blood. I see then that he has no hands any more. The woman is standing over him with her gun. She is pointing it at Mawakiya's face.'

'She saw that you were looking at her, but that didn't stop her?'

'No. She was not afraid at all. She shot Mawakiya between his eyes. Her gun is very small but very loud *bang*! and his forehead disappear. She load her gun again and then she shoot him in his nose, and the rest of his face is disappear, too.

'I feel sick to see what the woman has done to him. He has no face any more, only big red hole. She say something to me but I do not know what it is. I am deaf at first, because of the noise of her gun. She picks up my blanket and uses it to wrap up Mawakiya's clothes, his suit, his dirty underpant, everything. I do not see what she has done with his hands, but when she goes, his hands are gone, too.'

'But she warned you that if you tried to leave the room, she would kill you in the same way as Mawakiya?'

'Yes,' said Lolade. 'And I thought that she could still do it, even if she was not there. I thought that she was a juju witch, because of her necklace, and because of the way she killed Mawakiya. He cannot go to heaven now because he has no hands to hold his spear and his shield, and he cannot wear warpaint because he has no face. He has to stay between this world and the next forever. They say it is like being drowned in a sack, you cannot breathe, but you never die.'

Katie said, 'Tell me something about Mawakiya. What was his real name?'

'I do not know. Everybody call him Mawakiya, because he was always singing, and always the same song. I once hear a woman friend of his call him Kola, but that is the only time. The first day when I come to Cork I meet only white men. They make me stay in this very cold bedroom for two days and all the time there is a big fat man watching me, even when I go to the toilet. His name is Bula-Bulan Yaro.'

'That means "Fat Man",' put in Faith. 'We know him. He's an illegal who does all kinds of odd jobs for the traffickers.'

'Bula, yes, we know him, too,' said Katie. 'He wallpapers brothels, drives the girls to the STD clinics, things like that. Not exactly criminal activities in themselves, but not very moral, either. Our Immigration Bureau have tried to deport him at least twice, as far as I know. I think his defence is that he's fathered a child by some divorced woman in Farranree. There's some human rights issue, anyway. He's pretty low priority, but we'll get him one day.'

Katie opened up her briefcase again and took out a manila envelope with more photographs in it. 'I'm not going to tell you who the people in these pictures are, Lolade, but I want you to look at them carefully and tell me if you've ever met any of them, or seen them. If you have, I want you to tell me if you can remember any of their names, or what they might have called each other, or anything they might have said that sticks in your mind. It doesn't matter if it didn't make any sense to you when they said it.'

She took out six photographs and handed them to Lolade one by one. Lolade frowned at the first one, and then gave it back. 'I have never seen these two men.'

'That's a relief. One of them is Chief Superintendent Dermot O'Driscoll and the other is Councillor Charles Clancy, the current lord mayor. That was just a test, I'm sorry.'

Lolade took much longer to study the second photograph. At last she tapped it emphatically with her fingernail. '*This* man came to see me when I was first brought to Cork. It was in a flat, with other girls. I don't know his name, but before he came the girls kept saying that "Himself will be here in a minute".'

'Nobody actually called him by his name when he was there?'

'I don't think so. But I was very frightened and I didn't know what was going to happen to me. I didn't listen much to what the girls were saying.'

'Did *he* say anything that you can remember?'

'He looked at me and smiled and said I was a cutie. I asked him what he want me to do and he is surprised that I speak good English. I told him that I had best teacher in my school, Mister Akindele. He said because I speak good English this would help me with my work, to be friendly with customers. Then he tell me to take off all of my clothes.'

'What did you say?'

'I say no. But he say it is important health check. He say I cannot work unless he is sure I am healthy, I don't have skin problem, something like that. One of the women was there in the room with us and she said to me that it would be all right, she would stay there. So I took off my clothes, but to do that in front of a strange man I feel very – I don't know the word. Like shame.'

'Embarrassed, of course,' said Katie. 'But what did this man say then?'

'He was very angry when he see me with no clothes on! He ask the woman how old I am. He said look at her, she is only a *kid*! He said, do you want me to get done? I don't know what he means by "done". He keeps saying, "I'll get done, you stupid woman! I'll get done!" I want to stop him being so angry so I tell him that I am already thirteen. But then he was even more angry. I do not know about the law in Ireland – I think he is angry because he believes that I am lying. I have a friend at home who was married when she was eleven, and her husband is forty-nine, so I thought it would make it all right. But he is still so angry. And I have no clothes on.'

The memory of it was making Lolade even more upset, rocking backwards and forwards in bed and hugging her knees tightly. Katie sat back and let her calm down.

'Come on, sweetheart, how about a drink of water?' she asked her. 'Perhaps you'd like to take a break for half an hour. I can imagine how distressing this is.'

'*No*, I will tell you! I *have* to tell you!'

'All right. Ssh, don't get upset. I understand. So what happened next, after Himself got so angry?'

'He called on his phone and in only a short time Mawakiya comes to the flat. I do not like Mawakiya, he looks like a kind of a devil, with one eye all red and bad teeth, and he smells of perfume. Himself says to Mawakiya, "Take this girl away and teach her all the tricks. Bring her back in five years' time."'

'So that's how you ended up in that dump on Lower Shandon Street, being prostituted by Mawakiya?'

Lolade whispered, 'Yes.'

Faith said, 'We have no idea how Mawakiya kept himself out of sight for so long. Now that he's dead, though, the girls he used to manage are coming to us and Ruhama and the social services and they're desperate for help. They have absolutely no money, of course. Some of them have hardly any clothes, and without him they're lost. And they're all so young, fifteen, sixteen. It's heartbreaking.'

'You can understand why Himself wouldn't take them on,' said Katie. 'He could have been charged with child-trafficking and defilement of a child under fifteen, both of which carry a possible life sentence. He might have been charged with reckless endangerment, too, and he could have been given an extra ten years for that.'

She passed Lolade another photograph. Lolade said, 'Yes, that is the same man. I don't know the woman.'

'How about *this* man? Do you recognize him?'

Lolade looked at the fourth photograph and nodded. 'I know him, yes. Six or seven times he came to have sex with me, but he never pay. I think he work for the man they call Himself. Three or four times I see him hit girls.' She held up her fist and turned it slowly around. 'One girl he pulled her hair like this, and twisted it, and twisted it, so that she scream and scream. Then he hit her head against the wall.'

Katie showed the photograph to Faith, and Faith crossed herself and said, 'Dessie O'Leary. *Mister* Dessie, the girls all call him. There is no word that I can use to describe that man without having to say five Hail Marys and brush my teeth with carbolic soap.'

Next, Katie held up the photographs of the man that Lolade had only known as "Himself".

'Michael Gerrety,' she said. 'And here he is with his wife, Carole.'

'Michael Gerrety!' said Faith, her nose wrinkling in disgust. 'Even more Hail Marys! Even more soap, too!'

'Ah, yes. But Lolade has just told us that Gerrety passed her on to a third party, i.e. Mawakiya, for the express purpose of him pimping her – what other interpretation could you put on "Take this girl away and teach her all the tricks"? And Lolade is only thirteen. In other words, we now have a first-hand witness statement that Gerrety is guilty of trafficking and reckless endangerment, at the very least.

'I can't give you any specific details at the moment, Faith, but we're seeking more evidence against him, and this can only help our case enormously.'

Katie replaced the photographs in the envelope. 'Lolade, you've been pure amazing. I know how hard this has been for you, but believe me, things will only get better. I'll come back to see you over the weekend so. I might have a few more questions to ask you, but the most important thing for you, girl, is to get yourself well.'

Before she went, she embraced Faith and said, 'As for you, Faith, you're a star. Thank you for what you've done for Lolade.'

'A star?' said Faith, and Katie could see the pain in her eyes. 'I was a *fallen* star once. But you know, Katie – even a fallen star can rise up into the sky again, rise up, and shine. Maybe not as pure as before, but just as bright!'

Twenty-two

Katie went down to the pathology lab before she left the hospital. A young, ginger-haired pathologist was staring glumly at a shadowy scan of a bowel tumour, but Dr O'Brien had not yet arrived. Katie was relieved, in a way. Dr O'Brien would have insisted on showing her the two mutilated homicide victims, and how he had pieced together the skin from their faces, and her stomach didn't really feel strong enough for gristle and connective tissue and the all-pervasive sweetness of decomposing flesh. She was having enough trouble keeping down the pineapple juice that she had drunk too quickly instead of breakfast. She left Dr O'Brien a note to call her.

Before she drove out of the hospital car park, she checked her text messages, of which she had fifteen altogether. Chief Superintendent O'Driscoll wanted to see her as soon as she arrived at Anglesea Street. Detective Sergeant ó Nuallán had found the body-art parlour where Mawakiya had been tattooed – but there were 'complications', which she didn't specify but needed to discuss 'asap!!'

Detective O'Donovan said that the CCTV picture of the young African woman that had appeared on the RTÉ News yesterday evening had attracted thirty-eight responses, one of which had been a proposal of marriage. However, none of the respondents had been able to say who she was, or where she came from, or where they might find her now.

The sketch artist, Maureen Quinn, had finished a preliminary likeness of Mawakiya's reconstructed face. She had scanned it and sent it over for Katie to look at, but she wasn't at all happy herself with what she'd done. 'I've made him look like a troll! I shall have to have another try!'

Garda press officer Declan O'Donoghue said that he had received a request from Branna MacSuibhne from the *Evening Echo* for an 'in-depth' interview on the Garda's war against sex slavery and vice – 'which Detective Superintendent Maguire personally promised me'. *Mother of God*, thought Katie. *Doesn't she ever give it a rest?*

From John, she had received a text that he had booked them an upstairs table for 7.30 p.m. at The Rising Tide brasserie in Glounthaune village. 'Hopefully at long last we can eat a dinner together??'

Katie skimmed through the rest of her messages, just to see who had sent them, but most of them were routine updates from Garda headquarters in Phoenix Park, in Dublin – advising her, for instance, that they were making a new push to bring down road casualties on 'Fatal Friday', which was always Ireland's worst day for traffic casualties. She could look at these later, although she did pause to read an invitation for her to give an after-dinner speech on 'Drugs and the Law' at a medical convention in Kinsale. She had attended one of those conventions before, two years ago, and she couldn't imagine anything worse than spending an evening with two hundred drunken doctors in dinner jackets, all of whom were convinced that their professional qualifications authorized them to grope every good-looking woman in the room.

She bought herself a latte and a cheese and tomato sandwich in the canteen. She hadn't even reached her office, however, before Chief Superintendent O'Driscoll opened his door and said, 'Katie! There you are! I was expecting you before!'

'Oh, sorry, sir. I went to the hospital first to speak to Isabelle. Well, it turns out her real name's Lolade. She's started talking now, thanks to a very fine Nigerian lady from Cois Tine. And you'll be delighted to know that she gave me some extremely damning evidence against Michael Gerrety and Desmond O'Leary.'

'Well, good. Look, you can tell me all about that later. Bring your coffee in here, if you like. I have my replacement here I'd like you to meet. *Temporary* replacement, any road.'

Katie was about to say, 'Give me a moment, Dermot,' but he opened his office door wider and sitting at his desk was a short, bull-necked man in uniform, who immediately stood up and held out his hand.

Katie entered the office, awkwardly putting her briefcase down on the floor next to the bookcase, and her sandwich on the shelf next to a leather-bound copy of *Offences Against the Person*.

'This is Superintendent Bryan Molloy from the Henry Street station in Limerick,' said Chief Superintendent O'Driscoll. 'He'll be keeping his hand on the tiller while I'm away having my treatment.'

Katie shook Superintendent Molloy's hand, and nodded, and said, 'Yes. We've met before, briefly. It was at that seminar in Tip on dealing with Travellers.'

'Well, that's right,' said Superintendent Molloy. 'I seem to remember DS Maguire here proposing some kind of a softly-softly approach to the Knackers. Winning their confidence, learning their cant, making sure their children go to school and stay there for more than five minutes.'

'I don't usually refer to them as Knackers,' said Katie. 'I think there's enough alienation between the Travelling community and the rest of us without that. I don't think 'softly-softly' is how I treat them, though. If any Traveller breaks the law, they get jumped on just as hard as anybody else.'

Superintendent Molloy let out a noise like a party balloon just before its neck is tied up. 'I love hearing female officers getting all disciplinarian! Fifty Shades of Blue!'

Katie remembered Superintendent Molloy very well. He had not only opposed all her suggestions for improving relations with the Travellers, he had stood in the bar all evening, loudly denigrating the appointment of women as senior Garda officers, well within earshot of Katie and her team.

She could remember almost everything he had said. 'Every Garda station needs somebody to make the tea and keep the place spick and span and blow the noses of the beaten wives who come in cribbing about their drunken husbands. That's what women are *for*! What are we going to do if they all get promoted upstairs? Make our own fecking tea, is it?'

Katie was rarely judgemental about looks. Michael Gerrety might be handsome, but he was far from pleasant. Superintendent Molloy, on the other hand, had all the appearance of a bully and he was one. His prickly hair was cut very short, grey at the sides and black at the top. His blue eyes protruded, even when he wasn't in a temper, and he had a way of staring at people in a belligerent way when they were talking to him, as if he couldn't wait for them to finish so that he could disagree with them.

He had a snub nose, with black hairs growing out of his

nostrils, and a pugnacious mouth. His ears were large and unusually crimson, and Katie couldn't keep her eyes off them when he was talking to her. She kept meaning to google 'very red ears' to see if they were a sign of high blood pressure.

Superintendent Molloy said, 'Dermot has been giving me the background to these two homicides you're investigating, the ones with their hands missing and their heads blown to smithereens. How's that progressing?'

'Oh, it's all coming together,' said Katie. 'We have a possible suspect, although we haven't yet identified her. I think we're coming close to a motive, too.'

'And what would that be, do you imagine? The suspect is African, isn't she?'

'Yes, and I think that could explain the way the victims have been mutilated, but I don't think it has much bearing on *why* they were killed. As far as we can establish, the African victim was a local pimp and all-round low life nick-named Mawakiya, while the white victim was probably a Romanian pimp called Mânios Dumitrescu.'

Superintendent Molloy raised his eyebrows. 'Ah ... so you think that this African woman might be a brasser, taking out her revenge on two pimps who had cheated her? It does happen. We had a case exactly like that in Limerick last summer. Three of the local hookers decided they were sick of paying so much of their hard-earned wages to their minder. They trapped his head in the door of some old fridge that was standing in his own front yard, and then drove a car into it. Didn't quite decapitate him, but nearly.'

'I have no evidence that our suspect is or ever has been a hooker,' said Katie.

'Oh come on, what else? African, and going after pimps like that? It's the logical conclusion.'

'It's an assumption and I don't make assumptions. It's assumptions that get cases thrown out of court. Look at those charges that were brought against those brothel-keepers last year in County Louth. The Gardaí failed to identify themselves when they entered the premises because they "assumed" that the brothel-keepers would know they were the law. The judge agreed that by failing to identify themselves they had nullified their entry warrant. Case dismissed.'

'Dah – that was nothing but a legal technicality!' said Superintendent Molloy, flapping one hand dismissively. 'What we're talking about in *this* case is a motive so obvious that you'd have to be lying in your scratcher with your head under the covers to miss it. All you have to do is find out which girls were working for those two scumbags – and *that* shouldn't exactly tax your pretty head too much. Just check their websites, if they have them, and their ads in the local papers, and you're halfway there.'

'We're doing that already, of course,' Katie told him. 'With Mawakiya it's a little more difficult, because he's been keeping himself under the radar.'

'Meaning what, exactly?'

'Meaning that a few people in the city have been aware that he's around, but for some reason he's never come to *our* attention before. There's a chef who works in one of the African restaurants on Lower Shandon Street, he saw him quite often, and apparently he always had a number of very young girls with him. A couple of minor drug-dealers knew him, too, as well as some juvenile offenders who were caught stealing tyres from Smiley's. But that was about his level. Petty pimping and petty drug-pushing and petty thieving, that's all. It seems extreme, to say the least, that one of his girls would go to the lengths of forcing him to cut off his own hand, then amputating his other hand, then blasting him in the face with two shotgun shells.'

She paused, but before Superintendent Molloy could interrupt her, she said, 'That's another thing. She shot them with quite a new type of Winchester shotgun shell, fired from what was probably a fairly newish type of handgun. A personal protection weapon, rather than some long-barrelled shotgun like you'd be taking out to shoot clay pigeons with. We have to ask ourselves where she acquired it – or how she even knew such weapons existed.'

Superintendent Molloy shook his head. 'There you are, Dermot! What I have always been saying? Give a woman a perfectly straightforward case to solve and before you know it she has it all tangled up like her knitting!'

Katie said, 'Well, Bryan, we can discuss this later if you like. I can show you all the pathology reports we have so far, as well as all the witness statements and forensic evidence from the technical lads.'

'Perhaps we could talk about it over dinner tonight,' said Superintendent Molloy.

'Excuse me?'

'I said, perhaps we could talk about it over dinner. I'm staying at Jury's at the moment until they can fix me up with somewhere more permanent. It would give us a chance to get to know each other better, and for you to brief me on everything that you have in hand.'

'I'm sorry, Bryan, I have a prior engagement this evening.'

'Oh!' said Superintendent Molloy, turning around on his heel as if he were appealing to a sceptical jury. 'And is this prior engagement more pressing than you and me discussing how we're going to tackle two high-profile homicides, with the perpetrator still at large? Not to mention a host of other serious criminal activities in this not-so-fair city?'

'I've said I'm sorry, Bryan, but it's an engagement I really can't break. I'm supposed to have a day off tomorrow but, if you like, I'll come in around eleven and do whatever I can to get you up to speed.'

Superintendent Molloy blew out his cheeks. 'That's the first time in my life a woman has ever turned me down. I'm shaken! Shaken to the core!'

'I'll see you tomorrow morning,' said Katie.

She picked up her briefcase and her sandwich and Chief Superintendent O'Driscoll opened the door for her.

Outside in the corridor, Katie said, 'How are you feeling, Dermot? You're looking a little washed out, if you don't mind my saying so.'

Chief Superintendent O'Driscoll gave her a weary smile. 'I'm bearing up, Katie. I've packed my pyjamas ready for hospital, tried to give Bryan all the background he needs, but I know that you'll give him your support.'

'Of course I will, Dermot. It's my job.'

Chief Inspector O'Driscoll reached behind him and closed the door so that Superintendent Molloy wouldn't be able to hear him.

'I know he won't be that easy for you to get along with. There are still too many in the force like him. But one of the reasons he got this job so promptly was because he has influential friends at Phoenix Park. Let me tell you this, Katie: if you really want to get ahead, try to stay on his good side. He could help you go a long way. If Noirin O'Sullivan could make it to Deputy Commissioner in Charge of Operations, so could you. You might even make Commissioner.'

'I can manage Bryan Molloy,' said Katie. 'I was married

to Paul, remember, and he thought that women were only good for two things, one of which was washing the dishes. It's you I'm worried about, Dermot. Promise me that you'll keep in touch and let me know how things are going, I'll come and visit you in the Bon Secours and bring you some of Ailish's barmbrack.'

Chief Superintendent O'Driscoll held out his arms for her and gave her a hug and kissed her. When he stood back, he had tears in his eyes.

'Do you know something, Katie,' he said, 'in all my thirty-five years in the Garda, this is the first time I've ever been scared.'

Twenty-three

She finished her coffee and was debating with herself whether she needed another cup when Detective Sergeant ó Nuallán knocked at her office door. She was wearing a faded denim jacket and a denim skirt, but her blonde bob was immaculate and shining.

'Ah, Kyna,' said Katie. 'I got your message about the tattoo parlour. I've just had to organize all these technical reports for Superintendent Molloy to go through. Have you met him yet?'

'Not yet. He'll be after introducing himself to everybody this afternoon. There's a special meeting in the canteen at three o'clock. But – yes – I know of him by reputation.'

'And?'

'And I know of him by reputation, that's all. He's an outstanding officer, that's what they say. He's one of the reasons they don't call Limerick "Stab City" any more.'

Detective Sergeant ó Nuallán looked as if she were about to say something else, but instead she stayed silent. Katie looked up at her and said, 'Is that it?'

'Yes, ma'am.'

'You know that if you work with me you can speak your mind. I don't give anybody down the banks for having an opinion.'

'No, ma'am.'

Katie was tempted to tell Detective Sergeant ó Nuallán exactly what *she* thought about Superintendent Molloy, but she had learned a long time ago not to give hostages to fortune, especially when it came to promotional politics. It was highly likely that Chief Superintendent O'Driscoll would never return to duty and that Superintendent Molloy would take over permanently, and also that Detective Sergeant ó Nuallán would be seeking to make her way higher up the ladder. Better to say nothing at all.

'All right,' she said. 'What's all this about Mawakiya's tattoo?'

'Well, it's very sensitive. I'd nearly given up, to tell you the truth. Then I visited this tattoo studio on French Church Street and one of the artists told me that he'd heard of a Thai tattooist who was operating out of a massage parlour on Grafton Street. He said he'd seen some of his work and it was very similar to Mawakiya's. A dragon or a snake starting at the genitals and winding its way around the body.'

She took her notebook out her jacket pocket and flipped it open. 'The massage parlour is called Golden Fingers and it's one of those advertised on Michael Gerrety's website. They have three Thai girls working there. They give legitimate massages, but for sixty euros extra they'll go the whole way.

'There's a back room there where this Thai tattooist does tattoos and piercings. He didn't want to speak to me at first, but then I told him I came from the Immigration Bureau and after that I couldn't shut him up. He said his name is Nok. I showed him the photographs of Mawakiya's tattoo and he said that he had done it, about eighteen months ago. He had known him only by the name of Kola.'

'That fits. Young Lolade heard him called Kola. Lolade, by the way – that's Isabelle's real name.'

'Nok said that Kola had been brought to the massage parlour by three of his friends. They were all regulars – like they would come in two or three times every month, at least, and sometimes they would bring more of their friends in with them. A couple of them had tattoos, but mostly they came for the massage. The *full* massage.'

'Did this Nok know who Kola's friends were?'

'The three that brought him in, oh yes. He knew them well. One of them was called Mister Dessie and he represented the owners of the massage parlour. He came in every day to collect the takings. The other two were called Ronan and Billy. Nok knew that because they both came to him for tattoos while their friends were having a massage. In fact, they both had the same tattoo, right between the shoulder blades. Guess what it was?'

'I don't know,' said Katie. 'A dragon? A picture of Bono?'

Detective Sergeant ó Nuallán passed over her open note book. 'There – Nok drew it for me.'

Katie picked it up. The tattoo design was a Celtic cross with a circle in the middle, and two curly intertwined letters in the centre, G and S. Around the outside of the cross were the words *Gharda Síotchána na h-Éireann*.

'A Garda badge,' said Katie. She was shocked. 'Don't tell me they were both gardaí?'

Detective Sergeant ó Nuallán took her notebook back. 'That's how Mawakiya appeared to stay unnoticed for so long. He wasn't unnoticed at all. He was simply being shielded by Ronan and Billy. Nok told me that he knew for sure they were guards because he had seen both of them in the street, in uniform.'

241

Katie frowned. 'If Ronan and Billy were friends with Dessie O'Leary, that means they must have known that Mawakiya was being used by Michael Gerrety to farm out any girls who were under the age of consent. Ten to one Gerrety was paying them to keep quiet about it – if not directly, then indirectly. Settling their mortgages for them, something like that. Paying for their kids to go to school.'

'I won't have any trouble identifying them, Ronan and Billy,' said Detective Sergeant ó Nuallán. 'I just thought you ought to know about them first.'

'Well, good thinking,' said Katie. 'We don't want Michael Gerrety to find out yet that we've established a connection between him and Mawakiya, or Kola, or whatever he called himself. It could well put Ronan and Billy at risk, and whatever they've done, I don't want them ending up in the river.'

'One more thing,' said Detective Sergeant ó Nuallán. 'I checked on the Dumitrescu house again this morning. The whole lot of them have definitely fled the nest. It wouldn't surprise me if they've already left the country.'

Katie said, 'That definitely increases my suspicion that our dead Romanian is Mânios Dumitrescu. And, of course, Dumitrescu did business with Michael Gerrety, too – mostly doing the direct opposite to Mawakiya and taking the older brassers off his hands.'

'That still doesn't bring us too much closer to who killed them, does it?'

'It could do.' Katie told Detective Sergeant ó Nuallán what Lolade had said about juju, and why Mawakiya's hands might have been cut off and his face obliterated.

Detective Sergeant ó Nuallán looked thoughtful and then she said, 'Our perpetrator did the same to the white victim, didn't she? That could be further confirmation that she's Nigerian and believes in juju.'

'How do you work that out?'

'It's only logic. If she had punished Mawakiya like that only because *he* believed in it, then she would have punished the white victim in a way that was appropriate to *his* beliefs. Since it's likely that he was Romanian, he was probably Eastern Orthodox, and they believe that sin is its own punishment, so all she had to do was kill him and he would have gone to hell anyway. He wouldn't have needed to have his hands cut off and his face shot away.'

'That's very erudite of you,' said Katie.

'It's just that I always try to put myself inside the mind of the perpetrator. If I can understand how they think, it usually helps me to work out who they are.'

Katie stood up, shuffling together the papers that she had been preparing for Superintendent Molloy. 'If you can discreetly find out for me the identities of Ronan and Billy, we'll have a further meeting to discuss what our plan of action is going to be. Your tattooist mentioned that they brought in other friends, so it's conceivable that there may be other officers involved. Until we know the extent of this, we need to handle it like an unexploded bomb, believe me.'

As Detective Sergeant ó Nuallán turned to go, Katie's mobile phone played *And it's no, nay, never – no, nay never no more—*

'Patrick?'

'Yes, ma'am. They've found another one. African male with his hands missing and his head shot to buggery.'

'Mary, Mother of God. Where?'

'He's in a furniture workshop in Mutton Lane, in between the Mutton Lane Inn and the English Market.'

'When was this?'

'Only about twenty minutes ago. The owner came back from his holliers a couple of days early and found him there, like. Bring your strongest scent. The stink's enough to make a maggot gag.'

'Give me ten minutes,' said Katie. Then, to Detective Sergeant ó Nuallán, 'I hope you don't have any plans for the rest of the day. We've got ourselves another one.'

Twenty-four

It had stopped raining and the streets were glistening in the sunshine. Three patrol cars and an ambulance and a van from the Technical Bureau were already parked at angles along the south side of Patrick Street. Gardaí had closed the street to westbound traffic and cordoned off the pavement between Princes Street and Market Lane. There were crowds at either end, silently waiting like guests at a funeral for the deceased to be carried out.

As Katie and Detective Sergeant ó Nuallán drew up outside, Detective O'Donovan came across and opened Katie's door for her. He looked sweaty and tired and his eyes were watering. He had a surgical mask around his neck and he smelled of Vicks VapoRub.

'Sorry to mess up your day, ma'am.'

Don't worry about messing up my day, thought Katie, *it's already been thoroughly ruined by the appearance of Bryan Molloy*. However, she smiled tightly as she climbed out of her car and said nothing.

Detective O'Donovan led them down Mutton Lane. The Mutton Lane Inn was closed, although the candles were still burning inside and the bar staff were peering out of the windows. At the far end of the lane, the entrance to the

English Market had been closed and screened off, too. Four or five uniformed gardaí were standing outside the open door to the furniture workshop, as well as one of the crime scene technicians in his pale green Tyvek suit, having a smoke. Beside them stood a worried-looking middle-aged man in a faded pink polo shirt. He had a thinning comb-over and spectacles stuck together in the middle with a grubby adhesive plaster. His nose was flaking with sunburn.

'This is the owner of the workshop, Gerry O'Farrell,' said Detective O'Donovan. 'Mr O'Farrell, this is Detective Superintendent Maguire.'

'I don't actually own the premises, only rent it, like,' said Gerry O'Farrell. 'This is such a terrible shock. I can't understand why anybody would want to use my workshop to do such a thing.'

'You didn't know the deceased?'

'Of course not! I never saw him before in my life! The size of him, la! I don't know *nobody* as fat as that!'

'How do you think the perpetrator gained access?' asked Katie.

'There was no sign of forced entry,' said Detective O'Donovan. 'Mr O'Farrell thinks the perpetrator must have somehow managed to copy his keys.'

'And how do you think they did that?'

'I hang my jacket up by the door, with the keys in the pocket, and on a warm day I sometimes leave the door open. That's all I can think of.'

'I'd better take a look at the deceased,' said Katie. She took a blue cotton scarf out of her bag, sprayed it with perfume, and tied it around her neck. Then she snapped on a pair of yellow surgical gloves.

'It's been such a terrible shock, like,' said Gerry O'Farrell, wringing his hands. 'I don't know what effect it's going to have on my business.'

'You came back early from your holiday,' said Katie. 'Any particular reason for that?'

'We were out in Gran Canaria, first holiday we've had in five years, but for some reason I had a really bad feeling that something wasn't right here at home. Apart from that, the food was very substandard, and it was far too hot there, and there were quite a lot of guests who made me and Maeve feel uncomfortable.'

'I'm sorry?'

Gerry O'Farrell glanced left and right, and then he quietly mouthed the word, 'Gays.' He paused, and then he added, 'In very small ...' He paused again, and then he said, 'You know, like, *Speedos*.'

'I see,' said Katie. 'Come on, Patrick, let's pay our respects to the victim.'

She tugged up her scarf so that it covered her nose and mouth, and Detective O'Donovan pulled up his mask, too. They stepped inside the workshop, which was so brightly lit with four arrays of halogen lights that all the furniture looked two-dimensional, as if it were cut out of cardboard.

Katie and Detective Sergeant ó Nuallán weaved their way through the maze of half-upholstered sofas and occasional tables and skeletal armchairs. The chief technician came over to meet them, enthusiastically rubbing his hands together as if he were delighted to have a really fascinating crime scene to work on.

'Hallo, Bill,' said Katie. 'What's the story?'

'Very similar to your man up at Ballyhooly Road. Both hands severed, face obliterated with at least two shotgun blasts, possibly three, because there's not too much of his cranium left. He was also shot in the knee for some reason. Interesting upgrade on the MO, though. This time the hands were severed with a circular saw.'

He led Katie over to the couch where the body was lying. The victim was African, although he was quite pale-skinned. He was seriously obese, with a huge belly and breasts almost as large as a woman's. He had been suffering from eczema, with dry patches of skin on his elbows which he had obviously been scratching. His arms were crossed, in the same way that the white victim's arms had been crossed up at Ballyhooly Road, with no hands to cover his genitals. His penis was very small, and circumcised.

'I wonder why he was shot in the leg,' said Katie. 'Maybe he tried to get away.'

She examined his knee, which was a blown-open mess of red flesh, as if somebody had emptied a can of chopped tomatoes over it. The technician said, 'There? See? The tibial artery's been tied up with string. Presumably the perpetrator shot him in the knee to stop him hopping off but didn't want him to bleed to death or lose consciousness before she had amputated his hands. I say "she" advisedly, of course.'

'I'd go along with that,' Katie told him. 'There's a very strong element of punishment in all of these killings, and there's no point in punishing your victim unless he *knows* that he's being punished, and what for.'

'You're flogging a dead horse, else,' said Bill, sagely, as if he had thought of that analogy himself.

Katie examined the rest of the victim's body. It was rippled with cellulite and covered in tiny red bruises, which made her think that he had been suffering from liver disease. Then she took a look at what remained of his head. She was inclined to agree that he had been shot three times, because his skull had exploded in all directions and his bones and brains and sinuses were all mixed up in the black horsehair stuffing of the couch. There were two or three gold teeth shining amongst the debris.

Detective Sergeant ó Nuallán was examining the blood-spattered table saw. 'I'm thinking that the perpetrator deliberately chose this workshop because she knew this saw was here. I mean, why else would she have chosen to bring her victim to a place like this, right in the middle of the city?'

'I agree with you,' said Katie. 'There can't be any question that she planned this in advance. For starters, she must have known that Mr O'Farrell would be away on his holliers and the workshop would be empty. Another thing: the first two killings took place on the victims' home turf, so to speak, if we're correct about their identities – locations where they would have been anyway. But this workshop ... she would have had to lure this victim here, or force him. She's armed, so it's possible she made him come here at gunpoint. That would indicate that she already had copies of the keys, rather than picking the lock when she got here. You couldn't pick a lock and hold a gun on somebody at the same time.'

'She might have had an accomplice,' Detective Sergeant ó Nuallán pointed out.

'Well, that's always a possibility, but we know that she didn't have anybody with her when she killed Mawakiya. I'll ask Bill to check the lock levers to see if there's any sign that they've been tampered with, just to make sure. Patrick – if you can find out who the letting agents are for this workshop. They would be holding keys for it, and maybe she somehow got access to those.

'Before you do that, though, give Ryan a call, would you? Have him start looking through the CCTV recordings for this section of Patrick Street for the past – what? – how long do you reckon this feller's been dead, Bill?'

The technician looked at the body thoughtfully, and then he said, 'Not as long as he smells like. No more than thirty-six hours, I'd say. I don't know what he's been eating, but it's his decomposing stomach contents and faeces, that's what's making him so rank.'

'Well, say thirty-six hours to start with,' said Katie. 'Get in touch with Stalwart Security, too, and ask them if they'll do the same for the English Market. They could just as easily have come in that way.'

She stood by the body for a while, and then she looked around the workshop. She was trying to imagine what must have happened here – what words must have been spoken between the perpetrator and her victim. *If only chairs and tables could talk.*

Detective O'Donovan returned, mopping his sweaty forehead with the back of his hand. It was uncomfortably warm inside the workshop, nearly thirty degrees, as well as smelling so foul. He told Katie that he had called Detective Ryan and also the private security company that monitored the eleven CCTV cameras covering the English Market. 'And I'm sure you'll be delighted to know that the jackals are outside, panting for a statement.'

'Oh, grand,' said Katie. 'I suppose I'd better go and throw them a bone.' She turned to Detective Sergeant ó Nuallán. 'You're going to stay around here for a while, aren't you? Have a chat with the staff in the pub, and whoever you can find in the market. You know what witnesses are like. They might well have seen something important but they have no idea what it was they were looking at.'

As she was about to leave, however, a young technician

suddenly gave a muffled shout from the other side of the workshop, 'Mobile phone!' he called out. 'Mobile phone!'

He made his way over, holding it up. Bill, the chief technician, said, 'Go and ask Mr O'Farrell if this is his, or if he knows anybody who might have lost it in here.'

The young technician came back a few seconds later, shaking his head. 'He says he never saw it before in his life.'

He passed the mobile phone to Bill and Bill passed it to Katie. It was a black iPhone 4. Its screen was badly cracked, but it was still working.

Katie said, 'Well – if this belongs to either the perpetrator or the victim, the angels could be smiling on us.' She returned it to Bill and he dropped it into a plastic evidence bag.

'Give us a couple of hours and we'll have this decoded for you,' he told her. 'Maybe even sooner. Are you heading off back to the station?'

Katie nodded. 'I'll be there till late now.' She had no choice. She would have to report this homicide to Chief Superintendent O'Driscoll and Superintendent Molloy, and then she would have to talk to the press office about how they were going to present it to the media. By that time, too, the Technical Bureau would probably have accessed the mobile phone. If it turned out to be the perpetrator's or the victim's, she and her team would be spending the following few hours assessing whatever information it contained – addresses, telephone numbers, emails, messages, apps.

As she came out of the end of Mutton Lane she was met by Fionnuala Sweeney from RTÉ, as well as Dan Keane from the *Examiner* and Branna MacSuibhne from the *Echo*.

'Afternoon, detective superintendent!' said Dan Keane, cheerily. 'Another "hands off" murder, is it?'

'Who told you that, Dan?'

Dan tapped the side of his nose. 'The usual little chirruping bird.'

'I'll be holding a preliminary media conference later today at Anglesea Street. I should be able to give you more of the details then. Meanwhile, all I can tell you is that the body of a male has been discovered in his upholstery workshop by Mr Gerry O'Farrell. The body has been mutilated in much the same way as the murder victims discovered this week at addresses in Lower Shandon Street and Ballyhooly Road.'

'You've put out CCTV pictures of a young African woman,' said Fionnuala. 'Have you been able to identify her yet?'

'Not yet, no. But she's still our principal suspect.'

'Do you think she could have been responsible for *this* killing, too?'

'It's too early for me to say, I'm afraid. The technical team still have a lot of work to do and we'll have to hold a post mortem.'

'But are you looking for anybody else in connection with these murders?'

'No, Fionnuala, we're not. But we're keeping an open mind. We still have no clear idea of the motive, or why the victims have all been mutilated like this.'

'Do you still believe the murders are connected to the sex trade?' asked Branna.

'I don't remember saying that I *did* believe that.'

'But both of the first two victims were pimps, and the girl who was found with the body at Lower Shandon Street was a prostitute, and the house on Ballyhooly Road was being used by two prostitutes, too.'

'Branna – I'm not denying the possibility that the perpetrator's motive is in some way connected to the sex trade.

Like I say, though, we're keeping an open mind. In spite of first impressions, the killings could just as easily have been motivated by drugs or money or plain old revenge for some perceived insult.'

'Do you think that they're ritualistic in any way?' asked Dan. 'I've been doing some background research, like, and there are several West African tribes who punish people by lopping bits off of them. Same with some Islamic countries.'

'I don't want to say any more until we've gathered more evidence,' said Katie. 'The press office will be in touch with you as soon as they can.'

Branna followed Katie to her car, her water-buffalo hairstyle bobbing as she walked. 'I really do need to talk to you,' she said.

'Later, Branna. Honest to God, I'm up to my neck at the moment.'

'But I've thought of a fantastic way of breaking open the city's sex trade.'

'Branna, I'm sorry, but it'll have to wait. I *am* concerned about prostitution in Cork, you know that. In fact, it's almost at the top of my list. Right now, though, I have three extremely high-profile murders to solve and more cases of thieving and drug-dealing and human-trafficking and fraud than you can shake a stick at.'

'When you hear what I have in mind, you'll regret so much that you didn't listen to me earlier,' said Branna, as Katie climbed into the driving seat.

'Well, if I do, I'll apologize. Meanwhile, I really have to go.'

She shut her car door, but as she started up the engine, she saw Branna mouthing something. She put down her window and said, 'What?'

'I said, if you don't want to listen to me, I'll go ahead anyway.'

Katie had no idea what she was talking about, and at this particular moment she wasn't very interested. She had dealt with keen young reporters before and she had learned that they always wildly exaggerated their stories, and most of the time they got all their facts muddled up. In spite of her sensitive nose for what Chief Superintendent O'Driscoll called 'cat's malogian', Katie liked to keep her investigations very low-key, and her evidence meticulously accurate. That was why her conviction rate was so high.

Back at her desk at the station, she rang John. He didn't answer, so she left a message.

'I'm so sorry, John! Sorry and sorry and sorry! There's been another murder and I have to stay. I don't know what time I'll be home. I may even have to spend the night here. Sorry.'

She pressed *End* and stared at the screen for a while. Ever since she had received John's message about dinner at the The Rising Tide, she had been imagining the two of them sitting in its upstairs dining room, looking out over the river as the sun went down. Now, she had a depressing feeling that maybe this was one 'sorry' too far. As John had said to her only two nights ago, 'You can only call a relationship a relationship, Katie, if the people who are supposed to be *in* the relationship are actually there to have it.'

Twenty-five

She went to Chief Superintendent O'Driscoll's office to find him emptying out the drawers of his desk.

'Where's Bryan?' she asked him.

'Bryan's still making himself known to the support staff. As if a forty-five minute introductory speech all about himself wasn't enough. You'd think that he reduced the crime rate in Limerick single-handed.'

'Fair play to him, Dermot. He did a lot to crack down on knife crime.'

'I suppose,' said Dermot. 'I just wish he wasn't so fecking full of himself.' He raked around in one of the drawers and eventually came up with a bottle-opener with an enamelled Garda badge on one end of it. 'This was my leaving present from Phoenix Park. Do you know what they told me? "We're giving you this because you'll have absolutely feck all to do in Cork, except eat crubeens and drink Murphy's and chase after runaway cows." They gave me this and a pair of green rushers, too. Jesus, if only I'd known.'

'We've got handless murder number three now,' said Katie. She told him all about the murder victim in the upholstery workshop, and he listened solemnly, although he continued clearing his desk and stowing all of his belongings into a cardboard box. A hairbrush, an electric razor, a roll of masking tape, some AA batteries and a box of staples.

'The mobile phone sounds promising,' he said. 'But you'll have to repeat this all over again to Bryan. He's the boss man now.'

Katie couldn't keep her eyes off the Garda badge on the end of the bottle-opener.

'There's something else I need to discuss with you, Dermot, and I'm not too sure how to broach it with Bryan.'

'Like you say, Katie, he's a decent officer, even if we are allergic to him. Come on, you've dealt with plenty of sexist pigs before now. All you have to do is to feed them a bucketful of swill now and again. Your record speaks for itself.'

'I just don't know how Bryan's going to react, that's all. I don't want him coming down like a ton of bricks and upsetting half the station and me getting the blame for being Sneaky MacSneak.'

Chief Superintdent O'Driscoll stopped packing away his notebooks and took off his glasses.

'What's this all about, Katie?'

Katie told him everything that Detective Sergeant ó Nuallán had found out from the Thai tattooist Nok – that two Garda officers had been seen socializing in the Golden Fingers massage parlour with 'Mister Dessie' O'Leary and Mawakiya, or Kola, or whatever his real name was.

'They never reported Mawakiya for any of the rackets he was running, like drug-dealing and fencing stolen goods, and they never reported him for pimping underage girls. What makes their misconduct all the more serious is that these girls had been passed on to Mawakiya by Michael Gerrety. Gerrety had refused to handle them himself because they were too young and might have jeopardized his Green Light campaign.'

'And they didn't speak up, these two, even when Mawakiya was found murdered?'

Katie shook head. 'Neither of them said a word. If they had spoken up and told us who he was, we could have been spared hours of work. We might even have been able to arrest this Angel of Revenge woman before she murdered Mânios Dumitrescu.'

'Do you know who they are?'

'Only their first names, Ronan and Billy.'

'Descriptions?'

'Apparently Nok said that all Irishmen looked the same to him. But he had seen them both in uniform in the city centre, on patrol together.'

Chief Superintendent O'Driscoll slowly sat down. 'I'm pretty sure I know who they are,' he said. 'Ronan Lynch and Billy Daly. Both of them have been in trouble over the years for various alleged transgressions. A couple of times for being overenthusiastic with the baton at public demonstrations. Another time they suggested to a motorist they might let him drive home drunk if he paid them an on-the-spot fine of two hundred euros. Then there's been some cases of inappropriate sexual advances to the wives of men in jail, or to young women facing charges of theft or prostitution.'

He leaned back and looked up at Katie with an expression like a regretful old dog.

'They're not what you'd describe as rotten to the core, Katie. Not at all. They've both done some excellent work, especially when it comes to community policing and dealing with young offenders. Let's just say that they've tended to take too much advantage of the privileges that go with being a guard. They seem to consider it's the perks of the job, like. If they accept some free hospitality here and there, or pocket a little money for turning a blind eye when a councillor's been speeding, they can't understand why anybody should be disapproving. Keeps the wheels greased, that's their attitude.'

'But they knew about Mawakiya, and what he was up to, pimping underage girls, and they did nothing.'

'Well, we can both guess why that was. If they've been hanging around with "Mister Dessie" O'Leary, then their ultimate paymaster must be Michael Gerrety.'

Katie said, 'I'm going to be talking to Kyna when she comes back, to see if she knows any more about Ronan and Billy, and then I think I'll have to talk to the two of them myself. Any evidence at all that Gerrety was aware that he was passing on underage girls for the purposes of prostitution will be absolutely invaluable. Reckless endangerment, at the very least.'

'It's a sad day, this, Katie,' said Chief Superintendent O'Driscoll, and she knew that he wasn't talking only about Ronan Lynch and Billy Daly.

'What I was really asking you is, how should I bring this up with Bryan?'

Chief Superintendent O'Driscoll stood up again and resumed his packing. He said nothing for a while, but Katie waited patiently for him to answer.

At last he said, 'Talk to Lynch and Daly before you say anything to Bryan. Tell them what you know and *insist* that they cooperate with you in nailing Michael Gerrety. If they don't, you'll make absolutely sure that the fertilizer hits the fan and they could end up losing a whole lot more than their jobs. Tell them you'd like to see how two bombos with Garda tattoos get treated by the residents of Rathmore Road.'

'And if they refuse?'

'*That's* when you go to Bryan. But not before.'

'Dermot, I know you don't like him. Neither of us do. But don't you *trust* him?'

'I told you, Katie. He's a decent officer and he's done a lot for Limerick. He's well-connected, too, and you'd be a fool to yourself if you fell out with him.'

'But?'

'Talk to Lynch and Daly first, and give them some time to consider. I don't think we'll ever get Michael Gerrety behind bars, but I still want to make sure that he's convicted.'

At that moment, Katie's iPhone played *And it's no, nay, never – no, nay never no more—*

'I trust that phone of yours isn't gloating,' said Chief Superintendent O'Driscoll.

She had hoped it was John calling her back, but it was Bill from the Technical Bureau.

'We've unlocked the phone we found in the workshop,' he told her. 'Are you going to give me an early Christmas bonus?'

'It's still July, Bill.'

'Oh, I know that, but you wait till you see what we've got there. The phone is registered to Owoye Danjuma, Top Flat, 33 Oliver Plunkett Street. Don't worry, we've checked, he doesn't actually live there. In fact, nobody does at the moment.

'You only have to look through a few of Owoye's messages to realize that he's usually known as Bula.'

'So that's who he is. Bula-Bulan Yaro. The Fat Man, in English.'

'You know him?'

'Oh yes, we know him all right. He mainly works for "Mister Dessie" O'Leary as a gofer and general odd-job man.'

'Well, that makes sense. There's about five million messages on this phone from "D", telling your man to do this and do that and go to the airport and pick up somebody's dry-cleaning and fix a door and God knows what else. I'll bring it on up to you anyway, and you can go through it for yourself. There is so much incriminating evidence in this thing, and so many names, you'll be arresting half of Cork.'

Katie said to Chief Superintendent O'Driscoll: 'The mobile phone they found in the workshop, it belonged to Bula, that big fat Nigerian gom who runs around for Dessie O'Leary.'

'I know, the one we can never get rid of. He sticks around like a bad smell, that man.'

'Well, he does now, I can tell you. That body in the work-shop, that's almost certainly him. But you know what that suggests, don't you?'

'I don't entirely, apart from the fact that all three of them were scumbags.'

'It suggests a pattern. All three of them were scumbags, yes, but all three of them were directly connected to Michael Gerrety. It's too early to say for certain, but that young girl Lolade said that the perpetrator called herself the Angel of Revenge. I have a strong feeling that she may be carrying out a vendetta here, picking off Michael Gerrety's people one by one.'

'She could be a prostitute herself,' Chief Superintendent O'Driscoll suggested. 'Maybe she feels that she was mistreated, or cheated.'

'She's probably Nigerian, because she actually called herself *Rama Mala'ika*, which is Hausa for "Angel of Revenge" – or at least that's what Faith told me. But that doesn't necessarily mean that she's a prostitute. I've been watching those CCTV sequences of her, over and over, and there's something about the way she carries herself. She's very attractive, and she's very confident in the way she walks. She's wearing a juju necklace, which may indicate that she's a practiser of juju rather than a follower. In other words, she's somebody who's *controlling*, rather than controlled.'

'That's interpretating a hell of a lot from a straight back and a seashell necklace. You ought to be a detective.'

'It's her entire body language, Dermot. She's determined, she's alert, she knows what she intends to do and she knows how to do it. She managed to get Bula into that furniture workshop somehow and cut off his hands with a circular saw. That wasn't done by any woman who's had her spirit broken.'

'It gives me the tingles in me wrists even to think about it,' said Chief Superintendent O'Driscoll.

'There's one thing more: she uses a very unusual weapon. The way Lolade described it to me, it was very small, and she had to reload it after only one shot. There are several handguns that can fire shotgun shells, like the Taurus Judge or the Smith & Wesson Governor, but both of those can fire more than one shot without reloading, and you could hardly describe either of them as small. So I'd be interested to know what kind of gun our perpetrator was using, and where she got it from.

'Her ammunition was very up to date, as you saw from Dr O'Brien's first report. So I may be wrong, and I may be totally misjudging this young woman, but I don't think she's a hooker, or ever was a hooker. All the same, there's no doubt in my mind that she's going after Michael Gerrety and his not-so-merry men, starting with the not-so-merry men and working her way upwards. What odds will you give me that "Mister Dessie" O'Leary is next on the hit list?'

'That gun could be a very good lead. Have you canvassed all of the gun traders?'

'Every single one from here to Dungarvon. No result at all. I'm meeting with Eugene Ó Béara tomorrow, but I doubt if I'll get anything out of him.'

'Oh well,' said Chief Superintendent O'Driscoll. 'It doesn't do any harm to keep in touch with the boys of the old brigade.' He paused, reflectively, and then he said, 'What are you going to do about Dessie O'Leary? Are you going to warn him that he might well be a target for this Angel of Revenge? And what about Michael Gerrety? Are you going to warn him, too?'

'I don't know,' said Katie – and she really didn't. 'I honestly think she'd be doing us a favour if she offed those two, don't you?'

'We're guardians of the peace, Katie, not judges. Remember your oath.'

'I do. I can still recite it word for word. But my oath doesn't include anything about my going out of my way to save callous and sadistic bastards from the consequences of their own criminality. Come on, Dermot, the oath has always been open to interpretation. We swear to God that we're not members of any secret society, don't we? – but half the senior officers at Phoenix Park belong to the stone sculptors down at the end of Molesworth Street.'

Chief Superintendent O'Driscoll shrugged his shoulders. 'I leave it up to your discretion, Katie. But be very careful how you handle this. Be doggy wide. It's beginning to look like two trains approaching from opposite directions, so don't get caught in the middle.'

She watched him pack the very last of his belongings, the silver clock that his parents had given him when he first graduated from Templemore.

'I'm going to miss you, Dermot O'Driscoll,' she told him. 'Without you, I'd still be trying to find out who hobbled the collection money from the Holy Family, or who's been pinching the knickers off Mrs O'Gallagher's washing line.'

He nodded. 'I'm going to miss you, too, Katie Maguire. I fought to have you promoted because I always believed that women have a much better nose for bullshit. Ha! I don't know how much you've learned from me, but I can tell you for nothing that I've learned a whole lot from you – mostly about the opposite sex. My wife says I've been a much better husband since you were promoted. She says I actually listen to her when she's talking. I have to admit that listening to her hasn't made her any more interesting – in fact, it's reminded me why I stopped listening to her in the first place. But there, you can't have everything.'

'You'll be back,' said Katie.

Chief Superintendent O'Driscoll looked around his office. There was nothing on the walls now except the rectangular marks where his photographs had hung.

He didn't answer, but his mouth was puckered tight and his eyes were glistening, and they both knew that he would never be sitting in this office, no, nay, never no more.

Twenty-six

It was nearly 11.00 p.m. before Detective Sergeant ó Nuallán came back to the station, and she looked exhausted. She slumped down in Katie's office and said, 'Jesus, I'm knackered.'

'Any luck with witnesses?'

'No. I must have talked to more than forty people, but nothing. I interviewed all of the staff at the Mutton Lane Inn and most of the stallholders in the English Market, and quite a few shoppers besides. Not one of them could remember seeing an obese African man accompanied by a thin African woman.

'One of the butchers said that he'd seen a really fat African woman with three thin kids, if that was any good to me. In fact, he said the kids were so thin he offered the woman some buckshee sausages to fatten them up a little, like her. After that, she screamed at him for almost five minutes, giving him a hard time for insulting her.'

'Let me get us some coffees,' said Katie. 'I think I'm badly in need a caffeine fix.'

'I'll go,' said Detective Sergeant ó Nuallán.

'No, no. You've been on your feet all day. I want to see how Horgan's getting on, anyway.'

On her way back from the canteen with a tray of five

coffees, Katie pushed her way into the squad room. Bill from the Technical Bureau had brought up Bula's iPhone and Detectives Horgan and Nolan were hunched over it together, making a record of every text and every email on it, and copying out its list of contacts.

Katie came across and set down a cup of coffee in front of each of them. 'How's it going?' she asked them.

'Oh, feck,' said Detective Horgan, leaning back in his chair. 'There's so much here, ma'am, it's going to take us all night and half of tomorrow, too.'

'Anything interesting?'

'So far, there's nothing that you could call directly incriminating. On the other hand, we might be able to link up some of the dates and times of the messages on here with cases that we haven't been able to close yet. For instance, your man was told to go to Spur Cross at 5.00 p.m. on the fifth of June to pick up a shipment of computers. Now what's in Spur Cross? Just a scattering of private houses, that's all. But on the third of June fifty-five Acer computers were stolen from Lee Electronics and there hasn't been a sniff of them since. So this could be a lead to who took them, and who fenced them, and where they went.'

'Any mention of Michael Gerrety?'

'Not so far. But there's loads from "D" telling your man that "M" wants him to do something. Here, look, on the twelfth of May "D" says that "M" wants him to go up to the airport and pick up "R" and two other passengers off of KLM 3173. Now, KLM 3173 is an evening flight from Brussels, and as we know, Brussels is a regular staging-post for trafficking girls from West Africa. After he's picked them up, your man is supposed to take them to Washington Street so that "M" can meet him there later to have a sconce.'

Detective Horgan sat back and stretched. 'It's all supposition, but that could well be an instruction from Michael Gerrety telling Bula to pick up a courier and two young girls, and that Gerrety will come along later to give them a once-over.'

'You're right,' said Katie. 'It *is* supposition. But keep at it. The more circumstantial evidence we collect, the better, and if there's *anything* in that phone that proves that "M" is Michael Gerrety, I'll buy you an iced doughnut next time.'

'Oh yes. Thanks a million for the coffee. I was gasping.'

Detective O'Donovan had arrived by the time Katie returned to her office. On the large side table where she usually spread out her maps he and Detective Sergeant ó Nuallán had laid out more than thirty large photographs. All pieced together, these formed a 360-degree panorama of the interior of the workshop, complete with Bula's headless, handless body lying on the couch in the middle of it, like a giant beige slug.

'That's grand,' said Katie. All of these photographs had been taken by the technicians to record any forensics they might have found – any blood spatters or fingerprints, any smudges or scratches – but Katie liked to use them to reconstruct the scene of the crime. To her, it was like an empty stage set after the play had finished and all of the actors had gone home. All except for Bula, of course.

She had often found that it was possible to work out what had happened, and in what sequence, by noting the position of the furniture, and where the bloodstains were, and other small details, like a knocked-over vase or a broken window pane. From the angle at which Bula had been shot in the knee, and the blood that had sprayed from the wound, she could see that the perpetrator must have been standing where the table saw had been located when she shot him. That meant that she must have dragged the saw up close to him *after* she had made sure that he was unable to escape.

She was still studying the photographs when Detective Ryan knocked at her door, looking more than ever like a schoolboy who has just finished all his homework. He was holding up half a dozen printouts.

'Got her,' he said.

He spread the pictures out on Katie's desk. They showed the south side of Patrick Street in between Burger King and Oasis. In the first picture, Bula could be seen emerging from Burger King in his yellow floral shirt, holding his takeaway box. In the next, a nun was talking to him, but the young Nigerian woman was standing by the window of Claire's fashion store, only a few feet away, and she obviously had her eyes on him. She was dressed in the same outfit of black T-shirt, black leather waistcoat and jeans that she had been wearing when she was tailing Mawakiya.

As Bula reached the corner of Mutton Lane, the young woman stepped up close behind him. He turned, and they appeared to be exchanging a few words. Although the image was fuzzy, Bula could be seen to be frowning. A man appeared from Mutton Lane and spoke to him, and then walked away. Bula then turned into Mutton Lane and the young woman followed him.

'I don't think there's any question now who we're after,' said Katie. She pointed to the clearest picture of the young woman and said, 'Have that one circulated as soon as you can, would you? I'll make sure that the press office gets it. *Somebody* must know this woman, and where she's staying. I mean, she's striking enough. You wouldn't miss her, would you, even in a crowd?'

'Depends what it was a crowd of,' said Detective O'Donovan. 'If it was nothing but African lashers, then maybe you would. By the way – talking of African lashers, I checked on the letting agents for Gerry O'Farrell's furniture workshop – Carbery's, on Grand Parade. There was an African girl working there and she was quite a looker. Red hair she had, almost the same colour as yours. She said that nobody could have had access to the keys to the workshop because all of their keys were kept in the office safe. So maybe O'Farrell was right and our suspect did take them out of his jacket and have copies made of them. I'll check with Cunneen's the locksmith's later.'

John was deeply asleep when she eventually eased herself into bed. The digital clock on the bedside table said 2.52 a.m. She punched her pillow and tried to make herself comfortable, but she was feeling hot and restless, and the inside of her mind was like a fairground, with everything that had happened during the day going around and around like carousels and whistling and clanging and thumping like dodgems.

She was almost asleep when John put his arm around her and cupped her breast through her nightdress.

'You're back, then,' he murmured. His voice was so rumbly she could feel it through the mattress.

'Yes. I'm sorry. We had another murder.'

'Tell me about it in the morning. I don't want to think about murder right now.'

'I'm sorry about The Rising Tide. I was really looking forward to it.'

'We'll do it next week. That's unless somebody else gets themselves whacked. But we can go out for lunch tomorrow, can't we?'

'We should be able to. I'll have to go in for an hour or

so in the morning. I'll need to talk to the media, and Dermot's replacement has arrived and I have to get him up to speed.'

'Oh yes? What's he like, this replacement?'

'If he was any more full of himself he'd explode. Bryan Molloy, his name is, from Limerick. He has a very low opinion of women, especially women gardaí, and women superintendents most of all.'

John gently squeezed her breast and rolled her nipple between his finger and thumb. She could feel his hardened penis against the small of her back.

'Obviously the man has no taste whatsoever. Either that, or he's a faggot.'

'John ...' said Katie, taking hold of his wrist and moving his hand away from her breast. 'You know I can't, not tonight. Give it a couple of days and I promise you we'll have an orgy.'

John kissed her shoulder and then he lifted her hair and kissed the nape of her neck. 'Okay,' he breathed. 'I guess everything comes to he who waits. Or he who waits eventually comes. Or something like that.'

He turned over on to his back. It was beginning very gradually to grow light, and Katie could hear wrens singing in the garden. She remembered that she had been taught at school that wrens were treacherous birds, because they had betrayed the Irish soldiers fighting against the invading Norsemen by beating their wings against their shields.

Treachery made her think of Ronan Lynch and Billy Daly, the two gardaí she would have to talk to tomorrow. She wasn't looking forward to that at all.

John laid his hand on her hip and gave her a gentle shake. 'You *will* find time to read my proposal for ErinChem tomorrow, though, won't you?'

'I'll try, John.'

There was a long silence, interrupted only by the chirruping of the wrens outside. Then John said, 'You know how much I love you, don't you, Katie?'

She wrestled herself around and held him close and kissed him. His cheek was prickly and he smelled of himself and some woodsy aftershave. 'I love you, too, John Meagher. *Tá mo chroí istigh ionat.*'

Twenty-seven

She found them sitting in their patrol car on Parnell Place, outside Mulligan's pub, eating bacon sandwiches and drinking tea. She had been told where they were by central dispatch and it had only been a short walk from Anglesea Street.

She opened the back door and climbed in before they realized what she was doing. The driver twisted around and said, 'What in the *name* of Jesus do you think you're up to, girl?' spitting out bits of sandwich as he did so, but then almost instantly he recognized her and said, 'Oh. Sorry. Apologies, ma'am. Took me by surprise, that's all.'

'Just as well I wasn't armed and dangerous, then?' said Katie.

'We was only having a bit of breakfast, like,' said the garda in the front passenger seat. 'Our shift started at six and the canteen's cooker was banjaxed.'

'That's all right,' said Katie. 'I don't expect you to go hungry. Not that I suppose you ever do.'

Before either of them could answer that, she turned to the driver and said, 'You're Billy, right?'

'Yes, ma'am,' said Billy, frowning at his partner as if to say *what's all this about?*

Billy Daly was black-haired, with heavy black eyebrows and blue eyes and a blob of a nose like Play-Doh. A double chin

271

bulged over his collar and his uniform looked much too tight for him, as if he had to strain to button it up every morning.

In contrast, Ronan Kelly was fair-haired and thin, with pale eyes and angular cheekbones and a sharp triangular nose. He appeared almost lipless, and he barely opened his mouth when he spoke, like a ventriloquist.

Katie said, 'You know about that Nigerian feller who was found murdered in Mutton Lane yesterday afternoon? Both of his hands cut off, and his head blown to kingdom come with a shotgun?'

'Of course, yeah, we had the full briefing this morning,' said Billy. 'What's the story on that, then?'

'The victim was an illegal immigrant named Owoye Danjuma, better known as Bula. He worked as a general dogsbody for Desmond O'Leary, better known as "Mister Dessie".'

'Yeah … that's right,' said Billy. His tone was growing increasingly cautious.

'As you know, we have a fair idea who the perpetrator is, especially since she doesn't seem to be going out of her way to conceal herself. Twice now we've caught her on CCTV. In fact, the pathologist suggested that she might have a reason for doing this all so openly. He thinks she wants to get her revenge on these scumbags, but at the same time she wants to make a show of the Garda for being so useless in bringing them to justice.'

'Well, that's one theory,' said Ronan Kelly. 'It could be that she's simply thick, like most murderers are, and doesn't realize she's making herself so fecking conspicuous. If most people knew how many CCTV cameras we have in Cork, you'd never get them walking down the street scratching their arses the way they do.'

'We have her picture, like, and we're keeping a lookout for her,' said Billy Daly. 'There's not a whole lot more we can do than that, is there?'

'You can keep tabs on your friend Mister Dessie,' said Katie. 'So far this Angel of Revenge has killed three of Michael Gerrety's people, and if she carries on, there's a strong possibility that Mister Dessie will be next. Maybe she even has her eye on Michael Gerrety himself.'

'What do you mean "keep tabs"?' asked Ronan Kelly.

'Make sure that you know where he is, twenty-four hours a day, and make sure that *I* know, too. He may be a piece of shite, but it's still our duty to protect him if we think he's in danger of getting himself murdered.'

'He won't be happy about that,' said Ronan Kelly.

'He won't be happy about what? Being kept tabs on, or being murdered?'

'He's not too keen on people knowing where he is, like, or who he's with.'

'Because why? Because he's wheeling and dealing all the time for Michael Gerrety, and Michael Gerrety likes to make out that his hands are clean?'

Neither Ronan Kelly nor Billy Daly answered that, but they looked at each other warily.

Katie leaned forward and rested her elbows on the backs of their seats. 'I don't expect you to *tell* Mister Dessie that you're keeping tabs on him. I want you to do it *discreetly*. But from now onwards, and I mean from *now*, today, this morning, I want to know his exact location, and as far as possible what he's doing there.'

'I don't mean to be disrespectful, ma'am, but how in the name of Jesus are we going to do that?'

'Don't try to play innocent with me, Garda Kelly. When

I called Mister Dessie your friend, I wasn't joking. Mister Dessie gives you two money and women and in return you conveniently fail to notice that Mister Dessie is trafficking underage girls and running all of Michael Gerrety's so-called massage parlours and health clubs for him. You two knew everything that Mawakiya was up to, and you knew immediately that it was him who'd been murdered on Lower Shandon Street. I imagine you knew that the second victim was Mânios Dumitrescu, too.'

Ronan Kelly and Billy Daly stayed silent, but continued to stare at each other, as if they were trying to communicate telepathically what they were going to do next.

'There's no point in your trying to deny any of this,' said Katie. 'I have too many witnesses and too much evidence against you. I'll have to file a full report later, but meanwhile you can mitigate your misdemeanours by keeping a close watch for me on Mister Dessie. I also expect you to report back to me anything you might hear him say, whether you think it's illegal or not.'

'What if he's ordering a pizza?' asked Ronan, bitterly, through that slit of a mouth.

'You're in no position to crack jokes, Garda Kelly,' said Katie. 'I'm talking about him calling for taxis to take women around the city, or arranging to meet flights from the airport, or booking doctors' appointments, that kind of thing. And, of course, anything that directly relates to sex trafficking or prostitution. And anything at all that relates to Michael Gerrety.'

'Well, would you believe it?' said Ronan Kelly. 'You've put me right off me bacon sangridge.'

'I'm sorry about that, but the fault is entirely yours, and what you choose to do now is entirely up to you. If you help me, I'll make sure that you get the credit for it when it comes to any disciplinary proceedings, which it will. It may even come to criminal proceedings.'

'We're not the only ones!' Billy Daly protested.

'Will you shut the feck up!' Ronan Kelly snapped at him.

'I'm aware of that, too,' said Katie. 'Meanwhile, what are you going to do? Are you going to assist me in this, or not? If you say no, you're not, then I'm going directly to Acting Chief Superintendent Molloy and reporting you.'

Both gardaí were silent for a moment, and then Ronan Kelly said, 'Why don't we just warn Dessie that this black bird is out to get him, like?'

'Because he'll start to take precautionary measures, such as walking around with a bodyguard, and changing his daily routines, and maybe carrying a firearm.'

'So? At least he won't get his hands chopped off and his head blown to bits.'

'What do you think I'm trying to do, Garda Kelly? I'm trying to catch this Angel of Revenge, but if Mister Dessie makes it obvious that he knows he's next on her list, she's going to keep well away, isn't she? She needs time to do the things she does to her victims, time and seclusion. She follows her victims very closely. She won't attempt to go for Mister Dessie if she sees that he's always going to have some minder with him.'

'How can you be so sure that he's next on her list?' asked Billy Daly. 'There's *dozens* of other pimps around the city, aren't there? Jesus – I could count them on the fingers of three hands.'

'Of course I can't be one hundred per cent certain,' Katie admitted. 'But it was Bula who made me believe that it was highly likely. Mawakiya and Dumitrescu, they were both pimps, yes, but Bula was nothing more than a gofer. All that the three of them had in common was that they worked for Michael Gerrety, handling girls for him. There's only one surviving person who does that for him, and that's Mister Dessie.'

'Michael's going to hit the fecking roof if this all comes out,' said Ronan Kelly, shaking his head. 'I don't honestly know what I'm the scareder of, losing my job or Michael losing his rag with me.'

Katie opened the car door and a warm breeze blew in, smelling of river. 'I'm going to meet Acting Superintendent Molloy now. Text me as soon as you find out where Mister Dessie is, and what he's doing. Copy the text to Detective Sergeant ó Nuallán. She knows all about this, and my meeting you here, and if I'm otherwise engaged she can handle any crisis that might come up.'

Twenty-eight

Acting Chief Superintendent Molloy was talking on the phone when Katie knocked at his open office door. He beckoned her in and then he covered the receiver with his hand and said, 'The door. Close it, would you, Katie?'

Katie thought, 'Close it would you, *please*, Katie' would have been appreciated, but she closed it anyway and sat down next to his desk. She looked around the office while he was talking and noticed that he had already put up photographs of himself shaking hands with various politicians, like Alan Shatter the justice minister and Kathleen Lynch TD, and local dignitaries like the mayor of Limerick, as well as his awards and his certificates.

Propped up in the corner next to the bookcase there was a leather bag of golf clubs.

'Pat – that's the way we're going to be doing it, whether you like it or not,' Acting Chief Superintendent Molloy was saying on the phone. 'No, Pat. *No*, boy! Absolutely not. I told you before. All right, then. Good. I'll talk to you later so.'

He hung up the phone and scribbled some notes on the pad in front of him. It was only then that he looked up at Katie and gave her a questioning look as if he couldn't understand what she was doing here.

'Good morning, Bryan,' said Katie. 'I see you're making yourself at home.'

Acting Chief Superintendent Molloy ignored that remark. 'I saw the appeal you put out on the TV this morning. It's a pity I wasn't afforded the courtesy of vetting it myself before it went out.'

'Oh, I'm sorry. I did ask Declan O'Donoghue to make sure you saw it.'

'Well, there must have been a failure in communication. As it was, I wasn't at all keen on the assumption that these murders are connected to the sex trade. The sex trade is a very prickly issue, both legally and politically, and it's not our job to make moral judgements. We're a police force, not some band of hymn-singing evangelists.'

Katie laid a blue manila folder down on his desk. 'Dr O'Brien tells me that he won't complete his post mortem on the third victim until later today, if not tomorrow, and the Technical Bureau haven't yet sent me their final report on the Mutton Lane scene. But this should get you up to date on all three homicides – forensics, autopsies, witness statements and CCTV printouts. I think you'll find from what's in here that the connection to the sex trade is undeniable.'

Acting Chief Superintendent Molloy reached over and took the folder, but didn't open it. 'Dermot told me that you weren't one to jump to conclusions. Meticulous, that's what he said you were.'

'Two of the victims were pimps and the third was an errand boy for the biggest organized prostitution racket in Cork. I hardly think I'm jumping to conclusions.'

'It's a question of *attitude*, Katie. We can't be seen to be prejudiced.'

'I don't understand what you're getting at. I'm not at all

prejudiced. I'm just making a logical assessment of the evidence. If two butchers and a butcher's boy were murdered, you'd begin to suspect that their killings were connected to the meat trade, wouldn't you?'

Acting Chief Superintendent Molloy stood up and walked over to the window. 'Times are changing, Katie. Public opinion is changing. The Garda have to be responsive to that.'

Katie said nothing, but waited for him to continue. She could sense that he was building up to making some important announcement, but one that he didn't think she was going to like. He kept his back to her, and both of his hands in his pockets, juggling with his loose change.

'I might as well tell you now. I'm cancelling Operation Rocker,' he said.

'You're *what*?'

'I'm cancelling Operation Rocker. In my opinion, it's outdated and misguided, and it's a waste of our precious resources. The chances of successful prosecutions are next to nil, and I believe that it will cause serious damage to our relationship with the sex-working community.'

Katie was breathless. 'Bryan – do you know how many months of surveillance have gone into this operation? Do you know how many women have put themselves at risk to give us witness statements? You talk about the "sex-working community", but do you have *any* idea how many of those women have been illegally trafficked, and have been forcibly drugged, or physically threatened, or both? Do you know how many of them are not even old enough to leave school, let alone work as prostitutes?'

Acting Chief Superintendent Molloy turned around, although he kept his hands in his pockets. 'I'm perfectly aware of the statistics, Katie. I went through all of the reports with

Dermot yesterday before he left. Yes – there are some women who are working in the sex trade less than willingly, but what choices do they have? If they didn't do that, they'd be destitute, and we'd either have to deport them back to Africa or Eastern Europe for a life of even greater destitution, or else we'd have to pay them benefits at considerable cost to the Irish taxpayer, who is burdened enough as it is, God knows.'

'I can't believe I'm hearing this,' said Katie.

'That's because you're looking at it from a woman's point of view. You're still a *bangharda*, Katie. It's the church's job to take care of morality, not ours. It's our job to protect people, regardless of who they are or what they're up to, and the best way to protect women in the sex trade is to make sure that it's all carried out in the open. If prostitutes have responsible organizers who give them somewhere safe to live and take care of their welfare, surely that's better than seeing them back on the streets.'

'"Responsible organizers"? Are you messing? Which "responsible organizers"? Men like Mânios Dumitrescu and Johnny-G and Terence Chokwu and Charlie O'Reilly? Men like Michael Gerrety?'

'Michael Gerrety for one deserves a lot more leeway. His Green Light campaign has been given considerable support from charities and social workers and from sex workers themselves. He's trying hard to take the stigma out of sex work, and from our point of view that can only be helpful. It means less women forced into prostitution. It means less violence and fewer sexually transmitted diseases. People will always sell and buy sex, no matter what we do. If we harass men like Michael Gerrety, Katie, we'll only succeed in driving the sex trade back underground, where it's so much harder to keep an eye on it.'

Katie said, 'You really believe that?'

'Yes, I do. And that's why I'm cancelling Operation Rocker.'

Katie stood up. 'I'll leave that file with you, anyway. I have at least twenty more major cases to go over with you, but I think we can leave them till Monday.'

'I'm quite prepared to go over them now. The sooner I catch up, the better.'

'Well, I agree, but you've just dropped a bombshell on me and I need to go away and think about it.'

'Don't tell me you're *upset*? This is purely a policy decision, Katie, nothing to do with personal feelings.'

'It's a policy decision that I totally disagree with, Bryan. Michael Gerrety is a conniving manipulative bully and a con man, and if you're seriously talking about letting him carry out his sex business unmolested, then you're more of a chauvinistic meb than I thought you were.'

Acting Chief Superintendent Molloy stood with his mouth open, his face growing gradually redder. For a split second, Katie thought that he was going to shout at her. Then, however, he took his hands out of his pockets and started clapping her, slow and mocking.

'Good girl! Well done! If there's one thing I like, it's a woman who's brave enough to speak her mind, even if it is all rubbish!

He stopped clapping and came up to her, taking hold of her elbow, although she immediately twisted it away.

'I can understand that you're angry and disappointed, Katie. I would be, too, if I was you. So, yes, let's leave the rest of the catching up until Monday. You can go home now and vent your spleen on some hoovering, or washing the curtains, or some such. I'll see you when you've thought about what I've said, and realized the sense of it.'

Katie took a deep breath, opened the door and left the office without saying anything. She was so angry that she could have kicked the wall as she walked along the corridor. She was so angry that she could have burst into tears. But she did neither. Acting Chief Superintendent Molloy had called her a *bangharda*, which was the outdated name for a female garda, and the last thing she wanted to do was give him the satisfaction of proving him right.

She met Eugene Ó Béara in The Ovens in Oliver Plunkett Street. He was sitting in a booth in the far corner of the bar with a half-finished pint of Guinness in front of him, talking to a shaven-headed young man in a green polo shirt. Eugene Ó Béara himself hadn't changed at all since Katie had last met him, although his curly hair, once chestnut, was now almost completely grey, and badly in need of a trim. He reminded Katie of Dylan Thomas, the poet, because even at the age of forty he had the face of a very spoiled baby.

He was wearing a black short-sleeved shirt that had seen better days and a Blackpool GAA tie. As Katie came across the bar he lifted his left wrist and peered down at his large Rolex wristwatch.

'Sorry I'm a little late,' said Katie.

'Budge up, Micky,' said Eugene. 'Let the lady sit down.'

The shaven-headed young man shifted himself along the bench seat and Katie sat down beside him.

'Detective Superintendent Maguire, this is Micky Corcoran. Micky, this is the celebrated Katie Maguire, the bane of all wrongdoers everywhere. You'll be joining us in a scoop, detective superintendent, especially since you'll be treating us?'

'I'll just have a Finches rasa,' said Katie. She took a

twenty-euro note out of her purse and handed it over. 'You two have whatever you want.'

Micky Corcoran took the note and stood up. He had acne-pitted cheeks and a long pointed nose and two silver studs in his left earlobe. As he went to fetch the drinks he gave Katie a sideways look over his shoulder and smirked at her, as if there was something about her that amused him.

'Why is it that whenever the shades want to know anything about illegally acquired weapons they always come to me?' asked Eugene. 'Those days are over now. The last thing I blew up was a balloon for my daughter's birthday party. We have beaten our AK-47s into ploughshares and our mortars into pruning hooks.'

'Oh yes, and pigs might recite the Lord's Prayer.'

Eugene's eyes narrowed. 'I have the distinct feeling that you're a little out of sorts today for some reason.'

'Well, your distinct feeling is quite correct, but it has nothing at all to do with the business in hand.'

'If somebody's upset you, detective superintendent, I have plenty of friends who could soften their cough.'

'Like I told you on the phone, I'm only interested in one sort of weapon. It's a small handgun that can fire shotgun shells. From what our witness has told us about it, it can only fire one round at a time.'

Micky Corcoran came back with the drinks. He gave Katie a glass with two drinking straws in it, as well as her bottle of raspberry cordial. 'I thought you'd want to drink it civilized, like.'

'Micky will know about your gun,' said Eugene. 'Micky, do you know of a handgun that can take shotgun shells, but it's only a single shooter?'

Micky swigged Satzenbrau lager out of the bottle. 'Yeah,

for sure,' he said, wiping his mouth with the back of his hand. 'That'll be your Pocket Shotgun. It's made by Heizer Defense in America and it only went on sale at the end of 2013, so there's not too many of them around yet. It's made of stainless steel or titanium but it's so fecking small that you can carry it in the pocket of your cax and nobody would even guess you'd got it on you. The only trouble is the recoil. Because it's so small it's got a kick like a fecking donkey.'

'Where could I get hold of one?'

'Has somebody upset you that much?' grinned Eugene.

'A handgun like that could have been used in a homicide,' said Katie. 'If I can find out where the perpetrator got it from, then it could help me to find out who they are. And if there's so few of them on the market, like you say …'

Micky took another swig of lager and screwed up his face in concentration. 'I don't know,' he said. 'I don't want to be dropping nobody into the shite, like.'

'I'm not after the person who supplied the gun,' said Katie. 'I just want to know who he supplied it to.'

Micky turned to Eugene. Eugene shrugged and said, 'She's a woman of her word, Micky. I'll give her that. But you don't want to be giving away valuable information like that for nothing, do you?'

Katie opened her purse again and took out two fifty-euro notes. Micky looked at Eugene, but Eugene stuck out his bottom lip and shook his head. Katie took out another two fifties.

'One more and I think you're there,' said Eugene.

Katie held out five fifties. Eugene reached across the table and took them. He gave two to Micky and tucked the other three in the breast pocket of his shirt. 'Go on, Micky,' he told him. 'Tell her who's been flogging them guns.'

'Colin Cleary,' said Micky. 'He showed me one about three months ago and asked me if I was interested, like, but I wasn't really. That's a gun for protecting yourself if you're worried that somebody's got it in for you, or else for getting your revenge on somebody close up and personal. I don't know where the feck Colin gets them from, but you know what he's like, he can get you a fecking tank if you want one.'

'I thought Colin Cleary had gone out of the gun-running business years ago,' said Katie. 'He retired, didn't he, and opened up that garden centre in Mallow?'

'Oh, he's still doing that. If it's weedkiller you want, or tomato plants, then Colin's your man. But he never lost touch with his contacts in America, or the Middle East.'

'He's a patriot, Colin, like me,' said Eugene. 'In spite of all this Good Friday shite, we're still looking forward to the day.'

Katie walked back to Anglesea Street, but she didn't return to her office. Instead, she went directly to the car park and climbed into her car. She took out her mobile phone and dialled Nifty 50 to find the number for Colin Cleary's garden centre.

'Cleary's Horticulture,' a woman answered when she was put through.

'Is Colin Cleary there?'

'Who wants to know?'

'Maguire's Fertilizer. He asked me to call him.'

'He's away till Monday. Somewhere in the UK. Birmingham, I think. I can give you his mobile number.'

'Thanks.'

Katie jotted down Colin Cleary's mobile number and then

rang it. As she waited for an answer, she noticed that seven or eight hooded crows had gathered on the roof of the building overlooking the car park. She knew that it was ridiculously superstitious, but she had always taken a gathering of hooded crows to be an omen of ill fortune.

Colin Cleary's phone rang and rang but he didn't answer it. Eventually Katie gave up. She would try again later, but she didn't hold out much hope that he would pick up. A man like Colin Cleary would always be suspicious of a number he didn't know.

She started the engine and backed out of the car park and headed for home.

286

Twenty-nine

When they arrived at her father's house it was Moirin who answered the door. She was wearing a startling summer dress with green and orange geometric patterns on it and which was six inches too short for a woman of her age.

'Well, now, it's *you*!' she said, as if she had been expecting somebody else and was disappointed to see that it was Katie and John.

'How are you, Moirin?' said Katie, stepping into the hallway. They exchanged air blown kisses. Moirin's hair was much shorter and spikier than the last time Katie had seen her, and Katie thought she was looking sharper and older, even though she was only in her mid-thirties.

'John, it *is* John, isn't it?' said Moirin. 'I lose track with Katie.'

'I've had the one husband, Paul, who's passed away, and then John,' Katie retorted. 'Is that too many to remember, or shall I write them down for you?'

'Come on through,' said Moirin, closing the front door. Katie's father lived in a tall, green-painted Victorian house in Monkstown, on the opposite side of the harbour from Katie, who lived in Cobh. Her mother had died four years ago and Katie had repeatedly urged her father to sell up and move to somewhere smaller and easier to maintain, but he had told her that his memories were here. In winter he said he could still picture her mother sitting on the second-to-bottom stair to put her boots on, and in summer he could leave the kitchen door open and imagine that she was still out in the garden, tending to her hollyhocks.

Although the house smelled old, it had aired out during the summer and no longer smelled so damp. When they walked through into the living room, they found vases of fresh yellow roses and gladioli all around and the furniture was gleaming with polish. Over the fireplace hung a dark oil painting of a group of people trying to find their way through a forest, which Katie had always thought rather sinister, but even this had a shine to it this morning and the people looked cheerful rather than lost. An appetizing smell of herby roast chicken was wafting through from the kitchen.

Katie's father came into the living room, holding Siobhán's hand.

'Katie, darling!' he greeted her. 'And John!'

Katie went over and kissed him. She was pleased to see how much better he looked. His white hair was neatly trimmed and although he was still thin and bony he seemed to have put on weight, and he was wearing a freshly pressed tattersall shirt.

'Siobhán, how are you, sweetheart?'

Siobhán was the third of the seven McCarthy sisters, and she looked very much like her father had looked when he was younger. She was round-faced and rosy-cheeked and green-eyed, with abundant red curls. She used to have innumerable boyfriends, and would flirt madly with any man who would give her the time of day. Last year, however, she had been struck violently on the head with a hammer by a jealous wife, which had left her brain-damaged. She was still sweet, and still funny, but now she had the mental capacity of a seven-year-old child.

'Katie!' she said, and hugged her. 'John! It's like Christmas!'

'How are you, Siobhán? I love your pink dress!'

'It's pink,' said Siobhán. 'Ailish and me went to Penneys to buy it!'

'What have you been doing with yourself, Siobhán? Have you been anywhere nice lately? Has Moirin taken you down to the beach?'

'Yes,' snapped Moirin. 'Moirin has taken her down to the beach, and to Tarzan Land in Perk's Entertainment Centre, and for walks every day in Green Park even when it's raining. She adores the maritime mural, don't you Siobhán? It's her favourite.'

'I like the mermaids,' said Siobhán. 'And I like the fishing men, too, and the fish. And I like the crabs.'

Now they were joined from the kitchen by Ailish, and Moirin's husband, Kevin. Katie had found Ailish through a local employment agency. She kept house for Katie's father, and cooked for him, and kept him company. She was a pretty, plump woman, with her grey hair tightly plaited, which made her look German.

Kevin seemed to be as despondent as ever. He was round-shouldered, with thick glasses and thinning hair, and none of his facial features seemed to belong to each other, like Mr Potato Head. He was wearing a new blue short-sleeved shirt that still had the creases in it from being taken out of the packet. Presumably Moirin had been too busy to iron it for him, thought Katie.

They all sat down in the living room. Katie's father and

Ailish went into the kitchen and they heard a pop. Shortly afterwards Ailish came back in, carrying a tray with glasses of champagne.

'Hey, is this some kind of special occasion?' said John.

'Of course it is,' said Katie's father. 'You've found yourself a job and you'll be staying here in Cork and you've made Katie very happy.'

'Well, I'm happy, too,' said John. 'Katie's a very special person. One in a million, and I love her very much.' He reached across the sofa and took hold of her hand.

When he had handed everybody a glass of champagne, however, Katie's father said, 'But ... there's another reason I've asked you all here today, and that's to make an announcement.'

'At last!' said Moirin. 'You're selling this house! Hallelujah! Oh – so long as you don't expect to move in with me and Kevin! We've got enough of a houseful with Nona and Tommy, not to mention Siobhán.'

'I can arrange the sale for you, Mr McCarthy,' Kevin volunteered in his flat, expressionless voice. 'The market's very slow at the moment, but I'm sure I can get you a decent price. How much are you thinking of asking?'

Katie's father smiled and shook his head. 'That's not what I was going to announce. I'm not selling up. I've been living in this house too long to think of moving, and it has too many memories for me. Of you, of your mother.'

'Then *what*?' demanded Moirin.

'*Moirin*,' said Katie. 'Let the poor man get a word in edgeways!'

Katie's father raised his glass and turned to Ailish, laying his hand on her shoulder. 'My announcement is – Ailish and me, we're going to be married.'

'Oh, *Dad*!' said Katie. 'That's wonderful! I can't believe it! You're actually going to get married? When?'

'Well done, sir,' said John, lifting his glass. 'You two guys deserve each other.'

Siobhán said, 'What's happening? Why is everybody so excited?'

'Dad's going to get married to Ailish,' said Moirin. 'You're going to have a new mummy now.'

'But I don't want a new mummy! I want my proper mummy!'

'Siobhán, darling, I'm not going to be taking the place of your proper mummy,' said Ailish. 'Nobody could ever do that. It's just that your dad and I love each other, and we want to spend the rest of our lives living together, as husband and wife.'

Moirin put her arms around Siobhán and hugged her. 'It's all right, sweetie,' she said. 'Don't get yourself upset.' Then she turned to her father and said, 'You could have broken it to her gently, for the love of God. Springing it on her like that! You could have broken it gently to *all* of us!'

'Moirin,' said her father, 'I thought you might be pleased for us.'

'Well, it's very plain that *you're* pleased, you and Ailish, but what about your daughters, the daughters you had with your previous wife, who you say that you miss so much?'

'Moirin,' said Katie. 'Will you shut your mouth for once? Dad's happy, and that's what's important, not what *you* think. Don't you dare spoil this for him. Come on, raise your glass for him and Ailish, and let's wish them well.'

'You seriously expect me to drink a toast to us losing our inheritance?'

'*What*? What inheritance? What are you talking about,

Moirin? Dad's found somebody to look after him, somebody he loves very much, and he's smiling again. Aren't you pleased about that?'

'What do you mean, "what inheritance?"' said Moirin. Siobhán was sobbing now, and making whooping-cough noises whenever she breathed in. 'What do you think will happen when Dad passes away? Who do you think this house will go to? It won't be *us*, will it? It won't be sold off and divided between his daughters, will it? Oh no, because there'll be a new owner, Dad's not-so-grieving widow, and who knows how much longer she's going to live here, and who she'll pass it on to when she goes, and who knows when that will be?'

Katie's father put down his glass of champagne. 'How can you say such a thing, Moirin? Is that what you really believe – that when I die I'm going to leave you nothing? I invited you here today to share my new life, not to squabble about my death.'

'Then deny it, Dad,' Moirin challenged him. 'Deny that you'll bequeath this house to Ailish when you die. What's it worth, Kevin, this house, even at today's values?'

'Four hundred and twenty-five thousand, easy,' said Kevin.

Katie stood up and went over to her father. He was staring at Moirin in disbelief and his jaw was working as if he had to finish chewing a piece of gristle before he was able to speak.

'Dad,' said Katie, and put her arm around him. Then she turned to Moirin and said, 'I think you'd better say sorry for that, don't you? How *could* you?'

'I'm supposed to be sorry for telling the truth?' Moirin retorted. 'Well, if I've told the truth, and you don't like the truth, then yes, I *am* sorry.'

'Get out,' said Katie's father.

'What?'

'I said, get out. Get out of my house, which is still my house, and which I can give to whoever I choose. Go on, get out, and take that harmless individual with you.'

'Dad, it doesn't have to come to this,' said Katie. 'For the love of God, Moirin, how could you speak to Dad like that?'

'Because he's going to marry his cleaning woman, that's why! Jesus! What if I'd come home one day and said I was going to marry the local road-sweeper? His cleaning woman! And she's going to inherit everything!'

Katie's father said, 'Get out, Moirin, before you make me say something I regret.'

'All right, fine, we're going,' said Moirin. 'Come on, Kevin. Come on, Siobhán. We know when we're not welcome.'

The three of them stood up and left, with Siobhán still sobbing. Moirin made sure that she slammed the front door hard behind her.

Katie's father sat down and he was shaking. Ailish was wiping the tears from her face with her apron.

Katie knelt down and took hold of her father's hands. He was still wearing the wedding ring from his marriage to Katie's mother.

'Don't be upset,' she told him. 'What you're doing, marrying Ailish, that's wonderful. You're both going to have such a good life together. Moirin's just one of those people who always makes the wrong choice and then regrets it. She thought Kevin was going to be rich and interesting, and he turned out to be hard-up and boring. She thought Nona was going to be beautiful and Tommy was going to be a genius. What happened? Nona has sticky-out ears and Tommy's dyslexic. I think she's been counting on her inheritance all her life to transform everything. Don't be too hard on her. She's just bitterly disappointed. I'll have a word with her when she's calmed down.'

Katie's father nodded in appreciation. 'You're a very tolerant woman, Kathleen. Very understanding. I never met a detective superintendent like you, not in all my years of service. Thank you.'

After lunch, John went into the kitchen to help Ailish wash the dishes and clear up, while Katie and her father sat together in the living room, finishing the Merlot they had drunk with their meal.

Katie told her father about Dermot O'Driscoll retiring, and about Bryan Molloy cancelling Operation Rocker. She also told him about the Angel of Revenge and her strong feeling that Mister Dessie was likely to be her next victim.

'You don't have any real proof of that, though?' he asked her.

'No, I don't. I may be barking up the wrong tree completely and she could have a different agenda altogether. It might be about drugs, or money. But she's Nigerian, and she's already murdered three of the scumbags who work in the sex trade for Michael Gerrety. It seems logical to me that she'll go for another one, and Mister Dessie is the biggest scumbag of the lot of them. Of course, I don't know for sure what her motive is, but since she calls herself the Angel of Revenge she's clearly paying them back for something they've done.'

Katie's father said, 'What you've told me about those two gardaí ... what did you say their names were?'

'Ronan Kelly and Billy Daly. I think they're weak and greedy rather than corrupt. They're not exactly the sharpest tools in the box.'

'Well ... I came across a few of those in my time. It's understandable. They're young men, not too well paid, and they're mixing all day every day with criminals who have flashy cars and willing women and money to burn. But ... can you really trust them to help you?'

'Kelly texted me about eleven last night to tell me that Mister Dessie was at Havana Brown's and then he texted me again at half past one to say that he had gone home to Togher with some girl. Admittedly, I haven't heard anything today, but that could be because Mister Dessie's still at home.'

Katie's father swirled his wine around his glass. 'If I were you, Katie, I'd be very wary of those two guards. I know you've told them that you'll speak up on their behalf if they cooperate with you to catch this Angel woman. But they're going to lose their jobs whatever they do, and they're going to be pretty sick about that, aren't they?'

'Don't worry yourself, Dad,' said Katie. 'I always keep my eyes wide open. What really concerns me at the moment is if I'm right not to alert Mister Dessie that he's likely to be next on the Angel's hit list.'

'Don't you think he might have worked that out for himself? He looks thick but there's no flies on Mister Dessie. I knew him when he was knee-high to a high knee and he was very, very cute, believe me.'

'Yes,' said Katie. 'But supposing Kelly and Daly don't keep me up to date with his movements, and the Angel manages to kill him, and I've done nothing at all to warn him?'

'If Mister Dessie does get himself murdered, why should you feel guilty? He chose the kind of life he's leading of his own free will and he's fully aware how dangerous it can be. I don't think there's anything morally wrong in using him as bait, especially when you're trying to apprehend a multiple murderer. Besides, the world wouldn't exactly be a worse place without Mister Dessie, would it?'

'I have to agree with you on that,' said Katie. 'But we're supposed to treat all people with equal respect, aren't we, no matter if they're saints or scobes?'

'That's what it says in the oath we took. But how can we be expected to respect people who don't respect themselves or anybody else? We can't, it's humanly impossible, and if we did it would make policing impossible, too. No, Katie, I think you should trust your intuition on this one.'

'So what do you recommend I do about Michael Gerrety?'

'Nothing, for the time being. If Bryan Molloy won't authorize Operation Rocker, the DPP will just have to go ahead with whatever evidence you already have.'

'I honestly don't think we have enough to guarantee that we'll get a conviction – especially if Gerrety gets to the witnesses, which he will. We'll just end up looking priggish and out of date and, worst of all, incompetent.'

'In that case, sweetheart, I would simply let it drop for now and bide my time. If Michael Gerrety comes to believe that he's above the law, he's going to overstep the mark one day, and then you'll have him.'

'I'm not so sure about that,' said Katie. 'He's a very careful man, Michael Gerrety. He has a keen understanding of public opinion, too. He knows which way the wind's blowing, especially when it comes to the sex trade.'

Katie's father took hold of her hand. 'I may not have reached your exalted rank in the Garda, Katie, but in all my years of service I learned one thing. Justice does have a tendency to get served, one way or another – sometimes in ways that you're not expecting at all.'

John came into the living room. 'You two ready for another glass of wine?'

'No more for me,' said Katie. 'I'm driving.'

'Oh yes, *and* you have my business proposal to read tonight, don't you? Come on, I'm starting work tomorrow. I really want to know what you think.'

'I promise you I'll read it this evening. Cross my heart and hope to die.'

'Crossing you heart will be enough, darling,' said John. 'Don't you dare to die.' He turned to Katie's father and said, 'The working title of my proposal is *Attracting Professional Endorsements for Online Medication.* I have to admit that I wouldn't want to read it, either, if I were her.'

Thirty

The following morning Katie and Detective Sergeant ó
Nuallán drove the thirty-five kilometres up to Mallow. It was
lashing with rain all the way up the N20, although it began
to clear when they turned into Cleary's garden centre.

They parked and walked up the steps that led to the office.
The garden centre had a row of eight large greenhouses, as
well as a long brick building that housed a cafe and shop.
Outside the shop rows of new wheelbarrows sparkled with
raindrops and there was a cluster of green-painted leprechauns. Although it was wet it was warm and there was a
strong fragrance of stocks in the air.

Colin Cleary was sitting in the reception area drinking
tea and smoking a cigarette. He was a bulky man, with
prickly grey hair and a face that looked as if an amateur
sculptor had tried to carve an Easter Island monument out
of beetroot and then stuck two bushy grey eyebrows on it.
He was wearing a chequered shirt with four buttons undone
so that the tangled grey hair from his chest was climbing
out of it.

'Can I help you ladies at all?' asked a spotty young receptionist. She was wearing a green overall with *Clearly Cleary's!*
embroidered on the pocket.

'It's Mr Cleary himself we've come to see,' said Katie. She

turned to Colin Cleary and said, 'It's been a while, Colin. What's the story?'

Colin Cleary frowned at her, blowing out a steady stream of smoke from the side of his mouth. Then he slapped his thigh and said, 'Feck me! There's one face I never thought I'd ever clap eyes on again! DI fecking Maguire!'

'Detective superintendent these days, Colin. That shows you how long it's been. This is Detective Sergeant ó Nuallán.'

'So what's the craic?' said Colin Cleary. 'I thought you was in Cork. Don't tell me they've demoted you to Mallow.'

'No, I'm still in Cork city,' Katie told him. 'Listen, I need to ask you a couple of questions in private, if that's okay with you.'

'Hey – I'm not growing nothing illegal here, DI Maguire. I mean, DS Maguire. You don't get much of a high from smoking hydrangeas.'

'It's not about the garden centre. Colin,' said Katie, and raised an eyebrow so that he could see that she was serious.

Without another word, Colin Cleary levered himself to his feet and beckoned Katie and Detective Sergeant ó Nuallán to follow him into his private office behind the reception area. When he closed the door, it was so cramped that there was barely room for the three of them. Most of the space was taken up by a large desk heaped with invoices and copies of the *Racing Post* and ripped-open envelopes, as well as a large black leather couch and a Star Galaxy pinball machine. The walls were cluttered with framed photographs of Colin Cleary with jockeys and racehorse owners from the Mallow racecourse.

'Now then, what can I do for you fair ladies?' he asked, taking another cigarette from a packet on the desk and lighting it. 'I might not be narrow these days, but I'm straight. I don't get involved with none of that political stuff no more.'

Detective Sergeant ó Nuallán took out her notebook and said, flatly, 'A Heizer Pocket Shotgun.'

Colin Cleary stared at her with one eye closed against the smoke from his cigarette. After a moment, he said, 'You got me, girl. Is that some kind of a riddle?'

'Let me tell you this, Colin,' said Katie, 'I'm not here looking to cause you any grief. Maybe they're not forgotten, but they're all in the past now – those shipments you arranged from Libya and all of that Semtex smuggling. What I urgently need today is some information to help me close three cases of murder, and I've been led to believe that you might have supplied the weapon that was used.'

'A Heizer Pocket Shotgun,' repeated Detective Sergeant ó Nuallán.

'Never heard of such a thing,' said Colin Cleary.

'Oh, come on, Colin, don't act innocent. I wouldn't have driven all the way up here to Mallow if my informant wasn't sound. He only told me on condition that I wouldn't press any charges against you.'

'They're very new, these pocket shotguns,' said Detective Sergeant ó Nuallán. 'I'm surprised you managed to get hold of one.'

'Nothing's difficult if you know the right people.'

'So you did get hold of one?'

'I might have done.'

'Maybe you got hold of more than one?'

'Aren't you straying off the point here, blondie? You came here to talk about the *one* gun, not several, so let's keep it that way.'

'So you did supply at least one?'

'Yes. It's conceivable.'

'When was this?'

'I'd say about three weeks since. But I'm only saying it's conceivable, not that I actually did it.'

'Well, purely for the sake of argument, let's suppose that you actually did,' said Katie. 'Who did you supply it to?'

'There was a young woman who turned up in a taxi just before we was closing up for the day. She was dark.'

'When you say "dark" ...?'

'I mean she was black. And she was *black* black. Black as the inside of an undertaker's undercrackers. But she was a looker, I'll give her that. Not like my fecking wife. If you think I've let meself go you should see Bridget. Holy Mary, Mother of God. These days I wouldn't climb on Bridget to hang wallpaper.'

'And this black girl, she asked you if you could supply her a handgun that was capable of firing shotgun shells?'

'She might have done, yes. She said she'd been given my name by a feller in Lagos I used to do a bit of business with. In fact, she showed me a note that he'd given her, to prove she was sound.'

'Did you ask her *why* she wanted this particular type of gun?'

'Are you codding? In all of my professional career I never once asked nobody what they wanted a weapon for. I supplied them, that's all. What they did with them, that was entirely their business. I'm not saying I was never political myself, but what you don't know can't break into your house and shake you awake at night.'

'All right,' said Detective Sergeant ó Nuallán. 'So what did you arrange to do?'

'She said she'd heard of the Taurus Judge, which is a large revolver which takes shotgun shells. I handled a few of them in my time and they're great guns but they're fecking enormous.

Even with only the three-inch barrel they weigh about eight hundred grams, and there was nothing of her. They do a lightweight alloy version, but the recoil from that would have knocked her into the middle of next week. That's when I might have suggested the Heizer. I didn't actually have one in stock, like, but I could get my hands on one in just a couple of days, with ammunition.'

'How much did you ask for it?'

'Seven hundred yoyos, cash.'

'Can you describe her?' asked Katie.

Colin Carey let smoke dribble out of his mouth and up his nostrils. 'I don't have to, do I? There's been pictures of her on the fecking telebox three times a day.'

'And it never occurred to you to get in touch with us and tell us that you'd sold her a gun?'

'Like I told you, DS Maguire, whatever I supply a customer with, I never ask them what they intend to do with it. I don't do it here, at the garden centre. I don't say, excuse me, cove, but you're not thinking of putting them two leprechauns in some kind of compromising sexual position, are you? I never did it when it came to armaments, neither, even if I happened to find out later what they'd been used for. I have me principles.'

'Colin, you missed your calling,' said Katie. 'You should have been a priest.'

'Maybe you're right. These days, even some of them young boys look more appetizing than my Bridget.'

'Did she give you her name?' asked Detective Sergeant ó Nuallán.

'She gave me a number to call when the gun was ready for her to collect. She said if somebody else answered but her, I should ask to speak to the girl in number three.'

'Do you still have the number?'

Colin Cleary leaned forward and made a desultory effort to look for it, lifting up two or three letters and a copy of the *Racing Post* from his paper-strewn desk, but then he sat back and shook his head. 'No, I doubt it. It was a Cork number, I remember that much. But that's all.'

'And who did answer, when you called?'

'Some old boy. He didn't give a name.'

'Can we go through your recent phone records?' asked Katie.

'I don't think so, DS Maguire. Not without a court order, like. And if you asked for a court order, the judge would want to know for what purpose, wouldn't he?'

'We would ignore all of the other numbers except for that one, even if they belonged to al-Qaeda. I give you my word on that.'

'You might give me your word now, but you'd still have all of them numbers in your possession, and one day one of them numbers might tally with some other number that you've been investigating, and then what? No, I'm sorry. I'm not saying I don't trust you, but I don't trust any wabboo and I've run me mouth off far too much already.'

'Very well,' said Katie. She stood up and waved Colin Cleary's cigarette smoke away from her face. 'Thanks a million anyway for what you've given us. You won't be hearing any more about it. On the other hand, I don't want to find out that you've been trading any more weapons illegally, because then I might be round here again, and I won't be looking to buy any fornicating leprechauns.'

'May trouble follow you all of your life, DS Maguire,' said Colin Cleary. The usual ending to that benediction was 'and may it never catch up', but Colin Cleary said nothing more, only smiled and blew out more smoke.

* * *

They climbed back into the silver Mondeo that they had taken from the car pool that morning, with Detective Sergeant ó Nuallán driving.

'I'd quite like one of those leprechauns,' said Detective Sergeant ó Nuallán. 'I could stand him in my window box, looking in, and pretend he was a peeping Tom.'

'I don't think your boyfriend would appreciate that very much,' said Katie.

'I don't have a boyfriend.'

'Oh, I'm sorry. I saw you talking to some young man outside the station the other day and giving him a kiss and I just assumed. I must stop jumping to conclusions. It's not like me at all.'

'That was my brother Liam. He came down from Wicklow for a few days to visit me. He's a darling.'

She started the engine and they drove out of the garden centre. As they did so, Katie turned around in her seat and said, 'I want you to get a court order to go through Colin Cleary's recent phone records as soon as we get back to the city.'

'Really? On what grounds?'

'On the grounds that he sold a weapon illegally which we suspect was used in the commission of three homicides, and which we also suspect may be used to commit even more.'

'Oh. Okay.'

'You're thinking that I'll be breaking my promise not to take this any further?'

'Well, yes.' It had started to rain again and Detective Sergeant ó Nuallán switched on the windscreen wipers.

'Well, don't worry about that. Three men have been unlawfully killed and no matter what trash they were, no Angel of Revenge had the right to take their lives, and that's all that matters. I'm not going to charge Colin Cleary with any offence, but he who lives by the gun has to understand that he can just as easily die by the gun.'

As they joined the N20 again, her mobile phone played 'The Wild Rover'. It was Garda Ronan Kelly.

'Your man left his house about fifteen minutes ago. He drove to Washington Street almost opposite the courthouse. He's entered an address there and it's one we suspect of being a brothel.'

'Are you there now?'

'Yes, we're parked in Cross Street, but we won't be able to stay here. There's been some kind of incident in the Paul Street shopping centre and we've been called to attend that.'

'That's all right. See if you can drive past later and check if Mister Dessie's car is still there. I'm just on my way back from Mallow at the moment, I'll be there myself in twenty minutes tops.'

'What are you going to do?' asked Detective Sergeant ó Nuallán.

'I'm not sure yet, but I'll get Horgan and Dooley to go round there now and keep an eye on the place until I get there. Once you've dropped me off, you can go back to the station and get that application for a court order in motion. You have all the information you need, don't you?'

Detective Sergeant ó Nuallán looked across at her. It was barely raining at all now and the windscreen wipers were making a squeaky, rubbery noise. 'You'll be careful, won't you?'

Katie was busy prodding at her mobile phone. 'What? Yes, of course I'll be careful.'

'She's armed, don't forget that.'

'I know. But so am I. And she only has the one shot, while I have six.'

Katie had the feeling that Detective Sergeant ó Nuallán was going to say something else, but she didn't. The sun suddenly came out and the car was filled with light.

Thirty-one

Zakiyyah's sleep was disturbed by the sound of her bedroom door being opened and then closed again. She lifted her head from the velveteen pillow and frowned around the room, but there was nobody there. Mairead must have just looked in to see if she was awake. The sun was shining outside, but she was exhausted and she let her head fall back down. She was aching all over and she felt so sore between her legs that she didn't even want to touch herself there. She knew that she smelled of stale sweat and rubber and semen and some strong musky aftershave that her last client had been reeking of, but she felt too weak to get up and take a bath.

She closed her eyes. Outside her door she could hear Mairead clattering in the kitchen, and Lotus Blossom talking in her sing-song voice. Lotus Blossom never seemed to stop talking, except when she had a customer in her room, and even then Zakiyyah had heard her chattering and giggling.

She could hear a man's voice, too, mumbling like faraway thunder, but she couldn't make out what he was saying.

She fell asleep and dreamed that she was sitting in her mother's kitchen at home, while her mother was rolling out *funkaso*, millet pancakes. She was trying to tell her mother that she needed to stay at home for a while, but her mother didn't seem to be listening and just kept on singing.

It was then that she was woken up again by the sound of her door opening. She raised her head again and rubbed her eyes and blurrily saw that a large man was standing in the open doorway. She sat up and said, 'I am so sorry, sir. What time is it? I had a very late night. Please come in.'

'State of you, la,' said the man. 'And you supposed to be seductive, like. Feck's sake. You look like something the dog's dragged in.'

Zakiyyah blinked and focused her eyes and saw that the man was Mister Dessie. He was wearing a short-sleeved white shirt and a jazzy purple tie, and chinos. His hands were thrust deep into his pockets and he seemed to be playing with himself.

'I am sorry, Mister Dessie. I was very tired and needed some sleep. My last customer did not leave until five o'clock.'

Mister Dessie came into the bedroom and closed the door behind him. 'That's nothing at all to be complaining about. The very opposite, in fact. That shows you're pulling the punters in, and if you're pulling the punters in you're earning the money, aren't you, girl, and that means you'll be paying us off all the sooner.'

Zakiyyah was wearing nothing but an orange T-shirt with a picture of a tiger's head on it, which she had borrowed from Lotus Blossom. She hugged herself and bent forward with her thighs closely pressed together. She didn't like the way that Mister Dessie was looking down at her and fiddling even more ostentatiously inside the front of his trousers.

'You know that part of my job is, like, quality control,' he told her.

She looked up at him. He was standing in front of the window and all that she could see was his silhouette. 'I do not understand.'

'It's simple. It's the same as the quality control like they do in the supermarket – making sure that all of the produce is up to scratch. What I do is, I go around all of the girls for Mr Gerrety and check that they're giving the punters value for money.'

'My customers all said I gave them pleasure. One of them said the very best ever.'

'Well, I'm delighted about that, darling. And you made a shitload of money yesterday, let me tell you – nearly eight hundred out of only seven punters. At this rate you'll be getting your suitcase back before you know it.'

Zakiyyah said nothing. All she wanted was her rabies shot, and then for Mister Dessie to leave so that she could go and have a bath. She wasn't sure what time it was, but Mairead had told her she had a customer booked for 2.30 p.m. and then another about half an hour afterwards, and she knew that there would be more after that, all evening and most of the night. She had heard the phone warbling constantly as customers made bookings from the Cork Fantasy Girls website.

She felt hungry, too, although she wasn't sure that she would be able to eat anything after her experiences last night. Just thinking about some of things that she had done made her stomach tighten.

Mister Dessie took off his tie and unbuttoned his shirt, baring his pallid, mole-speckled paunch.

Zakiyyah looked up at him and said, 'What are you doing?'

'*You*, darling. That's what I'm doing. I'm just checking that you're giving our valued punters the kind of satisfaction they expect. After all, we have our reputation to think of. We don't want our punters logging on to the internet and saying that our girls are shite, do we?'

He prised off his tan suede loafers and then unbuckled his belt and dropped his chinos, pushing them off with his feet and kicking them across the floor. Now he was wearing nothing but pale blue Marks & Spencer's briefs.

'There you are, girl. I'll let you take these off for me.'

Zakiyyah looked at the angular swelling of his erection. Bile rose up in the back of her throat and she had to cover her mouth with her hand. Mister Dessie smelled of sweat and fenugreek, and she could guess that he had been out for a curry last night.

'Come on, then, I haven't got the whole fecking day.'

She saw her hands rise up in front of her as if they were somebody else's hands, and take hold of the waistband of Mister Dessie's underpants. Those unrelated hands pulled the waistband downwards, over his white, cellulite-dimpled thighs, and down to his knees. Now his reddened penis stuck up in front of her, with a crumpled scrotum and thick black pubic hair. She could faintly smell urine and Savlon antiseptic cream.

'How about a gobble to start with?' he said, resting his hands on his hips.

'You must put on a condom,' said Zakiyyah.

'Don't worry about that. The punters have to wear condoms because you don't know where they've been, or what they've been dipping their wicks into. But me, I'm family, and I'm FSAI certified. Besides, I like to see a girl swallow. What's the point of a gobble if the girl doesn't swallow?'

Zakiyyah saw her hand take hold of Mister Dessie's penis and she shuffled herself nearer to him. As she did so, she glanced down and saw that he was still wearing his white socks. Mairead had told her that some Cork men wore white socks to show that they were IRA, or Republican sympathizers anyway. She found herself staring at his crimson glans and wondering how her life had possibly come to this. White socks, red penis. It was like some absurd nightmare. She closed her eyes and opened her mouth and leaned forward with her tongue sticking out.

There was a sharp rattle of curtain rings, and then a woman's voice said, 'Stop. Leave go of him.'

Zakiyyah opened her eyes. A slim young black woman all dressed in black had stepped out from behind the curtain where she hung her clothes. She had a red scarf tied around her hair and she was wearing a necklace made of seashells and animals' teeth and claws. She was holding a small gun in both hands, and pointing it at Mister Dessie.

'What in the *name* of Jesus?' said Mister Dessie. He reached down to grab his briefs, which were still around his knees, but the woman snapped, '*No* ... do not pull up your pants. Take them off.'

Mister Dessie hesitated, but the woman took a step towards him and aimed the gun directly between his legs. 'Take them off, or you will never need to wear them ever again.'

Mister Dessie slowly removed his briefs, lifting one leg at a time. His penis was already drooping and even his scrotum had shrunk, as if his testicles were trying to hide themselves inside him.

'I *seen* you,' said Mister Dessie. 'I seen you on the TV news. It's you, isn't it? You're the one killed Kola and that dumb-arse Romanian gom.'

'Sit on the bed,' said the woman.

'Oh yeah? And what are you going to do about it if I don't?'

'I will make a woman of you. How would you like that? I will blow off your manhood and then everybody will have to call you "Miss Dessie".'

'How the feck do you know my name?'

'I know all of your names. I know all of you. Mawakiya, Mânios Dumitrescu, the one they call Bula, you, and Michael Gerrety. The others, too, who run your sex business, Bobby Devlin and Patrick O'Halloran and Razvy Cojocaru, but I am not concerned with them. Now, do what I tell you and sit down on the bed.'

Mister Dessie reluctantly sat down, keeping both hands cupped underneath his belly. 'Don't think for one moment you're going to get away with this, you bitch.'

'Why? What will you do? Send Bula after me?'

'That would be a start. Bula could fecking tear you limb from limb.'

'I do not think so, Mister Dessie, because I did it to him first. The dead man who was found in Mutton Lane on Saturday? That was Bula.'

Mister Dessie stared at her and his eyes looked even more bulbous. 'That was Bula? Are you messing with me?'

'No, that was Bula. Have you heard from him since Saturday?'

'You fecking killed Bula?'

'He cried before he died. He cried, and before I shot him in the face he asked for his mother.'

The woman beckoned to Zakiyyah and said, 'What is your name?'

'Zakiyyah.'

'Very well, Zakiyyah. You should go now and wash yourself. Take your clothes with you and get dressed in the bathroom. Do not come back into this room. Wait for me in the living room and I will come and get you when I have finished with Mister Dessie.'

'I don't know what the feck you have in mind,' said Mister Dessie. 'Whatever it is, you're not going to get away with it.'

From the hook behind the curtain, Zakiyyah quickly took down the only dress she had, which was light green with red roses on it, and out of the cardboard box on the floor beneath it she took a clean pair of white knickers. She had no bras and she had no shoes. Mairead had taken her only pair of shoes away from her. 'You're never going anywhere, girl. What do you need shoes for?'

Zakiyyah padded barefoot along the corridor to the bathroom. Before she closed the bedroom door behind her, the woman took the key out of the outside of the door and locked it from the inside, all the time keeping her gun pointing at Mister Dessie.

'This is fecking ridiculous,' said Mister Dessie. 'I don't know what we've all done to vex you so much, but we must be able to work something out.'

'You could bring my younger sister back to life.'

'What?'

'My younger sister Nwaha. You and your friends, you took my younger sister and you made her a prostitute. You hurt her, but most of all, you shamed her, and she could not bear that shame, which was why she took her own life.'

'I never even heard of any fecking Nwaha. You can't blame me.'

'She was a beautiful girl with tattoos of flowers on her hands. You made her do what you wanted to do to Zakiyyah. You made her swallow.'

'Feck's sake. That's – that's what sex is all about, isn't it?

Men shoot and women swallow. That's what makes men men and women women.'

'Well, you are soon going to find out what makes women women. This gun is small but it is loaded with a shotgun shell and when I shoot you, you will have nothing left between your legs but rags. You make jokes about women with rags. Now you can find out what it is like.'

Mister Dessie started to stand up but the woman straightened her arm to make it clear to him that she would pull the trigger if he tried to attack her, and he quickly sat down again.

'What do you want, then?' he asked her. He was beginning to sweat badly and the perspiration was sliding down his sides from under his arms.

'I am *Rama Mala'ika*, which means Avenging Angel. I want revenge for my sister. You cannot make me believe that you do not remember her.'

'Yes, well, maybe I do. Flowery tattoos on her hands. Yes. I didn't know what her real name was. She was Desiray on the website. Look – I'm dead sorry that she killed herself. We try our best to look after the girls, like. Michael Gerrety insists on it. We put a roof over their heads and we feed them. They get protection from any punters who are langered, or abusive, or psychos. We supply them with condoms and we make sure that they get regular medical check-ups. There's always going to be some girls who go on the game, that's the way of the world. If you can't stop them, at least take care of them, that's Michael Gerrety's motto.'

'My sister Nwaha never wanted to be a prostitute. She wanted to be an artist.'

'What more can I say to you? I'm sorry. I've heard that

you accept compensation in Africa, don't you, if somebody accidentally kills a member of your family, like runs them over or something? How about it? I can pay you. I can pay you thousands. I have cash on me now.'

The woman shook her head. 'Life is not all about money, Mister Dessie. Whatever you think, people cannot be bought and sold.'

Mister Dessie found it impossible to read her expression. She was unnervingly beautiful, so beautiful that she hardly looked human – as if she had been carved out of ebony and then polished and polished until her skin shone. Her eyes were heavily lidded and her lips were slightly pouting, but her face gave absolutely nothing away. Nothing that he could understand, anyway.

'I will take another part of your body, if you do not wish to lose your manhood. But you will have to give it to me voluntarily.'

'Name of Jesus, what the feck are you talking about? What part of my body?'

'Your left hand,' she said.

Mister Dessie held up his left hand and stared at it as if he had never realized he had one. 'My left hand? What? I don't understand you.'

'I want you to cut off your left hand and give it to me. If you do that, I will not turn you into a woman.'

Up until now, Mister Dessie hadn't noticed the metal hacksaw handle protruding from the right-hand pocket of her leather waistcoat, but now she lifted it out and held it out to him.

'You're asking me to cut my own hand off? Serious?'

'You do not have to. I can always shoot you now and get it over with. It depends how you wish to live the rest of

315

your life. With only one hand, or as a eunuch. It is no worse than the choice that you offered my sister.

Mister Dessie looked at the hacksaw and licked his red rubbery lips.

'I will give you five seconds to make up your mind,' the woman told him. 'One ...'

'How long's he been in there now?' asked Katie.

'Over an hour,' said Detective Horgan. He checked the clock on the instrument panel. 'And ... yes! ... I'm happy to say that he's overstayed his time on his parking meter by seven minutes. I can call traffic if you like and have them come around to give him a ticket.'

'Don't bother,' said Katie. 'I don't want him to get any inkling at all that he's under surveillance.'

'Fancy a sweet, ma'am?' said Detective Dooley, turning around to offer Katie an open bag of Emerald Caramels.

'Not while I'm on duty.'

'Oh.'

'For goodness' sake, I'm only joking. You can have one yourself. Those things always stick to my teeth.'

A patrol car pulled up close behind them and Garda Ronan Kelly climbed out and walked up to them. Katie put down her window and said, 'So – what's the story?'

'Nothing much. A bunch of knackers were trying to hobble bottles of booze from Tesco's and then putting up a fight about it when they were caught. Cautions, no arrests. Don't want to be accused of discrimination against the Travelling community, do we? Thieving bastards.'

'Mister Dessie hasn't reappeared yet,' said Katie.

Garda Kelly checked his watch. 'That's queer. This time of day he's always on his rounds, collecting the takings. He usually spends no more than five minutes at each of the knocking shops, and then he's straight back to Amber's.'

Katie was tempted to say, *I'm glad you're so well-acquainted with the daily routine of Michael Gerrety's messenger-boy*, but she didn't want Horgan and Dooley to catch any hint that Ronan Kelly and Billy Daly had been much friendlier to Mister Dessie than they should have been.

She climbed out of the back seat of the car and took Garda Kelly to one side, next to the courthouse steps. 'Why don't you give Mister Dessie a call, see what he's up to? You can think of some reason, can't you, like you'll meet him for a drink later, something like that, because you've got something important to tell him.'

'Supposing he says yes? What have I got that's important to tell him?'

'You can tell him that the body that was found in Mutton Lane was Bula. It hasn't been confirmed yet officially, but I don't mind him knowing. That's if he hasn't guessed already.'

Garda Kelly took out his mobile phone and rang Mister Dessie. He waited and waited, but there was no reply. He tried again, but this time Mister Dessie's phone was switched off.

'He's not answering.'

'He doesn't know that you've been tracking his movements?'

'No, I doubt that. We've been dead careful. And the times we've talked, he's been sounding normal. Not suspicious, like. Billy was on the phone to him only this morning.'

Katie shaded her eyes to peer at the rust-coloured building across the street. All of the top floor windows were covered with net curtains, so it was impossible to see who was inside, or what they might be doing.

'He still hasn't come out,' she said. 'Maybe I'll go in and see what he's up to.'

'They'll reck you, won't they? Then you'll have to explain what you're doing there, and that's going to let the cat out of the bag.'

'Not necessarily. All I have to say to him is that I want to ask him a few questions about Bula. I don't have to say anything about the Angel of Revenge being after him.'

She looked back across the street. 'Besides,' she said, 'now that Molloy has pulled the plug on Operation Rocker, I'd like to take a lamp inside and see what kind of a set-up Michael Gerrety's got in there. All of his brothels that I've seen so far are scruffy and smelly. So much for treating his sex workers like royalty.'

Garda Kelly said, 'We're keeping our side of the bargain, me and Billy.'

'Yes, you are,' said Katie, 'and I appreciate it.'

'If you collar this woman, like, and it's because of our assistance, would you maybe see your way clear to forgetting our association with Mister Dessie?'

'You mean, would I not report that you and Billy took bribes from Michael Gerrety?'

Garda Kelly looked away, down Washington Street. 'That's about the shape of it, yeah.'

'I've told you that I'll speak up on your behalf, and I will.'

'But you'll still report us?'

'Mawakiya was prostituting thirteen-year-old girls, Ronan, and you and Billy knew it, and you took money to turn a blind eye. How can I possibly not report you?'

Garda Kelly looked back and stared at her, his thin lips tightly pursed. 'Okay,' he said, after a moment. 'Message received and understood.' Then he walked back to his patrol car.

Katie went back to Detectives Horgan and Moody. 'I'm going to try to get inside,' she said. 'I'll give you a shout if I run into any problems.'

'Wouldn't it be better if I went?' asked Detective Horgan. 'I could make out I was a punter.'

'I think this needs a woman's approach,' said Katie. 'Besides, I don't trust you. You'd be playing the part of a punter with a bit too much enthusiasm.'

She crossed the street and went up to the brothel's front door. She was about to ring the bell when a moped stopped at the kerb beside her and a Domino's pizza delivery boy climbed off it. He took his bag of pizzas off the rack at the back of the moped and came straight up to the door and pressed the bell.

'Who is it?' asked a disembodied voice from the intercom.

'Domino's. Got your pizzas.'

The door buzzed open. The boy pushed his way inside and Katie followed him.

Thirty-two

Mister Dessie held up the hacksaw and said, 'I can't.'

'You can't? Why?' said the woman. 'Are you afraid of the pain?'

'It's just not fecking natural to cut your own fecking hand off.'

'Are you worried that you're going to cry, like Bula cried, and ask for your mother? "Mama!" That's what Bula said, "Mama, help me!"'

'You leave my mother out of this,' said Mister Dessie.

'Oh, you think your mother would be proud of you? Look at you! Look at what you have become! You are fat, and you are ugly, and you have no soul! I wanted to make sure that you would not be accepted in heaven, but I think you have already done that yourself.'

'I said to leave my mother out of this, didn't I? My mother was a saint. Brought us up all on her own, all five of us.'

'Do *you* have children?'

'Not yet, no.'

'Unless you cut off your hand, you will never be able to. I have counted to five and you have not yet started to cut, so I am going to shoot you between your legs.'

Mister Dessie laid his hand on the bedside table and then closed his eyes. '*Saint Anthony, consoler of all the afflicted, pray for me,*' he whispered. '*Saint Anthony, whom the infant Jesus loved and honoured so much, pray for me. Amen.*'

'Are you ready now?' the woman asked him.

Without opening his eyes, he dragged the hacksaw across his wrist. It made a rasping sound as it tore through his skin and dark red blood welled up immediately.

'Shit, Christ, shit, that hurts!' he said, clenching his teeth. He sat there, panting, and at last he opened his eyes and looked at what he had done.

'That hurts too much. I can't do it. That hurts too fecking much.'

'Here,' said the woman. There was a dog-eared guidebook to Cork city on the window sill. She held it out in front of his face and said, 'Bite on this. Then you won't scream or cry out for mama.'

He stared at her with utter hatred, but she continued to hold out the guidebook as if she were prepared to wait all day. Eventually he leaned his head forward and gripped it in between his teeth.

'Now,' she said. 'Be strong, Mister Dessie! You're a strong man, aren't you? Show me what you can do!'

Mister Dessie pulled the hacksaw back, and then pushed it forward. He was biting so hard on the guidebook that he almost bit right through it, and his eyes filled with tears. He stopped for a few seconds, his belly rising and falling as if he were bobbing in the sea. Suddenly, though, he seemed to be possessed by a terrible rage and he started to saw at his wrist with such fury that blood sprayed up the wallpaper and even spattered the window.

It took him less than half a minute to cut through his wrist. His hand dropped on to the carpet with a soft thud.

He tossed the hacksaw to one side and fell back on to the bed, shaking, his amputated wrist held up in the air. He was smothered in blood and he was angrily tearing shreds of guidebook pages out of his mouth.

The women bent down and picked up the hacksaw. She wiped the handle on the curtains and then stood by the bed for a while, watching Mister Dessie waving his bloodied stump around and spitting out paper. Her expression was completely dispassionate, but her lips were moving slightly as if she, too, were saying a prayer – but a prayer of thanks.

It was then she heard a rapping at the door.

'Mister Dessie? Mister Dessie, are you in there?'

Mairead turned to Katie and said, 'I shouldn't really be disturbing him.'

'He won't be asleep, will he?'

'Well, no, but he'll be likely giving Zakky a bit of a pep talk. She's just started here, you know, and he'll be showing her the ropes.'

'The ropes? I bet he will. Do you want to give him another knock? I really need to talk to him.'

Mairead wrapped her gold robe tighter around herself as if she was going to need its protection when an angry Mister Dessie opened the door and demanded to know what she wanted. On the other hand, Katie had shown Mairead her ID after she had come upstairs behind the Domino's delivery boy, and Mairead was equally afraid of her, and of Michael Gerrety, too. If Himself found out that she had let the Garda into the flat without a warrant, then she would be lucky if all she suffered was some bruises and her nipples twisted and a couple of broken ribs.

'Mister Dessie! I'm sorry to be disturbing you, Mister

Dessie, but there's a lady Garda officer out here wants to have a word with you urgent-like.'

Mairead tried the door handle, and rattled it, but it was locked. 'It's never locked, not usually,' she told Katie, and her voice was becoming increasingly panicky. 'It's the health and safety regulations, you know. And the fire hazard, like. And in case there's any trouble. Not that we have any trouble here, don't be thinking that.'

She knocked again and called out, 'Mister Dessie! Zakky! Zakky, would you open the door, would you, girl? I've got the guards out here! Zakky!'

There was still no answer from inside the bedroom. At that moment, however, the bathroom door opened just behind them and Zakiyyah appeared in her orange tiger's head T-shirt with a towel wrapped around her head.

'Did you want me, Mairead?'

Mairead stared at Katie and then turned around and stared at the locked bedroom door. Then she turned back and stared at Zakiyyah.

'Your room's locked and I've been knocking but I can't get an answer. I thought you were in there with Mister Dessie. Is Mister Dessie still in there?'

Zakiyyah nodded. Katie went up to her and put her hand on her shoulder. 'Zakky? Is that your name?'

'Zakiyyah. But they call me Zakky.'

'What's going on here, Zakiyyah? Is Mister Dessie in your bedroom?'

Zakiyyah nodded again.

'What's he doing in there, Zakiyyah? Mairead here thought he was in there with you.'

Zakiyyah's bottom lip began to tremble and two large tears rolled down her cheeks.

323

'There's no need for you to be upset, Zakiyyah. I'm a Garda officer, police. I'll look after you. Just tell me what Mister Dessie is doing.'

'For the love of God, Zakky!' snapped Mairead. 'Just fecking tell us, will you?'

'Mairead,' Katie cautioned her. 'No need for that.'

Zakiyyah wiped her eyes with the corner of her towel and said, 'Mister Dessie came in to see me. I was asleep, but Mister Dessie woke me up.'

'All right, then what?' said Mairead. 'Holy Mary, Mother of God, you'd get more sense out of a plank of wood!'

'Go on, Zakiyyah,' said Katie, gently. 'Mister Dessie woke you up and what did he do after that?'

'He wanted a gobble. He said he wanted to make sure I was good at it.'

'Well I've heard some fecking lines,' said Mairead, shaking her head.

'Did you do it for him?' asked Katie.

Zakiyyah shook her head, so that her towel slipped. 'There was a lady in my room. She was hiding behind the curtain. She came out and she had a gun and she told Mister Dessie to stop.'

'There was a lady hiding in your room with a gun? What did she look like?'

'She was black, the same as me. She was wearing black clothes. She had a necklace that was all made of bones and things.'

'And you say she had a gun? What did the gun look like?'

Zakiyyah held up her two index fingers, only about four inches apart. 'Very small, like a toy gun. Only I don't think that it was a toy.'

'So she came out from behind the curtain and told Mister Dessie to stop. Then what happened?'

'The lady told me to get out of the room and to go and have a bath and put my dress on. So I did. Well, I've had a bath. I haven't put my dress on yet.'

'It didn't enter you head to come and tell me what was going on?' said Mairead. 'Jesus, girl! If you had two brains you'd be twice as stupid.'

'The woman said not to tell anyone,' said Zakiyyah. 'I didn't know what else to do.'

'Is there any other way out of that room?' Katie asked Mairead. 'Is there a fire escape, or a ladder, or a roof you can climb out on to?'

'There's a fire escape, but you couldn't get out of the window. The little fanlight opens, but Mister Dessie had the main window bolted shut because the girl in there before kept getting out and running away. Three times she done that. Chinese, she was, and always crying, too.'

'So – as far as we know, both Mister Dessie and the woman are still in there?'

'I'd say so, yes. They must be. There's nowhere else they could have gone to.'

Katie called Detective Horgan. 'It looks like Mister Dessie's still here, but our suspect could be here, too. It seems like she got into the flat somehow and was waiting for him to show up. She's locked in one of the bedrooms with him and according to a witness here she's armed with that shotgun pistol she used on the other three victims. We've tried knocking but there's no response so far.'

'What's the plan, then, ma'am?'

'Have Dooley go around to the rear of the building. Apparently there's a fire escape there that gives access to the bedroom window. The window's supposed to be bolted shut but she may try and break the glass and escape, especially since she can fire shotgun shells.

'Call for armed back-up and then you and Garda Kelly come up here. I'll have the front door opened for you.'

'Right you are, ma'am.'

'There's several girls up here, too. I'm not sure how many.'

'Four,' mouthed Mairead, putting up four fingers. 'That's including meself.'

'There's four girls and I'll be evacuating all of those immediately. Tell Garda Daly to take them to his patrol car, but call for a van to pick them up and take them to the station. Ask for two female guards to take care of them. And make sure they're treated with respect.'

'Yes, ma'am.'

By now Lotus Blossom had appeared at her bedroom door. 'What is happening out here?' she said crossly. 'I have a customer inside and all of this noise is putting him off.' She made a drooping gesture with her finger.

Elvira came out, too, wearing only a red and black corset with dangling suspenders. 'Mairead? What's going on?'

Katie turned to Mairead and said, 'I want all of you out of here now. If you're not decent throw something on as quick as you can and get out. Get your customer out, too.'

'But he has paid me one hundred and sixty euros already! It is for one hour special service!'

'Then give him a refund, or a voucher for next time. But get him out.'

Zakiyyah went into the bathroom and immediately came back out, struggling to get into her rose-patterned dress. Katie gave her a hand to tug it down and zipped up the back for her.

'Now, *go*,' she said. 'I don't want any of you getting hurt.'

Zakiyyah clung on to Katie's sleeve and said, in a low voice so that Mairead wouldn't hear her, 'Please – after this, will you help me? I don't want to come back here. Please.'

Katie gave her a quick, tight smile and nodded. 'Don't you worry. I'll see you back at the Garda station later. Stay there, and don't let anybody take you away. Nobody – not even anybody who says they've come from social services. Tell them you're not allowed to, because Superintendent Maguire wants to ask you some questions.'

'Superin—?'

'Just say Katie Maguire. Now, get out of here.'

A balding man in glasses came out of Lotus Blossom's room, zipping up his trousers. He glanced at Katie and Katie recognized him as a city councillor. She pretended not to have realized who he was and turned back towards Zakiyyah's bedroom.

Mairead was the last to leave. Before the door closed behind her, Katie could hear feet clattering up and down the three flights of stairs. Detective Horgan and Garda Kelly must be on their way. She lifted her nickel-plated Smith & Wesson revolver out of the holster attached to her belt and cautiously approached the bedroom door, holding the gun in both hands with the muzzle pointing upwards.

She listened intently, although she didn't press her ear against the door in case the woman suspected she was out there and fired a shot through it.

She was sure that she could hear a mewling noise. It sounded like a cat that wanted to be let in out of the rain. Then she heard a woman's voice, although she couldn't make out what she was saying.

Detective Horgan burst in through the door at the opposite end of the corridor, closely followed by Garda Kelly. At the same instant, Katie heard the key turning in the bedroom door and it was opened up wide. The young black woman was standing there, with her right arm held out straight. The sunlight was shining through the window behind her, so that Katie was momentarily dazzled.

'Stay there, do not move!' said the woman. 'You move, I shoot him!'

It was then that Katie saw that Mister Dessie was lying on the purple velveteen cover of the king-size bed, naked and white and fat, and smeared all over with blood. He was holding up both of his arms in the way that a drumming toy monkey holds up its arms, except that he couldn't have held any drumsticks because he had no hands. He was mewling and sniffing and occasionally coughing.

The woman had a black plastic bag tied to her belt. In her right hand, she was holding the small Heizer pistol that Colin Cleary had sold to her.

Katie pointed her revolver at her and said, 'Drop that weapon, please.'

The woman leaned sideways a little so that she could see down the corridor. Detective Horgan had stopped outside the bathroom door and taken out his SIG Sauer automatic.

'Has everybody else gone?' the woman asked.

'There's nobody here but you and us,' said Katie. 'Please drop the weapon. I don't want to have to shoot you.'

'Tell those two men to go into that side room and close the door.'

'I can't do that. They're Garda officers and they're here to carry out their duty.'

'If they come any closer, I will shoot Mister Dessie in the

head and kill him. I think you understand that I will do that without any hesitation.'

'You killed Mawakiya and Mânios Dumitrescu and Bula.'

'Yes, of course. I have their hands to prove it. I intend to kill all of them.'

'When you say "all of them" …?'

The woman's right arm didn't waver. 'Tell those two men to go into that side room and close the door. I will give them five seconds and then I will shoot.'

'You realize that if you do that I will have to shoot you.'

'That will not stop me from killing Mister Dessie, and then you will be responsible for his death.'

Katie said nothing for a moment. She looked towards the window, but there was no sign of Detective Dooley out there on the fire escape.

'One,' said the woman. Then, 'Two.'

Without turning around, Katie called back to Detective Horgan, 'Horgan? Can you two go into that bedroom, please, and close the door after you? I'll give you a shout when I need you. But call a white van. Mister Dessie's in here and he's hurt.'

'Ma'am?'

'It's all right. Nothing to worry about. We're having a little negotiation here, that's all.'

Detective Horgan and Garda Kelly looked at each other and both pulled faces, but Detective Horgan shrugged as if to say, *She's the boss*, and they both went into Lotus Blossom's bedroom. As soon as she heard them door close the door behind them, Katie said, 'Okay? What happens now?'

'You explain to me why you did not punish these men for what they did to my sister.'

'Well, I would if I could,' said Katie. 'But I have absolutely no idea at all who your sister is, or what these men are supposed to have done to her. I don't know who *you* are, for that matter.'

'My name is Obioma Oyinlola. My sister is dead. Her name was Nwaha, which in my language means "second-born girl". She was very beautiful and she was a very talented artist. She was not political like me.'

All the time she was talking, Mister Dessie was moaning, and gradually his moans were growing louder and longer and more agonized.

'Love of God—' he gasped. 'Love of God, what have you done to me?'

'We need to get this man to a hospital,' said Katie. She reached into her pocket and took out her iPhone.

'*No!*' said Obioma. 'If you so much as press one single number on that phone, I swear that I will shoot him with no hesitation.'

'I've already asked my officers to call for an ambulance. I just wanted to make sure one was on its way. He could die from loss of blood and then you'd be charged with four murders. You're looking at a life sentence as it is.'

'What did they give to my sister? That was more than a life sentence. They took her life away from her – everything that made her feel proud of herself, and womanly, and talented, and pure.'

'Tell me what happened then,' said Katie, much more quietly, although she kept her revolver pointed at Obioma's heart.

'My family comes from Lagos. My father was an English teacher at Lagoon Secondary School. We were two sisters and a brother, but my brother died when he was only five years old and because of that my sister and I became very close.'

'Love of God, help me!' groaned Mister Dessie. Obioma glanced at him briefly but then turned back to Katie.

'My sister and I loved each other, but we were always different. She was always sewing and painting while I was playing adventure games with boys. When I was seventeen I fell for a boy who was active with MEND, and that was when I became political.'

'MEND? What's MEND?'

'It is the Movement for the Emancipation of the Niger Delta. An armed force of activists, fighting against the government and greedy big oil companies. We believe they should be giving their profits to the poor and disadvantaged people of Nigeria instead of creaming them off for themselves. They have polluted our land and given us nothing.'

'Yes,' said Katie. 'Now you come to mention it, I've heard of them. But they've been responsible for all kinds of terrorist attacks, haven't they? Shootings and kidnappings and piracy and bombings.'

'It is the only way to make the government and those big monopolies listen to us. It was MEND who taught me to fight. But anyway, that is not why I am here. My sister is why I am here.'

'Go on.' Katie knew that the best chance of getting Obioma to give up her gun was to listen to this and then show understanding. She had once sat in Fitzgerald Park in a steady downpour for three and a half hours listening to a would-be building society robber with a sawn-off shotgun and an elderly woman hostage.

Obioma said, 'My sister showed some of her embroidery at an exhibition in Lagos and a man came up to her and said he ran a design studio in Italy and would she come to work with him? She would make very good money and might even become famous.

'She went, and that was the last we heard from her for

nearly a year. Then my mother and father received a long letter from her. She had managed to get a friend to send it for her. I suppose you could say it was a suicide note.'

For the first time, Katie saw some emotion on the woman's face. She tilted up her chin a little and breathed a little more deeply, but still her right arm remained steady. The muzzle of her pocket shotgun was only about three feet away from Mister Dessie's head and from that range and that angle she would blow three quarters of his face off with one shot. It was possible that he would survive it, but who would want to spend the rest of their life with no hands and only a quarter of a face?

'In this letter, my sister told us how she had been tricked and beaten and trafficked to Ireland. She listed everything that had been done to her, every act of rape and violence, and how her will had been broken. But she named every name. She named the man they called the Singer, Mawakiya. She named Mânios Dumitrescu. She named Bula. She named this man, Mister Dessie. She named them, and she described what they looked like, and she gave us the addresses where they lived.

'Two months later we were told that Nwaha had drowned herself in the river. Actually, she had drowned herself on the day after writing that letter, but it took the Irish authorities a long time to discover who she was.

'That was when I decided to come here and to be *Rama Mala'ika,* the Avenging Angel.'

'Well, I can understand your anger and your bitterness,' said Katie. 'But why didn't you simply bring your sister's letter to the Garda? We would have taken action if we had been given evidence like that.'

'Because I read everything I could find about those men,

and the sex business they run in Cork, and I saw that time and time again they had been brought in front of the courts and nothing had happened to them. Oh, they had sometimes been fined, or had some of their profits confiscated. But the men who drove my sister to kill herself deserved a much greater punishment than that. They deserved to suffer, and die, and then to go to hell.'

Katie could faintly hear sirens outside. It would only be a few minutes before an armed back-up team would be storming in here. There was still no sign of Detective Dooley on the fire escape outside and she could see this ending badly.

'Is Mister Dessie the last on your list?' she asked Obioma.

'Please,' slurred Mister Dessie, at the sound of his name. 'Love of God, help me. Please. I'm dying here. I can't stand the pain.'

'These four I have punished so far, they were only servants,' said Obioma. 'I have been saving the master until last. I wanted him to know *dread*! I wanted him to think, "When is this Avenging Angel coming to kill me?" Because he will know that I am after him. I will make sure of that.'

'Who are you talking about?' asked Katie. 'Who do you call "the master"?'

'Michael Gerrety, of course. I do not know why you even had to ask me. It was Michael Gerrety who made my sister a slave and a prostitute. It was Michael Gerrety who was responsible for her suicide, more than anybody. And do you think that the courts will ever punish him for it?'

Katie said, 'I'm sorry, Obioma, but this is all over. You won't be able to go after Michael Gerrety because I'm going to have to arrest you now on multiple charges of homicide. I can understand your motives, but nobody can take the law

333

into their own hands, no matter what their victims might have done.'

Obioma stared at Katie and Katie thought that she had never seen an expression like that on anybody's face, ever in her life. It sent a crawling sensation down her back. Obioma had become *Rama Mala'ika*. She *was* the Avenging Angel. This was what implacable anger looked like in the flesh.

'Please give me the weapon,' said Katie, holding out her hand and taking a step forward.

Obioma fired. The bang was so loud that it made Katie jump, and she almost fired herself as a spontaneous reaction. Mister Dessie's face burst open and he was instantly turned into a bright scarlet Elephant Man, with his cheeks and his forehead in bloody lumps.

He didn't cry out, because his mouth had vanished, but the shot hadn't killed him. He was bouncing from side to side on the bed and thrashing his arms around and making a gargling noise.

'Drop the weapon and put up your hands!' Katie told Obioma, and she was almost screaming with the shock.

Detective Horgan and Garda Kelly came jostling out of Lotus Blossom's bedroom and into the open doorway. Detective Horgan pointed his automatic at Obioma and cocked it.

'Jesus,' he said, when he saw Mister Dessie. 'We've called for a white van already. But Jesus.'

Katie approached Obioma, pointing her revolver at her heart. Obioma kept her eyes on her, but at the same time she reached into the pocket of her leather waistcoat and took out a black shotgun shell. She broke open her pistol, eased out the spent cartridge, and slid in the new one.

'I said drop the weapon,' said Katie. 'If I had followed my training, I would have shot you dead by now.'

Obioma raised one perfectly arched eyebrow. 'The choice is yours,' she said calmly. She raised the pocket shotgun and pointed it against her own right temple. 'I am going to walk away now. If you try to stop me, or shoot me, I will shoot myself. Then you will have to explain to your superiors and to your media how you allowed such a thing to happen. You shot a woman who was threatening not you, but herself? You will also lie awake at night and ask yourself the same question, over and over. You will never be able to forget me. I have killed men who had personally done me no harm, oil workers who were only doing their job, and I can still see them now.'

'Put the weapon down,' Katie repeated. 'I don't want to shoot you, but I will.'

'No, you will not,' said Obioma. 'I can read it in your face. And your colleague will not shoot me, either, because he does not want all the complications that will go with his shooting me when you would not.'

Katie said nothing, but she couldn't help thinking, *Whoever trained you in MEND, they trained you well. Not only do you know how to kill, but you know how to survive.* She knew from her own experience that the best way to escape from a dangerous situation was to take the riskiest option open to you.

Obioma took a step towards the door, and then another one, circling around Katie with the muzzle of the Heizer still pressed against her forehead. Detective Horgan looked at Katie as if to ask her if he should try to grab the gun and wrestle Obioma to the floor, but Katie shook her head. Obioma was right. If she blew her own brains out, the Garda would look reckless and incompetent – and unsympathetic, too, especially since she had been on a mission to avenge her dead sister and had killed only pimps and low life. It wouldn't help, either, that she was beautiful. *Gardaí Provoked 'Avenging Angel' To Shoot Herself.*

Obioma reached the door and Detective Horgan stood aside, while Garda Kelly retreated into the corridor.

Katie said, 'You are not going to get away with this, Obioma, I swear to God.'

'We will see,' said Obioma. 'All I want to do is punish those men who deserve punishment. Then you will never see me again.'

With that, she backed quickly along the corridor to the front door of the flat, opened it, and was gone.

Katie said to Detective Horgan, 'If any back-up's arrived and they see her coming out of the building, tell them to let her go and not to follow her. The last thing we want is her shooting herself in the street.'

She turned to Mister Dessie, who was lying still now and had stopped making guttural noises. His face was so hideously disfigured that she could hardly bear to look at it. There was nothing she could for him even if he wasn't dead, but he certainly looked dead.

'Mother of God, what a mess. Chase up that ambulance, can you? Jesus. I've made a bags of this, haven't I? I should have shot first and thought about the moral issues afterwards.'

'Back-up's just arrived, ma'am,' said Detective Horgan. 'They haven't reported anybody at all coming out of the building. The paramedics are here, too.'

'What happened to Dooley? He was supposed to come up the fire escape.'

'I don't know, ma'am. I've lost contact with him for some reason.' He looked at Katie seriously for a moment – very seriously for him – and then he said, 'I think you did the right thing, myself. Mister Dessie's nothing but a total shite and them other three shites were nothing but total shites. If you ask me, that girl has done us all a favour.'

'She said she was after Michael Gerrety next.'

'In that case, good luck to her. He's the biggest shite of the lot of them.'

There was knocking at the front door of the flat. Garda Kelly went to open it and two gardaí from the emergency response unit came in, wearing Kevlar vests and carrying Heckler & Koch assault rifles. They were followed by two cautious-looking paramedics.

'Better call the Technical Bureau, too,' Katie told Detective Horgan. 'Can you stay here? I'd better get back to the station and report this mess to Molloy.'

Detective Horgan was about to say something, but then he changed his mind. Katie laid a hand on his shoulder to show him that she understood.

One of the armed gardaí came out of the kitchen holding up a tan leather briefcase. 'I think I just won the lottery!' he said. 'There's thousands in here!'

Thirty-three

Acting Chief Superintendent Molloy sat back in his chair with his fingers steepled and listened to Katie's account of what had happened at Washington Street without interrupting her. When she had finished he said, 'You should have shot her first. You know that. We had some trouble with armed gangs in Limerick and that was the only way to deal with them. At one time we had the ERU exchanging fire with them like the gunfight at the O.K. Corral.'

'I'm ninety-nine per cent sure that she still would have shot Dessie even if I *had* shot her first,' said Katie. 'She's been trained by this organization called MEND, which is one of the most violent and well-armed groups of activists in the whole of Africa.'

Acting Chief Superintendent Molloy screwed his finger into his ear and then took it out and examined it. 'Under the circumstances, Katie, I have to admit that you probably followed the most sensible course of action. If that young woman had shot herself the PR complications would have been horrendous. As it is, we'll have to be very discreet about Dessie's death. I suggest we simply say to the media that he was discovered dead in a flat that he had been viewing, and that our perpetrator must have followed him there.'

'It's not just any old flat, Bryan,' said Katie. 'It's one of

Michael Gerrety's brothels, and the media are certain to know that. They'll also know that Dessie O'Leary was Michael Gerrety's right-hand man and that there's an obvious connection between all of these four homicides. We won't be able to suppress that side of the story. There's even some young trainee reporter on the *Echo* who's hot on Gerrety's trail. She never leaves me alone.'

'All right. That's as maybe. But I still want you to play this right down. Michael Gerrety is innocent until he's proved guilty, and to be perfectly honest with you, I don't believe he ever will be. I know that we're guardians of the law, but Ireland isn't a police state yet. There's live and let live.'

'Why don't you make a statement to the media?' said Katie. 'There's time to make it for the Six-One News.'

'No, no, that's all right, I have a meeting this evening. I'll let you handle it. Just make sure that you collar this Avenging Angel woman before she gets anywhere close to Michael Gerrety. And don't dilly-dally next time. You have every reason to suspect that she's armed, even if you can't actually see the gun. So shoot her on sight.'

'I've put out some new CCTV pictures of her. Somebody must know where she is. She's very distinctive-looking.'

'That's grand. And I've warned Michael Gerrety himself to watch out for her, and to be extra careful with his security.'

'You've *warned* him?'

Acting Chief Superintendent Molloy frowned at her. 'Of course I've warned him. That's the sensible thing to do, wouldn't you say, when a man has been targeted by a four-times murderer?'

'Absolutely,' said Katie. 'Of course it is.'

'Well, not only that, after what's happened today, I'll be

posting a couple of armed officers outside The Elysian, twenty-four hours a day, until we catch this woman.'

Katie left his office and stood in the corridor for a moment. She felt as if the floor were sliding underneath her feet. She was a senior Garda officer. It was her sworn duty to uphold the law. Yet when Acting Chief Superintendent Molloy had told her that he had warned Michael Gerrety about the threat to his life, and that he was going to post gardaí outside The Elysian to protect him, she had felt an unexpected surge of frustration. Anger, even. Katie wanted to see Obioma arrested and charged for murdering four men. But she also wanted to see Michael Gerrety punished, and she had a dark, dark feeling that if Obioma managed to kill him, real justice would have been done.

She walked back to her own office, opened her cupboard and studied her reflection in the mirror on the back of the door. She thought she looked reasonably attractive today, in spite of the shock that she had experienced in Washington Street. Her hair was glossy at last and behaving itself, and she liked her new smoky purple eyeshadow. She also thought that she looked surprisingly calm and unflappable, although she didn't feel calm at all. It's not my job to hate anybody – not thieves, not con men, not drug-dealers, not murderers, not pimps – so why do I hate Michael Gerrety with such intensity?

Out loud, she recited, 'I hereby solemnly and sincerely declare before God that I will faithfully discharge the duties of a member of An Garda Síochána with fairness, integrity, regard for human rights, diligence and impartiality, upholding the constitution and the law and according equal respect to all people including that dirtbag Michael Gerrety.'

She heard a light cough behind her and turned around. Detective Sergeant ó Nuallán was standing in the doorway.

'Oh. Kyna. Didn't hear you. Sorry.'

'That's all right,' said Detective Sergeant ó Nuallán, trying not to smile. 'Myself, I can never remember all of that attestation oath.'

'Not even that last bit about Michael Gerrety? Anyway, come on in. What have you got for me?'

'Colin Cleary's telephone call – the call that he made to inform our suspect that her pocket shotgun had arrived.'

'Brilliant. So you got your court order?'

'The judge gave it to me in less than half an hour and wasn't even particularly interested in why I wanted it. I think he'd had a heavy lunch. Eircom sent me a PDF of Cleary's phone bills with no messing at all. There were only two Cork city numbers that Cleary called just the once. One of them was Quinlan's, the Honda dealers out at Victoria Cross, but that was three weeks ago. The other number he called eight days since, which would tally with our suspect's first visit to Cleary and the time it took him to get hold of the gun for her.'

'Do you have an address?'

Detective Sergeant ó Nuallán handed Katie a torn-off page from her notebook. 'A house called *Sonas* on the Lower Glanmire Road, just east of the railway bridge. I Googled it and it's the last one on the terrace. I must say it looks awful dismal for a house called "Happiness". Grey paint, dirty net curtains. There's only the one phone number, but by the look of it it's divided into flats because there's three bell-pushes by the front door.'

'Good. That looks a likely place for Obioma to be hiding herself.'

'Obioma? That's her name?'

'That's what she told me, anyway. She told me her

surname, too, but I don't remember that. Oily-something. Or maybe I've got that mixed up in my head with what she told me about herself. She belongs to this armed activist group in Nigeria that's fighting the big oil companies, like Shell. Stealing their oil, blowing up their refineries, that kind of thing.'

'Lord lantern of Jesus. Serious?'

'That's what she told me, anyway.' Katie briefly described her encounter with Obioma. She told Detective Sergeant ó Nuallán how Obioma had shot Mister Dessie, and how she had allowed her to leave without trying to arrest her.

'... but if she's staying in this house on the Lower Glanmire Road, we should be able to detain her there tonight. And it should be no later than tonight. If she's determined to go after Michael Gerrety, the sooner we catch her the better.'

Detective Sergeant ó Nuallán gave Katie a sideways look when she said that. 'You mean Michael Gerrety the dirtbag?'

'That's the very one,' said Katie, without smiling. 'As soon as O'Donovan and Horgan get back, we'll sit down and work out our tactics. It's not going to be easy to keep a watch on the house before we go in there because that's a busy main road and you don't usually get people footering around on the pavement going nowhere. We could go house to house asking if any of the neighbours have seen her, but again there's a risk that she could see us. I think the best plan will be simply to go in there, two or three in the morning, wham, and if she's there, she's there, and if she isn't, it's apologies all round for breaking down your front door and disturbing your dreams.'

'O'Donovan said he'd be back about six,' said Detective Sergeant ó Nuallán. 'Is Horgan still at Washington Street?'

'Yes. *And* Dooley. I don't know what happened to Dooley. He was supposed to cover my back from the fire escape outside but he never showed up and I haven't heard a word from him, either.'

Katie checked her watch. 'I'll tell you what you can do now. You can help me to talk to the women we evacuated from the brothel. Don't be judgemental and don't push them too hard, but see if you can get any incriminating evidence about Michael Gerrety out of them. Anything will do, even if he just made racist remarks to one of them, or threatened them in any way.'

'Oh, you really like him, that Michael Gerrety, don't you, ma'am?' said Detective Sergeant ó Nuallán.

'I'd like to serve his head up on a plate with an apple stuffed in his mouth,' said Katie. 'Mind you, that would be an insult to pigs.'

The four women they had evacuated from Washington Street were waiting in the visitors' room downstairs. Mairead had her arms tightly folded over her bosom and a bored, impatient expression on her face. Lotus Blossom and Elvira were both reading magazines. Zakiyyah was sitting at one end of the beige leather couch with her legs tucked up underneath her. She was hugging a cushion and looking anxious.

Katie said, 'Sorry we've kept you waiting so long. Would any of you like a cup of tea or coffee or a lemonade?'

'We want to get the hell out of here, that's all,' snapped Mairead, hoarsely. 'We have dozens of clients that we should be attending to.'

She held up her mobile phone and said, 'I've arranged for another flat for us to go to, temporary-like, until you people have finished sniffing around, but it's going to be a fecking madhouse.'

'We're just going to take some witness statements from you, then you'll be free to go.'

'I've got nothing to say at all.'

'What was the purpose of Desmond O'Leary's visit to your flat?' Katie asked her.

'Social. It was a social visit.'

'When you say "social", was he expecting any sexual services from any of you?'

'It was social. Like he just came by to have the bants, that's all.'

'Did he come to collect money from you?' asked Detective ó Nuallán.

'I'm sure I don't know what you're talking about.'

'A briefcase was found in your kitchen with more than seven thousand euros in it.'

'I wouldn't know about that.'

'You advertise yourselves on the Cork Fantasy Girls website and men come to your flat for you to offer them sexual services.'

'No,' said Mairead. 'That's not the way of it at all. We advertise companionship for lonely men and maybe a massage if they want it. Nothing else. Sometimes we might get friendly with one of them, and then things might go a little further than a massage, but that's purely personal, like, between the girl and the client, nothing to do with business. You can't arrest anyone for flahing.'

'Did Michael Gerrety train you to say that, if ever we pulled you in?'

'Michael who?'

'Oh, stop. You know Michael Gerrety as well as I do. He

may do it through a holding company, but he rents the flat you live in and he runs Cork Fantasy Girls and a whole lot of other sex businesses besides, like Amber's.'

'I'm not saying nothing until I have a lawyer.'

'All right,' said Katie. 'I think that's enough for now in any case. If we have any more questions for you, we'll drop in to see you.'

'You'll have to give us advance warning, like.'

'What? In case we catch you *in flagrante*?'

'What?'

'In case we catch you in mid-flah, that's what I meant. Now all I want to do is take your names and a few personal details and then you can go. The Technical Bureau will have your flat sealed off for two or three days, but we'll let you know as soon as you can go back.'

'Oh, thanks a million.'

Katie took Lotus Blossom over to the other side of the visitors' room and sat her down at a side table. She took out her notebook and said, 'Full name, please.'

While she was writing it down, she said, without looking up, 'This sex work, are you doing it willingly?'

Lotus Blossom looked anxiously across at Mairead, but Mairead was busy talking to Elvira.

'I don't know any other work,' she said.

'Are you being mistreated at all? Are you being given drugs against your will, or beaten, or threatened with beating?'

'I am fine. I don't know any other work. Most of the men like me.' She suddenly giggled and said, 'They say to me, "I always thought Thai girls have pussies that go sideways!"' Then she looked serious again. 'What else would I do?'

'You're sure about that?' said Katie. 'I don't disrespect

you for what you do, Lawan, but I want you to know that if ever you want to stop doing it, there are plenty of people who will help you, me included. Here – this is my private number.'

When she had finished with Lotus Blossom, Katie took Elvira's full name and details and asked her the same questions. Elvira denied that she was on any kind of drugs, but she was glassy-eyed and her voice was slurred, and none of her answers bore any relation to the questions that she asked her. When Katie asked her if she was being threatened to carry on working as a prostitute, she said, 'Yes, and fish might fly.'

She took Zakiyyah over to the table last of all. Zakiyyah was nervous and fidgety and kept biting her lips and playing with her pink glass bangle.

'That's pretty,' said Katie.

'It has the spirit of my *Orisha*, Ochumare. He is the god of rainbows, and he takes care of children.'

'Well, it seems to me that Ochumare is doing his stuff for you today. You don't want to go back there and do that sex work, do you?'

Zakiyyah shook her head. 'It makes me sick. And those men. They smell, and they hurt me. They hurt my bottom so bad.'

Mairead stood up and said, 'Are you finished with her now, Mrs Detective? We need to get out of here. We're going to be in all kinds of shite even as it is.'

'Don't tell me that Michael Gerrety's going to be giving you a hard time for missing a few hours' work?' said Katie. 'It wasn't your fault that Mister Dessie was murdered, was it?'

'Come on, girl,' Mairead told Zakiyyah. 'You've got that

Greek feller coming this evening, the one who asked for you special.'

Katie leaned across the table and said to Zakiyyah, very quietly, 'You and me, we're both going to stand up now. When we do, I want you to shout out, "How dare you call me that!" and then I want you to slap my face.'

'I can't do that!' said Zakiyyah, wide-eyed.

'Yes, you can. Just do it. If you slap me, I will have to arrest you for assaulting a Garda officer and Mairead won't be able to take you back with her.'

'Are you *done* now, for the love of God?' said Mairead. 'Her life story can't be that long!'

Katie stood up and then Zakiyyah stood up, too. For a moment, Katie thought that Zakiyyah wouldn't find the courage to do what she had asked her. But then she suddenly screamed out, '*What did you call me? What did you call me? How dare you call me that!*' and she slapped Katie hard across the right cheek.

For a moment there was stunned silence. Then Detective Sergeant ó Nuallán stepped forward and caught hold of Zakiyyah's wrists, pinning them behind her back.

Katie pressed her hand against her face and said, 'Right! That's it! I'm arresting you for assaulting a police officer in the execution of her duty! DS ó Nuallán, take her into custody. I'll talk to her later.'

Mairead came over and stood in front of Zakiyyah and Detective Sergeant ó Nuallán, blocking their way. 'You can't do that!' she spluttered. 'She can't – you just can't *do* that!'

'We can, and she has, and what's more, you can't stop us,' said Katie. 'Now, since you're so anxious to get back to your clients, I suggest you go. I wouldn't want to charge you with obstruction.'

'This is fecking outrageous!'

'Slapping a detective superintendent is outrageous. Now, push on, will you? You'll find a guard waiting for you in reception to drive you wherever you've arranged to go.'

Mairead and Lotus Blossom and Elvira left the visitors' room and the door slowly swung shut behind them. Detective Sergeant ó Nuallán let go of Zakiyyah's wrists and Zakiyyah burst into tears. Katie took her into her arms and hugged her and shushed her.

'You're all right now, darling. Everything's going to be grand. No more of those horrible men for you, I promise. We'll arrange to send you back to where you came from, and in the meantime we'll make sure that you have some good people to take care of you.'

Detective Sergeant ó Nuallán said, 'I *thought* that was a set-up! Smart thinking! But you should see the state of your face, ma'am! Everybody's going to think you and your partner had words!'

Katie laid her hands on Zakiyyah's shoulders and smiled at her. 'Detective Sergeant ó Nuallán will take you to the canteen now and get you a drink and something to eat if you're hungry. Meanwhile, I'll arrange somebody to come and collect you. They'll give you somewhere to sleep tonight, and clothes, and anything else you need.'

Zakiyyah wiped her eyes and sniffed and nodded. 'Thank you. I am really sorry if I hurt you. I did not mean to slap you so hard.'

'Oh, don't you worry about that. It didn't hurt very much and it'll fade in a while. It made it all the more realistic.'

'What about my rabies shot?' asked Zakiyyah. 'Mister Dessie gave me a rabies shot every day, so that I did not get sick.'

Katie and Detective Sergeant ó Nuallán looked at each other.

'Is that what he called it, a rabies shot?'

'He said you have squirrels in Ireland that can bite you and make you sick with rabies.'

'Rabies shot,' said Katie, disgustedly. 'We'll have to send her to A&E immediately to find out what those scumbags have been shooting her up with, before she starts suffering withdrawal symptoms. My God, if anybody ever got what they deserved, that Mister Dessie did. I almost wish I'd blown his face off myself.'

Detective O'Donovan returned to Anglesea Street around 6.45 p.m. and Detective Horgan arrived back shortly afterwards.

Katie meanwhile had been talking to Garda Sergeant Kenneth Mulligan about assembling a team to raid the house on Lower Glanmire Road in the early hours of Tuesday morning. He recommended six gardaí altogether – at least four of them armed, since Obioma was known to be carrying a weapon – two to be posted at the back of the building and four to enter the front. The back yard was easily accessible because it overlooked a loading dock stacked with containers and a slipway into the River Lee.

Detective O'Donovan came into Katie's office to report on another case he was working on. Thousands of euros' worth of electricity had been stolen from the mains on the Shanakiel Road in Sunday's Well so that a development of nine new town houses had been enjoying heating and lighting for free for six months.

When Detective Horgan appeared, he looked pale and tired and he needed a shave. He told Katie that the technical team had completed their preliminary examination of Zakiyyah's bedroom, and that Mister Dessie's body had been taken away. Unlike the three previous murder scenes, where the victims' clothes had all been missing, they had found Mister Dessie's still lying on the floor.

'His hands were gone, though. She must have taken those with her. She didn't toss them out of the window because they weren't to be found in the alley at the back.'

'Now I come to think of it, she had a black plastic bag tied to her waist,' said Katie. 'She could have been carrying his hands away in that. *Erghh*! Makes me craw sick just to think about it.'

'Oh – Dooley, by the way,' said Detective Horgan.

'Yes, *Dooley*! What on earth happened to him? The whole thing might have turned out different if Dooley had managed to appear outside the window – although I doubt it. That Obioma isn't scared of anything as far as I can make out. But where is Dooley? We're going to need him tonight.'

Detective Horgan was trying not to smirk. 'That fire escape has a gate with barbed wire on the top of it, so that people can't access it from street level. Dooley tried to climb over it – well, he *did* climb over it, but his trousers got caught on the barbed wire and he fell and fractured his ankle and lost his phone.'

'Oh God, poor Dooley. Where is he now?'

'The Mercy, the last I heard from him, waiting to have his ankle put in plaster.'

'He could at least have got in contact with me and let me know.'

'I think he was kind of embarrassed about it, like. We found him lying on top of a heap of old milk crates in his underpants, shouting out for help.'

'Hope you took some pictures,' said Detective O'Donovan. 'You could put them on Twitter. "Cork 'tec caught in Trousergate scandal."'

'Don't you even think about it,' said Katie. 'If you do that, *you'll* be the ones shouting out for help.'

She stood up and switched off her desk lamp. 'Right, I'm going home now to get something to eat. We rendezvous with Sergeant Mulligan's team at 02.00 hours in the car park outside Kent station. Double-check your firearms before you come out. This woman may have only one shot in her weapon but, believe me, you don't want to be the one that she hits with it. Not unless you want to go home without a face.'

Thirty-four

The clock in the hallway was chiming nine by the time she unlocked the front door. Barney came snuffling up to her as usual with his tail slapping against the radiator. John came out of the living room holding a bottle of Satzenbrau. His hair was messed up and his blue shirt was crumpled, but he came up to her smiling and gave her a kiss.

'I did get your texts,' he said. 'It was just that I was in meetings and I couldn't start prodding away at my iPhone.'

'That's all right. Sorry. It's been a hell of a day.'

'I saw something on the news. Another one of those pimp killings, huh?'

'I was there when she did it. Face to face. Listen, I really don't want to talk about it right now. Have you eaten?'

'I had some minestrone soup. I wasn't too hungry, to be honest. How about a drink?'

'I can't,' said Katie. 'I have to go out again about one-thirty. We think we've found out where the suspect lives and I've set up a raid.'

'Jesus. I'm so glad I don't have your job.'

Katie went into the living room and sat down. The nine o'clock news was still on, with the sound turned down, but they were showing an interview with a worried-looking dairy farmer in West Cork. John said, 'Anything I can get you?'

'I wouldn't say no to a cup of tea, if you could put the kettle on. I'll have a sandwich or something later, but not just yet. How was your day? I feel terrible. Your first day at ErinChem and I couldn't even get home early to make you something special.'

'Hey – if some crazy black lady wants to go around blowing people's heads off, I can't blame you for that.'

'But how did it go?'

'It went okay.'

'Only okay? Did they read your proposal?'

'Yes. Well, Aidan's deputy did. I guess he's my immediate boss. Guy called Alan McLennon.'

'What did he think about it?'

'He said it was much too upfront. Too much in your face. He said if I wanted to get endorsements from the Irish medical profession, I should cajole more. That was his actual word – 'cajole'. Sweet-talk them, don't be so direct. Make it sound more like craic than a sales pitch.'

'Well, you have been living in America for years. He should take that into account.'

'I guess you're right. Cork must be the only place in the world where people say "I will" when they mean that they absolutely won't. But – I don't know. ErinChem's a modern, well-financed company producing cutting-edge pharmaceutical products and they keep insisting that they want to update their sales strategy, yet their thinking about marketing is still so old-school. Aidan even calls it "the interweb".'

'John – it's only your first day there. You'll drag them into the future, don't worry.'

'Yeah. I guess so. Let me go put that kettle on.'

* * *

353

Katie made herself a corned-beef and tomato sandwich but she could only manage one bite. She kept seeing Mister Dessie's face exploding.

She took a shower and then changed into jeans and a dark grey cotton sweater which was loose enough and long enough to hide most of her holster. For the rest of the evening she and John sat together on the couch, watching a crime drama on television but not really following who the cops were chasing, or why. It was just lights flickering and people running and angry-looking faces. John's head began to press so heavily on Katie's shoulder that after a while she had to nudge him and say, 'Hey! You're squishing me there, boy!'

There was no answer. '*John*?' she said, but then she sat up a little and saw that he was fast asleep.

She eased herself off the couch and then tiptoed around and switched off the television and all the lights in the living room except for a single pink-shaded lamp. She covered John with a quilt that she brought in from the bedroom, and kissed his cheek. He murmured, but he didn't open his eyes. He must have been under such stress, worrying about his new job and worrying about her, but he had probably felt that he couldn't talk about it too much. The problems of developing online marketing for indigestion tablets hardly compared with hunting down a woman who cut off her victims' hands and almost blew their heads off.

She shut Barney in the kitchen and then she left the house, closing the front door very quietly behind her. It was a cool night, cooler than it had been recently, and there was a soft breeze blowing, as if it were trying to whisper something to her. It was very clear, though. The moon was shining behind the trees and its reflection was glinting in the harbour.

As she backed out of her driveway and headed northwards

on Carrig View, the road that led up the side of Passage
West, she saw a car's headlights switched on about two
hundred yards behind her. The car pulled away from the
kerb and followed her. It kept its distance as she drove up
the winding roads of Fota Island, but just before she reached
the main dual carriageway, it accelerated until it was almost
tailgating her. She had to click down her rear-view mirror
so that she wouldn't be dazzled.

'Jesus!' she shouted. 'What are you trying to do, you eejit?'
She stamped her foot down on the accelerator and pulled
away. The other car fell back, making no attempt to stay
close up behind her. There were only four or five cars on the
road at this time of the morning, but when she looked in
her mirror she couldn't distinguish which car it was that had
been tailing her.

'Ah, come on, girl, you're getting paranoid,' she told
herself. There were several times when she had been convinced
that she was being followed, especially when she was involved
in prosecuting members of one of Cork's criminal gangs. Her
husband, Paul, had suffered fatal injuries after her car had
been rammed into the River Lee, and when other drivers
came too close behind her it still gave her a deeply uncomfortable feeling.

She arrived at Kent train station. Four patrol cars were
already parked outside, as well as three unmarked cars
belonging to Detective Sergeant ó Nuallán, Detective
O'Donovan and Detective Horgan.

Sergeant Mulligan came over to Katie as she climbed out
of her car.

'Good morning, superintendent. We're all ready to go.
We'll be sending two men round the back of the house first,
and when they confirm that they're in position we'll go in

for the smash and bash. We've been keeping a discreet watch on the property all evening but nobody's been in or out of it. There were lights on downstairs until 22.03, and somebody watching television in the first-floor flat until 23.26, but it's all dark now. There's a bedsit in the attic with a dormer window in the roof but we've seen no light from that at all.'

'Very good,' said Katie. 'You've briefed your team on what they're up against, haven't you? A very highly motivated woman with terrorist training. We know for certain that she has one firearm, this single-shot pocket shotgun, but it's quite possible that she may have others. However, I very much want her taken alive. She can provide valuable evidence for further prosecutions.'

Detective Sergeant ó Nuallán walked over. She was wearing a dark brown hoodie and black jeggings and ankle-boots.

'Mother of God,' said Katie. 'If I saw you in the street dressed like that, I'd probably arrest you on suspicion.'

'I just thought you'd like to know that I contacted Mary ó Floinn at Nasc,' said Detective Sergeant ó Nuallán. 'One of their volunteers took Zakiyyah for a drugs test. I haven't heard the results yet, but Mary said that afterwards she would take her to the same family that are looking after that Romanian girl you saw.'

'Little Corina, yes.'

'She shouldn't be staying with them for very long – just long enough for Nasc to sort out Zakiyyah's legal rights and locate her family in Nigeria and arrange to send her back there, if that's what she wants.'

'Good,' said Katie. 'There's a few saintly people in this world after all.'

Detective O'Donovan came up wearing a blue Kevlar vest

and carrying two more. 'Here you are, though I don't know what earthly good these will do you if this Angel of Vengeance tries to blow your head off like Dessie O'Leary and those other langers.'

Sergeant Mulligan raised his hand to indicate to Katie that two of his officers were now in position at the back of the house. Katie and Detective Sergeant ó Nuallán got into Detective O'Donovan's Mondeo and they followed the four patrol cars, with Detective Horgan following behind them. It wasn't far to the house called *Sonas*, only five hundred metres under the railway bridge, but they took the cars to block off the road.

As soon as they slewed to a halt outside the house, the armed officers scrambled out of their patrol cars and went rushing to the front door. They didn't knock or ring any of the doorbells, they just swung at the door with a 35-pound Ram-It. The door was old and rotten and it was torn off its hinges with the first blow, crashing flat on to the hallway floor.

The officers screamed, '*Armed gardaí! Armed gardaí!*' and stormed into the house with their flashlights criss-crossing. They battered open the first door they came across, on their right, and jostled into the ground-floor flat. Katie approached the front door and she could hear an elderly man shouting, 'What the *feck* is going on here? What are you doing knocking me fecking door down in the middle of the fecking night?'

The lights went on and Katie stepped into the hallway. She saw a white-haired man in blue-striped pyjamas watching helplessly as the officers went from his living room to his bedroom to his bathroom, opening every cupboard door and even crouching down to look under his bed.

Two more gardaí had already climbed the narrow staircase

to the first-floor landing and were smashing down the door to the flat above. She heard a woman shouting and a baby screaming. She went into the ground-floor flat and approached the elderly man in his pyjamas.

'Detective Superintendent Maguire,' she said, showing him her badge. 'I'm really sorry we've disturbed you like this, but we're looking for a very dangerous young woman.'

'What?' he blinked. 'Who did you say you were? I can't see a fecking thing without me glimmers.'

'I'm a detective, sir. I apologize for breaking into your flat like this, but we're trying to catch a criminal and we suspect that she's armed. A young black woman, who sometimes dresses all in black. Is she staying in this house? Have you seen her?'

'The black girl? Of course I've seen her. Up and down stairs all hours of the fecking day and night in those clompy great boots of hers. I don't sleep well as it is.'

'Have you seen her today?'

'This morning I saw her. She comes clomping down the stairs and slams the front door. I'm not racist meself but she's enough to turn you that way.'

Katie heard more shouting and crying upstairs, and when she turned around she saw Detective Sergeant ó Nuallán heading towards the stairs. 'Listen, I'll have to leave you for a moment. I'm sorry about the damage. We'll have somebody around to fix your door first thing.'

'And what am I supposed to do now? Go back to bed and try to sleep while any thief who wants to can just stroll in off the street?'

'I promise you we'll make your flat secure before we go,' said Katie. 'You'll be compensated, too, for any distress we've caused you.'

With that, she went back out into the hallway and climbed the stairs. The officers had battered open the door of the first-floor flat, too, and Detective Sergeant ó Nuallán was in there, trying to calm down a hysterical young mother and her screaming baby.

'How can you *do* this?' the young mother was protesting. 'How can you just break into my flat? I have a five-month-old *baby*!'

The officers came out of her kitchen and squeezed past her in their bulky Kevlar jackets. The other two gardaí had already gone up to the attic and smashed down the door, and Katie could hear them walking about above her head. One of them shouted down, 'Clear! Nobody in here, Sarge!'

'I'm really, really sorry to have upset you and your baby like this,' she said to the young mother. 'My name is Detective Superintendent Maguire and I'm in charge of this operation, so if you want to blame anybody you can blame me.'

'But you've no right! You can't just burst in on people like this and break down their doors!'

'I'm afraid we can. We have a warrant for forcible entry. It's that Nigerian woman we're after.'

'Why? What's *she* done? She's been staying in the top flat, not with me.'

'She could be very dangerous,' said Katie. 'Haven't you seen the TV news at all? She's a suspect in four cases of homicide.'

'My TV's broke. My ex said he was going to fix me up with a new one, but he never keeps his word.'

'Well, we believe that she's already killed four people and she intends to kill more. She carries at least one gun that we know about and we know that she won't hesitate to use it.'

The young mother had been patting and rocking the baby

and it was beginning to calm down now. 'She only moved in here a couple of weeks ago. She used to smile and say hello but I never saw much of her. I wouldn't have minded having a chat, you know, because I'm stuck here all day with little Miley and I hardly ever get to speak to nobody. What am I going to do about my door? My landlord's going to go mental.'

'Don't worry about your door, we'll get it mended for you tomorrow. Or today, now. Did she ever have any visitors, this black woman?'

The young mother shook her head. 'I never saw anybody go up there apart from her.'

Detectives O'Donovan and Horgan had been up into the attic and now they came to the door. 'Looks like she's done a runner, ma'am. Nothing left up there except for a few tins of food and some towels.'

'Well, I won't be sorry if she's gone,' said the young mother. 'There was always such a smoky smell when she was cooking. African food, I suppose it was.'

Katie went up the steep, narrow stairs to the attic. It had two dormer windows, one overlooking the street and the other at the back, overlooking the loading dock and the river. At one end there was an unmade sofa-bed with a bunched-up duvet on it. In the middle stood two armchairs, one upholstered in mustard yellow and the other in grubby red, with a teak coffee table in between them. At the far end there was a kitchenette, with a counter made of chipboard, a small stainless-steel sink and an oven.

The walls and the sloping ceilings were papered with hunting scenes, with large brown damp patches in between them.

Detective Sergeant ó Nuallán came up, too, and looked

around. 'Looks like she's definitely gone. Think she might have given up on Michael Gerrety?'

Katie was looking at the tins of food that had been left underneath the kitchen counter. Locust beans, cassava, crabmeat. There was also a large bottle of palm oil, three-quarters empty, and a brown paper bag of wood chips.

She opened the oven door. It smelled strongly of smoke and inside it she found a baking tray with a wire rack in it and a layer of wood chips on the bottom. Katie picked some up and sniffed them. They were damp and very pungent.

'What do you think she's been cooking with these?' she asked Detective Sergeant ó Nuallán.

'She's been smoking spare ribs or something, probably. That's how you do it if you don't have a barbecue and you want to do it indoors. You soak the wood chips with water and then you just cook your meat very slowly.'

They looked carefully around the attic. There was a battered chest of drawers in one corner, but all of the drawers were empty except for two AA batteries and a reel of red cotton.

'I don't think she's given up on Gerrety,' said Katie. 'If she was driven enough to do what she did to those other four men, she's going to make sure that she gets him.'

'But we have him under guard now. She won't be able to get near him.'

'More's the pity.'

Detective Sergeant ó Nuallán looked at Katie narrowly. 'You'll get him one day. Just wait and see.'

She was back home by 5.55 a.m. John was still asleep and she was tempted to climb back into bed with him, but she was afraid that she would fall asleep herself and she had too much to do. As soon as she got into the station she would have to prepare a full report for Acting Chief Superintendent Molloy, and also brief the media.

The sun was shining so she took Barney out for an early walk along by the river. She felt light-headed with tiredness but she couldn't stop thinking about Obioma and what she was going to do now. She wouldn't be able to get into The Elysian Tower to attack Michael Gerrety at home, and he would almost certainly make sure that he had bodyguards with him whenever he went out.

It was possible, however, that Obioma was very patient. She was trained in guerrilla tactics and she could be prepared to wait for days or weeks or even months before she went for him. They couldn't keep guards outside The Elysian indefinitely. The budget wouldn't run to it, and apart from that the media would start asking awkward questions about what they were doing there. Why should they be protecting a man like Michael Gerrety when the ordinary citizens of Cork needed protection against housebreaking and mugging and drunken misbehaviour in the streets?

She returned home and put on the kettle to make herself a cup of coffee. John appeared from the bedroom, bare-chested, scratching and yawning. She put her arms around him and held him close.

'I love you, you know,' she told him. 'I'm sorry I've been so tied up lately. It won't always be like this, I promise.'

John stroked her hair. 'You smell of fresh air,' he said. 'You smell of Ireland.'

She looked up at him. 'Are you still wanting to go back to America?'

He shrugged. 'Let's see how the job goes. It wasn't exactly an ideal first day, but I'm sure I'll find my feet. You know

what it's like being a newbie. Everybody resents you, especially if you tell them that they're stuck in the Stone Age.'

'You didn't say that, did you?'

'Not in those words. But I implied it. Because they are.'

'Oh, John,' she said, and kissed his chest. She didn't say,
'Please make this work, for my sake.' She knew that it had
to work for him, and him alone.

Thirty-five

Almost the whole of the next day was taken up with paper-work. Just before lunchtime, Katie had completed her file on last night's forcible entry into the house on Lower Glanmire Road, and she took it in to Acting Chief Superintendent Molloy.

He flicked through it, and sniffed, and then he said, 'I'd also appreciate up-to-date reports on all your ongoing cases.'

'*All* of them? Serious? That's going to take a few days.'

'The thing of it is, Katie, I need to know that our manpower and our finances are being deployed in the most efficient way possible. I've already started to go through Dermot O'Driscoll's files and I'm sorry to say that I'm less than impressed. Far too much wastage and inefficiency. I need to assess which current cases of yours are worth pursuing and which ones we could drop. There's a few that I've earmarked already.'

'For instance?' asked Katie.

'Take this Mayfield Lodge Care Home case. It's not worth going after a care home for mistreating old folk if those old folk have all passed away and can't testify against them. The owners have promised to make improvements, so there's no real point in prosecuting them. Or this alleged bribery by Finbar Construction. It's a waste of resources to chase a council planning officer for accepting a sweetener from a developer if the development has turned out to everybody's satisfaction. Society has a way of curing its own ills, Katie. People are prepared to mend their ways if you point out to them what they've done wrong. It's not up to us to be too punctilious.'

'If society can cure its own ills, Bryan, that pretty much makes us redundant. We might as well pack it in and go home.'

Acting Chief Superintendent Molloy looked up at her with his eyes bulging. 'Was that supposed to be humorous?' he said. 'It's a truism, isn't it, that women don't know how to be funny?'

'It wasn't supposed to be humorous, no. But I can tell you a joke if you want me to.'

'I don't need any more jokes from you, Katie. The way you've been handling these Angel homicides is already a joke. I admit you saved us some media embarrassment by not shooting your suspect when she threatened to kill herself, but you should have shot her the second you saw that she was armed. You said, "Drop it," didn't you? When she didn't, you should have instantly taken her out, *blam*, end of story. Then nobody could have complained.'

He picked up the file that she had just put down on his desk, and then dropped it again.

'From what Sergeant Mulligan's told me, you made a right bags of last night, too. Before you go smashing people's doors down looking for suspects, it's always worth checking that your suspect is actually inside.'

Katie kept her eyes on his forehead so that she wouldn't have to look into his eyes. 'There was every likelihood that she was there, and we had no other way of telling for sure.

Besides, she's armed and dangerous, and when a suspect is armed and dangerous you don't go politely ringing the front doorbell and asking if they're home.'

'All right, let's leave it like that for now,' said Acting Chief Superintendent Molloy. 'Let me have those case updates by Thursday.'

'I'll do my best, sir, so long as nothing more important comes up.'

Katie could see that she had irritated him by calling him 'sir', but he let it go. She was quite aware, however, that he wouldn't forget it. He was notorious for bearing grudges, sometimes for years, and she had already annoyed him, on a daily basis, just by being a woman.

Detective Dooley came into the station in mid-afternoon, with his left ankle in plaster and on crutches. Katie gave him a hard time for not informing her immediately what had happened to him when he had fallen off the gate, but then she set him to work preparing reports on all of their current cases.

'In that shape you can't go running after bank robbers,' she told him, dropping a stack of files in front of him. 'So, here – you might as well make yourself useful.'

Detective Dooley looked at the files and his shoulders sagged.

Just before 5 p.m., John texted her and said, 'Will u b 18 2nite?'

'Don't think so,' she texted back. 'All quiet so far.'

'Gd,' he replied. 'We need 2 talk.'

She knew what he was going to say. She had expected it ever since she had let it slip that she had only managed to set up his interview with ErinChem because Aidan Tierney owed her a personal favour. Even if the job had gone well from day one and Alan McLennon had thought his proposal was the berries, John was too proud and too independent to have accepted that he hadn't been offered the position on his own merits. He had left the family farm to go to America and started his dot.com pharmaceutical business because he had been too proud and too independent to work for his father, so what could she expect from him?

As she drove home, though, she had a feeling that was close to being grief.

It was still warm and sunny, so they sat in the back garden with a drink while Barney sat close to Katie's chair with his tongue hanging out, panting.

John said, 'I know I haven't really given ErinChem much of a chance. The position is perfect for me, and all of ErinChem's products are excellent. But I know that it's not going to work out.'

'You said that they're backward when it comes to their marketing strategy,' said Katie. 'But surely you can modernize their thinking, can't you, given time? Can't you give it just a month or two? Then, if you're still not happy, we can put our heads together and think of something else you can do. Tyco are going to be starting up again in Cork, maybe you could work for them. Or maybe you could set up on your own, like you did in San Francisco.'

John leaned forward so that his basketwork chair creaked and held her hand. She was still wearing the emerald-set ring that he had bought her to celebrate his decision to stay in Ireland. 'Katie, I'm in love with you, darling, and I know you can't leave your job. But the problem isn't with ErinChem. It's with me.'

'You feel belittled because I called in a favour to get you the interview.'

'It's not that,' he said. 'It's much more profound than that.'

'It's us? There's something wrong with our relationship? I'm never at home, is that it? You know that I have to work unpredictable hours.'

'It's not that, either, although of course I'd like to see much more of you. It's not you, darling. It's Ireland.'

'I don't understand. What do you mean, it's Ireland? You're Irish. You were born here. This is your home.'

John shook his head. 'Once you leave Ireland and make a life for yourself someplace else you always fondly think that you can come back. You remember your pals, and the craic, and the pubs. You can almost smell that damp peaty smell, even when you're thousands of miles away.

'But what I've found out is, Katie, that you can't go back. Once you've left, you've left, and no matter how nostalgic you feel, it can never be the same again. I feel like I've come back to the house that I grew up in, but I've got my nose pressed against the window and I can see all of my family and my old friends inside, laughing and dancing and having a good time, but I can never go back in to join them.'

Katie blinked, because she didn't want John to see that she was close to crying. 'So what are you saying?' she asked him. 'You want to go back to America?'

'I don't even think that it's a question of wanting to. I *have* to. That's where my future is. I just can't stay here, in my past.'

Katie said nothing for a long time, her head bowed, staring down at the orange brick paving with the groundsel growing up between the cracks and listening intently to the bees that swarmed around the buddleia, and Barney's endless panting.

High above her a plane was scratching its way across the sky. Perhaps by saying nothing and concentrating on the ordinary world around her she could make time come to a stop. But she had known from the beginning that it would come to this. She had never wanted to face it, but now the day had arrived.

At last, still holding his hand, she said, 'I've turned this over in my mind so often. Over and over and over.' She didn't look at him. She didn't want to see those agate-brown eyes.

'And?'

'And you know what the answer is, John. I can't leave any more than you can stay.'

'What if I begged you?'

'Don't beg me. Don't ever beg me to do anything. You're too proud a man for that.'

'What if I asked you to marry me?'

She couldn't answer. Her mouth puckered and the tears started to run down her cheeks. He stood up and tried to take hold of her, but she flapped her hands and waved him away. 'Don't,' she said. 'Just don't.'

'Katie, the last thing in the whole world I want to do is hurt you.'

'You can't help it,' she said. 'It's not your fault. It's life. It's what life does to us.'

She stood up and went into the kitchen, tearing off a sheet of paper towel to wipe her eyes and blow her nose. John followed her and laid his hand on her shoulder. She didn't push it off, but she didn't turn round, either.

'Look,' said John, 'I'll stay at ErinChem a while longer. You're right. I haven't even given it a chance. Maybe I was a little sore about your fixing it up for me.'

'No,' she said. 'You know what you have to do. I shouldn't have tried to make you stay here in Ireland. I was being selfish.'

John put his arms around her and held her close. He kissed the crown of her hair and said, 'I love you, Katie. I adore you. I will never find anybody else like you, ever.'

'Yes, you will. And you'll marry her and have fifty-five kids and you'll live happily ever after.'

It was then that John started to cry too. 'Oh, shit, Katie. What am I going to do?'

Katie tore off another sheet of paper towel and dabbed his eyes. 'You're going to go, John. You know you are. Like you said, you have to.'

She smiled at him, and gently touched his cheek. 'It's going to hurt, boy,' she said in her strongest Southside accent. 'But only for a while.'

'Yeah,' he said, trying to get his breath back.

'Listen,' she told him, 'I think I'll go over and see my father for a bit. I won't be too long, only a couple of hours. The last ferry's at ten o'clock anyhow.'

'Okay,' said John. 'Maybe that's a good idea. I'll see you when you get back.'

She kissed him, and then she kissed him again. 'It's not that I don't want to be with you,' she said, very softly, her face so close that she couldn't even focus on him. 'It's just that if I stay here, I'll have to be brave.'

Thirty-six

She took the car ferry from Carrigaloe Pier across the river to Glenbrook. The crossing took only four minutes and it saved a circuitous half-hour drive on the N25 and N29. She stood by the railing with her face turned towards the setting sun and her eyes closed. In fact, she was praying. *Oh dear God, why are you doing this to me?*

She had called her father in advance to let him know that she was coming. As soon as she turned into his driveway and parked behind his old brown Volvo estate, he opened up the front door and waved. She climbed the front steps and gave him a hug. He was looking so much better since he had announced that he and Ailish were going to be married. His eyes looked brighter and he seemed to be standing up straighter, as if the pain that he had felt after the death of Katie's mother was easing at last.

Ailish appeared from the kitchen and hugged her, too. She was wearing a splashy summer dress in yellows and reds and a necklace of giant red beads.

'Well, to what do we owe the pleasure?' said Katie's father. 'We only just saw you on Sunday. This is an honour!'

'Have you eaten, Katie?' asked Ailish.

'No, I haven't yet. It's been one of those days – as if *every* day isn't one of those days.'

'I should have brought that lamb stew I made this morning,' said Ailish. 'I was going to freeze it for the weekend so I left it cooling off at home. I only live two minutes away and it wouldn't take long to heat up.'

'That's a great idea,' said Katie's father. 'Why don't you nip back home and fetch it? I think I could do considerable justice to a bowl of lamb stew. How about you, Katie?'

'I'm not all that hungry, Da, to tell you the truth.'

'Oh, you wait till you smell it! Here, Ailish, here's my car keys.'

Katie said, 'Really, Ailish, you needn't trouble yourself. I wasn't going to eat tonight anyway.'

'Oh, behave!' said Katie's father. 'There's nobody comes round to my house now without being fed. Ailish has made sure of that, haven't you, darling? You should taste her sausage coddle!'

'All right,' said Katie. 'But look, why don't you take my car? It'll save me having to move it.'

She opened her bag and handed Ailish her keys. Ailish said, 'You're sure?'

'Of course. It belongs to the Garda and it's fully insured for anybody to drive it.'

Ailish said, 'All right, then, thanks. I won't be long!'

When she had left, Katie and her father went into the living room.

'Drink?' asked Katie's father.

'I wouldn't say no to a glass of red wine if you have one.'

He stopped and frowned at her. 'What's wrong?' he asked her.

'What do you mean, "What's wrong?" Nothing's wrong.'

'You don't normally come across to see me on the spur of the moment like this.'

'Oh, I can't pay a visit to my own father without something being wrong?'

He came up to her and laid his hand on her arm. 'You're upset about something,' he said.

'What makes you think that?'

'Because I used to be a detective inspector, that's what, and I can read people's body language. You're tense, you're fidgety, and you're dying to tell me something but at the same time you're not at all sure that you want to because if you do you'll burst into tears.'

Katie said, 'I'm not going to cry, Da. Crying isn't going to change anything.'

'It's your John, isn't it?' he asked her.

'Yes.'

He nodded and said, 'I thought so. I could tell that, when you came round on Sunday. He kept saying how happy he was, but I could sense that he was very stressed. I mentioned it to Ailish afterwards.'

'He wants to go back to America. He says he'll never settle here. He wants me to go with him. He even asked me to marry him.'

'So why don't you?'

Katie sat down. 'Come on, Da, we've been through this before. There's something in life called a sense of duty and unfortunately I've been born with it. I probably inherited it from you.'

Katie's father looked at her sadly. 'There's something in this life called happiness, too, but not many of us get to enjoy it. I was lucky enough to find great happiness with your mother, and I've been extra lucky a second time to find it with Ailish. You should grab it while you have the chance.'

'How about that glass of wine?'

Katie and her father had been sitting and talking together for nearly half an hour before Katie glanced up at the clock on the mantelpiece and said, 'Ailish is taking her time.'

'I think her daughter's staying with her at the moment. They probably got chatting.'

'How old is her daughter?'

'Thirty-one. And she's a big girl, too. Not surprising, with Ailish for a mother. That woman never stops putting food in front of you.'

'Well, you be careful. I don't want a fatso for a father.'

Another ten minutes went past but there was still no sign of Ailish. Katie's father said, 'I hope she hasn't had a puncture. That hill where she lives is absolutely riddled with potholes.'

'Give her a call on her mobile,' said Katie.

Her father picked up his iPhone and touched Ailish's number, but immediately they heard a ringtone in the kitchen. Next he tried her home number, twice, but nobody answered.

'So where the devil has she got to?' he demanded. 'It's only a minute there and a minute back. I think I'd best go look for her.'

'Why don't I go?' said Katie. 'It's beginning to get dark now and you know what your eyesight is like.'

Katie's father took his car keys from the table in the hallway and gave them to her. 'Give me a call if she's had a flat tyre or something else is holding her up.'

'Of course, Da.'

She climbed into her father's Volvo estate and gave him

a wave as she backed out of the driveway. The sun had gone down behind the houses now and the sky was damson-coloured. Katie couldn't help hearing John's words in her head. *'It's not you, darling. It's Ireland.'*

Ailish lived less than a kilometre away, at the top of a hill overlooking the river. Katie had only just turned into her road when she saw flashing blue and red lights up ahead. Patrol cars, and an ambulance. *Oh God*, she thought. *What's happened up here?* She changed down and accelerated up the hill until she reached the first patrol car. She parked halfway up the kerb and opened her door.

A guard came over to her with his hand raised. 'Nothing to see here, ma'am.'

'Detective Superintendent Maguire, from Anglesea Street,' she told him, and showed him her badge.

'Oh, okay. A car's gone off the road, that's all, and into somebody's garden.'

She followed him up to the scene of the accident. Deep tyre tracks ran diagonally across the grass verge, showing where the car had left the road. It had crashed through a low brick wall and plunged down a steeply sloping garden, hitting the front of a bungalow. The impact had been enough to damage the brickwork and dislodge one of the double-glazed windows.

Katie saw at once that the car was hers. The driver's door was open and a paramedic was kneeling beside it, while a second paramedic was standing close by. Three more gardaí were standing around, talking to the owners of the bungalow, a couple in their mid-fifties, and a tall, lugubrious-looking man who was probably their next-door neighbour.

Katie stepped over a flower bed and made her way around

the back of the car. She went up to the driver's door and saw that Ailish was still sitting behind the wheel. The airbag had deployed, but Ailish was slumped forward with her face turned sideways so that she was staring at Katie with her eyes wide open. She was deathly pale except for a red mark on her forehead where the airbag had hit her.

'Detective Superintendent Maguire,' said Katie, as the paramedic looked up at her. 'I know this woman. In fact, this is my car. She just borrowed it.'

'I'm sorry,' said the paramedic, standing up. He was a short, stubby young man, with a very slight squint, so that Katie wasn't sure if he was looking straight at her or not. 'I can't tell the cause of death for certain, but I'd say it was probably cardiac arrest. She was already dead when we arrived.'

'Aren't you going to get her out of there?'

'Her feet are trapped under the pedals. We're waiting on the fire brigade.'

Katie stood and looked at Ailish and Ailish stared back at her with her pale blue eyes, unblinking. Ailish with her braided hair and her splashy summer dress and her necklace of big glass beads. Her arm was lying across her lap and her watch was still working. It was almost impossible for Katie to believe that this had actually happened. She couldn't even begin to imagine how her father was going to take it, or how she was going to tell him. *There's something in this life called happiness, but not many of us get to enjoy it.*

After a few seconds she turned away and stepped back over the flower bed. Two of the gardaí were crouched down now, examining the back of the car with their flashlights. The rear bumper was split and scuffed, and there were three deep dents in the bodywork.

'All that damage is new,' said Katie. 'There wasn't a scratch on this car when she took it away.'

'When was that exactly?'

'About forty minutes ago. She looks after my father, who lives at West View House. She borrowed it to go back to her own house to fetch a stew for us, for supper.'

'But it was totally undamaged before then?'

Katie looked at the split in the bumper. 'I'd say that she was rammed by another vehicle, and very hard.'

'So what? You think this could have been deliberate, like? I mean, she could have suffered a heart attack and stopped unexpected and whoever was coming up behind her crashed into her but they didn't want to stay around when they saw her go careering down into this garden. They could have been over the limit, like. That's the usual pattern.'

'No, this car has been violently rear-ended more than once. Even if you're drunk you don't do that.'

'Road rage?'

'Possible, but not very likely. Why would anybody have road rage halfway up an empty street in Monkstown?'

'But why would they do it deliberate? It doesn't make sense.'

Katie looked around. 'Were there any witnesses? Did anybody see this happen?'

'No. They was either in their gardens or indoors eating or watching the telly.'

'All right. But I don't want this car moved until the technicians have taken a look at it. I'll call them myself. Make sure that you tape it off and that nobody touches it.'

A fire appliance arrived, with its diesel engine roaring and lights flashing. Katie climbed up the garden steps and went back to her father's car. She sat in the driver's seat and called the Technical Bureau. When she had done that, she sat for a while and tried to think what she was going to say to her father.

It was going to be difficult enough to tell him that Ailish was dead, only two days after they had toasted his announcement that they were going to be married. But her father had been a police officer, too, and after he had recovered from the initial shock he would be urgently asking her the same question she was now asking herself.

Who would have deliberately rammed Ailish? She was a 64-year-old widow, a cook, and a home help. Who could have wanted to do a woman like that any harm?

The only conceivable reason she had been targeted was because she had been driving Katie's car.

Thirty-seven

Michael Gerrety was sitting in his basement office at Amber's when Trisha came down the spiral staircase from the shop and said, 'Michael, there's somebody up here wants to talk to you. It's a girl.'

'Did she say what she was after?' he asked, without looking up. He was busy totting up his accounts. There was usually a fall-off in income during the summer months, but this year business had been very steady. He guessed that fewer Corkonians had been able to afford a foreign holiday and so they had been obliged to get their jollies at home. His Washington Street premises didn't compare with brothels in Gran Canaria or Magaluf, but you didn't have to fly to get there, and if you wanted to get hammered after getting laid it was only a short walk to the Long Island Cocktail Bar at number eleven.

Trisha shrugged. 'All she said was, she was looking for work.'

'She's white, is she?'

'Yeah, why?'

'No reason. What does she look like?'

'Not too bad at all, I'd say.'

Michael turned around to his minder and said, 'Sounds harmless. Let's get a sconce of her, shall we?'

Charlie was sitting in the corner by the large grey safe, reading the *Sun*. His black hair was neatly cut and he was dressed in a crisp white short-sleeved shirt and well-pressed black trousers. He could have been handsome, but his face was unnaturally beige and there was a deadness about it, like a dummy in the window of a menswear store.

'Molloy says it's a darkie you have to watch out for,' he said. He had a distinct Limerick accent but no intonation in his voice at all. When one of Michael's creditors had threatened him, Charlie had said, 'Come here, boy, and I'll kick the heart outa ya,' but he had said it so flatly that it was difficult to tell if he meant it or not.

There was a loud clumping of wedge-heeled sandals on the spiral staircase and then the girl appeared. She was young, about seventeen or eighteen Michael would have guessed, because she still hadn't quite outgrown her puppy fat. She was pretty, though, with a heart-shaped face and curly ash-blonde hair. She was wearing a very short white mini-skirt and a sleeveless black satin top. Michael sat back in his chair and noted with appreciation that she was very big-breasted.

'Well, hello,' he said, dropping his ballpen on to his desk. 'And what's your name?'

'Are you Mr Gerrety?' the girl asked him, glancing nervously from Michael to Charlie and back again.

'That's me,' said Michael. 'Don't be taking any notice of him, he's just part of the furniture, aren't you, Charlie?'

'That's me,' said Charlie, without raising his eyes from his newspaper. 'Charlie the chair.'

'My name's Branna. A friend of mine told me you could help me find work.'

'Here, sit down, you don't have to be nervous,' said Michael. 'What kind of work are you after?'

Branna sat down on the very edge of the bentwood chair on the opposite side of Michael's desk, with her knees together and her feet splayed out. 'Like, you know, escort services, that kind of thing.'

'Have you done anything like that before?'

'No, never. I was working at Dunne's up at Ballyvolane for a while, but then they accused me of taking make-up which I never did but they sacked me anyway. I did a bit of waitressing and then a bit of bar work but the money's rubbish, and my friend said that you paid really good money.'

Michael smiled. 'You can make good money if you work through me, but you have to earn it. You have to meet a lot of different men and you have to be nice to them, which is not always easy.'

'I think I'd be good at it. I really do. I've always been a great listener. Anyway, they take you out and stuff, these men, don't they? Buy you meals and drinks and all that. I wouldn't mind if some of them were boring.'

'Sometimes they want something in return for taking you out.'

'You mean like sex?' said Branna. 'I'm not a total innocent, Mr Gerrety. If a man's given you a really good evening out, there's nothing wrong in it at all. He deserves a cuddle, you know, or whatever.'

When she said that, she parted her knees a little. Michael didn't look down, but kept his eyes fixed on hers.

'What if that's *all* he wants? What if he's not interested in taking you out for the evening, but just wants the sex?'

Branna lowered her eyelashes for a moment and gave a small, self-satisfied smile that Michael couldn't interpret. He liked to believe that he could read women better than books – not that he ever read books. Branna's expression, though, was like a hieroglyph. It meant something. It might even have meant something significant, but he couldn't understand what.

Charlie said, 'Ten past eleven, Mr Gerrety.'

Michael checked his watch. 'Shite, I didn't realize it was so late. I have an important meeting at the Maryborough like ten minutes ago. Listen, Branna, why don't you come and see me at home so that we can discuss everything in detail? I can tell you how you can use my website to advertise your escort services, and what it'll cost you, and what you're likely to be earning after all of your expenses. I won't try to finagle you at all. I'm the straightest guy in the business. You ask anyone.'

'Expenses?' asked Branna. 'What expenses?'

'Well, for instance, do you have a place of your own, a place that's suitable for bringing a man back to? If a feller's bought you dinner at the Hayfield Manor he's going to expect something a bit classier than a bedsit with a single bed heaped up with teddy bears and a poster of Pa Cronin on the wall.'

'I'm sharing with a friend at the moment. You know, because I'm so broke, like. It's my friend who suggested I come to see you. I expect she can't wait to see the back of me.'

'There you are, you see, you'll need a decent room, and I can provide you with that, but I can't let you have it buckshee. That's what I mean by expenses.'

He stood up, took his wallet out of his back trouser pocket and handed her a business card. 'That's where I live, The Elysian. I can't see you tonight because I have to go to a charity banquet, but make it tomorrow evening, say around seven? There's guards on the door outside but I'll let them know that you're expected. Show them that card and they'll let you in.'

Branna stood up, too. 'I'm excited now,' she told him.

'Well, you're a very good-looking young lady if you don't mind my saying so. I think you'll be raking it in. How old are you, incidentally? You don't mind my asking but some girls these days look a whole lot older than they really are.'

'Yeah, like my girlfriend,' said Charlie.

'I'm nineteen,' said Branna.

Michael gave her a paternal pat on the back and guided her towards the spiral staircase. He stood at the bottom as she went back upstairs so that he could see up her skirt. Charlie came and joined him and said, 'Yes or no?'

'Thong,' said Michael.

'Oh well. Halfway there.'

'Come on,' Michael told him. 'We're going to be late, and you know how much I hate to be late. It gives people the chance to cut the back off you before you arrive, and then they're all sardonic smiles and you don't know why.'

'If I catch anybody smiling at you like that, boss, I'll give them a kick in the back of the forehead, don't you worry.' He hesitated, and then he said, 'What's "sardonic"? Is that looking at you like a fish, like?'

Thirty-eight

'We've found the vehicle,' said Detective Sergeant ó Nuallán, solemnly.

Katie was standing by her office window, staring at the Elysian Tower with its dull grey concrete and its shiny green glass. It made her feel like a knight in a fairy story – a knight who can see the wicked king's castle in the distance, but who is bound by a spell not to enter it, and so is powerless to put an end to his reign of evil.

It was raining, but only softly, although the hooded crows that were clustered on top of the car park would occasionally flap their wings in irritation.

'Where?' she asked.

'The shopping centre car park at Ballyvolane, burned out. The only thing was, the front wasn't too badly burned, and there was damage on the bumper that matches the rear of your car, as well as traces of blue metallic paint, which we've already sent off to be analysed.'

'What was it?'

'Nissan X-Trail 4×4. It went missing from Nolan's Construction at Dennehy's Cross two days ago.'

Katie turned away from the window and went back to her desk. 'Whoever stole it, they were after me. I don't have any doubt about that. Nobody saw it being stolen, I suppose?'

'It happened at night, apparently. The wire fence around their building yard was cut through.'

'I wonder if it was Obioma,' said Katie. 'Like, it was a very terrorist thing to do. Take out the leader of the people who are looking for you, and throw them into a state of fear and uncertainty. While they're all flapping their hands and running around in circles, she can go in quick and complete her mission – which is to kill Michael Gerrety.'

'You really think she would target you like that?'

'Yes, I do. She looks beautiful, and she's already eliminated four people without whom we all agree the city of Cork is a much better place, but she's utterly and completely ruthless. What's more, she's totally unafraid. I really believe that if I had shot her in that flat in Washington Street, she would have blown her own brains out just to make sure that I suffered for it.'

Detective Sergeant ó Nuallán came a little closer. 'How's your father?' she asked.

Katie made a face. 'How do you think? He's in bits. I stayed the night with him last night and all I could hear was him howling. I've never heard a man howl like that before. It was like a dog baying at the moon.'

'And how are you?'

'Me? I'm very upset, of course. I didn't know Ailish very well, but she took such good care of my father and I hadn't seen him so happy since my mother passed.'

'I wasn't talking about Ailish,' said Detective Sergeant ó Nuallán. 'I meant you and John. How are you coping with that?'

Katie frowned at her. 'Me and John? What about me and John? That's none of your business, Kyna.'

Detective Sergeant ó Nuallán said, 'I'm sorry, ma'am. I

apologize. I didn't mean to stick my nose in, considering your rank and all. It's just that your John phoned me this morning and asked me to keep an eye on you and make sure that you were okay.'

'I don't believe this,' said Katie. 'I'm surprised he didn't phone the *Echo* as well. Then everybody would have known about us.'

'I'm really sorry, but he said you had mentioned my name to him and seemed to believe I was reliable. Which I take only as a compliment – not as a free pass to interfere in your personal life.'

'Go on, then,' said Katie. She was finding it hard to keep her voice steady. 'What did he say to you?'

'If you'd rather I just backed off—' said Detective Sergeant ó Nuallán.

'No, tell me what he said to you. Please. I want to know.'

'All right. He said that you were breaking up, the two of you. He said that he couldn't stay in Cork because he didn't feel at home here any more, but he couldn't expect you to go to America with him because of your job.'

Katie took a deep breath, and then she said, 'Well, yes. That's right. That's about the shape of it. Was that all he said?'

'He asked me to make sure that you were all right. Just keep an eye on you, like.'

'Well, thank you, Kyna. I expect I'll survive. I don't really have much of a choice, do I?'

Detective Sergeant ó Nuallán's eyes were glistening with tears.

'He also said that he loved you more than life itself, and that whatever happened he would never forget you, ever.'

That was more than Katie could take. Standing in front

of Detective Sergeant ó Nuallán she started sobbing, her fists clenched in frustration that she couldn't stop herself. She simply stood there with her eyes squeezed tight shut and the tears pouring down her cheeks,. Her chest hurt so much that she was hardly able to draw breath.

Detective Sergeant ó Nuallán put her arms around her and hugged her very close. Katie knew how wrong this was, but she desperately needed somebody to hold her, whoever it was. Detective Sergeant ó Nuallán shushed her and stroked her hair and very gently rocked her. Katie could smell her floral deodorant and feel her breasts pressing against hers. She hadn't felt so comforted for as long as she could remember, and perhaps the wrongness of it made it all the more comforting.

She lifted her head up and opened her eyes. Detective Sergeant ó Nuallán was smiling at her tenderly.

'Katie,' she said, so softly that Katie could hardly hear her, and then she kissed her on the lips.

Their kissing was tentative at first, but then Detective Sergeant ó Nuallán ran her fingers into Katie's hair and kissed her harder, and slipped her tongue into her mouth. They kissed for almost half a minute, more and more passionately, holding each other close. At last they let go, although their fingers trailed together as if both of them were reluctant for this to be over.

'Well,' said Katie. 'What can I say to you? That was lovely.'

Detective Sergeant ó Nuallán said nothing, and Katie thought she could understand why. She didn't want to say that she was sorry, because she wasn't, but at the same time she didn't want to admit how she felt about Katie, because she probably didn't know how she felt herself. Not only that, but Katie knew that she adored her job and didn't want to jeopardize it.

'Why don't you go and see how the Technical Bureau are getting on with the Nissan,' Katie suggested. 'And ask Detective Ryan to check if it appears on any CCTV in the past couple of days? If they stole it in Dennehy's Cross, it's likely they drove it past Victoria Cross or Magazine Road or else they took it round the South Ring, and there are cameras at all of those locations.'

Detective Sergeant ó Nuallán nodded, and said, 'Yes, ma'am. I'll have Horgan check with the pathologist, too, to see if he's completed his post mortem on Mister Dessie.'

Katie smiled at her. She could still feel the tears drying on her cheeks, and still taste Detective Sergeant ó Nuallán's lip gloss. 'Thank you,' she said. And then she said, 'Thank you,' again, and they both knew what that was for.

Thirty-nine

Detective Dooley called her just after 4 p.m. to see if she could help him make sense of some scribbled notebook reports. While she was standing over his desk trying to decipher a witness statement that looked as if it had been written in the dark, in the rain, Katie's iPhone played *And it's no, nay, never – no, nay never no more –*

It was Acting Chief Superintendent Molloy. He sounded more like a barking bull terrier than a man.

'I've just this minute had a call from Michael Gerrety. He's had a package delivered and he says he feels *threatened* and *disgusted* and what are we going to do to protect him? He says he's going to make an official complaint about the way in which we've been handling these latest homicides because they represent a direct threat to his organization and to him personally and neither he nor anybody who works for him has been found guilty of any legal transgression whatsoever.'

'No, they haven't,' Katie retorted. 'And they probably never will be, either, now you've put a stop to Operation Rocker.'

'I don't need that kind of back-chat, Katie, thanks very much.'

'So what's *in* this package that has threatened and

389

disgusted the saintly Mr Gerrety so much? Don't tell me it's a picture of Mary Magdalene. I know how offended Mr Gerrety is by prostitutes.'

'Don't try to be funny with me, either. It's hands.'

'What did you say? *Hands*?'

'I would guess without seeing them that they're the hands that were amputated from your four homicide victims.'

'Holy Mary, Mother of God,' said Katie. 'You told him not to touch them, didn't you?'

'I didn't see the need. I don't think he's going to touch them with a bargepole.'

'All right, then. I'll personally go over to The Elysian and collect them. Maybe you could kindly call Mr Gerrety for me and tell him I'm coming. I assume you have his number to hand?'

'That's not another of your jokes, is it?'

'No, it's not. None of this is funny, Bryan, and Michael Gerrety is the unfunniest thing that has happened to Cork since I was on traffic.'

She took Detective O'Donovan with her. She would have taken Detective Sergeant ó Nuallán because she knew a lot more about the finer details of all four homicide cases than he did. After what had happened between them this morning, though, she thought that it wouldn't be a bad idea to give themselves some breathing space. Apart from that, for all of his bluster about respect for sex workers, Michael Gerrety was deeply contemptuous of women and she wanted to have a man by her side when she spoke to him.

The Elysian Tower was only a block away, so they walked there, under umbrellas that were clattering with rain. The two uniformed gardaí outside the building saluted Katie as she approached.

'A package was delivered to Michael Gerrety about half an hour ago,' said Katie. 'Who brought it?'

'Only a messenger from DHL,' said one of the gardaí. 'We signed for it and took it up to him.'

'Didn't it look at all suspicious?'

'All it said on the box was "meat, perishable", and the name of some beef farm in Kerry. We thought it was probably them steaks you send away for.'

'You're supposed to be protecting this man,' said Katie.

'Yeah, from some black woman. Nobody said nothing about boxes of beef.'

Katie closed her umbrella and shook it and the garda opened the wide glass doors for her. As they went up in the lift to Michael Gerrety's apartment, Katie said, '"Nobody said nothing about boxes of beef." Jesus. I sometimes wonder what they're teaching them at Templemore these days. It didn't occur to him that box might have contained a bomb, as well as steak?'

Detective O'Donovan shook his head, 'Don't be too hard on him, ma'am. He was only following his orders. If he'd been told to look out for a box of beef, he'd have been on it like that,' he said, snapping his fingers.

'Yes, well, personally, I almost wish that it *had* contained a bomb. That would have killed at least three birds with one stone.'

They reached Michael Gerrety's floor and rang the bell at the door of his apartment. It played the opening bars of 'If I Were a Rich Man'. Michael Gerrety's wife, Carole, opened it, unsmiling. She was a short, chubby woman, and she was wearing a wraparound dress in shiny purple silk which didn't seem to fit her anywhere. Her face was Canary Islands orange, with emerald-green eye make-up and scarlet lips. She smelled strongly of Jōvan Musk.

'You'd better come in,' she said, making no effort to hide her hostility. 'Himself is taking a call at the moment.'

As they entered the apartment, Katie could see Michael Gerrety in what appeared to be his study, pacing up and down as he spoke on his mobile phone.

'No, feck that,' he was saying, waving his free hand around. 'No, absolutely not. Well, you can stick it up your grannie's arse as far as I'm concerned.'

Katie looked around. She had seen these apartments advertised in magazines and on the internet, but she had never been inside one. The outside walls were all glass, floor to ceiling, with a wide balcony outside overlooking the city. She could see the River Lee and all its bridges, from the Eamon de Valera Bridge to the Passover, and the spires of Saint Finbarr's Cathedral and the Holy Trinity Church, and the bell tower of St Anne's in Shandon, which had given her the inspiration for Isabelle's nickname.

Beyond that, she could see the green hills surrounding the city, as far as the airport to the south, with heavy grey rain clouds trailing across them like dirty petticoats.

All of the furniture in Michael Gerrety's apartment was leather and chrome and glass, and the floor was highly polished oak. On the wall behind the dining table there was a large semi-abstract painting of a purple nude, with crimson nipples.

Michael Gerrety at last came out of his study. Today he was wearing a jazzy open-necked shirt and chinos, and was holding a half-smoked but unlit cigar. 'Superintendent Maguire! The Boss Lady herself! I'm pleased to see that Bryan takes this so serious.'

He held out his hand, but Katie ignored it. 'This is Detective O'Donovan,' she said. 'He's been one of the leading investigators in all of these homicides.'

'Well, I won't try to shake *your* hand, detective, since the Boss Lady doesn't seem to regard this as a social call.'

'Do you want to show me the box?' Katie asked him.

'Oh, it's *beyond* disgusting,' put in Carole Gerrety. 'Me *gorge* rose when I saw what was in it.'

'Here, it's in the kitchen,' said Michael Gerrety, and led them through. The kitchen was pale lemon-yellow and gleaming and full of all the latest equipment. In the centre stood an island counter, topped with polished marble. On top of the counter lay a white cardboard box, only a little larger than a shirt box. The brown tape that had sealed it had been roughly cut open, and its lid was still half an inch open.

Katie and Detective O'Donovan approached the counter and looked at the box from all sides.

'You've opened it, obviously,' said Katie. 'Apart from that, though, you haven't touched its contents?'

'Are you messing with me? Not at all. When you see for yourself what's inside, you won't want to be touching it, either. It's savagery, that's what it is. Savagery! And not only that, it's an out-and-out threat. It's like saying to me, this is what's going to happen to you if you don't watch yourself, or even if you do.'

Katie sniffed, and said to Detective O'Donovan, 'Can you smell smoke?'

'Oh, I can't stay in here, it's turning my stomach,' said Carole Gerrety. 'Why don't you just take the horrible thing away and let's be rid of it.'

Detective O'Donovan sniffed, too, and then he leaned

closer to the box and said, 'You're right, that's definitely smoke.'

'I don't smell anything at all,' said Michael Gerrety.

'That's because you smoke cigars,' said Katie. 'But this isn't cigar smoke.'

'Smells more like a barbecue to me,' said Detective O'Donovan.

Katie looked at the label on the box. All of the usual DHL labels and barcodes were stuck to the top of it, but there was also a label with a picture of a green pasture on it, and two grazing black cows. The lettering said Phelan's Finest Dexter Beef and gave an address and an email in County Kerry.

Katie took a pair of latex gloves out of her pocket and pulled them on. Then, using her ballpen, she lifted the lid of the box and folded it back. The inside was lined with bubble wrap, and when she opened the bubble wrap she found eight human hands. They had been neatly tied together in pairs with thin black satin ribbon, palm to palm, as if they were praying.

There were two white pairs and two black pairs, one very dark but the other paler. The white pairs and the darker of the black pairs looked shrivelled, while the paler black pair was bloated and blotched.

All four of the left hands had rings on their fingers, some gold, some silver, three with semi-precious stones – a garnet, an onyx, and a yellow heliodor. The black right hand and the bloated right hand were also wearing rings. The ring on the black right hand was plaited gold, although it was only cheap because the gold had started to wear off, while the ring on the bloated right hand was a silver skull with red glass eyes.

Michael Gerrety came a little closer and pointed at the skull ring. 'That's Desmond O'Leary's. The ring, any road. I couldn't tell you for certain if the hand is his.'

'Do you recognize any of the others?'

'How do I know? They're *hands*, that's all. If you had your feet chopped off, I'll bet that even your husband wouldn't reck that they were yours.'

Katie didn't tell him that Paul was long dead and buried: she didn't want to give him the pleasure. 'This one has a quincunx tattooed on it,' she said. 'Are you sure you've never seen that before?'

'A *what* does it have?'

'A quincunx. Four outer dots arranged in a square with a fifth dot in the middle. It's a prison tattoo mainly, because it represents a person trapped inside four walls. And it's mostly seen on Romanians.'

'Well, I can't lie to you and say that I don't know any Romanians, but I never saw that tattoo before.'

Katie folded back the bubble wrap and closed the box. 'We'll be taking these away then and examining them more closely. I'm not one hundred per cent sure who sent these or what the sender was trying to imply by sending them to you, but for the time being we're continuing to keep guards outside and we do recommend that you take your personal security very seriously.'

'What do you mean you're not one hundred per cent sure? It's that Nigerian woman, isn't it? That's what Bryan said. He said that she'd even admitted it to you and told you why she was doing it.'

'Did *you* know her sister?' asked Katie. Detective O'Donovan was carefully sliding the cardboard box into his forensic evidence bag, but when she said that, he stopped and looked up, waiting to hear how Michael Gerrety was going to answer her.

'What kind of a question is that? How could I know her sister if I don't even know *her*?'

'It's because of her sister that she's after you. That's what she says. Her sister was called Nwaha and she drowned herself because she was so ashamed of what you and your minions had turned her into.'

Michael Gerrety pretended to think for a while and then he said, 'No. Sorry, superintendent. Can't help you, I'm afraid. What did you say her name was again?'

'Don't bother,' said Katie. 'Come on, Patrick, let's get this evidence over to Dr O'Brien. It won't take him long to work out who these hands belong to. He's got the bodies that go with them.'

Michael Gerrety showed them to the door. As he opened it up, he said, quite casually, 'Bryan Molloy said that you were seriously considering dropping those thirty-nine charges against me.'

'Oh, did he now?'

'He said that it was a waste of public money and the court's time to pursue them any further – what with all of your evidence being nothing much more than hearsay and malicious gossip.'

'He told you that, did he?'

'Well, we were discussing it, like, at the golf club. We both agreed that it was better to be realistic about sex work.'

'Realistic? Is that what you call it? So if some poor Nigerian girl is trafficked away from her parents and forced to have sex with countless numbers of dirty old men, so that in the end she's so mortified by what she's become that she throws herself into the Lee, that's "realistic", is it?'

Michael Gerrety smiled at her and Katie knew why. He was smiling because he was sure that he would never have to appear in court on any of the charges that had been filed against him. He was smiling because she hated him but he had beaten her, whether the hands fitted the bodies or not.

'Thanks for coming, superintendent,' he told her. 'And thanks also for the warning. I'll keep my eyes open for any vengeful young Nigerian women. Bye bye, then. Good luck.'

Katie and Detective O'Donovan walked back to the station. It had stopped raining for now but more clouds were rolling in from the south-west, as dark as slate, and it would soon start pouring again. 'You'll have those sent to Dr O'Brien asap, won't you?'

'Of course. Are you going up to have a word with Molloy?'

'No, no, I'm not,' said Katie. 'I'd only lose my temper and there isn't any point. Gerrety's right, really. We don't have enough evidence to be certain that he'll be convicted, and even if he is, he'll only get a fine, which he can afford, and have some of his assets confiscated by the CAB. Without the evidence we would have got from Operation Rocker, we're stymied.'

'So what do you plan to do? You're not going to give up on him, are you? That wouldn't be like you, if you don't mind my saying so.'

'It wouldn't, would it? No, I'm not giving up on Michael Gerrety, ever. Right now, though, we have to catch this Angel of Revenge or Avenging Angel or whatever she calls herself, so let's just concentrate on that.'

Forty

She had intended to stay with her father that night, but she didn't finish work until 9.45 p.m., and when she rang him to tell him that she would be late, he said not to worry about him. He was still very shocked and distressed, but Ailish's daughter had been around to see him and in any case he would rather be alone for the moment. And, yes, he had eaten something. Ailish's daughter had brought him a chicken pie.

She stayed overnight at Anglesea Street. The room was sparsely furnished and there was only a single bed, but there was a kettle and some teabags and some sachets of instant coffee and hot chocolate. She undressed and put on the plain white nightgown that she kept at the office, and then made herself a mug of chocolate.

She knew that she shouldn't allow herself to get stressed about Michael Gerrety, but after sitting on the bed for a few minutes sipping her chocolate she stood up and parted the curtains and looked out. There, in the rain, stood The Elysian Tower, its windows lit up in a chequerboard pattern because so many of its apartments were still unoccupied. At the very top, though, she could see the lights of Michael Gerrety's apartment.

In a way, she believed that dropping the charges against

Gerrety was the right course of action for now. If they made a bags of this prosecution, it would be much more difficult to get him back into court at a later date even if they managed to gather some much more convincing evidence against him.

What was nagging her, though, was how it was ever going to be possible for them to get hold of that evidence, now that Acting Chief Superintendent Molloy had cancelled Operation Rocker. It also seemed as if Molloy had become buddies with Gerrety at the golf club.

She closed the curtains and drained the last of her chocolate. When she had brushed her teeth, she rang John. She had already texted him and told him that she would be staying in the city.

'How are you?' she asked him.

'Fine. I'm fine. I've just got off the phone with Nils Shapiro.'

'Oh, your pharmacy friend in LA.'

'That's right. He still wants me on board. He's very keen.'

'I see,' said Katie. 'Maybe we can talk about it tomorrow, when I get back.'

'I don't know that there's too much to talk about.'

'Well, you know me, I can always find something to talk about. My mother was always asking when I was ever going to shut my mouth and eat my dinner.'

'How did she expect you to eat your dinner with your mouth shut?'

'I'm not in the mood for jokes, John.'

'No, sorry.'

'Talking of dinner, have you had any?' she asked him.

'You're not my mother, Katie.'

'No, I'm not. In fact I'm not anything at all to you, am I?'

'Katie—'

'I'm sorry. I didn't mean that. It's been a long day. I'll see you tomorrow so. Goodnight.'

'Katie—' he said, but she switched off her phone. Maybe it was rude, and unkind, but she was beginning to feel that when he said he didn't love Ireland any more, what he really meant was that he didn't love her. Well, he did, but not enough to give up his life in America. She supposed she couldn't blame him. He wanted sun instead of rain, blue skies instead of grey. He wanted boundless opportunity, instead of 'Ah well, we've suffered many times before in the past and we've learned to put a brave face on it, like.'

She climbed into bed. The sheets smelled of laundry instead of her. She closed her eyes and almost instantly fell asleep.

'Smoked,' Dr O'Brien said.

'*Smoked*?' she said, looking at the eight hands laid out in a line on the stainless steel table in front of her. 'You mean, like bacon?'

'That's correct. Or kippers. They haven't been done in a proper smoker, though. I'd say a normal domestic oven. But it's desiccated them enough to preserve them for a while – these three pairs, anyway. This fourth pair haven't been smoked at all. Well – you can tell by the shape they're in.'

'But they all fit the wrists of our four victims?'

'No question at all,' said Dr O'Brien. 'Every one of them, a perfect match, like a jigsaw. Or Lego maybe. Would you like me to show you?'

'No, thanks, Ailbe,' said Katie. 'I'll take your word for it.'

It was almost noon. The sun was shining in through the clerestory windows of the pathology laboratory, so that it looked almost like the interior of a church. All of the congregation here, though, were lying on trolleys under green sheets and had already gone to the place for which they had been praying all of their lives.

Dr O'Brien picked up Mawakiya's left hand and turned it over. 'Apart from the left hand of victim number three – the one you call Bula, is it? – the left hands of all the other victims were amputated very raggedly, almost certainly using a hacksaw. I thought before from the condition of their wrists that they had cut off their own left hands, but now I am almost certain of it. With Bula it's impossible to say, of course, because his left hand was detached with a circular saw.'

'Well, we know for sure what the motive was for cutting their hands off,' said Katie. 'Revenge, as you said, Ailbe, right from the very beginning. And they were sent to Michael Gerrety either as a threat or as trophies to show him what she had done to the people who worked for him, or both.'

'I think in this case, both,' said Dr O'Brien. 'Not that it falls within my mandate to have an opinion. But it was common in many parts of West Africa for hands to be amputated as a punishment. In the colonial days they did it to prove to their white bosses that the punishment had been duly carried out. Well, it would have saved them from dragging in the whole body, wouldn't it? In the Congo, they also used it as proof that expensive ammunition hadn't been wasted. Even brutality has to stick to a budget.'

Katie would normally have taken the South Ring Road back to Anglesea Street, but she had to go into the city centre to do some shopping at the Paul Street Tesco. She needed dog food for Barney and washing-up liquid and cheese and fresh bread. She also felt like doing something totally normal, like pushing a shopping trolley around to the sound of piped music, so that she wouldn't have to think about John and severed hands and Obioma and Michael Gerrety.

She turned into Washington Street, past the courthouse. As she was passing the building that housed Michael Gerrety's brothel, she saw the front door open and a woman step out. To her astonishment, she realized that it was Obioma. Her black, Medusa-like hair was untied, but she was still wearing a black T-shirt and black jeans and boots, and that black leather waistcoat. She looked up and down the street, as if to make sure that nobody was watching her, and then she started to walk towards Grand Parade.

Katie stepped on her brakes and the van behind her blew its horn at her. It pulled up beside her and the passenger yelled out, 'Learn to drive, you stupid cow! You almost had us up your arse there!'

Katie took no notice. Obioma was crossing Grand Parade and heading towards Patrick Street, and walking very quickly. The traffic lights were red, but Katie drove through them, turned left, and pulled her car up on to the pavement outside Finn's Corner sportswear shop. She climbed out and started to run across the road, although she had to stop when a car came around the corner and almost hit her.

'Are you after dying, you daft bitch?' the driver shouted at her.

She didn't say anything but dodged around the back of his car and reached the pavement on the opposite side of the road. However, Obioma must have heard the driver's brakes screeching and him shouting at her, because she turned around. The instant she saw that Katie was coming after her, she started to run.

Katie started running, too. Patrick Street was crowded

with lunchtime shoppers and she had to jink and sidestep to avoid bumping into them.

Obioma collided with several pedestrians and Katie heard them calling out after her in protest, but then she left the pavement and started to run in the road. Katie followed her and almost knocked a cyclist off his bike.

The two of them ran along the middle of Patrick Street, with shoppers turning round to stare at them. Obioma was about fifty metres ahead of Katie, and even though she was wearing high-heeled boots she was running very fast. Katie felt as if she ought to shout, '*Stop her!*' but she knew from her experience as a young garda that people never reacted quickly enough, and that Obioma would be two streets away before they realized what she wanted them to do. Besides, she was too short of breath.

Obioma ran into French Church Street, a long narrow pedestrian alleyway that would lead her to Paul Street. Again, she was colliding with people as she ran, and she knocked one woman's shopping all across the pavement, but that didn't slow her down. In fact, she seemed to Katie to be running even faster. Katie herself was fit, and exercised regularly, but by now she was panting hard and she was very conscious of her holster slapping against her thigh. Her vision was jiggling like a hand-held camera and the shopfronts and cafes all along the street were becoming a blur.

She reached Paul Street and looked left and right to see where Obioma had gone. There was no sign of her anywhere, although Katie guessed she had probably turned right because that part of the street was more crowded. She started to jog towards Academy Street, trying to glimpse Obioma's snake-like hair bobbing up and down ahead of her.

As she jogged, she took out her iPhone so that she could call for back-up. Obioma was in the city centre, on foot, and patrol cars could encircle the area within a few minutes. She slowed down to a walk to switch it on, but as she did so Obioma stepped out of the darkened doorway of a men's hairdresser's called The Crop Shop and hit her. It was a stunning chop with the edge of her hand which struck Katie on the cheekbone and sent her stumbling backwards across the pavement.

Obioma stalked after her and hit her again, with the left hand this time, striking her left ear. Katie pitched over on to her shoulder and dropped her iPhone. Obioma immediately stamped on it, twice, and crushed it.

Katie's head was singing and her vision was even more jumbled than when she had been running, but she managed to reach for her gun and tug it out of its holster.

Obioma stood over her. A crowd of shoppers had already started to gather around them, and Katie could hear one young man calling out, 'Catfight! Come and see this, boy! Catfight!'

Katie propped herself up on her left elbow and pointed her revolver at Obioma. 'You're under arrest,' she told her. She could feel her right eye closing up already.

'Or what?' said Obioma, looking down at her. 'You will shoot me, in front of all of these people, with the risk of hitting one of them as well? I don't think so, detective superintendent. Besides, I don't think you're the shooting kind.'

Now that Katie had produced her gun, the shoppers who had crowded around closest to them started to shuffle backwards. 'I'm a Garda detective,' Katie announced, without taking her eyes off Obioma. 'Will somebody please dial 112 and somebody go looking for a guard. And, please, all of you, clear out of here now, as quick as you can.'

Several of the onlookers took out their phones and started prodding, while the rest of them began to disperse, but far too slowly, as if they were reluctant to miss out on any of the action.

'Will you push on!' she snapped at them. 'I'm making an arrest here!'

Obioma, however, was giving Katie that haughty, heavy-lidded look. 'I have a mission to fulfil,' she said. 'You know what I am sworn to do, and I will do it. There is only one way that you can stop me.'

With that, she turned around and started to walk away. The crowd parted to let her through, pushing at each other in their effort to keep clear of her in case Katie started shooting.

She turned the corner into Academy Street and was gone. Katie stood with her gun in her hand, pointing at nothing. Then she lowered it and slid it back into its holster. Obioma was wrong. She *was* the shooting kind. She had shot a killer before, and fatally wounded him, but that had been in a moment of high stress, when her own life had been in danger. She was not going to shoot a woman in the street in broad daylight in front of at least a hundred bystanders, especially since that woman had presented no obvious threat apart from hitting her, and especially since she would have had to shoot her in the back. That would have been summary execution.

More than that, she was keenly aware that Obioma wasn't afraid of her. When she pointed her gun at most suspects that she arrested they would put up their hands and give up immediately, but Obioma didn't care if she shot her or not. Her fearlessness made her invulnerable.

She heard sirens. A patrol car appeared at the Academy Street end of the street, and then another two at the opposite end, in Saint Peter and Paul Place, even though that was a pedestrian precinct. She heard running feet and saw yellow high-visibility jackets making their way towards her through the crowd.

Her head was throbbing and she felt that the pavement was ebbing and flowing underneath her feet. An elderly priest came up to her and put his arm around her. She could smell the mints on his breath.

'You look very pale, my dear. Take some deep breaths, that's it. Look, there's a bench over here. Come and sit down. That's a fierce terrible bruise on your cheek there and no mistake.'

She sat down, and the priest sat down next to her. Two gardaí came up to her, and at least one of them recognized who she was.

'Who did this to you, ma'am? Do you know where she might have gone now?'

'Yes, officer,' said Katie. 'I know who did it. I know where she's going, too. But God alone knows how we can stop her.'

Forty-one

Detective O'Donovan came into her office and said, 'You're going to love this, ma'am. But then again, you're probably not.'

'Has she been caught yet?'

'Not a sniff of her anywhere, I'm afraid. We've had thirty-five guards and the dog unit out searching for her. They were even looking in the ladies' toilets in Dunne's. That caused a bit of screaming, so I'm told.'

'Well, she managed to outwit us before, didn't she, Patrick, in Washington Street? Never even left the building after she shot Mister Dessie. No wonder we didn't see her coming out of the front door, she never did, and she must have been staying in that empty flat ever since. We did search that flat, didn't we?'

Detective O'Donovan nodded. 'We did of course, yeah. But it was probably just a quick look in and all she would have had to do is hide herself in a wardrobe or under the bed or somewhere like that.'

Katie gently touched her right cheek with her fingertips. Her eye was swollen and tender and she knew that by tomorrow morning she would have a huge black eye. She had taken two Nurofen, so at least her headache had subsided. 'So what's this thing that I'm going to love but probably not?'

'We've just brought in your two favourite gardaí, Ronan Kelly and Billy Daly. They're downstairs in the interview room.'

'Brought them in? What do you mean, you've brought them in?'

'They were arrested at Ringaskiddy about an hour ago, trying to board the Swansea ferry with a load of drugs on them. I don't know exactly how much, but there was heroin and racemic methamphetamine and so many pills you could have opened a maracas factory.'

'Holy Mother of God, what did they think they were doing?'

'They were emigrating. They knew you were going to report them for corruption, so they decided to make themselves scarce. They would have got away with it, too, except that one of the sniffer dogs was being taken off duty and started barking at them as they walked past.'

Katie stood up. 'Right, I'll go down and talk to them. I can't believe those two. They walked through the stupid wood and got hit by every branch.'

Detective O'Donovan raised his hand and said, 'Wait, ma'am. There's something more.'

'Don't tell me. What?'

'After they were stopped at Ringaskiddy, Daly's car was found in the ferry terminal car park. Apparently he was just going to leave it there. It was only an old Honda Civic and he isn't married or nothing so it's not as if he has a wife or a partner who would have needed it.'

'So?'

'So a Honda Civic stopped across the street from Nolan's yard at Dennehy's Cross at the same time as the Nissan X-Trail was stolen – the one that rammed your car.'

'Really? Why didn't Ryan report that as soon as he saw it?'

'Because it only stopped for a couple of minutes, and you can see that the driver is making a call on his mobile. Then it drove off.'

'Don't tell me it was Garda Daly's car?'

'I'm sorry to say that it was. It didn't look like he was doing anything in particular, but he could well have been keeping a lookout while Kelly cut the wire and then he was checking on his mobile that he'd managed to break into the X-Trail and get it started.'

Katie didn't know what to say. If Garda Kelly and Garda Daly had stolen the X-Trail, they had done it with the deliberate intention of using it to run her off the road and kill her. More than likely it had been them who had been following her when she left her house to go to Kent station and had come up so close behind her as she joined the main road to Cork.

They had been stupid enough to ram her car while it was going up a hill, with no certainty at all that the crash would be fatal. If she had been driving, instead of Ailish, she would probably have survived it. It was only Ailish's bad heart that had killed her.

Katie took a deep, deep breath.

'Are you okay, ma'am?' asked Detective O'Donovan.

'What do you think? Let's go down and have a word with those two, shall we?'

Ronan Kelly and Billy Daly were sitting at the table in the interview room, both looking frowsy-haired, unshaven and dejected. A burly uniformed garda was standing by the door with his hands behind his back, staring at the ceiling. He knew them both well, of course, but he was under instructions not to say a word to them.

When Katie and Detective O'Donovan entered the room, neither of them looked up. Katie said to the garda on the door, 'If you could wait outside, please.' She didn't want everybody in the station to hear the details of this interview before she had even had a chance to discuss it with Acting Chief Superintendent Molloy and decide what charges they were going to bring.

Katie and Detective O'Donovan sat down opposite the two gardaí. Ronan Kelly glanced up and saw Katie's bruised eye and Katie thought she caught him giving the ghost of a smile.

'Patrick, would you?' she said, and nodded towards the recording machine. Detective O'Donovan switched it on and Katie said, 'Interview with Garda Ronan Kelly and Garda William Daly.' She checked the clock on the wall and added the time and the date.

'Now, we're going to switch that off and talk informally,' she said.

'Ma'am?' said Detective O'Donovan. 'I just switched it on.'

'Well, switch it off again, please, and go right back to the beginning.'

When Detective O'Donovan had done that, Katie propped her elbows on the table and laced her fingers together like a judge about to pass sentence.

'You two clowns tried to kill me,' she said.

Billy Daly said, 'That wasn't us! Swear on the Bible!'

'Will you shut your trap, Billy!' said Ronan Kelly. 'Saying it wasn't us is just as bad as saying it was.'

'Jesus, you two are thick,' said Katie. 'How you managed

to qualify as gardaí I can't understand for the life of me. I'm surprised you know which end of a baton to take hold of. You're not only thick, you're greedy and immoral and a disgrace to your uniforms. And to think the both of you had the Garda badge tattooed on you.'

She paused, and then she said, 'There's no point in you trying to deny what you did. You knew I was going to report you for taking bribes from Michael Gerrety. So you thought you could save your miserable skins by getting rid of me.

'Instead of that, you killed a perfectly innocent and happy woman. She was somebody's mother and even more than that, she was soon to be somebody's wife.'

'That was hardly our fault,' said Ronan Kelly out of his slit of a mouth. 'How were we to know that you weren't driving your own car? It's not as though we're fecking psychic.'

'So you admit it?'

'I'm not saying nothing. We might have done it and we might not. I thought you said this was just an informal discussion, anyway. Testing the water, like. Seeing where we stand.'

'There's no question where you two will be standing and that's in the dock. What were you planning to do about Detective Sergeant ó Nuallán? She was the one who first told me that you were taking money to look the other way.'

'What does it matter? We made a right hames of it, any road.'

'We were going to do the same to her,' put in Billy Daly. 'The same only different, like.'

'I fecking told you to shut your fecking trap,' said Ronan Kelly.

'We have CCTV evidence of you stealing the Nissan

X-Trail from Nolan's Construction,' said Katie. 'We have forensic evidence that it was the Nissan that collided with the rear of my car. That was done deliberately, so we're not just talking manslaughter.'

She opened a folder in front of her. 'Not only that, we have witness statements that confirm that you were paid substantial sums of money by the late Desmond O'Leary on behalf of Michael Gerrety in order not to interfere with any of his trafficking of girls under the age of legal consent or illegal immigrants. You were treated to sexual favours, too, free of charge. We also have evidence that you knew of his drugging and beating of unwilling sex workers.'

Both gardaí sat silent for a while, staring down at the table in front of them like two admonished schoolboys. In reality, Katie had no substantive evidence that the money that Mister Dessie had given them had come from Michael Gerrety, even though it was highly likely. There was nothing in the folder in front of her except for a report on stolen farm machinery in Maglin. However, they would be facing a charge of unlawful homicide and she reckoned they would do anything to mitigate the punishment they would receive for that.

Ronan Kelly frowned at Katie and he almost looked remorseful. *Briseann an dúchair tri shúile an chat*, she thought. *A cat reveals its character in its eyes*. If he wasn't remorseful, then he must be bitterly regretful for having been so self-indulgent, and such an easy mark for Michael Gerrety's bribery. Sitting here in this interview room, about to be charged with serious crimes, what had he got out of it, after all? Some money, which had all been spent, and some drunken sex, which was all over and washed off. A tattoo, too, which would make him an obvious target in prison.

'If I tell you a few things, give you some leads, like, would that make it any easier on us?' he asked.

'It depends on how useful they turned out to be, these leads.'

'Well, I know you've been after Michael Gerrety. I know about Operation Rocker, like, and how Molloy was after calling it off, and how you weren't exactly delighted.'

'Word gets around, doesn't it?' said Katie.

'Bryan Molloy and Michael Gerrety have known each other for years. I don't think they've ever made a secret of it. Michael Gerrety started off his sex business in Limerick, remember, when Molloy was just a sergeant. He gave Molloy regular kickbacks to keep the law off his doorstep, and that's how his businesses did so well.

'He's been paying him ever since. I don't know how much, but a fair heap, I'd say. In return, Molloy uses his contacts in Dublin to put pressure on the politicians to change the law about sex workers. Gerrety thought that Chief Superintendent O'Driscoll was one almighty pain in the arse, and when Molloy was appointed to replace him he thought that all of his Christmases had come at once.'

'Have you any proof at all that Michael Gerrety has been bribing Bryan Molloy?' asked Katie. 'Any evidence that would hold up in court?'

Ronan Kelly turned to Billy Daly. Billy Daly rasied one eyebrow and then he leaned over and whispered something in Ronan Kelly's ear. Ronan Kelly listened, and nodded, and then he turned back to Katie and said, 'It depends.'

'It depends on what offences I charge you both with, is that what you mean?'

'Something like that.'

'Tell me what you've got and I'll tell you what concessions I might make,' said Katie.

At the back of her mind, she was seething with anger and hatred for these two men. They had killed Ailish, and they had intended to kill her, and they had destroyed her father's happiness forever. Not only that, they had dragged the honour of An Garda Síochána through the dirt, and if it wasn't for the Garda oath of attestation that she had taken she would have quit her job and gone to America with John.

In spite of that, her training and her experience kept the door to the back of her mind firmly closed. Showing how angry she was would only be counterproductive. She wanted Michael Gerrety, and the only way to get him was to keep calm – almost disinterested.

'They took my phone off me,' said Ronan Kelly. 'They took my phone off me, but it's all on there. Recorded, like.'

'Okay …' said Katie. 'Patrick, would you be good enough to go and fetch Garda Kelly's phone for him.'

Detective O'Donovan left the room and Katie was left with Ronan Kelly and Billy Daly.

'You might have got away with it if you hadn't had all those drugs on you,' she told them.

'We didn't have any choice, did we? We hardly had any money between us, so we were going to sell the stuff to keep us going.'

'Where did you get it?'

'Off of one drugs bust and another, over the past year or so,' said Ronan Kelly. 'Like we would hand in about a half of what we seized and keep the rest. We sold a lot of it off, but we still had a fair bit left. Maybe ten or eleven thousand euros' worth. This is totally off the record, mind, and if you ask me again on the record, I'll deny it.'

'Where were you going?' Katie asked him.

'Liverpool, to begin with. We've got a few friends there.'

'And then what?'

'I don't know. If you want to know the truth, I think we've made a fecking pig's dinner of everything. I've learned one thing: you don't need much in the way of brains to commit any kind of crime, but you have to be a genius to get away with it.'

Detective O'Donovan came back with Ronan Kelly's mobile phone in a clear plastic evidence bag. He handed it over and Ronan Kelly shook it out of the bag and set it down on the table. He touched the voice memo button and sat back with his arms folded.

They heard fiddle music playing faintly in the background, and a bodhrán drumming, and laughter, and glasses clinking. Then they heard Ronan Kelly saying, 'We've sorted that (unclear) at Carroll's Quay.'

Another man's voice said, 'Yeah, Billy told us. That's grand. We appreciate it.'

'I mean, what a fecking eejit,' said Ronan Kelly. 'You don't go into a knocking shop with your wallet stuffed full of cash. What do you expect is going to happen? Anyway, we persuaded the feller to drop his complaint.'

'What did you say to him?' asked the other man. 'You'd be forced to tell his missus, something like that?'

'We tried that,' Ronan Kelly replied. 'Trouble was, he said he wasn't married. So we told him the girl was underage and we'd have to charge him with defilement.'

The other man laughed. 'Dowtcha boy! And you know what's really, really funny about that?'

'Go on, Dessie. What's really, really funny about that?'

'She is underage! She's only fourteen!'

'Oh, for feck's sake, you (unclear).'

'Anyway, Michael's shown you his gratitude by giving you another hundred yoyos each.'

'Tell him, any time. We're only doing our job upholding the law.'

'As long as it's the law according to Michael Gerrety, he'll be happy.'

Katie said, 'Got him! You can turn that off now. I don't need to hear any more.'

Ronan Kelly reached forward to switch off his phone, but Detective O'Donovan snatched it away first and dropped it back into the evidence bag.

'I'd be interested to know why you recorded that particular conversation,' said Katie.

'Oh, I recorded plenty of others, just to be on the safe side. You're never quite sure where you are with people like Gerrety. But this is the only one that's out-and-out incriminating.'

'We have plenty of interviews with Dessie O'Leary on record,' said Detective O'Donovan. 'We won't have any trouble matching the voice.'

'So what's it worth?' asked Ronan Kelly. 'I mean, that's pure gold, as evidence, you have to admit. It's only second best to having a video of Michael Gerrety handing us the money in person.'

'It's highly incriminating, I agree,' said Katie. She could feel her heart beating harder, but she was trying to stay dispassionate. 'I'll tell you what I'll do, I'll forget about the drugs.'

'You'll forget about the *drugs*? Is that all?'

'Garda Kelly, I have to bring charges of corruption against you. It wouldn't make any sense for me to charge Michael Gerrety with bribing you, would it, if I didn't also charge you with accepting those bribes?'

'Well, thanks for nothing at all,' said Ronan Kelly. 'Just don't expect me to give you any other evidence.'

'I won't bring any charges of reckless endangerment,' Katie told him.

'*What*? How could we be guilty of reckless endangerment?'

'You were aware that girls under the age of sixteen were being trafficked for sex. You did nothing to stop that trafficking. In fact, you facilitated it, even though you were police officers. I'd call that reckless endangerment, wouldn't you? And the penalty for reckless endangerment is ten years inside.'

Ronan Kelly said, 'I'm not saying another word. I withdraw everything that I've said to you and I won't give another interview without it being recorded and a lawyer present to represent me.'

'I don't honestly care,' said Katie. 'You're a pair of worthless dirtbags and you're going to be punished for killing a wonderful woman who didn't deserve to die. You've given me everything I need and if I never see you or hear from you again, either of you, that will suit me very well indeed.'

'Do you know what you are?' said Ronan Kelly. 'You're a fecking witch, that's what you are. We shouldn't have tried to make you crash your car. We should have burned you at the stake.'

Forty-two

Branna pressed the doorbell outside Michael Gerrety's apartment and it played 'If I Were a Rich Man'. She stood there, wondering if she was making a terrible mistake, and if she ought to run back to the lifts and escape from The Elysian Tower as quickly as she could. It had seemed like such a brilliant idea when she had first thought of it, getting the inside story on Michael Gerrety's vice empire by pretending that she wanted to be a sex worker, but she was beginning to lose her nerve.

She was wearing a pink mini-dress that she had taken up two inches to make it even shorter, and the same wedge sandals as when she had first approached Michael Gerrety at Amber's. She had back-combed her hair in a Miley Cyrus style and stuck on false eyelashes, although they made her blink as if she were facing a barrage of flash photographers.

Michael Gerrety opened the door himself. 'Ah, there you are,' he said. 'Why don't you come along in? Brenda, isn't it?'

'Branna,' she said, stepping inside. The sun was going down and the apartment was filled with orange light.

'Branna, my mistake,' said Michael Gerrety. 'Would you care for a drink, Branna?'

'Just a lemonade, if you have some.'

'Oh come on, how about a splash of vodka in it? It'll relax you.'

'What? All right then, but only a splash.'

Branna looked around. She could see Carole Gerrety sitting outside on the balcony with a tall glass of Pimm's, talking on her iPhone.

'This is pure amazing, this flat,' she commented. 'And the view you have!'

Michael Gerrety came out of the kitchen with her drink. It was in a frosted glass, with lots of ice and a slice of lemon. 'I have to pay for it, though, the view,' he told her. 'Nothing comes for nothing in this world. I'd say without a doubt that I'm probably the hardest-working man in Cork. If not the country.'

He sat down on one of the tan leather couches and beckoned for her to sit down next to him. 'Now I've got the chance to see you close up, you're a very pretty young lady,' he told her. 'You should do very well for yourself, depending on what you're prepared to offer.'

'Like I told you, Mr Gerrety, I'm not an innocent. I've had three boyfriends and I've done it with all of them.'

'All right,' said Michael Gerrety. 'Supposing I said, I'll give you a hundred euros if you give me oral sex, right now. I'll take it out and you get down on your hands and knees and gobble it for me, and then I'll spray it all over your face.'

Branna felt as if her stomach were going down in the lift and leaving her behind. There was Michael Gerrety, lolling back on the couch in his green and white striped silk shirt and his chinos, smiling at her. Supposing he actually took out his penis and expected her to suck it? But then she thought, his wife's out there, sitting on the balcony. He can't expect me to do it if there's a chance that she's going to turn around and see us.

'Without a condom, a hundred and twenty,' she said, although her throat was so tight that she could hardly speak.

Michael Gerrety laughed and slapped his thigh. 'I like your style, Branna! That's a bit above the going rate, but like I say, you're a pretty girl and you'll probably get it. Is there anything you won't do? You know what I'm talking about, don't you? If a client wants to piss on you, or vice versa, or if he wants to bring a friend along for a threesome, or even a foursome?'

'I don't care what I do, Mr Gerrety, so long as they treat me with respect, and so long as they pay me.'

'That's perfect, Branna. That's exactly the right attitude. And that's why you've made the right decision, coming to me. If you'd tried to set up on your own, you wouldn't have the website advertising that I can offer you, so you wouldn't get nearly so much work. Apart from that, and more important, you wouldn't get the protection that goes with it. All of the girls who work through Cork Fantasy Girls are very well looked after.'

He finished his drink, and then he said, 'I've had a little trouble with staff lately. I've lost one or two of them. But I'm hiring some new fellers and they'll take good care of you, I promise.'

Branna tried to smile. 'That's grand, Mr Gerrety. When do you think I'll be starting?'

'Give it a couple of days. We have to set up your web page and get you online. There's a room free on Carroll's Quay and you can move into that as soon as you like. We should think of a working name for you, too, shouldn't we? How about Roxanne? Or Godiva? I like that – Godiva! That's what we'll call you.'

Branna nodded, dumbly. She was close to panicking. She had all the evidence she needed on the voice recorder in her bag and all she wanted to do now was get out of here. Although Michael Gerrety appeared to be so relaxed and so matter-of-fact about her working as a prostitute, it was his very nonchalance that frightened her most of all. Here he was, sitting in this luxury apartment as the burning orange sun sank over the city, asking a seventeen-year-old girl if she would allow men to sodomize her and urinate all over her, or even worse, and yet he was treating their conversation as completely normal.

'There's one more thing,' he said. 'We'll give you a medical examination before you start. Cork Fantasy Girls is always very responsible when it comes to sexual health. You'll be given examinations regularly after that, usually about once a month, or at any time you feel that a client might have passed something on to you.'

'When you say "given" ...?' asked Branna.

'Oh – I don't mean given for free. You have to pay for each examination, of course. But you won't notice because they're automatically deducted out of your earnings, like everything else. Your website, your rent for your room, the gas you use, the electric, your food, your condoms, your wipes. But you'll still be making more money in a day than you would have made at Dunne's in a month, and you won't be paying any tax or social insurance, so you won't have anything to complain about.'

'All right,' said Branna. She stood up and said, 'I'll wait to hear from you, then.'

'No, you won't,' said Michael Gerrety.

'What?'

'You won't hear from me unless you give me your mobile number.'

'Oh, no, of course not. If you have a pen I'll write it down for you.'

Michael Gerrety reached across the coffee table and handed her a silver ballpen. 'Here, write it on this magazine.'

He watched her while she was leaning over the table, writing. When she handed him back the pen and the magazine, he said, 'What are you wearing, underneath that dress?'

Branna said, 'A bra. I always have to wear a bra.'

'Anything else?'

'No.'

'Lift it up, then.'

'What?'

'Lift up your dress and let's take a look.'

Branna turned around. Carole Gerrety was still on the phone.

'Go on,' said Michael Gerrety. 'You'll be doing it professionally from next week.'

There was something hard in Michael Gerrety's expression that made Branna think that this was a test. She didn't think that he suspected her of not being genuinely interested in becoming a sex worker, but this was a way of making sure that she had no inhibitions about showing herself off to strange men.

She took hold of the hem of her dress and lifted it up to her waist. Michael Gerrety looked at her for a long moment and then he said, 'Good. That's how the punters like it. I'll be giving you a call, then, as soon as everything's been arranged.'

He paused, and then he said, 'That's grand. You can let it down now. Don't want the missus to see you flashing your gash, now, do we?'

'I'll see you after, then.'

'Well, not me myself. I don't personally run this business on a day-to-day basis. But somebody will be in touch with you on my behalf and get you sorted.'

He laid his hand on Branna's shoulder and steered her towards the door. 'I want to thank you for coming to see me. I wish all the girls who worked through my website were as wholesome as you are, and I mean it, you're really wholesome. And you're very pretty with it. I certainly wouldn't kick you out of bed for eating crisps.'

They hadn't reached the door, however, before the doorbell played 'If I Were a Rich Man'.

Michael Gerrety called out to Carole, 'Are you expecting anyone? Carole! Carole, will you get off that fecking phone for one minute! Are you expecting anyone?'

Carole didn't hear him, and the doorbell chimed again. 'Jesus,' said Michael Gerrety. 'It's probably the Chinky she ordered.'

He opened the door. As soon as he did so, without any hesitation, Obioma stepped into the apartment and shut it behind her. She was all in black, as usual, except for a white scarf knotted around her hair. She was pointing her pocket shotgun directly at Michael Gerrety's face.

'How the *feck* did you get in here?' Michael Gerrety demanded. 'Carole! Call the guards! *Carole*!'

Carole was still on the phone and still she didn't hear him. Obioma said, 'Get back, Mr Gerrety, and sit down on that couch there.'

But Michael Gerrety seized Branna and pulled her in front of him, gripping both of her arms so tightly that she couldn't twist herself free.

'What are you going to do then?' he said, ducking his

head down behind Branna's. 'Blow this poor girl's brains out? Carole! Will you get off that fecking phone, Carole. Can't you see what's going on here, you dozy mare! *Carole!*'

Michael Gerrety backed towards the open door that gave out on to the balcony, pulling Branna after him.

'Leave go of me!' squealed Branna. 'Leave go of me! Leave go of me!'

But Michael Gerrety dragged her out on to the balcony and now Carole looked around and saw what was happening.

'Call the guards!' Michael Gerrety panted. Branna was throwing herself from side to side and bending herself around and kicking back at him, and he was having to use all of his strength to stop her from breaking away.

Carole said, 'Name of Jesus, what's going on? Who's this?'

'I said call the fecking guards! She has a gun, for Christ's sake!'

Obioma stepped out on to the balcony, too. She pointed her pocket shotgun at Carole and said, 'Drop the phone!'

'What?'

'I said drop your phone or I will kill you!'

Carole opened her hand and her phone fell to the floor. 'Now,' said Obioma, 'go to the end of the balcony and kneel down with your back turned and say nothing.'

Carole did as she was told. Michael Gerrety was still wrestling with Branna, but he managed to say, 'You're not getting away with this, you bitch!'

'You don't think so?' said Obioma. 'Mawakiya did what I told him to do and cut off his own hand. So did Mânios Dumitrescu, and Bula, and Mister Dessie. I sent you the proof that they had done it, didn't I? Did that scare you, Mr Gerrety? Did it make you fearful that I would come to you and make you do the same?'

'Leave go of me!' gasped Branna, and then she screamed out, '*Help! Help! Somebody help me! Somebody help me!*'

'Nobody will hear you up here, my darling,' said Obioma. 'But I am not going to harm you. You have done nothing. It is this man, Michael Gerrety, that I want to punish. This is the man who took my sister Nwaha into slavery and made her a prostitute.'

'What do you want?' Michael Gerrety asked her. 'Just tell me what you want and you can have it.'

'They all said that. All four of those human slugs who worked for you. "Don't hurt me, don't hurt me, you can have anything! I will give you all the money I can lay my hands on! Just don't hurt me!"'

'Listen, I can give you a hundred times more than they could,' said Michael Gerrety. Branna was jerking her head back now, in an attempt to hit him in the face, and he was having to dodge from side to side. 'Will you keep still, you stupid bitch!' he shouted at her. 'Do you want to get me killed?'

'Yes!' she screamed back at him. 'Yes, I do! I'm not a prostitute at all! I'm a reporter, for the *Echo*, and I'm going to see you damned for what you do!'

'So you're a fecking liar, as well as a slag?'

Obioma said, 'Let her go, Mr Gerrety. You cannot hold on to her forever. My sister killed herself because of what you did to her, and now is the time for you to be punished for it.'

'If you think you can make me cut off my own hand, you're badly mistaken. Nobody in the whole of my life ever made me do anything that I didn't want to do, and you're not going to be the first.'

Obioma said, 'There is a saying in Nigeria, Mr Gerrety.

He who shits in the road on his way to the farm will meet flies on his way back. You can never escape the consequences of what you have done.'

Carole suddenly started to cry. It was like the crying of a small, terrified child, rather than a middle-aged woman.

Obioma said nothing, but waited for Michael Gerrety to answer her.

Forty-three

Katie arrived outside The Elysian with Detective Sergeant ó Nuallán and Detective O'Donovan.

She went up to the two gardaí who were standing outside the front door and said, 'What's the story? No more suspicious packages, I hope.'

'Only the usual residents in and out,' said one of them. 'Apart from that, one pizza delivery, one CD from Amazon, and a letting agent.'

'A letting agent?'

'She was after taking pictures of one of the apartments, that's what she said. She was black, and I'll tell you, she was some beour. But she didn't fit the description of the suspect and I checked her ID. She was in and out of here in five minutes, if that.'

'Which letting agency did she come from?'

'Carbery's, on Grand Parade.'

'When was this?'

'I don't know. I'd say she left about twenty minutes ago.'

'Describe her. What colour was her hair?'

The garda looked uncomfortable. 'It was, like, red, like yours. I mean, you couldn't really miss it, a black woman with red hair. I mean, it must have been dyed, like, you know.'

'Full marks for logic, officer,' said Katie. Then she turned to Detective O'Donovan and said, 'Sounds suspiciously like your African lasher who said that she didn't give Obioma the keys to O'Farrell's furniture workshop. What other ways can you get into this building, officer, apart from this one?'

'There's a door for the maintenance staff, but only the maintenance staff have a key for that, and then there's a door from the basement garage, but that has a keyless combination lock and only the residents know the combination.'

'But you could open the garage door from the inside, even if you didn't know the combination?'

'You could, yeah. I took a look in there meself this morning – just checking that nobody had wedged the door, like, or messed around with the lock so that it didn't close proper.'

Katie said, 'Okay. As it happens, we're here to bring Michael Gerrety into the station with us for questioning. Stay here for the moment, but if we need you upstairs we'll call you.'

As they waited for the lift, Detective O'Donovan turned to Katie and said, 'What are you thinking, ma'am? Are you thinking what I think you're thinking?'

'You mean, that your African lasher might have lied to you about the keys to O'Farrell's workshop, and that she might have come here to let Obioma into the building? Well, we'll soon find out, won't we? If we find Michael Gerrety with no hands and half his face blown away, we'll know that we've been outsmarted.'

They went up to Michael Gerrety's floor, walked along the corridor and approached the front door of his apartment. Katie raised her hand to indicate that they should be quiet and pressed her ear to the door.

'I can faintly hear a woman crying.'

'If you listened at half the doors in Ireland you could probably hear a woman crying,' said Detective Sergeant ó Nuallán.

'I don't know. Maybe it's just the Gerretys having a row.'

She pressed her ear to the door again, but now the crying had stopped. She heard a man's voice, and he sounded angry, but then there was silence.

'Oh well,' she said. 'Whatever's going on in there, here goes nothing.'

She pressed the doorbell and the chimes played 'If I Were a Rich Man'.

They waited, and waited, but nobody opened the door and there was still silence inside the Gerretys' apartment.

'Try the doorbell again?' suggested Detective O'Donovan.

'They'd have to be deaf or dead not to have heard that,' said Katie. 'Something's happening in there and they're deliberately not coming to the door. Kyna, there's a caretaker's office in the lobby, can you go down and get a master key? And bring one of those guards up with you. Tell the other guard to stay on the door in case I'm wrong and Obioma hasn't managed to get inside.'

Katie and Detective O'Donovan stood well away from the Gerretys' door while Detective Sergeant ó Nuallán ran back along the corridor to the lift.

'What's the plan if she is in there?' asked Detective O'Donovan.

'I have no idea, Patrick. It isn't easy to stop somebody who doesn't care at all if they live or die.'

They waited, and listened, and Katie heard a girl's shrill voice calling out something that sounded like '*Don't – don't do that!*', but after that there was silence again.

Detective O'Donovan said, 'Sounds like there's somebody

else in there, apart from the Gerretys. Let's hope this isn't going to be messy.'

They heard the lift whining, and then Detective Sergeant ó Nuallán was back, with one of the gardaí from the Elysian Tower's front door, his high-visibility jacket rustling as he jogged close behind her.

'The master key,' said Detective Sergeant ó Nuallán, holding it up. 'The caretaker was very reluctant to let me have it at first, but then I threatened to arrest him for obstructing a police officer, and he was most cooperative after that.'

As quietly as she could, she inserted the key into the door and turned it. Katie took her revolver out of its holster and stood to one side as Detective Sergeant ó Nuallán gingerly pushed the door open. To Katie's relief, neither the bolts nor the safety chain were fastened, so there was no need to kick it.

She put her finger to her lips and they entered the Gerretys' apartment without saying a word. Normally, they would have stormed in like they had at Lower Glanmire Road, shouting out '*Armed gardaí!*', but she had no idea of what they were going to find here, and Obioma was so different from the usual armed suspects they encountered that she wanted to proceed with the utmost caution.

Outside the floor-to-ceiling windows in the living room it was almost dark, and the sky was the same prune colour as Katie's bruised eye. Although the sun had gone down, the balcony outside was lit up and they could see Obioma out there, pointing her pocket shotgun. Only two metres in front of her stood a young blonde girl in a very short pink dress. She appeared to be struggling, but she was being forced to stay in front of Obioma by Michael Gerrety, who was holding her arms. Behind Michael Gerrety, at the very far end of the balcony, Carole Gerrety was kneeling on the floor with her back turned and her head bowed.

'Let's take this very, very easy,' said Katie. Keeping her revolver raised, she crossed the living room towards the open balcony door. She was only halfway there before Obioma caught sight of her, although she kept her pocket shotgun pointed at the girl in the pink dress, and Michael Gerrety.

'Obioma,' said Katie, stepping out on to the balcony. 'You need to put that weapon down, Obioma.'

'I am here to finish my punishments,' Obioma retorted, in a challenging tone. 'This man deserves to die more than any of the others.'

'Detective Superintendent Maguire!' gasped the girl. Katie quickly glanced at her. She hadn't recognized her without her water-buffalo hairstyle.

'*Branna!* What in God's name are you doing here?'

'She's a lying conniving bitch, that's what she's doing here!' Michael Gerrety put in. 'Now arrest this fecking black madwoman, would you? That's your job, isn't it? Keeping us citizens safe?'

'Leave go of me!' Branna shrilled at him. 'Make him leave go of me!'

'Oh, absolutely, and get myself shot dead? No thanks, girl! Come on, DS Maguire! Do your duty before somebody gets killed!'

Branna jerked her head back again, and this time Michael Gerrety wasn't expecting it and she hit him with a sharp crack on the bridge of his nose.

'Jesus!' he shouted, and two streams of bright red blood poured from his nostrils and dripped from his chin. By way of retaliation he gave Branna a violent shaking, but he didn't let go of her arms.

'Obioma!' said Katie. 'This is all over now. Branna's an innocent girl and I don't want her hurt.'

'Innocent?' raged Michael Gerrety. 'She's just broken my fecking honk!'

'I am not going to put down this gun and I am not going to leave here until this man is dead,' said Obioma. 'I will take away his face and cut off his hands so that he cannot be accepted into heaven, and then my mission will be finished. My sister Nwaha will be able to sleep in peace.'

'I'm not going to let you do that, Obioma,' said Katie.

'You will not stop me. You could not stop me before and you will not stop me now.'

With that, she took a step nearer to Branna and Michael Gerrety, with her pocket shotgun aimed directly at Branna's face. Then she took another step, until the muzzle was almost touching Branna's forehead.

'Are you going to be a man, Michael Gerrety, and let this young woman go?' she said. 'Are you going to take the punishment that you deserve?'

'Oh, I will, yeah!' said Michael Gerrety. His voice was panicky and bubbly with blood. 'You're mad, you are! You're touched in the head! DS Maguire, aren't you going to arrest this nutjob?'

'If I have to kill one to kill the other, then so be it,' said Obioma.

Over five seconds passed during which nobody spoke and nobody moved. Off to the south, an airliner rumbled as it took off from Cork airport. Tears were running down Branna's cheeks, while Michael Gerrety was keeping his head down behind her and his shoulders hunched.

Close behind her, Katie heard Detective Sergeant ó Nuallán whisper, 'My God. She's going to do it, isn't she?'

Katie fired. Obioma spun around, thrown off balance by the impact of the .38 Special bullet, and also startled. Her arm swung around, and she tried to aim her pocket shotgun at Katie, but Katie fired again, and this time she staggered backwards and hit the balcony railing with a clang.

Then, whether she did it deliberately or not, she rolled and toppled over the railing and disappeared. She didn't cry out, she simply disappeared. Katie reached the edge of the balcony just in time to see her hit the pavement, seventeen storeys below.

'Oh my God,' said Detective Sergeant ó Nuallán. She reached out and laid her hand on Katie's arm, but Katie pushed it away. Her ears were ringing from the two gunshots and her wrist hurt from the recoil.

Michael Gerrety released his grip on Branna's arms and Branna sank to her knees on the floor and started sobbing – agonized, lung-wrenching sobs. Detective Sergeant ó Nuallán and Detective O' Donovan helped her up on to her feet and took her into the living room. Carole Gerrety stood up and went to the railing and stared down into the street, both hands held up to her face in horror.

Katie turned to Michael Gerrety. He was smearing the blood from under his nose with the back of his hand. 'Don't think it's broken after all,' he said. 'Just a bad nosebleed. Bitch.'

Katie returned her revolver to its holster. She was still partially deafened. '*You* did this,' she heard herself say to him. 'This is what happens when you treat human beings as if they were only put on this earth to make money for you.'

Michael Gerrety put his arm around his wife's waist and said, 'I'll ignore that remark, detective superintendent, considering you just saved my life. Are you all right, Carole? Jesus.'

Katie took another look down to the street below. The garda from the front of the Elysian Tower was kneeling down next to Obioma and several bystanders had gathered, although they were keeping their distance.

Detective O'Donovan came back out on to the balcony and said, 'I've called for an ambulance and the technical boys.' He nodded towards Michael Gerrety and said, 'What about him?'

'What does he mean, what about me?' asked Michael Gerrety.

'The reason I came here this evening was to take you in for questioning,' said Katie.

'Questioning? What about? Jesus, you never leave me alone, do you? You're obsessed, you are.'

'I need you to answer some questions about payments made by you to certain police officers in exchange for their turning a blind eye to some of your illegal activities.'

'*What?* What illegal activities? I never did anything illegal in my life.'

Katie said, 'Under the circumstances, we'll leave it until tomorrow. But I'd appreciate it if you'd make an appearance at Anglesea Street sometime in the morning. You can bring Mr Moody with you, if you wish.'

'This is harassment! I almost got myself killed there and now you want me to answer questions about illegal activities which I've never even done! You're fecking *obsessed*!'

Katie followed him into the living room. Branna was sitting on one of the couches, still crying, while Detective

Sergeant ó Nuallán had her arm around her and was trying to calm her down.

'All right,' said Katie. 'We'll leave you in peace for now. There'll be some technicians up here shortly to lift fingerprints and scuff marks from the balcony, if there are any. Otherwise, Mr Gerrety, I look forward to seeing you tomorrow.'

Michael Gerrety was still dabbing at his nose. Before she left, Katie leaned close to him and said, very quietly, so that nobody else could hear her, 'Actually, you're right, Michael. I *am* obsessed. I'm obsessed with finding you guilty of every disgusting deed you've ever done and showing you up in public for what a revolting louse of a man you really are.'

She smiled at Carole Gerrety, who smiled back at her, and then she turned around to Detective O'Donovan and said, 'Let's go, Patrick. I need to pay my respects to Obioma.'

'Your *respects*, ma'am?' said Detective O'Donovan, as they went down in the lift.

'Well, not exactly respects. But I killed her and I need to see her. She may have been a murderer, but I could understand her anger.'

As they reached the ground floor she looked upwards. 'She didn't get her revenge against Michael Gerrety, but I will, I swear to God.'

Out in Eglington Street, Katie made her way through the crowd that was beginning to gather. She didn't push, just gently touched people's arms and said, 'Excuse me, excuse me,' until she reached Obioma's body.

Obioma was lying on her side, almost as if she had simply decided that she was tired and needed to have a sleep on the pavement. Her eyes were open and she looked puzzled, but still beautiful. Her arms and legs, however, were all at impossible angles, and the back of her skull was smashed so that blood and brains were sprayed all the way across to the kerb. She must have fallen from the balcony head first, and it was over seventy metres to the ground.

Katie knelt down beside her. The garda who was already crouching there said nothing, but looked across at her in anticipation, almost as if he expected her to say a few words of benediction – *In nomine Patris et Filii et Spiritus Sancti* – but all Katie said was, 'I'm sorry,' and carefully reached out to close Obioma's eyes.

Forty-four

She stayed in the city all night – first at the Elysian Tower, until the technicians had finished measuring and photographing Obioma's body, then at Anglesea Street, writing out a preliminary report on the shooting and then briefing the media.

She didn't manage to return home until 10.35 a.m., without having slept at all. Even so, she would only have time for a shower and a change of clothes and a sandwich before she would have to return to the station to interview Michael Gerrety. She had provisionally arranged with his lawyer, James Moody, that they would meet at 3.30 p.m. She had warned Mr Moody that if Michael Gerrety failed to appear he would be arrested.

James Moody had said, very haughtily, 'My client quite understands his civic responsibilities, detective superintendent. You don't have to threaten.'

John was waiting for her when she came through the door. He was wearing a light gabardine windcheater and khaki chinos and his blue Samsonite suitcase was standing in the hallway.

'Hell's bells,' he said. 'Look at your eye.'

'How can I look at it?' she said. 'I can hardly see out of it.'

She hung up her jacket. Her revolver had been taken away

from her at the station as a matter of procedure, but it would be returned to her once the shooting had been thoroughly investigated.

John said, 'Are you okay? You look terrible, if you don't mind my saying so.'

'I know I do. But that gives you one more reason for going, doesn't it?'

'Katie—'

'Oh, no,' said Katie. 'Who could possibly blame you for leaving a wet miserable country full of priests and prejudice and pigs' trotters when the only person who's keeping you here is a terrible-looking red-haired detective who never comes home at night?'

John tried to hold her but she pushed him away.

'Katie—'

'Just go,' she said. 'We've said everything to each other that we're ever going to say. There's no point in going over it all again.'

She sat down in the living room that John had been going to redecorate and Barney came up and sat in front of her, cocking his head to one side as if he were asking her what was wrong.

John stood in the doorway, saying nothing.

'What time's your plane?' Katie asked him.

'Three-thirty.'

'Oh. That's when I'll be questioning Michael Gerrety.'

John said, 'You shot that woman? That Obioma?'

'Yes.'

'What's it like? I mean, what does it feel like, when you have to do that? Like, *kill* them.'

'Don't ask me that, John. I've had enough of dying. And just at this moment, I feel like I'm dying myself.'

John waited a little longer, one hand on the door frame, looking at her sadly. Then he laid his keys down on the table in the hall and picked up his suitcase and left, closing the front door very quietly behind him.